Under the Frangipani Tree

Anthea Syrokou

Cover Design by BespokeBookCovers.com

Anthea Syrokou
Under the Frangipani Tree
ISBN-13: 978-0648157472

antheasyrokou.com

For anyone with a dream!

Under the Frangipani Tree (Julie & Friends, Book 3) can be read as a standalone or as part of a series, following on from the delightful *Eventually Julie (Julie & Friends, Book 1)* and *The Greek Tapestry (Julie & Friends, Book 2)*.

Eventually Julie (Julie & Friends, Book 1)

Julie has had enough! At 27, she feels overwhelmed with the "shoulds" her family pile on her, and an office job that she detests. It doesn't help that she's carrying her "baggage of unfinished business" with her, weighing her down even more … making it impossible to see clearly and dig herself out of the rut her life has become.

When she finally decides to take action, a chance encounter presents her with an opportunity to deal with her messy past, so she sets off to Paris to find the answers that can set her free, and live a life full of meaning and passion. Julie loses herself in the sights and smells, and in the beauty of travelling in one of the most romantic cities in the world. She opens her heart to love, and begins to be true to herself … until she discovers a secret that sets her right back to where she began; uncertain about life — about love!

When Julie arrives back home to Sydney, she needs to make some serious decisions, or risk missing out on true love … and finally having the career she always wanted.

Join Julie and her delightful and witty friends on a journey of fun, adventure, and passion. Set in and around Sydney, as well as London and Paris, Eventually Julie is a "finding yourself" romance that deals with being stuck in a rut and eventually finding the right ingredients to live a life that is true.

"This has been one of the nicest books that I have read all year! Chick Lit at its finest I'd say!"

Whispering Stories Book Blog

"I liked how the story flowed smoothly and kept the interest until the last page. I really enjoyed it and I'm eagerly waiting for the next book in the series."

Liina reads

"Author Syrokou writes in a clear and compelling way and her scenes of Paris and London are vivid and dynamic."

Readers Review Room

"A good read. I need to read more by Anthea!"

The Rambling Boho

"A sweet, light-hearted chick lit book that will remind you of Eat, Pray, Love in the best ways possible."

Comfy Reading

The Greek Tapestry (Julie & Friends, Book 2)

Maria and her older sister, Nicki, were childhood friends with Dimity, the girl who lived across the street. Growing up in Sydney, they even came first in an art project with a tapestry they made by hand, which depicted island life in Greece. They believed nothing would separate them - but would sadly find that nothing was a tall order. When Nicki and Maria's parents uproot them to move to Greece, leaving Dimity behind, they discover that even the strongest friendships can disintegrate.

Now, almost twenty years later, each of them has their own life. Dimity lives in a designer house with her sexy husband, an industrial designer named Malcolm, and their two daughters. She loves Malcolm, but is tired of playing the accommodating wife and daughter-in-law. In need of change and inspiration, she sets off to Greece.

Maria has both the career and the family, but still feels the need to prove herself to her mother. After her mother hides invitations to her cousin's wedding in Greece from her, Maria is spurred into action. She is sick of her mother's interference and heads to Greece in search of answers.

Nicki also has a successful career, but she and her husband, Marco, are unable to have what they really want - a child. Needing a change in life, she follows her sister to Greece, and stays in a peaceful, historic village outside the town of Ioannina.

As Maria, Nicki, and Dimity each try to untangle their complex lives, will they find their way home and weave their own beautiful reality?

Fasten your seatbelts and get ready to join the fun in magical Greece!

"Anthea's new novel reads like you're watching a very well made chick-flick movie! Someone make a movie out of this, please."

The Rambling Boho

"This book nails life on the head, and I'm grateful for it being written."

A. Miller (Amazon review)

"She created such a lovely and captivating vision of Greece, that I almost put the book down and bought my flight to Athens!"

J. Henry (Goodreads review)

"Once again Anthea Syrokou delivers a beautiful story and one that will stay with me for a long time to come."

Whispering Stories Book Blog

"I felt drawn into it – immersed, in fact – to the point of feeling that I was part of the story, and that the characters were people I knew intimately."

B. Underwood (Amazon review)

"In nature's infinite book of secrecy
A little I can read."

– William Shakespeare, *Antony and Cleopatra*

CHAPTER ONE

A kookaburra laughed as it nestled into the eucalyptus tree's cavity and seized Cassandra Jensen's attention from her phone's screen, as the bird cast its territorial warning to other birdlife: Stay away.

"So, what do you think? Don't you think it's the most beautiful place for a wedding reception? Ryan and I fell in love with it the moment we saw it," her friend, Cynthia, asked from the other side of the screen.

Cassandra's gaze combed the parameter of the rich land. The kookaburra's cackle continued, though it wasn't yet dawn or dusk, and embellished the rustle of leaves and the omnipresent sound of grasshoppers, which created a cello-like harmony. She wondered why the native bird fended off unwanted intruders at that peculiar time of the day.

In the nearby river, dainty ripples shone with lustre. The graceful, dance-like movements reminded Cassandra of how soulmates seamlessly flowed through life —sometimes swimming with the current and sometimes against it — in their own world with eyes only for each other. Hills of emerald and golden brown contrasted with the ambient, flowing water, and created a stillness that seemed distant and eerie. Yet the green slopes, which resembled outstretched arms, gave the impression that they welcomed those in its presence. The fresh grass added to the abundant natural life around it.

Cassandra hugged her cream-coloured linen jacket around her waist as she gazed in wonderment at the nearby vineyard, which burst with vitality. The familiarity of the serene landscape made her feel at home.

She scanned a pebbled path which led to the renovated grand entrance of a restaurant. The old, stone wall oozed history from the German pioneers of the land, who arrived to that particular part of Australia with their loved ones and their few belongings. Armed with ambition, they planted roots in the fertile soil and evolved together as a community.

Cassandra feasted on the beauty. How she had loved growing up with the history of the wine harvesting country towns and villages of the Barossa Valley in South Australia.

"So, what do you think?" Cynthia queried, and a lovely image of her friend appeared on the screen.

Cassandra snapped out of her reverie. "It's gorgeous," she exclaimed. "I remember going on family picnics nearby. My parents always visited the nearby cellar for a good bottle of red." A heavy sigh emerged from somewhere deep inside. She wondered why that had happened so often lately; why she sighed at the thought of her youth and her upbringing.

"Anyway, I hope you like the invitation. I can't wait to see you again. And you can bring that handsome fiancé of yours. It's a shame you couldn't be my bridesmaid. Though I know you're busy planning your own wedding. Plus, Ryan has so many young sisters eager to fill the role. I think they actually wanted me to catch them looking at bridesmaid dresses so I would pick up on the hint. Seriously though, who would have thought we'd be getting married at similar times? I know you're coming anyway. I just sent the invitation so you can have one to keep. It's lovely, isn't it? I really think we chose the right ones …"

Cassandra opened her mouth to interpose. Her friend was so positive Cassandra would be attending the wedding. She looked at her desk, at all the client files, and thought of an excuse. How could she leave her clients? She also couldn't miss the Sydney counselling conference coming up. She always attended them.

Cynthia continued talking as Cassandra's heart rate continued to climb. She would break her friend's heart if she gave any indication that she mightn't be able to accept the invitation. Cynthia's face glowed as she stood in front of the robust vineyard in the summer heat. Her long, brunette hair swayed in the breeze, and a trace of perspiration showed on her smooth forehead. It must be hotter there than it was in Sydney, Cassandra thought.

Cynthia's hazel eyes matched the greens, browns and golds around her. The blushing pink and peach roses in the huge charcoal planter behind her highlighted her rosy cheeks, which shimmered with hope.

"It's going to be so much fun, Cass. I can't wait to see you. You can also bring Julie and Maria along. I had so many conversations with them when you shared the North Sydney terrace house and when I visited last year. I know you're close to them. It can be like a holiday for all of you. It's an ideal time of the year to do that. Some people are still not back at work yet. I'm still recovering from New Year's Eve."

Cassandra thought of her friends and her heart lightened. It would be wonderful to take them both to the place where she grew up, so they could share a magical day with her childhood friends. It would be wonderful. So, why did she want to run away from it? Why did she want to hide the invitation in a drawer and never look at it again?

Of course, she was happy for Cynthia, but she was anxious about being part of the wedding. The kookaburra called out again and she attentively listened to it. The thought tugged at her heart. Why would it call out at that odd time of the day?

"Cass … are you still with me? You seem a million miles away. If you're worried about Julie and Maria bringing their partners, they're invited as well. I wanna share this day with everyone!" she said, enthusiastically. "And I just received a response from Josh. Josh … It's been ages since I've seen him. He's still working in New York … as a photographer. I'm sure he's still as hot as he was back in high school. It's been a while since we've seen him. At least we caught up with him when he returned a few years ago. That will be so wonderful … for you to catch up with him … don't you think? You two were great friends. I'm surprised you didn't keep in touch. Anyway … I've gotta go. The manager at the restaurant needs to go over some catering things. I'll see you soon. I've got a lot of pre-wedding parties to plan as well. See ya …"

"See you, Cynthia. Bye. We'll talk soon. Good luck …" Before she could finish her sentence, the image on the screen had disappeared … just like he had. The words still rang in her ears. *Josh might be there.* He said he might be attending … he might agree to go to their wedding, even if he was working all the way in New York. She wondered if he was hesitant to respond to the invitation just as she was.

Cassandra looked at the piece of gold cardboard. It was silky, elegant, yet not too opulent. Two rings were embedded on the front and the side was adorned with an elegant gold ribbon, which was tied in a perfect bow. It almost looked too precious to disturb. Too good to be true.

The tiny, gold booklet within contained the beginning of a story; the first chapter of the friends that sat next to her at roll call every morning.

She had looked at similar invitations for her own wedding. She breathed a heavy sigh. She knew the signs: the heart palpitations, the heat on her face, the uneasiness that overtook her every time she thought of wedding invitations.

The phone on her desk startled her with its sharp ring. Her fiancé Connor was calling from his office down the hall.

They started their counselling practice in an art-deco building nestled in with the trendy coffee shops along Oxford Street. Cassandra loved knowing he was just down the hall during their work day, as she offered her undivided attention, and non-judgmental ear to her clients.

As emotionally draining as their counselling roles could be, they thrived on helping others find balance in their lives: to find contentment. Cassandra knew she was good at her job, but applying the same techniques to her life was more difficult than having her clients apply them to their lives. A heaviness pressed at her heart lately, and she wasn't sure why.

"Nice invitations," Connor said as he stood at the door.

"Oh," she said, taken aback. "When did you get here? I was just about to answer the phone."

"You took a while to answer, so I knew you didn't have any clients. How about going out tonight?" he asked. "It's been a while. I know I've been slacking off with the wedding stuff. I thought it might be a good chance to catch up. It's not fair that you're doing most of the work …" he trailed off as he walked towards her.

She looked back at the invitations. She was unable to meet his eyes. That familiar and unwelcomed inner turmoil caused her hands to slightly tremble. He neared her and placed his soft lips on the nape of her neck, working his way to her mouth as he gently turned her to face him. He wrapped his toned arms around her waist and Cassandra's skin tingled. Connor had always been able to do that, ever since they had become study partners for their counselling course just over two years ago.

She reciprocated and kissed him with the same intensity. She decided to let go of all the feelings that were holding her captive, instead surrendered to the momentary comfort of an impulsive physical gesture: he stroked her waist, her hair, and teased her with desire. *But then what?* The thought rapidly appeared in her mind and the momentary, impulsive, burning desire fizzled away as the negative energy succeeded in consuming her.

Then what? The thought pestered her and held tight to her mind.

She met Connor's searching, concerned aqua-blue eyes. He breathed heavily; he read her as though she was one of his clients. His ability to remain neutral was betrayed by the line that creased his forehead, like a faint crevice on cement that hadn't set properly. Cassandra thought it looked out of place against his smooth, stubbled skin.

"What is it, Cass?" he asked as he stroked her face. She nervously pondered his gaze. The river of speculation in his eyes threatened to reveal the confusion that one innocent question carried with it. Connor's eyes mirrored her every apprehensive, confused thought.

Cassandra unlocked her eyes from his, fearful that he would read those fragile thoughts. She trembled as she played with the ribbon on the invitation. A silky, ash blonde strand of hair fell from her loose ponytail. Connor's gaze softened. She adjusted the perfect ribbon and stifled a tear as she contemplated if her friends would have many joyous moments. Would the ribbon tie their life into a beautiful, neat package or would it become a restraining knot? She felt that tight, asphyxiating knot in her stomach and her skin broke out into a shiver as Connor's strong arms turned her toward him and pulled her into him.

He aligned his eyes with hers and stroked her hair. "It's okay, Cass. Whatever you're thinking right now, it'll pass. You just need to clarify it, to bring it out into awareness."

"I know," she said. She wanted to confide in him about how she felt, but her confusion embarrassed her. She was the controlled one. The one her friends came to for advice.

"Anyway, why have you got the air-conditioner on if you're wearing a jacket? No wonder you look flustered," he said.

"I just felt hot … and then I felt cold … after I turned it on. Those things never adjust to the right setting," she said in a forced, flippant voice. The truth was that she had felt agitated and hot a lot lately. She was never happy with the temperature. Her unsteadiness worried her. Connor pretended to read a file on her desk, while his focus stayed on her back.

"Hey," he said in a smooth voice. He fingered the material of her jacket. She felt the heat from his nearness: his warmth and compassion. She looked into his eyes and managed an affectionate smile. "I think I'm just in a sentimental mood. It must be from talking to Cynthia. I guess the past just came back to me."

Connor gave her a half-smile. "You can't hide anything from me, Cass. I know you …"

Guilt washed over her like a tidal wave and she felt herself drowning in his deep, mesmerising pools of aqua-blue. Tears welled as he searched for answers.

I can't do this to him ... worry him like this, she thought. She impulsively wrapped her arms around his neck and pressed her lips into his. She kissed him fervently. A sudden desire to make things right came over her: to push the uncertainty aside and enjoy the moment, to ride the wave until it crashed to the shore. Connor was the love of her life. He deserved her undivided attention. She was being silly. It was supposed to be the most joyous time of their lives. I won't deprive him of the excitement, the happiness of planning our life together.

"Wow! What was that?" he asked with a flirtatious and relieved smile. "It's good that I closed the door ... and that we don't have any clients for the rest of the afternoon."

"I can't help it when I see you. Let's go out tonight," she continued with the same enthusiasm. "You're right! It'll be fun to get away from all this work and let our hair down," she added.

He stopped himself from responding as he looked into her pleading eyes. He wasn't convinced that she had recovered from her uncertain and negative mood.

Her cheeks ached from her blinding smile. She wanted him to believe her; she mostly wanted to believe that the uneasiness would go away.

His smile spread like sunshine as he came around. He leaned in and his soft, full lips spoke to her as they moved with her own. He didn't need to respond. She got her answer as he picked her up and placed her on the desk. Charged with urgent desire, he deepened the kiss.

"Come on ... let's get out of here," he finally said, in between heavy breaths.

The piano in the Oxford Street restaurant calmed Cassandra's senses. The melody massaged every fibre of her being. She looked at Connor's approving gaze through the smoky air. She admired him from across the small, round table. The candlelight illuminated his handsomeness: his light brown curls fell over his forehead, and his smile added to the flame's warmth. How could she be uneasy with the thought of marrying this wonderful man? It didn't make any sense. Everything would be okay. *I'll make sure it's okay, like I always do,* she thought as her hands shook.

"So, tell me about this wedding we're invited to."

Cassandra cleared her throat and looked at the waiter approaching them with their order.

"Oh, the wedding … um … I don't think we can make it. We can't just leave our clients. Aren't you at a critical stage with one of yours? And I really think we should go to that counselling conference coming up. We don't want to fall behind … I think it's crucial we keep up with these things."

"That's true. But there'll be more conferences, Cass. This is your friend's wedding. I don't know about you, but a few days at the Barossa Valley sounds great to me. We can move a few appointments around and make it work … like they say, 'if there's a will, there's a way' …" he trailed off when he noticed Cassandra's eyes slanting. "There is a will … isn't there? You do want to go, don't you?"

"Of course, I'd love to go. Cynthia was one of my best friends back home. It's just … the timing. Anyway, can we talk about something else? I just wanna relax and enjoy each other's company. It's been a brutal week. I'm exhausted!"

"Fine with me. Are you sure you aren't coming down with something? You seem a bit flushed." Connor sat back in his chair and sipped his beer.

"It's stuffy in here …"

"I thought you liked it here."

Cassandra looked at the waiter with a smile as he placed the salad and the herb bread onto the centre of the table. Connor stared at her.

"I get it … let's change the topic. It's this wedding talk, isn't it? You're stressed out about it all getting done in time. We've already found a great place for the reception, with a view of Sydney Harbour. I just can't wait to plan our honeymoon. Remember how much fun we had in Europe?"

Cassandra's eyes alighted to the mention of Europe. They had fun exploring many countries. She would have loved to take off with him right then.

Connor smiled. "Remember that time in Rome when we were eating at that outdoor restaurant and a scooter startled you, and …"

"… I bumped into the little boy sitting next to me and his ice cream fell. It went all over his shirt and the cone landed on his shoe. He had the biggest tantrum … in front of the whole piazza. His mother wouldn't stop giving me an evil glare. I thought she was going to throw her marinara all over me. I do remember how good you were under such stressful circumstances, you know, playing mediator. You gave the woman one of your charming smiles and she calmed right down. I couldn't blame her though. That tantrum would have made any parent blush … her face had turned tomato red, not unlike the tomato salsa in her marinara."

"I had to intervene. You caused quite a scene," he teased.

"Well … the way you handled that toddler, and his mother, with such grace … such finesse … I knew then that you'd make a great husband … and an excellent dad …" Cassandra looked down at her plate.

"You can say it, Cass. I'd make a wonderful dad. Why is it so hard for you to tell me that? I can feel you slowly slipping away from me lately. I don't want to feel that we have to hide certain things … that certain topics are taboo. I know that's important to both of us. The liberating feeling we get when we learn why many shy away from being their true self is what attracted us to our profession. To not listen to the 'shoulds' and …"

"… 'oughts', and 'musts', and 'ifs' … and to trust their instincts and clarify what their values are. You're right, Connor. I guess we counsellors need to be reminded about that as well sometimes. I can say it. I can say what I truly believe … that you would make a great husband and an exceptional father. It's really not that. I honestly don't know what it is. Thinking about our holiday has cheered me up though. Why don't we look at some of our videos and photos when we get home? Just chill and reminisce?"

"Sounds like a great idea. I do have one question though," he said, moving closer and taking her hand into his. He stroked her hair and looked at her with intent. "If our holidays make you happy, then why do you refuse to go away? The Barossa Valley sounds wonderful. Remember how much fun we had at many of the vineyards in the South of France, and in Italy? It would be so wonderful to go back to where you grew up … to see your family home. It would be good for you too. It's been a while since you went back, and I've only seen your parents once when they came to Sydney for our engagement party …"

Cassandra tensed. The restaurant closed in on her. She unbuttoned the top button of her olive-coloured silk blouse. The waiter arrived with their mains. She could smell the buttery, white wine sauce and eyed the slices of orange around the grilled salmon. It sat on a bed of brown rice. She had looked forward to having a nice dinner, but her appetite had completely abandoned her. She opened her mouth to talk.

"Would you like some pepper?" she heard the waiter ask her.

"Um … sure … yes, please." She snuck a glance over at Connor. Concern was evident on his face. His lips were pressed together, and his eyes were serious. She thanked the waiter and diverted her attention to the plates on the table. She looked up at Connor. He hadn't said anything to the waiter as he left. All he saw was her.

He leaned closer to her. His fingers intertwined with hers. "You do want to see your parents, don't you? What is it? You're trembling."

"Of course, I want to see my parents. I don't know what came over me … again. Anyway, they're overseas, remember? I don't even know if they'll be there when we're supposed to be there."

"Maybe you're overworking yourself. You don't want to burn yourself out. Some counselling cases can be draining. I hope you're remaining disengaged, to a point at least, and setting strict boundaries. I know how hard it can be not to worry about clients, even after work hours. I think a holiday will do you wonders. Let's just do it."

He pressed his lips to her hand before leaning to kiss her. She caught a whiff of his masculine cologne. Something about the way he had said it made her want to let him in … to have him see the world where she had grown up and to meet the little girl that grew up amongst the vineyards, robust hills, and wide open spaces. It was Connor, the love of her life, and she would say yes … she so wanted to capitulate to his pleas. "We'll see," she finally managed.

"We'll see? I guess that's a start. I'm sure you'll come around."

Cynthia's words then entered her mind. *Josh might also be attending … you two were such great friends. I'm surprised you didn't keep in touch.* She remembered Cynthia's words very clearly. *Might,* she reassured herself. At that moment it dawned upon her that she didn't know how she would feel if that *might* change to *will* or *won't.* She didn't know how to feel about it. These feelings were unfamiliar and, surprisingly, came out of nowhere. Well, if she was being honest with herself, she knew perfectly well where they were coming from: the emotions she'd repressed over the years were being called to the surface. What a hypocrite she was, telling everyone to invite such feelings out into awareness, and yet she didn't want to acknowledge her own. What she did acknowledge was the familiar gnawing in her chest. Her thoughts were diverted to the lone call from the kookaburra that now sounded in her ear. *Why was it calling at such an odd time?* she wondered. Those, like her, who had grown up hearing its laughter-like call, usually at dawn or dusk, knew that the kookaburra wasn't really laughing. That type of call was a territorial warning, for trespasses to stay away.

CHAPTER TWO

A big, orange balloon fastened to a plastic white wand waved in the air, held by a long, slim hand, which also held two crystal wine glasses. Cassandra watched the balloon and the wine glasses move down the tall kitchen cabinets as Maria stepped off the white timber two-step stool with as much care and dexterity as a magician's assistant on a tightrope.

Maria looked incredulously at the wine glasses and balloon. She moved a strand of long, auburn hair away from her face and tried to catch her breath. "I never thought I would be holding an orange balloon and wine glasses at the same time in my kitchen! I mean, what are the chances? I guess that's what being a mother involves. Here's to multitasking," she added with a grin, trying to look as though she was bothered by it. "Running your own business makes multitasking easier. And the delegation of tasks. Which reminds me, I need to tell Antonio to buy some more carrots and celery for Thomas' soup. And we might be out of nappy wipes ... he just stepped out to visit a friend."

Casandra smiled at her friend as she looked up from her magazine. She knew the truth behind her friend's half-smile. She knew how much Maria was enjoying the motherhood journey. She hadn't failed to notice Maria scratch her nose as she completed her sentence. Her green eyes were beaming with pride. It didn't take a qualified counsellor to work that out. It was written all over Maria's face. She was enjoying being a mother and Mrs Reyes. She watched Maria with an amused smile as Maria placed the balloon on top of the stepping stool. The long, plastic wand that held the balloon fit snuggly in the carry-top opening of the stool.

"Thomas doesn't want it in his room in case it pops while he's sleeping, and for some reason we just left it here ... and after a week, of course, it's still here. I don't see this balloon deflating any time soon."

"Julie will have a field day when she sees it's still there. It doesn't go with the neutral colours in the kitchen," Cassandra mused.

"Oh, don't you worry about that. She noticed it the moment she stepped in the kitchen a few days ago. 'There's no excuse for that … whether you're busy or not. Once you stop caring about your environment, it's difficult to go back', she had warned me with a forced smile on her face, but her eyes said it didn't bother her. Not as much as my mother would be bothered by Thomas not learning Greek."

Cassandra gave her friend a questioning gaze.

"Well, she's not that bad these days. It's funny how things and people can change. My sister, Nicki, keeps saying that. And that applies to all of us, really," Maria continued as she poured the chilled rosé into the glasses. They had decided to have a toast between them to bring in the new year since they didn't get a chance to do it on the actual night itself. Maria, Antonio, and Thomas had spent New Year's Eve with her parents and Nicki and her husband in Melbourne.

A heaviness crept into her chest. She pressed it down as she inhaled and exhaled. "Just half a glass for me, thanks. I've got to drive back," she reminded Maria.

"Look at me for example," Maria continued, placing the wine bottle back on the bench, and glancing at the balloon as though it symbolised her life and the woman she'd become: like she was floating through life, dealing with the problems as they arose, trying to keep afloat.

Of course, she was as svelte as ever, thanks to her yoga and Pilates classes. And her bohemian lifestyle and love for herbal tea ensured she was glowing. Cassandra commended her friend for keeping up with her positive and nurturing holistic ways; they made her mothering journey that much more rewarding. Maria was more relaxed than she had ever been. Turmoil stirred inside Cassandra at the thought of how, not so long ago, *she* was the one who was relaxed in her own skin. She couldn't suppress the feeling that she was the balloon: she was ready to burst, but empty within.

"Well, I never thought I'd see you making Greek cakes and pastries. Or have so many photos on show from your trip to Greece."

Cassandra eyed the photo of Maria, Antonio and Thomas in Mykonos. Maria's love was reflected in her sparkling eyes; the shimmer matched the majesty of the stars in the sky and the luminance of the sea. She continued to study the photo. Maria's wavy hair floated in the wind, resembling waves in the ocean, as she stood on the cobblestone courtyard, her tanned legs in her laced-up sandals. Antonio's tanned arm was around her waist as she held Thomas. Three of the famous windmills had been captured in the background, symbolising their family unit. The windmills spun in the wind. They would spin through life together, Cassandra thought, completing each circle and then beginning anew, dealing with each problem together. Cassandra could almost feel the wind and the salty, sea air just by gazing at the beautiful image. Tears welled as if the musty, pulsating wind had stung them.

Maria cleared the marble bench-top of exfoliant bottles from her shop, Eventually You, Thomas' toys and Antonio's graphic design work. She scrubbed at some carrot puree from the kitchen tiles above the cooktop. Cassandra had walked into a toddler's food blending disaster when she had arrived at the North Sydney terrace house that Saturday afternoon.

Maria opened a pantry draw. "Oh my God! I found Mr. Potato Head! I've been looking everywhere for him. I can't believe Thomas put him with the real potatoes," she said, hugging the toy in her chest.

Cassandra smiled as she looked back down at the interior design magazine, wanting to hide the sudden tears that welled in her eyes. "Wow! Everything in this magazine looks so beautiful … and unique." She smiled with incredulity as she suppressed a tear. She couldn't believe how emotional she felt lately.

"Thinking of renovating the apartment?" Maria queried as she opened the fridge. "I guess now that you're soon to be married it makes sense that you would want a change," she continued.

Cassandra looked at her with her mouth agape. "Umm … not really …" she began, looking back down at the magazine, trying to find her words.

As she looked up again, she saw Maria placing a tray on the kitchen bench. "Ta da," she sang with a beaming smile. "Let's dig into this. I made it yesterday. I even sent a photo to Mum. Do you know my mum is on social media now and we keep posting all the food and cakes we make? Maybe we should start a blog or better still, a vlog together: *From the rustic ovens of Greek villages to your home kitchen, we bring you … Effie and Maria's Greek Organic Cooking Adventure …*" Maria was in stitches. "Actually, I told her that would be a wonderful idea for their restaurant. Maybe my dad can make guest appearances. Although, they're doing quite well on their own without my input. Would you believe my parents' restaurant had recently been featured in the '*Best places to eat in Melbourne*' section of a travel brochure? It would be fun though …"

Cassandra smiled at Maria. She had never seen her so excited about working on a project — with her mum, of all people. They'd had their differences, but they'd worked through them and now Maria was on the other side of it, making jokes. She eyed the tray. "Very impressive! You can never have enough *baklava*. I guess we can't waste all your effort. And we have been pretty healthy even if it's the silly festive season," Cassandra reasoned.

"You're always the voice of reason," Maria said with conviction, "so, let's take your advice this time. *Kali Orexi!*"

"*Kali Orexi,*" Cassandra replied, the broad smile she had tried to stifle appeared.

"What?" Maria asked with a mock offended expression.

"It's great … seeing you so … happy, or content, rather … that may be the right word. You've come so far since we lived together," Cassandra said, admiring the tall, ornate kitchen ceiling of the Victorian terrace.

"I guess I was a bit grumpy back then," she said and passed her a slab of *baklava*, having given up on cutting it in even rhombus-like shapes like her mum did.

Cassandra looked at it with wide eyes. She really had heeded her advice. "You didn't have to give me such a big piece. Your piece is half the size. Soon, I'll be walking down the … um …" She looked at her plate. She could feel Maria's gaze on her.

"… aisle?" Maria finished her sentence for her. "You will be doing that, but I don't think you should be too concerned about your weight. Um … don't get me wrong … but you are looking a bit thinner than usual," she said with caution in her voice.

Cassandra felt her cheeks growing warm. She knew where the conversation was headed and she wanted to steer it back to the direction that it came from. Maria was one of her closest friends and she was always direct with her and Julie. After years of knowing her, Cassandra had become used to Maria's ways; as in the past, she would still either avoid confrontation or she attacked with all her might. She awkwardly took her fork and placed a small piece of the sweet in her mouth, the syrupy pastry seducing her mouth instantly. "Mmm … this is so good!" Cassandra said, needing to digress but meaning every word of what she'd said.

Maria decided to continue with her previous remark instead. "It must be the stress of planning the wedding," she suggested. "I can help you with that … and Julie is great with these types of things. She'd love to help. Over the years you've helped us with our love lives, being the wise counsellor in the group. It's about time we repay you. I'm just glad you changed your mind about postponing it. You and Connor were so flat out setting up the practice that Julie and I were a bit concerned about it. Nicki said that when a couple love each other, they find a way to make it work. It got me thinking and I really hoped you two were okay. But here we are talking about your wedding again, right? So …”

“So …” Cassandra managed, remembering how lost Nicki had been before she and Connor had helped her. If she had made the comment after finding out, maybe others had felt the same way. Maria certainly did. It seemed like they knew something Cassandra didn’t. This was new territory for Cassandra. She was used to knowing things before other people did … especially when it came to her love life.

“You’re fine now. So why do you look so … so dreamy? In fact, you’re always dreamy-eyed lately … but not the in-love dreamy-eyed … more like dazed or confused, um … kind of in your own world, so to speak,” Maria blurted out. ‘What’s up with that?”

Cassandra dared to look into her friend’s eyes. Part of her thought it was funny that Maria was making so much sense. Maria’s questions had brought up other questions, which clarified that she had no obvious reason to be upset. Though there was something that lingered inside of her: something like a child demanding to know why she couldn’t enter the secret room her parents kept her away from. Of course, a child would damage all the precious, sentimental things inside that had sat in dusty solitude: all of the beautiful, painful and sorrowful memories. The secret room in her heart had shut some time ago, but that faint nagging voice was determined to unlock it. Her face warmed with shame. She was a counsellor and yet refused to unlock the door.

A scene from the very kitchen she was in returned. She was direct with Julie about the guys she dated and her family’s interference. At that time, Cassandra had opened up to Julie and Maria about how she felt about Connor; she had everything figured out. Julie and Maria had been too concerned with their problems. Maria was right, they had changed. But her change was not what she anticipated for herself.

Why am I feeling this way? It must be all this talk of Cynthia and Ryan's wedding and the idea of returning home. That's when things got all out of control, she speculated. She'd found out about their wedding a while ago, but back then, she'd thought it was so far into the future. Now it was all so real … as was her own wedding. Now that she thought about it, that was when Connor and she had decided to postpone their wedding. Why was that? *Yes, there was the practice, and so many clients, but why have I not been back home for so long? Why did the thought of it affect me so much? To the point that I would postpone my own wedding?* Everything was fine until they had set an official date. Their wedding was back on. Until, now … now that Cynthia kept including her in her wedding plans back home … those uneasy feelings had returned. "Maybe you should be the counsellor," she finally said, meeting her friend's gaze.

"Um … I don't think that'll ever happen. I think you'll always be the counsellor in this group. Although I am a lot more mellow than I used to be, and I could offer each client a cup of herbal tea to relax as we search for answers together. A counsellor and a client always work as a team, don't they, Cass?"

"Yes … they do," she matched Maria's mischievous smile. Her eyes then scanned the packages on the bench. "So many packages of tea … and I've never seen those before."

"Oh … those? They're some soaps from one of the new brands I'm stocking at Eventually You. I have some soaps and moisturisers from Greece. I must say," she said, becoming animated, "… the idea to have the new skin-care range … the ones infused with olive oil … you know, from that supplier I met in Athens? Well, they've been such a hit this past year. I've decided to extend the range."

Cassandra remembered when Maria told them about the business deal she'd agreed to with one of the shop owners in Greece. She had stocked many of their oil-infused organic products in Eventually You, and sold many of the Australian certified organic brands: incense oils, soaps, and many other healing products. "You know what?" I might stop by the shop on Monday and have a look around. I need some incense oil … and maybe some more candles. I could do with more aromatherapy in my life. I've always believed in a holistic approach to life."

Maria looked at her friend, her cheeks flushed with pride. "Sure … it's funny how we all offer something to the group. We work well together and have fun together. It's a shame Julie couldn't join us. She called and said she had some work commitment."

"We can't keep her away from her job lately. Can I have a look at these teas?" Cass asked, walking over to the exotic looking packages.

"Knock yourself out. Right on cue," Maria then added as she took a sip of wine. "It's Thomas. He's awake from his nap."

"Great. I can't wait to see him. I've missed him."

"You're such a devoted godmother. Thomas is so lucky to have you in his life … and Julie … and my sister … and many of my other beautiful friends … and my dad …"

"… and your mum?"

"Yes, even my mother. Did I tell you she had a conversation with Thomas on the phone the other day … and he used some Greek words?"

"I can imagine that went extremely well?"

"I nearly had to tell my dad to sedate her," Maria chuckled. "You'd think she won the lottery. I guess some things never change. Although she played it cool and instructed Thomas to learn Spanish as well, since his father is from Chile, and that it's very important that he doesn't forget his English. She made sure I heard that part."

Cassandra laughed. "I'm really happy for you, Maria," she said, and looked away.

Cassandra lifted one of the packages as Maria walked toward the hallway. As she looked up, she caught her friend gazing back at her. They both smiled at each other before Maria walked away looking thoughtfully towards the timber floor.

After perusing the stock, Cassandra walked around the house. So many memories, she thought, as she sauntered into the lounge room. The walls were still touched with the same pale blue hue that Julie had chosen. The writing desk was still there, facing the window showing the friendly, robust, vibrant garden. How many times did they ponder life as they gazed out of the big, French windows as the sun blanketed them with its warmth? She turned and faced the tall, heavy, antique mirror. *I guess I have become slightly thinner than usual*, she thought. She touched her face. It felt warm again even if the air-conditioner had cooled the house. It was as though her skin was blushing with guilt, with fear, or some deep uncertainty. *I'm a counsellor*, she told herself. *And I'm so fearful and uncertain, and what's worse, I won't even open up to anyone … even to another counsellor.*

She heard a distant repetitive birdcall, a faint cry. No other bird responded. They didn't hear its muffled and timid call. Maybe it didn't want to be heard, she thought.

She continued into the dining room, her flat sandals clacking over the timber floor boards. As her silk, terracotta-coloured summer dress caressed her smooth legs, her spirits lifted. She wanted to feel free like she had the previous summer. The dining table spoke to her: it had been, on many occasions, the focal point of attention as friendly and jovial faces enlivened it with unfeigned laughter and conversation. It was like an open book waiting for someone to leave their mark on it with words that meant something to someone in the room. And, when the ink dried, more words would be written, nurturing it with new stories as people gathered around it, just like they had written their story that afternoon. His eyes had looked at her with such desire, such longing.

"So, one of the aspects of Gestalt therapy theory deals with is unfinished business. Something has to be completed before something new begins. This means they cannot start something new if they haven't resolved the prior problem. The unfinished business needs to come out into awareness, otherwise it hangs around in the background and doesn't allow the individual to be in the here and now," Connor had commented.

"That's right," she had responded. "It all makes perfect sense … we all need closure in our lives, whenever possible, otherwise we can't focus entirely on the here and now and move on in an effective way …"

"It does make sense. Thanks to you, Cass." Cassandra remembered him saying something along those lines.

"Well, you did tell me about Cognitive Thought Restructuring," she recalled saying at one point. She remembered watching a strand of wavy, light brown hair fall onto his forehead. His full lips remained pressed together. His eyes shone with feeling. He'd handed her the textbook. A tingle had spread over her skin, causing her to shiver with delight. His skin on hers felt so good, so potent.

"Are you cold?" he'd asked as a smile formed, before his eyes became serious, thoughtful, intently looking into hers. Cassandra was mesmerised by the aqua-blue. She felt like she had deep-dived into a tropical reef and found pearls in sacred, precious oyster shells. She wanted to dive into them to see what treasures they hid inside; and the pain they hid.

She also wanted to show him her pain, her joy, and her every desire. That's how she felt around him. He had reignited her need to know everything about a person. Connor stirred those undisturbed and unexplored emotions that lurked within her. He had awakened the most intense feelings inside of her; feelings and desires that had remained dormant for so long, hiding on the ocean floor. And yet, she couldn't even talk to him now. She wasn't even sure that she wanted to uncover her inner feelings. She had forgotten about them until now.

They had looked towards the hallway as Julie had walked in and offered them tea or coffee. Cassandra had introduced Connor to her as her new study partner. Julie had been eager to meet him. She too could see the chemistry between them.

Thinking of that particular study session made her realise that her childhood memories had been locked and bolted for too long. They're always there. *They've never left me and won't go away until I deal with it or I won't be able to focus on the here and now ... on Connor and our life together.*

They've always been with me, she told herself. *I'm just aware of it now.*

"Cass ... it's snowing outside ... Cass ... Where's your fairy godmother, Thomas? Has she gone off to far away and magical places?"

Cassandra jolted. "Really, is it? I mean, what? Snowing? Maria ... What are you talking about?"

"You were a million miles from here, Cass." Maria looked concerned as Cassandra turned to her from where she stood next to the dining table.

Cassandra stretched her arms out to hold Thomas.

"I mean, you nearly believed that is was snowing in Sydney ... in summer! I was calling out to you for a while," Maria added, while passing Thomas into Cassandra's arms.

"I was just thinking about when I met Connor here. You know, reminiscing about the past. We had so much fun in this house. But now we can create new memories with this little sweetie. You and Antonio and Thomas ... it's so right that you managed to buy this house when it went on the market. I hope it's always in our lives. It has a lot of meaning to me ... I think to all of us. It's when we all started our lives as young adults, straight out of university. Where we all met."

"We don't plan on leaving anytime soon. I'm just grateful you and Julie let us move in here."

Cassandra hugged Thomas, who had just spotted Mr. Potato Head.

"Mr. Potato Head," he screamed, before freeing himself from his godmother's grasp.

Cassandra laughed as she watched him waddle his way to the toy. "Well, it was the perfect time for me and Connor to go away and do our European stint. We became so adventurous that year. One minute I was in an Italian boutique becoming familiar with all the baby clothing brand names in Italy while looking to buy something for Thomas, and next, Connor and I were camping by a lake in Sweden. We were living our dreams …" Cassandra trailed off.

"Well, I wouldn't mind another holiday. It's been a while since we all went to Greece. You did go crazy with the clothes you bought. You've definitely spoilt Thomas."

Cassandra hung on Maria's previous sentence; that she wouldn't mind another holiday. She thought of Cynthia and Ryan's wedding at the Barossa Valley. Cynthia had invited all of them and said it would be the perfect holiday. "Well, how could I resist? There were so many cute baby clothes," she said, repressing her previous thought.

"You didn't finish your *baklava* …" Maria accused her.

"Why don't we have it outside? It's been a while since I've sat in the garden. We can also have some coffee and play with Thomas on the grass … we can sit around the bird bath, you know, like we used to when we'd eat our breakfast or lunch on the outdoor table. Can I borrow this interior design magazine? Will Julie mind?"

"Sure … she forgot it the other day. She won't mind. She's finished with it." Maria gave Cassandra another inquisitive look.

"What?" Cassandra asked.

"You're just very sentimental. I guess it's the fact that you're taking the big leap … you know, the marriage leap. Julie will be the only one left to take that leap. To tell you the truth, I would have thought I'd be the last one to get married. In fact, I never even anticipated that I would get married. You're probably just thinking of your days of being single. Anyway, I thought you'd be looking at wedding magazines instead. How's the planning going? I'm surprised you're discussing anything else. If it's because I'm not into all the hype, don't hold back on my account."

An image of Cynthia's invitation came to Cassandra's mind. She scratched her nose inadvertently before looking back up at Maria. Cassandra walked in front of her and led her to the garden. "It's okay. I just want to sit amongst nature for a while. Nature has always made me feel happy," she said. The warm air kissed her skin as she stepped onto the patio.

"You have to take us to your hometown one day. I've seen so many pictures of the vineyards, but I haven't been there yet. You need to go back there, Cass."

****

Connor leaned forward to take in the beauty of the languid lake. Boats swayed as the gentle waves disturbed their peaceful slumber, while floating at the jetty nearby. A fisherman cast his fishing rod, diverting both Connor and Cassandra's attention to the line, which was already several metres over the water, where it landed with a gentle splash. The sun streamed shyly over the lake before running back to its hiding place, intermittently casting its kind, glorious spring warmth, embracing the trees, the flora, and the fauna, and the reposeful few people that enjoyed the day. Even the rowers in the canoes were relaxed, as they glided by like a sweet breeze, each stroke performed with gracious dexterity. The sunlight brushed Cassandra's skin as her elbows rested on the soft picnic blanket. Her shoulders and head were raised away from the ground. She looked at the canoes and heard a lamentable cry from the baby nearby; it too was disturbed from its slumber. She pulled Connor towards her, making sure the back of his head softly touched the blanket, and she nestled herself in his arms, resting her head on his chest. She couldn't believe that they were actually in Sweden.

"Lake Vänern ... is that what this lake is called?" she asked Connor.

"Yes ... it is. Apparently, it's the largest lake in Sweden and the third largest in Europe. I read that an Old Norse tale from Iceland's *The Prose Edda* was most likely based on this lake."

Cassandra looked at Connor's stubbled jaw as he spoke. "You're so sexy when you become factual ... like when we used to study together. I remember *Prose Edda*. I loved that tale. It's so cleverly written even if I had an excruciatingly hard time getting through it. It's the same lake?"

"It's breathtaking, isn't it? Just like you are, especially at this very moment." He faced her. "I've never seen you look more radiant ... and definitely pretty ... especially with all those daisies in your hair," he said. His jaw tightened as he combed her ash blonde sunlit hair with his long fingers. "Look at you ... in your white summer dress," he said with admiration. "What fairy tale are we in ... Cass?" His voice almost sounded drunk, as though the lustre of the sun touched it and cast a magical spell on it, causing it to be in a lucid, beguiled state; it carried traces of beautiful pain — complete awareness of the moment they were in, that they were sharing together. "Sometimes it actually hurts ... looking at you. It's as though I can feel everything you feel ... what you're thinking, just by looking into those pale blue eyes. At times, I have to force myself to look away. It's too intense ... the feelings that you make me feel. Like the beauty of this lake ... it's too real and so ... I don't know ..."

"Affecting? Maybe even poignant? It makes you truly feel and explore feelings that you never knew existed within you?" she continued his thoughts. "Like when you have too much happiness ... it can make one sad because it magnifies the fact that it can vanish ... but it also highlights how wonderful it can truly be if you let yourself feel it and to be enraptured by it ... to delight in it."

"Yes, exactly. How did you know the words I was after?"

"Because they're the words that come to my mind whenever I look into your breathtakingly mesmerising eyes," she said with a smile. "Seriously, Connor. I know how you feel. Eyes can tell a thousand stories; more than words could ever tell."

They looked at each other for a while without moving. She flinched as a gull flew past her. As she lifted her hand to push a strand away from her eyes, she felt his soft lips on hers. He pushed her into the warmth of the blanket. His hands aroused desire with their touch. Warmth filled her. She couldn't get enough of his kisses, his touch. She felt his stubble on her neck as his mouth navigated her skin. She pushed him back, breathing heavily with desire. "Connor … not here … with families nearby."

"We're only kissing, and we're so far away from them. The tree is even hiding us," he said with smiling eyes. "Plus, you never shy away from public displays of affection. I've never met a woman more liberated than you when it comes to these things … in touch with what she desires."

"That's only because of you. You're the one that brought it out of me. You're the one who liberated me. I feel like I can't be more myself than I am when I'm with you. Do I make sense?" she asked. He kissed her in response. She knew what that kiss meant. It meant that he understood what she meant, what she felt, even when she had trouble expressing it.

"Come on … let's go back to our room," he said with intense, pleading eyes.

"What about seeing that medieval castle … Läckö Castle? And we also said we'd go on those canoes … the swan or duck canoes. I hope they're not only for display," she said softly, searching his eyes. "And, speaking of tales, remember that book we were going to look for from that local author?" Their eyes talked to each other for a while. "I guess there's always tomorrow," she managed, as he took a daisy out of her hair.

"Do you know daisies are a flower in a flower? The yellow centre is actually a flower, not a bud?" he remarked as he placed it on his nose.

"And do you know they don't actually have a heavenly scent like many assume they do?"

Connor's lips curled upwards as he smelled the flower, obviously agreeing with her comment. "You're right. The smell … well, it's interesting. Who cares, they're beautiful just like you." He then sprinkled the petals on her, before he ravaged her with small successive kisses. "Yes, Cass. There's always tomorrow. Lucky for me, there'll be many tomorrows that we spend together."

"Cass … you're still here?" Cassandra turned and came face to face with Maria. She was standing in front of the terrace house. Cassandra had decided to take a stroll around the old neighbourhood when they had said their goodbyes. She looked at her watch and realised that twenty minutes had passed since then. Just as she was about to enter her car she had thought of Connor: how much fun they had together when they took time off to explore Europe right after they'd completed their counselling course. "I thought I'd take a stroll before heading back home. I've got nothing planned tonight anyway."

Maria gave her another one of her studious looks before she spoke. "Well, lucky you. I've got to get ready for another one of Antonio's work dinners … with all his trendy, graphic design friends. I'm too tired to socialise. At least you and Connor can have a relaxing romantic night together."

Cassandra opened her mouth to talk before her eyes fell on a gorgeous, white frangipani tree across the street. "How long has that tree been there? I can't believe I never noticed it before. I love frangipani trees. They're so friendly and summery. I've always felt safe around them … kind of like I can trust them with my feelings."

Maria just stared at her. "Okay?" she managed, giving her a playful grin. "I have to remind myself that you and Julie would get a bit carried away with the counselling talk. So, you talk to trees now?" she asked, stifling a smile as Thomas ran up to her from where he was playing in the hallway. Maria picked him up. "It's been there for a while, but a white van is usually parked in front of it, so you probably missed it. It used to be small, but now it's finally thriving. Anyway, I'm glad I caught you. Julie just called. She's sorry she missed our get-together. The tennis match is on tomorrow, so bring Connor, and Julie and I will bring our beaus as well, okay? Bright and early. No excuses from anyone. Is that understood!" she stated rather than asked.

"Yes, Mum," Cassandra teased as she kissed Thomas on the forehead and dashed to her car. *Yes, I will have a romantic night with my beau*, she thought to herself. The white daisies with the yellow centres in her hair came to mind, and she turned to look at the white flowers with their yellow centres on the white frangipani tree while she drove out of the parking spot in the beautiful sun-drenched, tree-lined street. She opened the car window and waved to Maria and Thomas.

"You're a frangipani tree, Cass," Maria shouted out when she noticed that she'd taken another look at the fragrant, exotic tree.

Perplexed, Cass stopped the car as she heard her words. Maria had already stepped back into the house. *What on earth is Maria talking about? Maybe the wine got to her. She's doesn't usually drink too much. Anyway, she was always saying funny things.* She pushed her thoughts aside, instead opting to concentrate on her evening with Connor. She had plans to have a gloriously relaxing and romantic evening with him. They had to get things back to how they were. They had to step back and take a breather, to forget about weddings for the night and celebrate being together. As opposed to what Connor had told her, that they needed to get back into it, she felt that there would be plenty of time to talk about such things. Besides, with a sweet and intuitive guy like Connor, she was surprised she wasn't sprinting to the altar. But tonight, there would be no wedding talk, just a carefree, relaxing evening. After all, didn't she give similar advice to her clients? That they should remember what got them together when things got too complicated? She had told Nicki that same thing not too long ago.

A message came through on her phone. A smile formed when she realised it was from Connor. She felt elated to tell him about her plans that she wanted to devote every minute to being in his arms that evening, just the two of them. She began to read the message with optimism in her heart, but her smile rapidly faded.

Cass, my parents are here. Actually, we're having dinner with them tonight. I know it's short notice but they're only in Sydney for a while before they head back to the country and they're so excited to talk about the wedding. They want to take us out since they didn't see us at Christmas. They won't take no for an answer. They kind of feel like they're out of the loop with our plans. So sorry, Cass. I hope you don't mind. They can't wait to see you and hear all about what we've done so far with the preparations. I hope you're up for it.

Love you! Connor xxx

CHAPTER THREE

"You'll make a stunning bride, Cassie. I can almost picture you. Connor is so lucky to have you in his life. You've made my son so happy," Mrs Olsen said, enthusiastically.

"She definitely will," Mr Olsen agreed, raising his glass for yet another toast. This time it was for predicting that she'd be a stunning bride on their wedding day. A few minutes ago, they had made a toast for the good weather they were having during their time in Sydney.

"You'll jinx it all, William. We shouldn't discuss these things before the wedding."

"Miranda … they're both counsellors. They don't believe in such superstitious things. How are your folks?" Mr Olsen digressed and turned to Cassandra.

"Um … they're great." Cassandra cleared her throat. "They're actually away for an extended holiday. They're visiting family in Norway and in Denmark. They have relatives there."

"Mrs Jensen was envious about our trip," Connor explained, "when Cass and I told her about our time in Scandinavia on the phone, she convinced Mr Jensen to go since they grew up in Denmark."

"They used to go to the same school when they were young," Cassandra continued. "They migrated to Australia when they were young adults. They already knew English, so I guess it would have been easier for them …" She felt all eyes at the table on her. She had started strong, but when an image of her father came to her mind, her breathing became heavy. She took a sip of her water. "It's a beautiful restaurant. Great choice," she said.

She met Connor's appreciative smile. She reciprocated it with one of her own smiles. When she had arrived home, he'd felt terrible, with a sheepish look on his face. Cassandra had told him that she was exhausted. The last thing she wanted to do was get dressed up to go to a stuffy restaurant. She, of course, refrained from mentioning that the last thing she also wanted to talk about was the subject of weddings. *So much for spending a quiet evening at home*, she'd thought.

However, to her surprise and relief, Mr and Mrs Olsen had chosen an outdoor restaurant at Balmoral Beach in Sydney's North Shore. She could hear the melodious waves as she and Mrs Olsen sipped tropical cocktails and while the men stuck to light beer, having volunteered to be the designated drivers. People strolled past on the promenade, glancing over at the enticing platters on their table, as they contemplated where they should eat. She looked at the horizon and could only think of beautiful, positive thoughts as she observed how the sky met the sea, creating a glorious display of beauty. It was turning out to be a relaxing night, apart from the lingering misgivings she carried within her, that had lately appeared sporadically.

She was surprised at how easily she could speak to Connor's parents. Mrs Olsen reminded her of her own mother … at least how she used to remember her. Over the years her mother, Isabel, had changed, becoming more reserved. Cassandra was surprised that she'd convinced her father to go anywhere, let alone overseas. Her father was not a man one could persuade easily, if at all. She remembered one of his friends at the real estate agency that he co-owned referring to him as a 'constitution'. "Hey Oscar, I think when they made constitutions to govern countries, they must have known someone like you. You're your own walking, breathing constitution. Once something's said or written, you'll never budge." Her father hadn't been impressed with Mr Dennison's teasing and had just barely managed a grin.

With a tight jaw and a loud voice, he'd defended his pride. It was always his way, to nurture his self-preservation. "If you can't govern yourself and stick to a plan, you'll have anarchy in your mind. When that happens, all that remains is an abandonment of morals. What's society without morals, a concrete plan of action, or a set of rules? Would you prefer that I was indecisive, frivolous, and self-indulgent? I haven't got time for that, Dennison. I'm a realist. Dreams are for the faint-hearted. For those that need people like me to do the important jobs, so they can pursue their dreams and walk around with their heads in the clouds, dressed in their own self-importance. The realists have to guide the dreamers out of the clouds before their vision is so blurred they can't see a thing."

Cassandra squirmed in her seat at the thought of his words as she took a sip of her strawberry daiquiri. She had also squirmed in her seat back as a twelve-year-old girl. She vividly recalled eating one of her mother's apple and custard Viennese pastries while the two men talked in the kitchen which shared a view with the mountains in the distance. Her stomach had rejected the sweetness of the pastry. She ran to the bathroom, feeling sick. Her body rejected the pastry the same way it had rejected his words.

How dare he tell us not to dream! Mum's a dreamer. She always told me to believe in fairy tales. She told me I can create my own fairy tales. Dreams aren't for the faint-hearted, she'd decided. *Dreams are for the brave.*

Since then, her mother had metamorphosed to a shell of the creature she'd been. She had no opinions, spending most of her days baking. She could always rely on having a freshly-baked cake or cookies after school. She would have gladly given back the sweets just to see her mother smile again. To see the glimmer in her mother's beautiful eyes again; it would be all the sweetness she needed in life.

Before that, Mrs Jensen used to direct her in plays, acting them out to their friends that would visit. She had taken Cassandra to many stage productions, sang with her, learned to play the piano together, and it occurred to her that while Cassandra was in her youth, her mother had abruptly stopped doing all those things. She remembered an incident when her mother took out all the costumes she was given from when she worked as an actress as a young girl on the stage back in Copenhagen. She had starred in many low-key productions of well-known plays and musicals, and she and her father had toured in Vienna, London, Paris, and other parts of Europe. Her mother went through all the costumes and told her all the stories behind them.

One afternoon, she had played the piano while her mother told her about the time she played the leading role for a production of *Annie*. The front door shut with a thunderous bang just as the lid of the piano she was idly playing had. For some reason, the light left the room, and her mother's eyes darkened. Her dad was home. The costumes had been hastily thrown back into the chest. Cassandra had seen sweat on her mother's pretty face; on her flustered shiny cheeks, although it was winter. "It's so hot in here. Turn that heater down, Cass, and hurry and tidy your room. You need to get started on your homework." Her eyes lost their shine; they were listless.

Cassandra remembered seeing a woman in a play by Henrik Ibsen with the same look in her eyes. She had watched the video where her mother, dad, and another male actor who she knew little about, were performing. She never forgot the name of the play. It was the legendary classic, *A Doll's House*. Cassandra thought that her mother's eyes looked the same as they did in the play, the same as the character she played: Nora Helmer. When her dad entered the room that day, and Cassandra looked into the darkness of his eyes as he avoided looking at her and her mother, she thought they reminded her of something. She realised then that his eyes also looked like the character he acted as in that particular play. He didn't play the role of the woman's husband. The other friendlier looking man played that role. He played the character of Krogstad, a character that caused a lot of trouble for the other characters. Cassandra got chills when she watched him play that role, the same way she had chills when she looked into those almost vacant eyes that day in a room that had been heated and was full of life, but had quickly become painfully cold and empty.

Why can't he be like the other actor? Why can't he have warm kind eyes like him? Like many of my friend's fathers have? she'd thought as she looked down at her feet, hearing his heavy footsteps head to the kitchen acknowledging her and mother with a *hello*, but never looking at them. Cassandra often wondered why he never purchased a pair of sunglasses if he despised the light so much, like many of his sleek-looking real estate colleagues wore. That day it occurred to her, as she watched the back of his smart, navy blue suit jacket while he marched down the hall; he did always wear sunglasses, even if he'd never owned a pair.

Cassandra would not allow anyone to make her lose the light in her own eyes. As a young girl, she was told that she had eyes the same colour as the sky. She'd decided that she wanted to stand as tall as the sky, and when the pale blue was replaced with a blanket of darkness as night set in, her eyes would reflect the sparkle of the stars just like many of the magical creatures in the fairy tales. She was no constitution, she would be flexible and adapt and she would move in whatever direction she chose without self-imposed restrictions, like her mother did when she played different roles. She would always shine and play the character she was truly meant to play in life.

"They say the Danes are the happiest people," Mr Olsen suddenly offered.

"I wish that were true," said Mrs Olsen. "I wouldn't have you sulking around the house just because the taxes have gone up, or the house needs painting. He just wants everything to be perfect. I think they mean the ones that actually live in Denmark, dear. Anyway, what a remarkable coincidence. Cassandra's parents are also from Denmark, like you."

"What are you talking about? I was born in Australia, just like you were. I was delivered in a hospital not too far from

Sydney two months after my parents moved to New South Wales. My name is Norwegian. I had a great granddad with the name Olsen."

"Your mum told us that it was from the Danish side of her family. She's told me the story so many times. You always mix these things up. You even insisted that my name, Walsh, was from the Scottish side of the family, when I know for a fact that my great granddad was Irish."

"I'm pretty sure my name came from my—"

Cassandra looked at Connor from across the table. It was time to intervene. Mr and Mrs Olsen could bicker over anything. Cassandra thought their honesty was healthy though, a far cry from her parents' relationship. "It's so great that you can discuss these things. I think it's admirable," she offered.

Mrs Olsen was about to respond to her husband's comment, but she was left with her mouth agape when she heard Cassandra's words. "Oh … why, thank you, love," she managed. She then took a sip of her daiquiri and gave her husband a friendly, slightly awkward smile. "Oh well … it's a Norwegian and a Danish name, I guess."

Mr Olsen reciprocated. "Let's drink to that," he said, jovially.

Connor raised his glass and gave Cassandra another appreciative smile from across the table.

Moments later, the sand massaged Cassandra's feet with every step she took. The sea sighed as though it was relieved that another day was over. Cassandra too felt relieved that the night wasn't as unpleasant or demanding as she thought it would be. Connor wrapped his arm around her waist. He looked so handsome and summery in his white, linen shirt and beige, chino pants. She leaned closer to him and he hugged her affectionately, sneaking a kiss on her hair as they strolled across the sand. Mrs Olsen thought it would be wonderful to take their shoes off and take a walk on the beach like many were doing. It was such a balmy night, and

Mr and Mrs Olsen had launched into a retelling of their honeymoon in Cyprus. They reminisced about their beautiful walks on the beach and they wanted to feel young and free again.

"You two should do more travelling. It gets harder when you have a family," Mrs Olsen suggested.

"Stop. You'll scare them … talking about kids already."

"I'm not telling them to have kids yet. I'm telling them to travel. There's a huge difference. Do you always have to twist my words?" Mrs Olsen retorted.

"They'll be off on their honeymoon before you know it, anyway. And they nearly spent a whole year in Europe after they completed their studies."

"We've been talking about travelling lately. Cass has been invited to her friends' wedding in the Barossa Valley. We might be going …" Connor trailed off, his eyes searching hers cautiously.

"That sounds marvellous. It's a shame your parents won't be there though," Mrs Olsen commented.

Cassandra looked down at her feet as her toes played with the soft, comforting sand. Connor stroked her back. She knew he had mentioned it to prevent his parents from having another disagreement. The moon illuminated the light in his eyes. He really was keen to go to her hometown. The wrench twisted her heart tighter at the thought. She felt torn. Part of her wanted to go back with him, but part of her still had serious reservations. He squeezed her hand, and pulled her close to whisper, "You look so beautiful, I can't wait to have you all to myself tonight." He stroked her arm and her heart lightened. His touch made her skin feel like it was on fire. It had been a while since that longing desire awoke her senses with such intensity. Her heart felt like it was floating. She longed to float with him in their own world. Maybe they could have the night she had planned for them after all.

She noticed that Mr and Mrs Olsen had witnessed their display of affection. The older couple looked at each other knowingly.

"I think we should call it a night. It's been such a pleasant evening. I hope you both enjoyed yourselves. We've got the hire car anyway."

"I wanted to stay and have another coffee," Mr Olsen began before Mrs Olsen nudged him on his arm with her elbow. He soon understood her sudden need to end the evening.

"Okay, William. We'll have our coffee before driving back to our hotel. Do you think it's wise this late though?"

A loud squeal came from behind them. "I want it!" the cry of a young girl rang through the promenade.

She shook profusely and stomped her feet with such vigour and defiance, it was remarkable that she didn't scare the seagulls that were scavenging around the nearby bins. Her body was tense, and her face was beetroot-red as she stood next to a toy stand that was selling a variety of toys. The girl obviously had her heart set on a scooter. A tall woman with shoulder-length hair pointed to the price tag of the scooter so the girl could see it.

"It's way too expensive to buy another one. We can't buy all the colours! We discussed this last time. They're scooters, not marbles."

"I want one that colour as well. You said you would get me another one." Her cry escalated when her mother didn't answer. It seemed to reach a crescendo before it decreased in pitch and volume and settled to heavy breaths and intermittent short sobs.

The woman placed a nervous hand on the young girl's shoulder, trying to comfort her. "Shh, it's okay. You already have one. I got you one last time …" she offered the girl.

The girl pulled away from her. "But I want one this colour … I never wanted the purple one."

Cassandra gave the woman a sympathetic, cautious smile as they stepped off the sand to put their shoes on. The woman continued to plead with the girl, lowering her voice, realising that many eyes were on them. She then nervously looked at the girl who seemed to be ready to try reaching a higher vocal tempo. Just before the squeal began again, she heard Connor's soothing voice.

"What's your name?" Connor asked the girl, leaning lower to hear her.

Cassandra and the girl's mother looked on with apprehension as Cassandra managed to strap her heels back on.

The girl breathed heavily, abruptly ending her loud cry. "Umm … Cassandra."

Connor raised his brows at his fiancée as she straightened. Cassandra smiled at him.

"Wow! Do you know that this lady's name is also Cassandra?" he said with confidence, knowing the task had been made easier.

The girl's mother also managed an apprehensive smile. "You have the same name as that pretty lady," she told her daughter, smiling at Cassandra.

"Do you like boats?" he then asked the girl.

"Yes. I saw lots of boats … I went swimming before," she then said in between heavy breaths.

"Wow, you're so lucky that your mum took you swimming. Your mum must be a very special person."

The little girl just looked at him like it was a trick question, before hesitantly responding with, "Yes, she is."

Cassandra knew she was coming around. She knew that her body was overwhelmed with hormones and chemicals and her brain didn't know what to do with them, but that a state of calm would eventually follow. One where negotiation and reasoning could occur. She watched him with admiration.

Connor eyed the toy stand and noticed some small boats on sale. He intentionally stood next to them and guided the girl to look in the same direction. He then looked at the sea where the boat swayed gently near the jetty. "I'd love to have a boat like that, but it costs too much money and it's way too big. It would take away all the space, and I wouldn't be able to buy all the other things I'd like to have."

The girl looked at Connor and then at the boats next to him. Her eyes widened and a smile began to form on her face. "I'd love a boat too. We can get one of these little ones. Look, Mum. They have the colour I want. Can I get one of these?"

Her mother smiled. Relief had washed over her face. Cassandra felt for her. She had dealt with many clients who were having challenging parenting difficulties. Connor had worked a miracle though. The tantrum was high on the scale.

"Thank you so much," the girl's mother said with a shy smile. You don't know how much you've done for me. You've spared me getting the biggest migraine."

"No problem," Connor said, giving her a sincere smile. "I'm happy to help."

The woman then looked at Cassandra and leaned in. "He's a keeper," she said when Connor was out of earshot.

"Bye," they both sang in unison to the woman. "Bye Cassandra," they said to the little girl whose face glowed amongst all the colours of the little boats reflected by the moonlight and the street lamps.

"Well, that was brilliant! I knew you were great Connor, but I never knew you were that good. You two are sure to make great parents," Mr Olsen said as he sat on a bench and put his shoes on.

"Now who's scaring them? You told *me* not to mention babies," Mrs Olsen protested.

Connor also put his shoes on. They hugged Mr and Mrs Olsen as they said their goodbyes and promised to keep them involved in the wedding plans. They gave each other a knowing smile as Mr Olsen insisted that she had brought up the subject of having children first. Before they knew it, Connor and Cassandra reached the car and Mr and Mrs Olsen's bickering had become a murmur.

"You were brilliant," Cassandra said before she stepped into the car. She couldn't wait to have him to herself.

CHAPTER FOUR

Cassandra wrapped her sheets around her tired body. It had been a surprisingly pleasant evening. Connor breathed contently, fast asleep beside her. Just as she dozed off, her thoughts prevented her from falling asleep. It was way past 1:00 am. With eyes closed, she thought of how she had begun to feel content and at peace again that evening. The little girl's flustered face came to her mind. Her face had quickly changed to one that was hopeful and open to suggestions. Connor did that, just like he had in Rome when she'd caused the boy's ice cream to fall. *Rome*, she thought. How wonderful travelling together had been. Her mind became free and unfettered at the thought.

Images appeared of cobblestone streets, the vibrant colours in gelato stands, water cascading from grand fountains, blue skies appearing like the heavens were speaking to anyone on the streets below gazing up at cathedrals, at columns, and at magnificent enormous statues. Flowers in full bloom, lavender fields like purple rivers. Through windows on country express trains, she saw blurring images that belonged to provincial towns as Connor and she sipped their morning coffee in a carriage bursting with animated discussion. Then ... stillness. The train rocked on the tracks while she sat languorously in her seat and listened to the soothing sound. Murmurings on the train had faded and the carriage had become a space for quiet and reflection. Green grass and brown leaves coated the open spaces and meandering paths in country villages leading to tranquil lakes. Sunlight streamed onto her face and onto daffodils and friendly, sunny daisies. White and yellow petals gracefully floated in the air before they landed on her, and Connor's dimpled smile ... his friendly, sunny blue eyes spoke to her.

Her head fell deeper into her pillow as though it was resting on sand. Blue skies in a tree-lined street appeared in her mind, with more yellow and white. "You're a frangipani tree, Cass." She heard the words and then drifted through fragrant, pure white petals. She was floating … swimming in petals. Branches reached out to her, inviting her to taste the sweetness of their milky, exotic flowers and to smell their fragrance. Her nose twitched. He looked at her: his lips so soft, yet hard as he kissed her with such intense and aching want. His fingers intertwined with hers and her skin shivered from his touch. She could still smell the sweet fragrance; it reminded her of walks to school, childhood summers, *him*: his hands caressing her warm face, and his long fingers running through her hair. It felt so right. She was now running her fingers through his messy, dark brown hair. Her heart fluttered, like butterflies had found their way to a stream of sunshine. Josh was all she'd needed. She felt the rocking of the carriages. He breathed heavily. Connor breathed heavily and she felt his nearness as he wiggled closer on the mattress between soft cotton sheets. Her heart raced.

In a fright she jumped up from her pillow. It was still dark. She looked around the room. Moonlight streamed through the curtains, illuminating the shirt Connor had thrown onto the armchair before he'd lavished her with passion. They'd arrived home late after their dinner with Mr and Mrs Olsen. They couldn't keep their hands off each other. They had such an urgent need to be together. They had been together until he'd dozed off and now she was facing the darkness by herself.

She climbed out of bed, her mouth dry. She needed water. She robotically wrapped her light robe around her and walked over to the kitchen, careful not to wake Connor. She poured some water from the filter on the fridge. Holding the glass with trembling hands, she took several sips, the cold water numbing her throat. Why was she thinking of him? After all these years? She placed her hand on her heart;

it still raced, no longer fluttered. She heard the words again: "Josh might be there. You were such great friends".

She looked at the dark, rectangular object on her desk — the invitation she'd left on the desk in the lounge room. There it sat and awaited a response. Like a bolt, it hit her. She had to respond. She couldn't ignore it forever. Everything around her seemed so quiet, just like the carriage she'd dreamed about. Her face warmed at the thought of how her mind had travelled to their time in Europe, then to the street where she lived with Maria and Julie, to the white frangipani tree, to the daisies, and then back … back to Josh …

She looked at the invitation again. How different everything appeared in the stillness of the night. Her busy day hadn't allowed her to process that her friend thought she was going to her wedding. She couldn't keep her waiting and she couldn't keep Connor waiting.

Through squinted eyes she switched the desk lamp on and took the invitation in her hands. Could this invitation hold the key to her confusion? If she untied the ribbon and responded, would it finally set her free?

You two were great friends. It would be great to see him again. Cynthia's words tangled her thoughts. She walked over to the cabinet. It was a contemporary piece created by an Australian designer Julie had worked with in Amsterdam. How far had Julie come with her uncertainties! She was in such a good place now without all her "unfinished business" clouding her vision. Not only did she have a great career, she had been in a healthy and happy relationship for years, and had fixed things with her family. Cassandra's heart ached. What Julie had said to Maria about the orange balloon came back to her as she opened the cabinet door. "There's no excuse for that … whether you're busy or not. Once you stop caring about your environment, it's difficult to go back." Her words hit a nerve. She needed to hear someone else's words, from a mind that was thinking clearly.

Cassandra, the *wise counselling student*, had taught Julie so much and now she was a qualified counsellor and needed to hear those words, to guide her out of the hazy state her mind was in.

She flinched at the sound of a car horn as a car sped through the street, while she took out one of the photo albums. She nearly fell backwards onto the grey, limestone tiles as she tried to pick up the heavy album from where it had sat undisturbed by anyone. She had pushed it right to the back: where it was hard to reach, where she couldn't see it. With a trembling hand, she brushed the dust from the top. One photo album was all she took with her when she left her parents' home. This small album contained snippets of her life.

She heard laughter and walked to the window to peer into the street below. They had forgotten to shut it when they got home. The people on the street talked to friends while leaving restaurants, or cinemas, or dinner parties at friends' apartments, or the many renovated terrace houses that Paddington was known for. It was such a different environment out there. It juxtaposed the quiet darkness inside the apartment. She watched as the woman walked to the entrance of a house. The young woman waited for the man, who appeared to be her partner, as he took some bags out of the car. He approached her with a smile of admiration.

She saw *him* smiling as well. She saw Josh smiling as she waited for him. The image appeared vividly. She remembered talking to Ryan as a fourteen-year-old girl outside the school gates, after coming back from her summer holiday. She remembered looking away from Ryan. The sweet fragrance from the frangipani tree above her smelled like summer and happiness. She immediately noticed his familiar walk in her peripheral vision. Turning, she gave him a warm smile, to let him know how happy she was to see him again. Giggling, she watched him as he walked over towards them. He always looked like he'd been frantically searching for something, as if he always misplaced things or was always running late. It was part of his charm and laid-back attitude. He was something she needed in her well-structured, curriculum-packed daily routine.

"Hey mate, you look like you've run a marathon!" Ryan had already voiced Cassandra's thoughts. Ryan also knew his best friend too well. It was Josh's redeeming quality and they always teased him about it.

She'd affectionately messed his long fringe, suspecting that his mother, who was always well-groomed, would have voiced her thoughts on his urgent need to visit a hairdresser.

"What are you looking at?" she enquired when he didn't respond. He studied her appreciatively. Even though they were only friends, it was clear he found her attractive. She too found him attractive: his honey complexion, the freckles his sun-filled life had bestowed upon him, his thoughtful hazel eyes, his slight goofiness and aloof attitude, his ability to see things differently and succinctly describe what he saw. He always observed everything around him. She had advised him to make sure he applied plenty of sunscreen on his face. He could be complacent about such matters.

"Hey, Josh. How've you been?" Cassandra asked and playfully messed his hair.

"Hey, glad to have you back, Cass. How was your trip?" he'd asked her.

Right before she'd answered, he turned around and looked at the road. His mum had dropped him off and had driven into the adjacent street. She disappeared. He had waved, but it was too late; she was gone.

"Hey, Josh." Ryan had messed his hair.

"Come on. Let's sit in the shade and catch up," she'd suggested. "We've got time before our first class."

"Don't mind me," Ryan had said with a mischievous smile. "I'll leave you two alone.

"Yeah, don't mind us. I'm sure you and Cynthia have lots to catch up on. Is that where you're heading?" Josh had teased.

So many memories, she thought as she turned the page with a trembling hand. She sat on the grey, suede couch, after shutting the window. There she was, all hopeful, in front of her family home with views of lush, rolling hills behind her. Her mother wore a yellow summer dress and hugged Cassandra. Cynthia's mother had taken the photo. She had stopped by the house to return the cookbooks she'd borrowed.

She looked at the next photo. Cynthia and Cassandra had been walking home from school. She remembered the street vividly. It was in their hometown of Tanunda. They walked home through fields of colour. Cassandra remembered the time they took a detour and headed to one of the vineyards. It was when Cynthia had confided to her about how much she loved Ryan.

"Should I really be getting serious with him? Now that we have our studies to think about? It's the last year of school …"

"Listen to what your heart is saying, Cynthia."

Cassandra loved listening to other people's problems. It was rewarding to help them see things clearly. She could relate when she heard how they felt.

"You understand, Cass. I can't talk like this to anyone else. I feel that I can say anything to you," she'd told her.

Cassandra was about to tell her something about her family life — how she felt like all the pretending was suffocating her — from not saying anything to her father and yet the silence saying too much. Her friend continued, to her relief. It seemed they always did. Cassandra was unsure whether to be offended or flattered by it. She knew that it had worked — that her smile would hide it all. They thought she didn't have problems, so they too placed her in the role of a friend who would always listen. She knew that she'd enabled them to give her that role, with her smile, and not speaking up or admitting that she too had something she wanted them to hear, about her own family life.

It saved her from revealing too much. She pushed it down; she wouldn't be able to find the words anyway. It ostracised her soul even more. Cassandra knew what was expected: that she would only be accepted and loved when she excelled at school. So, she stuck to her strict schedule to ensure she always performed her best in her studies, and her extra-curricular activities.

She hesitantly turned the page and saw his eyes: her father's. Of course, they weren't looking at the camera. It was as she remembered him. Then she saw her mother's beautiful face. Her smile seemed forced as they both stood outside by the creek, where they'd had a picnic with friends. Mr Jensen had to keep up appearances, after all; he co-owned the leading real estate agency. He was a member of the community. She'd taken that photo. Tears welled up and her cheeks trembled at the realisation. *He didn't look at the camera because I was behind it.*

Her vision blurred. A bird call from the window startled her. She hadn't shut it properly. It was the soft, deep *oom oom* that would often keep them up in the night. Connor had once laughed when she'd thrown her pillow towards the window, as its continuous cry got on her nerves. "Imagine your clients saw you now," he'd said, and he'd continued laughing, before she threw the pillow at him in a playful way. Connor had told her it was a Tawny Frogmouth. "Of course, it is," she'd said with a mischievous grin.

Connor stirred amongst the sheets. She sat still, not wanting to wake him. He stopped moving. The bird continued its pitiful call. This bird never seemed beautiful to her. Its sombre cry was more of a nuisance: a bitter reminder rather than a joyous song. It was the same melancholic and accepting cry that bothered her. It acknowledged that that's all it would ever be: how everything around it would be, as it called every night. Its surroundings and the people near it accepted its dullness as they accepted their own.

She despised its dullness. Even if everything around it changed and everything in people's lives changed, they would still hear it every night. They didn't have a choice. *That's probably how Mum felt*, she acknowledged between tears.

She carefully studied the photo. The day before the photo was taken, he had been so angry. Her mother had tried to calm him, of course. Mr Jensen hadn't forgiven Cassandra because she had come home late the previous night — after being with Josh.

"All the sacrifices ... for what? For nothing!" he had stomped back to his private office. The office concealed a window to the garden and a bar: a garden he seldom looked at and alcohol he never consumed. If he did, he pretended he didn't as though it was a sin to enjoy oneself. When her parents purchased a bottle of wine, it was usually for the guests. Her mother irregularly drank a glass or two, but he would often cast his judgment on her glass, and she would then pour it down the sink. He lived in his own dark tunnel. "You are definitely your mother's daughter," he'd scoffed, looking down at his feet as he walked. "You think with your heart, not your head. Your selfishness will drag others down with you. I won't be dragged down ... not again. You stay away from that Josh kid! He's not for you. He and his mother have their minds more in the clouds than you and your mother do. If that's possible."

"Oscar, calm down! All of Tanunda will hear you," her mother had cried before shooting him a hurt glare as he stormed out of the room. Cassandra had thought the look was also one of disgust. It was then that Cassandra realised her mother had a lot of repressed anger.

Cassandra's heart had fallen to the floor, not because of how he treated her, but because she hated seeing her mother so pitifully weak. She felt oddly happy that her mother revealed her anger towards him. Maybe she would finally speak out. She was sick of her mother pleading with him or keeping out of his way, lest they disturbed his silence. If it was any more silent, they'd be living in a monastery, she'd thought as she played with the necklace Josh had given her. It was a grungy piece, not really her taste, but she loved it because it had belonged to him. It had sat on his sun-kissed chest. He wanted her to wear it. He had kissed her for the first time outside the school gates. *Oh Josh, how much fun did we have together? How in love were we?*

She saw his eyes now as her long slim fingers turned the page. She took the photo out of the sleeve to take a closer look. He was handsome. Soft, thoughtful, hazel eyes looked back at her. She hugged it to her chest. They'd had a strong connection. He made life bearable. Holding onto the photo of Josh, she continued looking at the album. A photo of Josh at the school disco with Ryan and Cynthia appeared. Another female friend stood next to them. His eyes were not as carefree in that photo. They had just come out of the 90s and everyone resembled the grunge bands that had emerged. Cassandra and Cynthia would often joke that they looked like the cast of *Dawson's Creek*: serious and intellectual. Cassandra knew there was more to Josh than this; the light had disappeared from his life just like she had.

A hand nudged her shoulder and she jumped. "Connor! You startled me!" she cried and her cheeks warmed. She hastily tucked the photo under the album, but it fell. *Oh no!* Her thoughts ran rampant. *Where did it go? It must have fallen under the cabinet*, she fretted.

She looked at the page that was still open. She now wanted to remember it all, but she had to shut it out, even if she wanted to stay in the album a bit longer. Her thoughts confused her.

Connor kissed her shoulder. She wanted to hold onto the memories. Why was that? Why did she want to remember them? Was it time for her to go back? But she had to stop.

Connor kissed her as her robe fell from her shoulder. Shame washed all over her. She saw her father's eyes judging her.

"That's your dad, isn't it? When he was younger? You never look at these. What made you want to look at them now?" he asked with a deep, sleepy voice.

Cassandra saw her father's face and hastily turned the page. She knew Josh might be in one of the photos.

"Come to bed," he said. "We have a tennis match tomorrow, remember?" He pulled her close and kissed her. She backed away; a wave of guilt threatened to drown her as her eyes fell on the silver, contemporary legs of the cabinet. She suspected the photo had fallen under it. It had to have. She needed time to snap out of that world. She had to place the memory back where it belonged.

"Tomorrow, we can let the games begin, but tonight I want you all to myself. We're on the same team, you and I."

She forced a smiled and, as he shut the window, she shut the album. As she looked away from the album, she noticed the photo on the side of the cabinet. She quickly picked it up and placed it in her handbag, before walking over to Connor.

"I'm yours always, Connor," she said, taking a quick glance at her bag. He pulled her close and guided her towards their bedroom. He switched the lamp off, and darkness returned. *Let the fun and games begin.* The words gnawed at her chest as he held her hand tightly as though he didn't want to let her go.

CHAPTER FIVE

Julie Canei sat beside Cassandra, trying to catch her breath as she placed her racket at the side of her chair. "Does George ever give up? I think I've had enough for one morning."

Cassandra smiled at her friend as she reached for her bottle of water. "He is a professional tennis coach who happens to own a tennis school. I think Antonio and Connor are pretending they're not tired. Poor dears." Cassandra laughed as she opened the bottle.

"You're right. Although I think George is also getting tired, but he's not letting on."

Cassandra was having such a wonderful morning, even if she was exhausted from her sleepless night. The tennis game was all she needed to breathe out all the negative energy and release the happy endorphins.

"Maria seems to be giving all of us a run for our money. I knew she was fit with all her Pilates and yoga classes, but the way she's running for those shots …"

"Well, I think you're in that category as well. Methinks you and George have been cheating and you've been getting extra training without our knowledge. The backhand slice you managed earlier … could it have been a more accurate angle? I think not."

"Speaking of looking good …" Julie said. "I've never seen a more stylish and classy tennis player. You've got a Ginger Rogers or Grace Kelly thing happening with your lob hairstyle loosely swept to one side. And those earrings …"

"My hair gets a bit wavy when I toss and turn at night. Anyway, Julie, I couldn't help but notice that you're wearing a designer canvas belt around your shorts and a matching designer sports bag."

"Okay, guilty as charged. But those earrings, they suit you. They make everything you wear look so stylish. And they definitely match with that blinding diamond on your finger. I'm glad it's back on … the wedding," she continued with sincerity. "The glow on your cheeks also matches that sparkle from the diamond. You and Connor have been more affectionate than usual …" she said with a wicked smile.

"Don't get too smart there, Jules. What happened to Maria and me interrogating you?" she asked, whimsically. Cassandra took another sip of water. "George looks so fit. I'm sure you get many women checking him out. Even mothers who drop their kids off for a tennis lesson? I'll bet they stick around to watch …"

"… and pretend they're looking at their phones, instead of his muscular legs," Maria added, as she caught the tail-end of the conversation. "Although, Connor has the philosophical, gregarious blue-eyed thing happening. Women would love to have him listen to their problems. It would be hard to disengage with someone like him. And he's obviously been working out. A lot," she added, while trying to catch her breath.

"And then you have Antonio, who practically has the whole team at his work drooling with every word he says in that sexy accent. He looks like he's dancing when he runs, the way he's flicking his long fringe to the side … it's like a seduction scene," Julie laughed.

Cassandra joined in as they caught all three men looking at their table. "What are you three laughing about?" Connor called out.

"Oh … don't mind us. We're just admiring your athleticism," Maria shouted back.

"Now they're pretending that they're playing an intense game, like they're at the Australian Open. Even that young woman is looking at them," Maria said between laughter.

"Maybe they're trying to impress her," Cassandra said. "They'd better not be when they've got three intelligent and stunning partners like us," Cassandra said, playfully. She was enjoying herself. The three of them always found something to laugh about when they got together.

"Although, the way we're carrying on, we sound like a group of immature tennis groupies," Maria added. "And you, being a wise counsellor."

Julie looked at the woman through her sunglasses with a half-smile on her face.

"Who cares? It's healthy to laugh at ourselves. And to be silly sometimes. I can't analyse everything all the time, can I? I'm a person, after all …" Cassandra trailed off, looking at the court.

Maria looked at her thoughtfully. "Of course, you are, Cass. Remember that you also have two wise friends that can offer you advice as well or, of course, simply listen," she said, pointedly.

"That's right," Julie added, still looking at the athletic woman who was wearing tights and a sports t-shirt.

"She is really toned, isn't she?" Maria acknowledged as she grabbed her water, sitting between Cassandra and Julie.

"Yes, she is …" Julie trailed off, looking back at her friends. "She actually works at the tennis centre. George just hired her … she's one of the new tennis coaches."

"Oh …" Maria replied. "You'd better go and join them before she does. There's only three of them playing now. They'll need a fourth if they're going to continue playing doubles …"

Julie gave her a questioning look. "What do you mean by that?" she asked. "She's a nice girl. I've talked to her a few times."

"Of course, she is, Jules. I wasn't implying anything different," Maria said.

Cassandra looked at Julie. She noticed that she looked agitated by Maria's comment. Her 'helping side' couldn't help but burst out of her. "How are you and George doing?" she asked. She was in her element again.

Julie looked at her instantly. Cassandra felt that she had startled her with her question.

"We're fine," she said rather quickly.

"That's good," Cassandra said with a smile.

"I mean … sure, we might have some issues … but what couple doesn't, right?" she said, looking from Cassandra to Maria.

"What types of issues?" Cassandra really wanted to know. She was surprised by her friend's comment.

"Maybe you've been away too long," Maria offered rather bluntly. "You know how you've been overseas so many times … I mean, lately. Not that it's bad or anything … I mean, it's great …" she added with a sheepish look, realising she may have overstepped.

"It hasn't been that often. Sure, I've been to Europe a few times. Interior design demands it. I have to keep up with the latest industrial designs if I want to be included in more of the bigger hotel and luxury house and apartment projects."

"… and the latest industrial designers?" Maria queried, obviously without thinking.

Julie looked hurt by her comment. "Are you still going on about my Amsterdam trip? You know it was all business. Yeah … I admit many of the designers I've worked with are hot, but George is the only hot man for me," she finished in a defensive way.

"Okay. You don't have to convince us. Calm down!" Maria said. "I didn't mean that. I was really talking about your boss. He's so generous with you, and sexy … and there I go again. Honestly, I'm just playing with you. George is all that and more. He's sophisticated and the way he talks … he's like a poet. And those enigmatic blue eyes. You have to be careful not to drown in them. But how does he feel about you working with so many sophisticated artistic designers in glamorous five-star hotels all the time?"

Cassandra's mind immediately went to the cabinet in her lounge room, where the photo album was kept. It was from one of those industrial designers they were referring to. Her mind went back to her dream that she had the night before. It shook her to the core.

"Are you okay?" It was Julie's turn to ask her that question.

Cassandra watched as George returned the tennis ball to Connor.

"I'm fine. I was just thinking about the cabinet. You know that we got it together from that same designer."

"Sure," she said before turning back to Maria. "Anyway, what exactly are you suggesting, Maria? Are you suggesting that George hired her just to make me jealous? He'd never do something so childish. He …"

"He loves you too much," Maria completed her sentence. "I know he does, honey. I was just teasing. You know me … I shoot my mouth off, without thinking. Forget I said anything."

"Sure," Julie said with a smile. "I've forgotten already," she said. "I know you didn't mean anything like that."

Cassandra caught Julie looking at the woman again. She wondered why she was still there, looking on at the match. As she smiled back at Julie, she knew her friend was asking the same question.

"How about you? You look like you're glowing. You and Connor couldn't keep your hands off each other on the court … and you are rather sleepy. You said that earlier."

"They're always affectionate," Maria offered. "I always said that being counsellors they would be able to communicate in more ways than one. And if talking about different counselling theories made you fall for each other, I guess it would be easy to be passionate in more romantic settings. Julie's right, though. You two are acting like you're on your honeymoon. There'll be time for that very soon. Have you planned your trip yet? I'd love to get away. An exotic getaway would be perfect right now … I'm still in holiday mode. We just had Christmas, and it's too soon to be all serious—"

"Didn't you just go to Melbourne for New Year's?" Julie reminded her. "Anyway, you think Connor and Cassandra are acting like lovesick teenagers, you should see how my sister was carrying on when I visited her at her and Brian's accounting firm. I've never seen two people get so passionate about numbers. I guess it can be fun for a couple to work together, like you and Connor do. But you're on to something, Maria. I think George and I are long overdue for a holiday. Maybe some time together will be good for us, since things have been a bit hectic. It would be great to have time just for each other. I can't believe I finally have time off and we haven't even planned to get away. Everything's probably booked out anyway."

"Not necessarily," Maria interjected. "People are going back to work now. Some hotels may still have good rooms available. Hey," Maria then said, turning to Cassandra. "Isn't Cynthia getting married soon? Isn't her wedding in a month or so? You'll be heading home soon after all. Please take me with you. Your hometown looks so picturesque."

Cassandra's phone beeped. Her stomach turned. Seeing her friends so excited about a holiday made her feel guilty. They were invited. She was being childish. She had to let them know. She looked at her phone. It was a message from Cynthia. Besides, Cynthia had mentioned that she'd send them some invitations soon anyway.

Hi Cass. Hope you're well. You won't believe what a great pre-wedding party I've got planned. I've booked the most gorgeous house and my dad agreed to pay for it. He wants to bring everyone together. It's overlooking the vineyard. I can't wait to see you all. Oh, before I forget, Josh might be able to make it. It's going to be so great to have everyone there. Please, tell your friends to come as well. I've just sent them the invitations. It's going to be so much fun. Hugs and kisses.

Cynthia

"Who's that from? You look pretty tense. Is anything wrong?" Maria asked.

Cassandra lifted her head from the phone and met Maria's inquisitive green eyes. The ends of her long auburn ponytail circled her face in the breeze. She then looked at Julie. She was looking at the young woman who spoke to George as she neared him. Cassandra caught Julie's eyes as they looked away from George. She had placed her sunglasses on her head. She looked somewhat vulnerable.

"Maybe we should get away," Julie managed to say.

Impulsively, the words spilled out of Cassandra's mouth. "Maybe we all should," she found herself saying.

Both women looked at her with eyes and mouths open.

"We're all invited."

"Invited? Where?" Maria and Julie chorused.

"Cynthia's wedding ... at the Barossa Valley."

Cassandra would have told them earlier had she known she'd be the cause of such jubilation. Julie and Maria looked like they were about to perform cartwheels across the tennis courts. It was as though Cassandra announced the news at the best time. What was more, her lingering reservations began to subside. Maybe she was being silly. It felt so good to make people happy ... to be spontaneous.

"Why didn't you tell us before?" Julie enquired.

"Cynthia is sending the invitations as we speak. I just decided that it might be fun to go now, on a whim," she said as she opened her bag to put her phone in. A ball flew past her just as she ducked out of the way. Her bag fell and spilled its contents.

"Oh my God! Cassandra! Are you all right?" Antonio called out. Connor and George followed Antonio to the outdoor table, but all Cassandra could see though was Josh. She couldn't believe this was happening. The picture of Josh had fallen to the ground and a breeze carried it away from her.

"Cass … are you okay? You look upset. Did you get hurt?" Connor asked.

"I'm so sorry, Cass! Do you need anything? Are you hurt?" Antonio asked.

Maria stared at the photo resting next to her sneakers. She snatched it up and placed it under her sports bag after a glance, to Cassandra's relief.

"I'm fine," she managed. Guilt overwhelmed her. *Josh … he'll probably be there.* She had told them it would be a great idea to go to the Barossa Valley, and now she couldn't take those words back.

It sounded great in theory. It would be wonderful, if only she didn't feel the burden she'd been carrying for so long in her chest. Now she was forced to face it.

She met Maria's eyes again, and then looked at Julie's concerned face, at Antonio and George around her, at Connor stroking her back. Her cheeks warmed. While they were concerned about her, all she could think about was the photo.

"Guys … it didn't even hit me. Don't worry about it. It's your fault, Antonio, for having such a powerful serve," she laughed, trying to push their concern, and them, away.

"Well, thanks Cass. I do have a powerful serve, don't I? What do you think, George?"

"It's pretty good. How do you feel about being a part-time tennis coach?" he teased.

"That's a great idea," Maria said, obviously not really hearing what George had actually said. She attempted to steer the attention away from the table. "Why don't you all finish your game, and we'll have something to eat after?"

"Sounds great. We can eat at one of the coffee shops by the beach," George replied. "How does that sound, pretty lady?" he asked Julie. "Is that up to your standard? You have been used to many of the finest hotels lately. Will our lovely Bondi Beach suffice?"

Julie smiled at him. "It's perfect. How can you complain with this glorious view?" She kissed him on the cheek as she glanced at the ocean. "I was also enjoying this view here too," she said, looking at him.

"We all were," Maria joked. "George, those legs—"

"Hey," Antonio said. "Connor and I have been working out too," he said, trying to look offended.

Cassandra managed a half-smile, after looking nervously at Maria's sports bag. She met Connor's eyes. They still looked at her.

"Are you sure you're okay?" Conner asked.

"I'm fine, just go finish the game, or your training session?" she replied. He didn't seem convinced. She wrapped her arms around him and kissed him.

"Hey, you two, there'll be plenty of time for that later," George said. "We've got a game on."

"Finish your game quickly. Cass has some great news to tell us. I think you'll all be excited about it," Julie suggested, her worry gone. She waved to the new, mysterious female coach, like she was suddenly a different woman.

Maybe she needs this time away more than she's letting on, Cassandra thought. She knew the feeling too well.

"I'll see you soon," Connor said. He kissed her again and it brought back memories of the previous night: of how close she felt to him in between the sheets. She wanted to feel safe in his arms, to wipe away what she was feeling, to show him how much she loved him.

He stroked her back before heading back to the court.

Maria had caught their moment of affection. She finally took the photo out from under her sports bag. She studied it for a moment. "He's handsome," she finally said. "So ... who is he? Or do I need to ask? It's Josh, right?"

Cassandra raised her brows. How did she know Josh?

"How do I know him? Cass, you told me the story ... about when you two snuck out of school and made a visit to your uncle's wine cellar. You both got drunk from drinking wine from a barrel. And you also told me about the time you got stuck up that steep hill at Eden Valley and there was a thunderstorm. Why do you look so surprised?

Remember when Cynthia came over and told us all those stories?"

Cassandra's eyes widened. She finally remembered. "That's right. Of course," she said, coming out of her trance-like state. She had to get it together or her friends would think she was hiding some dark secret.

"So, you carry a photo of him in your bag?" Maria asked, glancing between Cassandra and the photo.

The conversation had drawn Julie's attention. She stared at Cassandra with curiosity.

"What?" she managed. "Of course not. I was just looking at some photo albums, and that one fell out. I found it on the floor and threw it in my bag. I hate seeing an untidy apartment, and we were running late. I think I've become like you, Julie," she said, trying to resist scratching her nose.

"Hey … are you saying I'm neurotic? That's the old Julie. I don't mind a bit of clutter or mess occasionally … it's cosy to have the lived-in feel sometimes."

Cassandra placed the photo into her bag and stood up. "Have they finished their match? I mean, their training session? George seems to be teaching them some skills. There are only three players left on the court since we all abandoned them. I really need a coffee. I haven't slept a wink," she added as she met Maria's curious eyes. She then closed her bag and locked eyes with Connor as he approached.

"Are we done … with all the games?" Antonio asked both men.

"Yeah, we're done," Connor replied, before heading towards her.

***

They found a coffee shop with groovy melodies and animated discussions from the patrons along Bondi Beach later that morning. Cassandra sipped her flat white coffee.

"This is so scrumptious," Maria shouted out. "Try this everyone. This custard chocolate bread thing is heavenly."

"So, we play a game of tennis and then we scoff down copious amounts of coffee and chocolate bread?" Cassandra enquired.

"Something like that," Julie said. "Anyway, let's get back to the topic of weddings. Would you believe we're all invited to Cynthia and Josh's wedding? Oh my God! What's his name? Ryan? That's it ... how embarrassing," Julie corrected, placing her hands on her face.

"And who, may I ask, is Josh?" George asked in his usual formal way. "He's not one of your creative and handsome industrial designer colleagues, is he?" George gave Julie a look of mock hurt.

"Oh, come on George, surely you're not jealous. We've discussed this ..." Cassandra heard the words, but the ringing in her ears blurred all the noises around her. It heightened and the space around her shrunk. She wished they'd chosen one of the outdoor tables. The suffocating feeling wrapped her in negativity. The conversation digressed. *Josh will probably be able to come to the wedding,* was all she could hear though. Then blurred images of the kiss, dreaming of him kissing her, and the photo under the cabinet. *If you don't take care of your environment ...* she saw smiles. Julie's pink lip gloss shimmered, along with her hazel eyes and light, golden-brown and shoulder-length hair. *The lip gloss colour really does suit her,* she found herself thinking. Then she looked at Maria. She was laughing at something George said.

Her father's face also came to mind. As did the image of the crying girl from the night before. The girl's face transformed into Cassandra's when she was the same age. Her father told her mother to calm down; everyone was looking at them. He told her to control her daughter, to stop being a friend over a mother. That's what he had said to her when she had asked her mother to buy her a toy. She remembered it clearly now. They were at a shop in the nearby cosy town of Angaston. Her father looked on impatiently. Cassandra's body had quivered; her heart fluttered. She cried, but not because of the toy. It had started that way, but at the age of six, she was scared of him: scared of the way he talked to her mother, the way he looked at her, like he would rather be anywhere else. She asked to have the doll because it looked so sad. She wanted to make sure it was safe. His answer made sure she never felt as though she belonged. She remembered the silence and her mother's laughter as she tried to make it better. She never forgot how she'd felt though.

She looked around the table. Her kind, smart friends laughed joyfully. She felt like she didn't belong in the happy picture, not like she usually did. She was so used to offering advice, but how could she offer any advice?

Her mother had told her, "a broken jug can't quench anyone's thirst", or, what was it? "A starving chef doesn't have the energy to cook for others. He has to feed himself first." She wished her mother took her own advice.

Cassandra always had a seat in the front row, but now she was fading to the back where the main performance is hard to see. She was obscured by the backs of people's heads: the people who only looked towards the front where the action is, where things got done, where people are noticed. She knew that when one fades into the background, only those who really know them notice and try to save them. She saw this happening many times with her clients.

Why did I agree to go back? My life is how I wanted it to be until now. I'm the person I want to be …

But am I really? she speculated. *Am I the person I really want to be? Did I really live up to my potential? Am I able to evolve and live without the obstacles holding me back? Relax,* she told herself. She didn't know if it would be good or bad that her parents would be away during the wedding.

"Are you okay?" she heard Maria's concerned voice.

Julie gave her an affectionate smile from across the long table.

Cassandra pulled herself out of the hole she was sinking into. "Yes. Thank you for your concern. Both of you." She smiled appreciatively and felt reassured that she had friends who wouldn't let her fade away.

"No problem. We're always here for you, like you've always been for us."

"Your wedding will be great," George said, from across the far end corner of the long table. "Another excuse to drink and act silly. I'm in," he added.

Cassandra's heart rate began to return to normal as Connor pulled her close and kissed her on the lips, wiping some custard away from her face. He squeezed her hand under the table reassuringly, and she knew he would always make sure she was not only in the front row, but always on centre stage.

"To Cassandra and Connor," they all sang, raising their coffee cups.

CHAPTER SIX

On that gloriously sunny Monday morning, Cassandra admired her nails as she typed away on her keyboard. She decided to start the week on a positive note. She had woken up early and tied her long, ash blonde bob into a chic bun. She had even managed to paint her nails a scintillating cinnamon brown hue. The diamond ring sparkled amongst her earthy-brown nails. Even in such harsh and old surfaces, she realised, such a beautiful diamond can be found. It told her that even in the harshest and dullest places, there is a glimmer of hope in the form of something magnificent, strong, resilient and aesthetically pleasing to the eye — enriching the lives of those who touch it.

Cassandra smiled at her thoughts. *Maybe I should be a poet.* Her analysing had become more intense than ever. *Now I'm analysing my nail polish*, she thought. It felt good to laugh at herself, to not take herself too seriously.

She liked how the diamond kept shining no matter what happened in her life or how uncertain she felt. It prevailed. Its light was always with her, as was Connor, and he would be her husband very soon.

She told herself that she had nothing to worry about. Being with Connor and her friends the day before reminded her of how much fun they had when they get together. It would be wonderful to spend time with them at the vineyards. The parties Cynthia was planning sounded exciting. It wasn't like she would be on her own. She wasn't a vulnerable girl anymore. There would be so much to do, so many sights to see, heaps of parties and restaurants to attend, and, of course, the wedding.

She decided that once that was over, they would take charge of their own wedding. She was a strong, caring and resourceful woman and would not drown in one drop of water. She could easily skip over it, she told herself.

She was excited to buy some scented candles and moisturisers at Eventually You later. She was determined to get her life back in order. She had made a decision to go back home, and she felt proud and recharged. *That's why I'd been anxious,* she told herself. She was used to taking charge of things, being proactive, not hiding behind excuses. Not doing things added to the stress. She told her clients that staying busy doing things they loved could be what they needed during long periods of inactivity and inertia, or if they felt lost.

Opening one of the client files to prepare for her next session, she sighed contently. This particular client had made great progress. Cassandra's guidance had helped her clarify many things about her relationship. A rewarding feeling came over her. It felt good to focus on helping others. Her phone rang and Ava at the front desk informed her that her next client was ready to see her.

Later that afternoon, Cassandra brushed through the George Street crowds in Sydney's CBD. She walked through the noise which filled her heart with energy. The city was alive: people had places to be, people to see, shops to entice them as they visually feasted on many of their offerings behind polished shopfront windows, which invited them in for a closer look. She loved visiting Maria at her lovely shop amongst all the excitement.

As she opened the door, she was met by a small fountain. The tranquillity welcomed her. The dissonance from the throngs of shoppers and the buzz of activity outside felt like it was so far removed from the world inside the cosy, cocooned space.

"You like?" Maria asked from behind the counter. A proud smile lighted her face.

"I definitely like," Cassandra responded. "It's that obvious?"

"Well … I'm used to it. Many have the same expression on their faces when they enter my invigorating and healing world," she said in a soothing voice, as though she was in the middle of teaching a yoga class.

Beautiful harp sounds came from the speakers as Cassandra placed her khaki bucket bag on the counter. She looked around, a feeling of peace enveloped her all over. Birdsongs followed, adding to the ambience. Cassandra felt like she was in the Scottish Highlands or amongst some Irish forest, smelling the freshness of the pine and oak as a Celtic flute and a tin whistle joined in. "Which one is this?" she enquired. "It's so beautiful and relaxing. I also love that other new-age piece you had last time. I think I could hear windpipes and pan flutes. I felt like I was on the mountains of Peru …" she ended her sentence with a sigh that revealed a hidden yearning.

"Looks like a holiday amongst the mountains is what you need … and I need. Julie was ecstatic to spend time with us, and some 'alone time' with George. Thanks so much, Cass. This is something we all need. Speaking of new-age music and lovely positive vibes, I can tell you where you can download the one you're referring to … and others that contain beautiful piano melodies that you might like."

"Great. I'll also have a look around. I really need some rose-hip oil, organic moisturiser, some incense oil, and perhaps a Neroli candle … or maybe sandalwood …"

"Wow! You're about to buy the whole shop. I might have to stop you, which is something I don't usually do. I think you're looking like your positive self again, Cass. I could tell that you haven't been yourself these days. Julie also mentioned it."

"Oh … really? So, I see I've been a topic of conversation. My, my, how things have changed. It wasn't too long ago that you were all coming to me for advice, but, you know what, it says a lot. You picked up on it, so that says you are true friends, and it also says that even us counsellors are actually human."

"Oh, really? I didn't know that. You mean, you too have insecurities … and feelings like the rest of us?" she teased. "Cass, you never need to hide from us. I think a change is needed. A different perspective, like you keep telling us. Everything is interconnected. We can't just heal one aspect of our lives and ignore the other parts."

"You're right about that," she said, as an image of the photo came back to her mind and then, strangely, an image of her father appeared. *Everything is interconnected,* she repeated in her mind. She wondered why the images appeared simultaneously when she thought of those words. She had to change perspectives. Maria was right. She would face her fears and confront them just like she told her friends and clients.

"Maybe you can visit me in my little world in Paddington … we could do some evening-dress shopping, you know, for the wedding? I think Cynthia's also planning a birthday party for Ryan … some type of dress-up party. She was always doing things like that in high school. There are so many unique clothes in Oxford Street, and we could also plan a shopping day here in the city and have lunch. The clothes here are so fabulously unique."

"Sounds great. I'm so glad for you, Cass. I'm glad to see that happy smile on your pretty face again," Maria told her after giving her a big hug as she led her to the glass door.

Almost an hour later, Cassandra sat up straight in her office chair, listening to her client. A young woman was having major communication problems with her partner. Another work day was nearly over. She hadn't felt so positive in weeks. Her decision to go back home to face the uncertainty and attend the wedding was obviously agreeing with her.

The small nagging voice appeared in her mind: *But they're not going to be there. He will though. Josh will probably be there.*

Cassandra moved uncomfortably in her chair as she listened to the words. She couldn't ponder them now. She had more pressing issues. Her client needed her guidance.

Always attentive for other's problems, but finding excuses for your own as usual. Good old carefree Cass goes through life helping others but never takes the time to help herself. A broken jug can't quench anyone's thirst.

She sat up straighter. She pushed her thoughts aside. She had to focus. Her client began to talk about an argument she had with her husband.

"So, you were upset that he was late again for another planned dinner? Is that right?" she managed to ask, reflecting the client's feelings, and trying her hardest to remain nurturing and facilitate a non-judgemental atmosphere.

Her client agreed and continued. "He didn't even see how much it meant to me. He never does. It's as though he's lost the light in his eyes … like he can't see clearly anymore … like he doesn't see anything around him. He used to be so easy-going and responsive."

Cassandra listened attentively. An image of her father came to mind, and then Josh. She recalled the day she saw him after her holiday, outside the school gates when they were both fourteen-year-old teenagers. It was a warm and sunny day.

"The light left his eyes," her client continued to say.

It also left your eyes, Josh. Right after that day, Cassandra found herself thinking. Her mind drifted again. She had to remain focused.

"The fact that he didn't acknowledge how you felt, that he didn't acknowledge your feelings, really hurt you? Is 'hurt' the correct word?"

"Yes, it hurt me … it always hurts me … the fact that he doesn't listen … truly listen to me. All I hear is silence. The silence is so loud, that I can't hear myself think sometimes because it just … I don't know … it does something to how

I feel about life, about myself … about him … I don't know what I'm trying to say," she said, despondently.

Cassandra tried to focus. "You're doing great. You're slowly clarifying how you feel and bringing those repressed feelings to the surface. You're ready to allow yourself freedom and to free your soul."

The woman uneasily smiled at her, but seemed relieved that she was going well. She had taken a while to open up and Cassandra knew she was now on her way to deal with all her repressed feelings. The guilt began to take over. Was she herself seeing clearly? Here she was on her high horse, guiding others with her wisdom and her knowledge, but was she practising what she preached?

The woman continued talking. Cassandra's mind drifted again. Dust floated in the sunlight streaming through the curtains that overlooked the busy street. The specks danced gracefully while Cassandra sipped water. She watched the performance as though the curtains were drawn for it to take the stage and dance in the spotlight. Each speck fell to the floor, onto pieces of furniture around the office. Often, she felt guilty: as though the dust was reminding her of her obligations, of her duties to have everything spic and span. There was no time to relax. She was the one that had to ensure that everyone around her was okay, even though the person cleaning the mess was an actual mess inside. Cassandra looked at her client.

She looked at her client's hair. She wondered if she would look better with a fringe. The top she was wearing did nothing for her complexion. It made her look pale and shortened her chest. She was shocked at her incompetence: not being able to focus on her client, judging what she was wearing instead. She couldn't focus on anything. Everything was hazy. A nervous, unclear feeling held her hostage again. She couldn't be free of the feeling. It wouldn't let her focus on the present. She thought of Gestalt therapy theory: not dealing with unfinished business leaves people incomplete.

Julie's words rang in her ear: "If you don't take care of your environment, it's hard to go back."

She looked at the dust again. She realised that it was always there. It seemed like an uphill battle, one that she could never beat. It was an omnipresent force, and why was it always her job to tidy everyone else's mess?

Once again, nothing suddenly gave her joy. Even the impending lunch and shopping trip with Julie and Maria: the planned night with Connor, the scented candles encircling them, the sound of windpipes. She knew the signs. A sign of inner-peace and contentment was usually evident in people who enjoyed the simple things in life: when even a cup of coffee gave them joy. This meant that people were truly at peace: content, not just happy, but at peace.

The sparkle of the client's ring blinded her vision. She looked at her own ring, amongst the earthy hue on her nails. She had told herself that it would always sparkle, no matter how uncertain everything around her was, and that it was birthed amongst adversity, but it would still shine. But here was her client who was wearing a ring, and yes it was sparkling, but the sparkle had left her marriage completely. It was now replaced with darkness: complete deafening, overwhelming silence. She grew up with the darkness … the silence. She couldn't breathe. She couldn't pretend anymore. She was not in a place to help others. She gazed over to the round clock on the wall. To her relief, the time was up for the session.

Her client placed her bag around her shoulder and stood up. "I've got to go away for a while. It's a work thing. I can't get out of it, so can I plan another appointment in a few weeks?" she heard her client asking.

As soon as she heard the words, Cassandra knew what she had to do.

***

She rushed along the busy street lined with clothing boutiques, coffee shops, restaurants, bars, bistros, but it all looked the same to her; like one blurry line of windows and doors. Although her legs carried her aimlessly, she knew that she couldn't go on like this. She wouldn't go on feeling like the wrench was twisting her heart tighter every day. She thought she could sugar-coat it and talk herself into believing that going back was a brave decision: that she was, in fact, taking control of her life again. She was lying to herself. She had to see him; to see the man that raised her but barely tolerated her existence. Only when the awards flowed and the trophies shined as they sat proudly on her bedroom bookshelf, did he pay attention.

"You see, Oscar." Mr Dennison had said one afternoon after she'd come back from school with an award for her piano performance. "She does excel when she wants to … she really is a great kid."

He had looked down at his cup of coffee and nodded. "I guess, she does … when she wants to."

She remembered Mr Dennison giving her a rather sympathetic look, like he understood her plight. She took the compliment even though she knew it would be difficult to receive another one. She would disappoint him again because it would be impossible to continually achieve top marks and trophies. She knew where she stood when he was silent: out of sight, out of mind. All he noticed was the bronze trophy, not the girl that craved affection: to be accepted for who she was, not what she did … to be accepted unconditionally.

Part of her didn't want to admit that she may have intentionally wanted to focus on other's problems to avoid her own. She was a fraud. She had to face her problems. She couldn't get married or continue being a counsellor while she felt like a fake. It was more than imposter syndrome. It was unfair to her clients, to Connor and to herself!

Her heart raced as she ascended the stairs of the landscaped entrance. Were they still overseas? She hadn't bothered to find out if they were planning to actually attend the wedding because she was too afraid to hear the answer. But why wouldn't they? Cynthia's mum and her own mum were good friends.

She pressed the 8th floor in the lift and tried to catch her breath. Connor was still with a client.

"Hi," she greeted one of her neighbours. He played in the courtyard with his young daughters while his wife was busy with business. He smiled back. She found herself comparing his fathering to Connor's.

She sat heavily onto the grey, suede couch facing the cabinet that housed her past. She cleared her throat. She heard a female voice at the other end of the line.   "Hello …"

Cassandra didn't answer. She couldn't find the words. She had talked to her mum on Christmas, New Year's, and birthdays. Her mother had called numerous times, but Cassandra was always busy, and it was mostly idle chit-chat.

"Hi. Mum?" she finally answered.

"Cassandra? Sweetheart … I'm so glad to hear your voice."

Cassandra's heart warmed. How could she have run away from this? How could she punish her mother when her mother had punished herself enough? "I'm glad to hear your voice too, Mum. So, when do you and dad get back home?"

"In around a week. Why? Are you asking about the wedding? If we're going? It's great that they're getting married. Cynthia and Ryan were always so in love … kind of like you and … Anyway, are you coming to the wedding? Cass? It would make me so happy. Cass, I need to know, are you coming home?"

"Yes Mum, I'm coming home." She gazed at the window, watching as a stream of intense light invited itself inside.

CHAPTER SEVEN

"Wow. When did you get time to do all this?" Connor walked over to her, gazing over the fragrant candles. Windpipes and the sound of a waterfall intertwined with gentle harmonious melodies and soothed the cosy lounge room.

"I visited Maria at Eventually You and the rest, I guess, is history," Cassandra replied. She placed her hand on the nape of his neck and caressed his lips with hers. She paused and looked intently into his eyes before she deepened the kiss.

Connor obliged with the same urgency. His lips moved to her neck and chest, planting quick kisses all over her exposed skin. They then moved back to her lips. "You smell so nice, kind of like a lavender field, like you've been immersed in flowers. So, what brought this on?"

"I thought I'd surprise you with a relaxing evening. We counsellors need to nurture our bodies and souls if we're going to be effective in our work."

"That's true," he said and looked at her sceptically.

"What is it, Connor? You don't approve?"

"I don't approve? Of course, I approve." He moved closer to her and stroked his thumb over her lips as he cupped her chin. He caressed her hair as his eyes scoured every feature of her face. "You're full of surprises lately. I love this side of you. I always have. You give so much of yourself when you're like this and you ask me if I approve?" he said as a warm smile spread over his handsome, chiselled features.

"I'm glad," she said. "I mean … I'm glad you want more of me, because that's what you'll be getting this evening." She slid the thin strap of her cream, silk nightie down her shoulder. She then placed her long, slim leg on the couch trying to strike a seductive pose as though she was in a soap opera. She swept her hair to one side in a messy way, adding to the image. She stifled her laughter as she nearly lost her balance.

Connor gave her a dimpled smile and laughed. He wrapped his arms around her waist and pulled her into him. "Did I tell you how much I love you?"

"Many times," she said, while stroking his face. "Since you love that I'm full of surprises …" she began awkwardly, "I have something to tell you … a decision I've just made."

"Well, I'm sure if it's like the surprise of agreeing to go to South Australia, I'm sure I'll love it."

"It is something like that. I've actually decided to go back earlier," she said and studied his perplexed face. "Alone … so your clients won't be impacted, and I've already called all of mine. I told them to organise calls via webcam if they really need to talk. I just feel like I need to go back and think …"

Connor stood still and attentively listened. He then hugged her and locked his eyes with hers. "Cass, I think that's a great idea. I've noticed you've been a bit lost lately. I think you do have some underlying issues that you need to finally address. I was certain of it when I saw you looking at the photo album in the early hours of the morning. I will miss you … really miss you though."

"You can join me a few days before the others join us. We can spend time together and the following weeks we'll be able to attend all the pre-wedding parties. Cynthia will be so happy that we'll be there so long and not just for her special day. She's really getting into this wedding business, which makes me think that I need … I need to complete something first …"

Connor looked at her knowingly. "Before you begin something new?"

"Yes," she replied.

Connor looked at the body oils and lotions sitting on the coffee table. He took one of the friendly looking bottles in his hand and opened the lid. "So, are these for us? Do they serve a purpose tonight?" he asked in a husky voice.

Cassandra laughed at his attempt.

"Okay, I might not sound as sexy as Antonio does with his accent, but I thought it was pretty good," he said and pretended to look hurt.

"It was better than good," she said, taking the bottle out of his hand. She unbuttoned his crisp, slim-fitting work shirt and rubbed oil over his chest.

Connor took her in his arms and led her to the bedroom. As her back rested against the firm mattress, she gasped at the effect Connor's experienced hands had on her body. She placed her head on the soft pillow and watched him work. He massaged her with the healing oil and she felt like she was back in the sunlight. *I need to do this ... to go back home,* she told herself. *It's the only way Connor and I can have more moments like this. It's the only way we can be healed,* she thought as she felt the sensuous, silky-smooth oil gliding over her skin, caressing her gently, healing her.

Early the next morning, Cassandra and Connor enjoyed sitting at an outdoor coffee table of one of the cafes that lined Oxford Street.

Cassandra sipped her coffee and felt recharged. She had felt so close to Connor the night before and waking up in his arms.

She finished her coffee. "I better get going if I'm going to make my plane. I have to be there in a few hours. I'll head back to the apartment and pick up a few things before I wait for the taxi outside our practice. I also need to pick a few files from the office," she said.

"You look so beautiful. This is definitely what you need. I think your confidence is coming back. I can't wait to join you in a few days. You're right though. We'd better end our leisurely breakfast. I've got a new client to see soon, and I don't want you to have to rush. I'll head back to the apartment with you to get my work bag."

Back at the apartment, Cassandra's phone beeped. "Can you get that, Connor? I'm brushing my teeth. It could be Julie or Maria. I told them I'm leaving soon."

"It's Julie," Connor called out. "She wishes you a safe trip and to call her when you get there."

"Can you send a text message back for me? Say thanks and that I'll keep in touch while I'm there," she mumbled with toothpaste in her mouth.

"Done," he said.

She heard nothing as she continued rinsing. After running a brush through her hair one more time, she rushed into the kitchen to have a glass of water. "Thanks for that," she said.

"No problem," Connor replied.

He sounded different, not so enthusiastic. "I'm going to miss you ... so much!" she said as she turned him and wrapped her arms around his waist.

He looked intently at her.

"So, you never told me ..."

"Told you what?" What is it, Connor?"

"Told me what made you change your mind ... about going back. That day when we were all playing tennis and you girls were talking at the table? It was then that you just decided to go, after I pleaded with you that it would be great for us. I'm just curious ... why was it that you decided to go then?"

"I don't know. I guess I heard how much Julie and Maria needed a holiday, and then I got a message from Cynthia ... Does it really matter though? I mean, aren't you so happy that we're all eventually going?"

Connor looked deep into her eyes. It was as though he was searching for an answer that she didn't yet give him.

"Connor, what is it, honey? Is it because I'm leaving you behind? You're the one who said I haven't been myself ... that it's odd that I haven't been seeing my parents. You know, I can tell that you sense how much the rift between my dad and I has been affecting me. You could always read me more than anyone has. That's why I am so blessed to have you in my life. You help me find out what's important to me. You make me realise that the only way I can evolve is to accept all aspects of me, including who I was."

His face softened. "Of course, I want you to go. I want the best for you, Cass. I always have and I always will. You mean the world to me."

She kissed him with feeling and desire. Between breaths she looked down at his silver watch around his wrist. An image of Josh appeared in her mind after the words she had told him.

He lifted her chin with his cool, smooth hand. "Look at me, Cass," he said. She tried to meet his eyes, but resisted for a moment. She could feel his stare on her and finally met his eyes. They remained locked for a moment. "Last night, you were so intense … more than ever. It was beautiful to see you looking at me so longingly, to trust me so much. Tell me, Cass. Where did all that come from?"

"What do you mean? I've always trusted you. I'm always uninhibited with you. I feel safe with you."

Connor just looked at her. "Sure … I know you do and I love that we can be like that with each other. I just don't want it to hide anything else you're feeling. I hope it isn't like a Band-Aid or even like you're trying to convince …"

"I know where you're heading with this. You think I'm trying to convince myself that I don't need to deal with anything, that I already have what I need and that I shouldn't hide behind basic needs because it won't heal what needs to be healed. Connor, I'm a counsellor … I know all that," she said with a lop-sided grin.

Connor looked away from her, his jaw clenched. "You do what you need to do," he said, softly. "Go fix things … with your … with him," he stumbled and searched her.

She froze. She couldn't look away from the hold his stare had on her. His eyes softened and a smile appeared on his face, bringing back the warm, caring, good-natured man she fell in love with.

"I will, Connor. I'll try to fix things, with him … with my dad," she added, a tremor threatening to give her away.

Later that morning, Cassandra hurried out of her office. She had instructed her taxi to be outside the practice they shared with a dental practice and acupuncture clinic. She eyed her luggage near the front door beside the reception desk and her heart rate increased with excitement and unease. The uneasiness persisted and the uncertainty took over. *Why am I doing this without Connor? Do I even need to go so soon? Why can't I wait for a few more days? Why did I have to go to so much trouble to rearrange things?*

Ava smiled at her behind tall, white roses that were arranged in a crystal vase. Cassandra had bought them from one of the local florists to make their clients feel calm because of the flowers' purity, humility, grace and compassion. They offered spiritual healing and sympathy to the space. Ava always looked at Cassandra and Connor like they had some pure, magical healing power, like they held the key to happiness. She often felt honoured to be placed on such a pedestal, but she was also uncomfortable because she knew too well that anyone who stands on a pedestal has nowhere else to go but down. It is almost impossible to maintain and deserve that level of adoration. It wasn't healthy. She now felt like she was not worthy of such an honour. What use was she to anyone at that moment? She smiled back at Ava and continued walking.

There was something about the way Connor had said goodbye that made her feel discomforted, like it was inconclusive and incomplete. What did he mean when he asked if she was trying to convince herself? When he asked if she was okay? A nagging feeling tugged at her heart. She thought he'd meant that she was trying to 'convince herself that she already has everything she needs' and that's why she had been tense the previous night.

Is that what he was trying to say though? Or was he wondering whether she was interested in him or not? Did he think she was only trying to convince herself of her desire for him? Her heart rate elevated. Was he asking if she was, in fact, trying to convince him? *No … surely not.* She dismissed it. She was being silly.

She grabbed her handbag and headed for Connor's office. She had to say goodbye to him again. It felt odd just to leave like that without saying another goodbye and kissing him again, to be in his arms again. She needed his strength to make her feel safe. She needed to convince him that she loved him. A bout of guilt washed over her. Her thoughts were confusing.

That's just great! she thought with despair. His new client was just walking into his office. It would look so unprofessional to interrupt them. Just as she was about to leave, her stomach turned. There was something about the woman. She looked familiar. *She must be around my mum's age,* she speculated. *Oh well, I'd better go. I have to wait for my taxi. I'll call him soon.*

As she stepped out into the warm embrace of the hot sun's rays, she kicked something with her sneaker and nearly lost her balance. She wanted to be comfortable, but she was not used to the bulky flat-form heel that was apparently all the rage. She looked down and a paperback stared up at her. She had almost kicked it off of the footpath. She quickly picked it up and brushed off the dirt. The author's words, story and soul were within the pages. She picked it up. Immersed in the cover, she looked up and came face to face with a woman.

"Excuse me," the woman said. "Cassandra Jensen? I can't believe I ran into you. Well, literally ran into you. Of course, I would, especially since you're outside your practice. What an odd thing to say," she said with a nonchalant laugh.

Cassandra met the woman's eyes. She did look familiar. The woman looked confident and happy. She was vivacious; brimming with positivity. Her energy was infectious.

"It's Kelly … you were my counsellor a while ago. I was having problems with my self-confidence?"

"Of course. Hi Kelly. I'm afraid I didn't recognise you. You look great and …"

"… and confident and invigorated, because of you. You helped me so much when I'd hit rock bottom. I was drinking. I was too scared to open my own business. I would barely leave the house and I practically lived in my pj's. After seeing you for a few months, I began to turn things around. I've never felt so comfortable to talk about my feelings with anyone other than you. Even with other counsellors. I was scared to trust them, but you have this quality … this genuine interest. The way you made me feel at ease … you created such a nurturing and safe environment to encourage me to open up. I'm so grateful. I've finally opened my beauty business and now I'm getting so many clients. I'm so proud of myself."

Cassandra couldn't believe what she was hearing. A feeling of pride and joy washed over her. *I did that for this woman. I helped her to feel confident in her own skin* again *and to follow her dreams.* Kelly was unrecognisable.

When Cassandra had first met Kelly in a counselling session, Kelly wouldn't maintain eye contact and now she was radiating a positive vibe. The energy made Cassandra feel as though she could climb the highest mountains and sing at the top of her lungs.

"Thank you. I'm glad I was able to help you so much, but please, you also contributed a great deal. I guided you to see things more clearly, and to remove obstacles that were hindering your growth. I helped you uncover what you already had. We worked as a team," Cassandra reassured her.

"Thank you so much, for everything. I can see you have to go somewhere, but I wanted to let you know. Do me a favour? Never stop helping. You have a gift; don't throw it away. It would be a waste of a talent. Anyway, have a great trip."

Kelly strode confidently down the street, with her bold colourful dress. Kelly was in the front row, no longer fading into the background. "Thanks, bye," she called back. *I won't stop helping others,* she told herself. *But in order to do that, I need to help myself.*

She decided to return the book. It probably belonged to one of her clients or Ava. *Great! It'll give me another chance to say bye to Connor …*

Her thoughts were interrupted by the taxi driver who had parked in front of her.

"Are you ready, Miss Jensen?" he asked her.

She took a deep breath and threw the book into her handbag. There would be no time to say goodbye to Connor, she thought solemnly. "Yes, I'm ready," she decided.

CHAPTER EIGHT

When Cassandra rolled down the window of the hire car, a gust of wind swept an ash blonde strand of hair across her face. As she drove through the hills, fields of green and gold flanked either side of the road. She was on her way to the Barossa Valley. She took a deep breath. She wasn't too far from where she grew up.

Two hours ago she had landed at Adelaide airport and nostalgia wrapped her in its sentimental arms. Old stone churches, cathedrals, cottages and streets full of shops and pubs, old and new, brought back her past. She and her friends had caught the train into the city of Adelaide and explored the busy streets amongst throngs of people, before heading back home to the country on many occasions.

The music kept her company as she sang to "Why Does It Always Rain On Me?" by Travis. Being on her own was liberating. She would soon be greeted by vineyards and wine cellars, and comforting, friendly country towns.

A familiar tall, rusty windmill caught her attention from afar. It juxtaposed the flatness of that particular strip of land with its imposing height. She loosened her grasp on the steering wheel, relaxing as the road emptied of all other traffic.

She admired the scenery changing from the views of her windscreen and review mirror and glanced at the dashboard to check the speed. For that moment, her only purpose was to get to her destination and enjoy the ride. Nothing else mattered as she sat in the driver's seat steering her way to her own past and to her future.

Sheep flocked together, idly grazing near a stream. Tall, leaning branches cast a shadow over the sun-drenched flow of water. It reminded Cassandra of lazy summers on the porch, eating ice cream or sipping iced tea with a Viennese pastry on the side that her mother had freshly baked, away from the unapologetic heat. The sheep, too, had found their own shade: their momentary shelter away from the scorching heat, to enjoy their meal.

The sting of summer has always been so intense in these parts, she recalled. It would leave its mark with vigour and in an unforgiving way that was brutal but also nostalgic and romantic. The romance of the land was found in its dents and rawness, in its flaws and its uniqueness. It was also found in its forgiveness, as fertile soil created new life, and colours were displayed in clusters as Mother Nature painted her masterpieces.

Cassandra breathed in the warm air before she closed her window to allow the air-conditioner to cool her perspired skin. Her hair waved ferociously as she turned the fan on high. The temperature outside was now in the high 30s — 39 degrees Celsius to be exact.

As the temperature reached a sweltering 40 degrees Celsius, the view outside the windscreen grew hazy.

She would soon go through Rowland Flat and then reach her hometown, Tanunda. She had booked a hotel room on late notice in the town, where she would visit before driving to her childhood home. Her parents wouldn't be there for a few more days.

She sang nonchalantly to another track from Travis called "Flowers In The Window".

The sweeping view from her windscreen was panoramic: blue sky with patches of white meeting fields of emerald, and a bold, familiar, yellow circle in the sky, showering everything below it with streams of gold light, creating patterns like a disco ball.

Cassandra sang louder, feeling like she was driving straight towards a movie screen or a gigantic billboard picture; that's how still and picturesque it all looked in the distance. The jingle continued through the speakers, and feeling nostalgic and moved, a tear streamed down her cheek as she passed a sea of cheerful, dancing daisies that waved to her. *How surreal is this? It does something to you,* she thought. The daisies reminded her of Connor, and she was momentarily saddened that Connor was now not with her to also savour the beauty of the rich land around her. Its beauty resonated with her and touched her to the core. It awoke her senses as she breathed it all in. She felt like she was being reacquainted with a warm, familiar friend.

"Rowland Flat," she said, aloud. She was now well and truly in Barossa Valley. She was nearly home. A vineyard appeared; its rows of green vines with its rich, burgundy-coloured grapes stood obediently in parallel rows allowing the sun to blanket them. They always reminded Cassandra of eager students dressed in uniforms, standing at their morning assembly. The historic Jacobs Creek sign came into view. It was the sign that pointed to the actual creek itself. She tried to see it more clearly as she continued her journey on the Barossa Valley Highway.

She thought of the time she'd hurt her ankle while running with her heavy school bag. Ryan and Cynthia had sat down next to the creek to comfort her. She'd fallen over a huge branch when Ryan had shared one of his witty jokes.

She pulled up in front of the creek, near some native river red gums, and opened the window on the driver's side. Cars passed her as she admired the beauty of the trees.

She opened the door and stepped out, her flat form sneakers making her yearn a pair of sandals. *On second thoughts, perhaps not,* she thought as she jumped over a nest of bull ants.

The restoration and replanting of blue gums, red gums, as well as other native Australian shrubs and trees had brought her surroundings back to their former glory. Frogs croaked from the creek's edge.

The heat soaked her as her mind trailed back to the day when Josh quickly rode his bike to the creek after Ryan told him Cassandra had been injured.

This was the log I sat on when he and I were nearly eighteen, she recalled, touching its rough surface. He had looked seriously at her.

Josh had changed over the years. By that time, he was no longer a carefree fourteen-year-old. He was still everyone's friend: the guy everyone got along with. However, at that stage of his life, he looked like he was carrying the weight of the world on his shoulders, not just his backpack. A heaviness hung over him; it was reflected in his eyes, in his half-smile. It was as though he was uneasy and hesitant to allow himself to be happy. His world had changed at the blink of an eye that day outside the school gates after he'd walked over to her. She had returned from her summer holiday and patiently waited for his arrival, under the tree that perfumed the air with its sweet milky flowers.

"Hey, Cass. Are you okay? I've got you now. You're gonna be fine. Just chill. Take deep breaths and we'll get you to the doctor's," he'd said, after jumping off his bike and racing to where she sat.

She was full of worry while her ankle throbbed. She was in pain, but she wished she could tell him that was not her only problem. She was so worried about what he would say, what her dad would say. He would not take the news that she had irresponsibly gone off with her friends without being aware of the 'imminent dangers' well. He would be angrier still that she missed doing her homework or practising the piano or flute straight after school. He was unnecessarily cautious for her, as though she was some delicate flower that would get trampled if she hung out with the sinister creatures and tall domineering trees in the wide, dark forest.

It was strange that he actually cared about her safety. She had thought it was because he didn't want her ruining his reputation in the community. To add insult to injury, if he saw her with Josh Sturgess … He hadn't approved of the entire family, including Josh's parents Lana and Ben.

Cassandra still didn't know why he didn't approve of Lana. Ben was laid-back and did as he pleased, which meant Cassandra's father wasn't impressed with his *blasé* attitude, but Lana was the opposite; she expected everything to be immaculate and she cared about appearances.

Anyway, how could Cassandra have complained when Josh had his own serious worries? Her guilt made her resistant to share her problems. His problems were a way for her to hide, as though his woes enabled her to avoid telling him the truth: she wasn't cheerful, confident and carefree behind closed doors.

She had looked into his pensive, hazel eyes, and wanted to tell him everything. Her heart ached. She felt like running off with him somewhere far away, somewhere where their problems would vanish, where they could feed off each other's love without judgemental eyes looking down on them. Even at seventeen, she had craved affection. She wished he would give her even more affection than he already had.

Her cheeks had ached while she desperately tried to hide how broken she was. The emptiness, for her, was too heavy to carry, unlike his burden — which was full of answers about life that he didn't think he would ever need to know or learn.

"I know that I'll be fine now, Josh. I'm always fine when I'm with you," she'd said with a shy smile between her tears.

Cassandra's eyes stung her with salty tears as she recalled the scene as though it had occurred yesterday. He had caressed her face with his smooth hand before continuing to nurse her wound. "What is it?" he'd asked her, flicking his long, dark brown fringe away from his face to see her clearly.

She'd managed another smile and said, "Nothing. I'm just glad you're here to help me."

He looked at her unflinchingly for a while. He seemed to be studying her before he looked back to her ankle.

He was always there to take care of her, and she of him. That would never change. It had been like that since they were children. *He was always there for me,* she repeated the words in her mind.

Her phone rang, startling her. It was Cynthia. She read the message:

Hi Cass. Thanks for confirming that your friends are all able to attend our wedding. I'm glad you let me know before they responded to the invitations. It means that I can now organise the rest of the seating arrangements. At least your table is easy to arrange … unlike some other tables. I don't want people to just sit there like they're at some forced team-building course. It's a shame that some couldn't make it though. Oh well, I'll just have to move some seats and people around. See you soon. Cynthia.

Cassandra had to know. She moved to the shade of the trees and typed a response.

Hi Cynthia. So, who in particular couldn't make it? I know my parents will be coming. Is it anyone I know?

Cassandra wandered to the car and waited for the response, deciding to freshen up at the hotel. Comfortable clothes were calling out to her. Her loose, cotton t-shirt stuck to her while her hair felt too dry from the humidity.

As Cassandra tied her hair into a ponytail, her phone beeped. Comfortably seated in the driver's seat, she turned the air-conditioner on and then fastened her seatbelt. She then turned the ignition and read the message with a fast-beating heart.

Hey Cass. Sorry. I can't believe I didn't mention this. It's Josh. Unfortunately, he won't be able to make it; some photography thing, and he might not be able to get a flight in time from N.Y.C. I'm not really sure what the reason is … he wasn't that clear. I think it might be too much out of his way. It's a shame though ... that he won't be here. You must be devastated. You were great friends.

Cassandra looked at the words, her heart palpitating. She diverted her attention to the log where he had nursed her wound. *Yes, we were great friends ... but we were a lot more. More than many ever knew.* "It is a shame," she said aloud. *But it's the way it should be,* she thought to herself. *You were my past, and my future is with the sweet, intelligent man I left behind. Did I do that for you, Josh?* Her heart gave the answer she feared. Its heaviness spoke volumes.

The empty feeling returned; the load too difficult to carry. He had refused to help her fill the void all those years ago, even when she returned to him in her twenties. She'd completed her studies at university and had worked as a teacher for a few years before she'd decided to study counselling instead. She'd thought they could finally have what they had once wanted.

A kookaburra flew past and made its way to its nest in one of the many trees where the rest of its family waited. They stayed with their partner for life. She recalled the lone call she'd heard when she was on the phone to Cynthia.

It's for the best, she told herself. It's for the best that he stayed away ... especially because I didn't. She had ignored the warning, but he never did. He was always aware of the *imminent dangers.* He had learned of their existence early in his life, which forced him to take more responsibility than he should have had to: to be more observant about the environment around him, to remain alert, to do it for his own self-preservation.

With that thought in mind, she drove back onto the open road. Holding the steering wheel tightly, a tear streamed down her cheek. She kept driving, trying desperately not to look back.

CHAPTER NINE

The sound of the travel bag's wheels travelling down the spacious tiled foyer got one of the cleaner's attention who was busy cleaning one of the hotel's ground-floor rooms. The woman looked up from her task of assiduously sorting sheets and Cassandra smiled at her before pressing the button of the lift. The cleaner reciprocated the gesture.

Waiting patiently for the lift, Cassandra scanned the wide, tiled corridor: the contemporary lounges, huge mirrors that reflected the outdoor breakfast area, and a lovely verandah that boasted a spectacular view of the vineyard near the resort. The view was so peaceful and rustic that she felt like recommending the hotel to some of her clients.

The elevator *dinged* and the doors opened, diverting Cassandra's attention. After letting some of the hotel's guests out: a family with two eager-looking, cheerful toddlers, and a middle-aged man wearing a polo top and a smart pair of shorts, carrying a bag of golf clubs on his shoulder, she entered the opulent lift. Excitement built inside her chest as she gazed at all the different floor levels from behind the polished glass of the lift. The hotel oozed a crisp, relaxed contemporary vibe. The views circling the hotel ensured that nature could be seen from most of the rooms, lounges and restaurants.

Cassandra had no intention of imposing on anyone. She had to build up the courage to visit her family home. Part of her knew that many had suffered worse plights growing up, but she couldn't help wonder if it all happened because of something she did. She had caught her father laughing, letting his guard down, on occasion.

When she entered the contemporary suit, she marvelled at the art prints on the wall and an unusual vase on the coffee table. She had chosen a wonderful room on short

90

notice. The heavy, pale grey curtains were open, revealing an impressive view of the vineyard and plush, green hills in the distance. The long resort pool was also in full view, as were many of the white outdoor chairs and tables, and the pool's bar.

Cassandra sat back on the sofa and took in the atmosphere. As beautiful as it was, she wished Connor was there; a romantic setting wasn't the same without him. *But he will be here in a few days*, she told herself. He would spend a few days with her in the hotel before they all rented one of the double-storey holiday houses together. Maria had made sure everything was ready for their stay.

It was also odd that she was staying in a hotel when her parents lived close by. What was even more odd was that she even had a set of keys to her family home.

She sent a message saying she had checked into the hotel room to Connor. He had sent her a few messages ensuring she was okay and telling her that he loved her.

"So, what do I do first?" she asked an empty room, eyeing her unpacked luggage. *Maybe I should sit by the pool and have something to eat,* she contemplated. It was nearly 3:00 pm and she hadn't had lunch yet.

Around a half hour later, she was strolling into the cafe sporting a kimono midi dress, a white, floppy hat, flip-flops, a beach bag around her shoulder and one of the hotel's blue and white striped towels. She felt like rejuvenating before she began her homecoming obligations. She hadn't even told Cynthia she was there, but as she would tell her clients, there's nothing wrong with pampering yourself first, in fact, it's healthy. Self-love is not selfish. It's the only way to nurture yourself so you can have time and energy for others. It was funny how many, including herself, walked around with false beliefs that she even had to remind herself to challenge. They would appear so rapidly. Disproving their validity was a constant challenge, but so well worth it. With her father shouting out so many 'shoulds' and 'musts' at her during childhood, it was a miracle she turned out the way she did. But she couldn't keep running forever. The past would always be there.

She hadn't confronted certain things from her past, but she would now, and she had done alright for herself regardless. She had followed her heart. She hadn't become like him. She believed in following dreams, being true to her values, and reaching her potential. She accepted and tried not to judge. She had become a counsellor to guide others with the techniques she learned, which encouraged self-acceptance, forgiveness, and evolving. She encouraged clients to pursue their dreams. He had tried to teach her to stop dreaming.

Why did you become like that, Dad? Did the same thing happen to you? Did someone tell you to forget your dreams? Did they tell you to live only to survive and that you weren't allowed to fly?

When he screamed at her, which he did on some occasions, she would at least have the opportunity to answer back. That look in his eyes, that she should do what is expected, was like a closed door. If she didn't have Josh … He was the one that would give her the look she needed, with his warm, accepting eyes. He would challenge the 'shoulds' and 'oughts', until she learned to challenge them for herself.

"But you're learning to play the piano because you want to, remember?" Josh had told her one day after school when they had stopped to have a drink at their local pizza hangout. They had continued talking as they'd stepped onto the footpath.

"Yes … I do want to," she'd replied, not being able to explain the silent power her father had on her, the way he made her feel like she would fail if she didn't do things his way, how she craved to be noticed. He wouldn't understand the shame she felt about who she was when he ignored her; when he looked at her trophies and failed to realise that the person who earned them had a heart, and feelings, and dreams. Before she'd completed her sentence, he continued his thoughts.

"Why do people imprison themselves? Why do they live with guilt and fear as though any path they choose or any decisions they make must be scrutinised and judged? They wait until they get some special pass telling them that they can enter, like they do in some night club, like their decision is only then valid? Sometimes, it's as though even the act of having a nap is rebellious, that you're a conspirator and have some dark secret to hide from the masses; that secret is that you are actually in need of rest."

Cassandra had looked at him thoughtfully. He understood, she realised. He saw how she felt even if they didn't directly address it.

"I don't know," she'd said. "I guess it's like when people pretend that they don't know something even when they do. It's like they all know but won't admit they know because it means they don't have to deal with it. Maybe it's too hard, or too messy … or too real," she'd replied. His eyes locked with hers when she'd finished talking. Ironically, it was like she had touched on something that they wouldn't admit.

"I can always talk to you. I mean, I rarely dare to talk to anyone the way I talk to you — deeply. There's feeling in every word you say."

"Can you, Josh? I mean, can you really talk to me? Tell me the things you can't tell others?"

"Yes, Cass, I can. About what you said earlier, sometimes people that truly know each other, know what the other is thinking before they even think it. Which may mean they're not really pretending. There's no need to say what they already know about each other or what they already feel."

She'd looked up at him, stunned by the way he looked at things. She would often catch him noting his thoughts down in the journal he carried.

He leaned in and stroked her hair. "Anyway, when you talk about pretending, do you also mean how much I don't want you to leave for Sydney in a few months? Tell me, Cass. Why does everyone leave in the end?"

She continued to look into his vulnerable eyes. His wavy fringe covered part of his eye as he moved his lips softly onto hers. She thought he would confide in her, but his lips spoke instead, of how much he yearned to feel close to her.

He pressed his chest against hers, deepening the kiss, and held her hand. She pressed her back onto the wall of a shop in the quiet street. She knew he would be her first eventually. She loved him, but she would have to let him go. She knew they would keep pretending. Just like when he said everything would be okay, even when she knew he was harbouring pain from that day at the school gates. He couldn't talk to her about why his eyes had become darker, why his heart had become less trusting.

She knew that love would not be enough for them. She feared that their pretending would lead to silence. Maybe he saw that too. Maybe he feared it like she did, but pretended he didn't. Maybe he had convinced himself that they really knew each other when, in fact, they knew nothing about each other's real life.

She sat on one of the outdoor chairs and caught a young, bare-chested man wearing board shorts looking at her as he sat near the bar. His friend also sat down after placing a tray of cocktails and beers on the small table. She caught him saying something to his friend, and then they laughed before they smiled at her, which made her uncomfortable. Before she could move to a table behind a large fern, the waitress came over. She clenched her fists as a family claimed the table she had her eye on.

The last thing she needed was a pair of immature larrikins rallying for her attention when all she wanted to do was to rejuvenate. No one should have to put up with such nonsense. She could pretend they didn't bother her or she could confront them, but why should she exert so much negative energy to that? It would only eat into her time and encourage more unwanted attention. That wasn't an option. The other option was to wait for a table to become available and take it. For now, she would have to stay where she was and suffer because she was hungry. The young, blonde-haired waitress who was waiting to take her order had such a warm smile, she couldn't help but smile back and place her order.

"I'll have the pumpkin and mushroom risotto and a glass of the Riesling, thanks."

The blond male stood and struck a strange pose, leaning an elbow on the concrete column that held the pergola up, placing his tanned leg onto it as well as he took sips from his beer. During the display, he continued glancing over at her table.

Just as Cassandra thought the strange position would make drinking a beer impossible, the man nearly lost his balance. Within a few seconds he was back on the column, attempting to sip his drink again.

She looked away when he caught her looking at him and went to check her phone before deciding to read the book she had kicked across the footpath.

The book made her think of Connor. *How I wish you were here, right now*, she thought as she admired the shimmer of her diamond next to the vibrant colours of terracotta, yellow and white on the cover of the book. *At least I can immerse myself into a story until my food gets here*, she thought. *And why should I let them ruin my lunch?* Her last thought gave her strength, and she received an extra boost when she noticed a message had come through. It was from Connor.

Thanks for letting me know, Cass. I'm about to have a session with the new client I was telling you about before you left. Have fun and stay safe. I miss you so much already. Tonight, our bed will seem so cold without you in my arms and the feel of your soft skin against me. I love you, Cass. Talk to you soon.

Connor xxx

Cassandra smiled to herself. It was as if she could conquer Mount Everest. A pair of nuisances were easily dealt with.

She thought about the client he had mentioned. *It must be the woman that had gone into his office before I left.* The older woman had looked so familiar. Cassandra couldn't remember where she'd seen her. *Oh well,* she thought as she opened the cover of the book, noticing that the blond-haired male was still glancing over to her table while emphasising his toned assets. He rubbed sunscreen over his muscular arms. Cassandra stifled a smile when the sunscreen bottle slipped out of his hands and came close to knocking his friend on the head. His friend looked less than impressed. She opened the cover and read the first page.

Peter couldn't breathe. He ran frantically up the hill. His ears buzzed, and his sneakers felt like they dragged him into the ground. He tried desperately to reach the top, but his aching feet did not agree.

A bird call from across the lake muffled his hearing. His heart throbbed, but he wouldn't cry. He wouldn't allow himself to cry even though his heart ached, and his stomach felt like someone had turned on the spin cycle.

"It's not true. This isn't happening," he told himself, but he wasn't a good liar. For the thirteen years he had been in this world, his life had been exactly how he wanted it to be — his friends, his school, his fam—

As he reached the top, the sun's rays hit him like rocks. He gasped for air, but his lungs felt like they were collapsing on him. It couldn't be possible. The words weren't real; he couldn't acknowledge them. They hadn't caused the sudden, overwhelming pain in his heart. Everything was supposed to be the way it always had been. Why would things change?

"Everything is the same," he muttered to himself. The words convinced him for a second, but his heart knew the truth even if his mind denied it. With each unbearable beat of his heart, he heard the cold, harsh words reiterating. "She's gone. She's gone …"

He rose up from his bundled state of despair and made out the log near the old stone bench where he'd sat many times before, and the lake in the distance; the lake where he had so many fond memories with his friends and fam … He couldn't breathe again. His eyes blurred out the scenery in front of him until it looked like an abstract painting. His tears created strokes on strokes of colour and the view became bleak as the tears increased with intensity. The scene no longer evoked fond memories of picnics, birthday parties, or cricket games. It was foggy, foreign and messy, just like his life had become.

"She's gone …" he said, louder this time. "She's gone … she's gone. She's gone!" he screamed, but there was no reply. There was no one by the lake that could reply; no one from the birthday party, the picnic, or the cricket game, and there would never be a time like that again, because she had left them — she had left him.

Everything disappeared from view as his tears became uncontrollable. Each tear felt like a nail hammering the reality into his heart. The long, brown strands of hair from his fringe stung his eyelids and irritated his sweaty face. He shivered even though the sun bit through his skin to his soul.

He surrendered to the ground which waited to embrace him with open arms. He fell into the arms of the welcoming earth. Sinking into it, he dug his nails into the dry dirt. He hugged his knees just like he had done as a young boy when he was afraid on a cold, stormy night. Huddled, he cried rhythmically. The crying comforted his heart. The tears expressed his pain, and his heart accepted it.

A tear slid down Cassandra's cheek. She hadn't expected to read such a sad story.

That's how Josh would have felt when his mother had left him at the school gates— for good.

Of course, no one said that she'd left him, his brother, and his father. Everyone went along with the story the family had concocted: she was on a trip to see family, but she'd be back. That day never came and eventually people stopped asking.

Whenever Cassandra had brought it up, Josh would disengage and his eyes would darken. He didn't trust her enough to tell her his secret, and so they continued to pretend.

She looked at the cover of the book. *Fragrant Streams* was the title. *How odd,* she thought. It was almost a sign that she needed to see him again. She wanted to help him. She needed to know why she wasn't enough; why he remained silent. She had loved him so much that it had scared her. She never knew that a love so strong could prevent two people from knowing who the other truly was. She never knew that it could lead to an emptiness that not even love alone could fill. Their love would have been unhealthy. It was better kept only in their memory.

What was she thinking? Josh wouldn't be there. No matter how much her heart ached, she knew better than to believe in signs. She had always told her friends that it was dangerous to believe in fate when free will was essential to life.

Cassandra snapped out of her reverie. She felt someone near her, but the waitress was at the table in front of her, not delivering her food. Panic struck her as she realised that it must be the annoying guys.

"Cassandra?"

Relief enveloped her at the feminine voice and she turned. "Bella Anderson! From French class with …"

"Mrs McNamara … the teacher that kept us back when we learned to construct sentences using directions in French. With the accent! We were so scared that we'd never be able to do it and wondered if she'd keep us there indefinitely."

Cassandra laughed at the memory. "She felt so sorry for us that she gave us some sweets from her trip to France. Bella … I can't believe I ran into you like this."

"It's great that you're back. You moved to Sydney, right?"

"Yes, I have, and you? Are you living in Tanunda still?"

"No, I married and moved to Adelaide for work. We come here in the summer holidays. It's just beautiful here. It's less busy this time of the year, and the kids love the aquatic-sized pool. Plus, I love my parents dearly, but spending more than a few days at mum's can get on my nerves."

Cassandra stirred in her seat. "Kids … you have children?" Guilt washed over her as she thought about seeing her parents.

"Yeah, my hubby is minding them in the pool. It's a shame to see you right before we're about to leave. Anyway, it's great to hear Cynthia and Ryan are getting married. They were so sweet in high school. I haven't kept in touch with that many friends from school so it's great to be invited to the wedding. Have you seen Josh?" she glanced to Cassandra.

"I'm engaged," she blurted and showed her engagement ring. Her heart raced at the sound of his name.

"Wow, you're engaged? That's great. You and Josh were one of the best suited couples in school. I know you two played the 'we're just friends' card, but I did catch you kissing in the back oval one day in the last year of school, and I don't think friends would kiss with such passion. I mean, it was hot."

Cassandra's cheeks burned. Bella's pitch had increased since high school. The two men smiled like they were impressed with what they heard. She cleared her throat and tried to regain her composure. "Um … I'm engaged to Connor. That's his name … my fiancé's name. I met him in Sydney. We've been together for a few years now."

"Oh!" Bella managed, sounding more surprised than embarrassed. "I thought you two would stay together. I mean, sorry, that was rude of me. I'm just surprised. He was so into you … really into you. Anyway, there I go again. I'm sure Con …"

"Connor," Cassandra immediately assisted.

"I'm sure Connor is also a great guy. You always attracted the deep thinkers. Josh had become so philosophical and lyrical over the years; I thought he'd definitely end up with someone just as perceptive, empathetic, I guess, and dreamy-eyed. You were always helping people. That's why you were given the name *Compassionate Cass* at the end-of-year school formal. The school committee made the name official."

Cassandra listened apprehensively to every word Bella uttered. She could hear the words loud and clear in her mind: *I thought you two would surely stay together.* It was as though Bella was disappointed that Cassandra would let a love like that fade away.

"Anyway … what did you end up studying? I'm in sales at the moment."

"I'm actually a counsellor. So is Connor," she replied. Her eyes teared as she looked at the pool where numerous kids were playing on long foam noodles. A man waved in their direction.

"Of course, a counsellor. I should have guessed."

"Is that your husband waving?" Cassandra asked, eager to end the conversation.

"Yes, we're running late. The kids wanted one last swim before we check out. You'll be at the wedding?"

"Yes, I will."

"See you then," she said and gave her a hug before striding back to her family.

"Here's your risotto," the waitress announced, jovially.

"Thank you," she said, trying hard to match her sincere smile.

Cassandra took a sip of wine and eyed the book next to her bag. She felt so hot and agitated. She decided she couldn't eat and would instead jump in the pool.

The men stood from their seats and headed in her direction.

"Cheer up, love," the fair-haired one said. "There's no need to be sad. Look at yourself. You're beautiful!"

Cassandra refrained from squirming in her seat. She managed a smile, not knowing how to respond to the idea that beauty equalled happiness.

"It's not your fault you broke that guy's heart," he continued.

Cassandra gave him a perplexed look, which begged the question: *How do you know whose heart was broken?*

"Of course, you broke his heart," he insisted. His friend behind him nodded in agreement. He was now a mind reader, she thought sheepishly at her false assumption of him being clueless.

"Well, opinions tend to vary," she managed, as the smell of mushroom and pumpkin comforted her.

"Yeah, I guess they can," he replied. "But the truth doesn't." His green eyes met hers. "The truth doesn't," he repeated and placed his sunglasses over his eyes.

Cassandra looked on with her mouth agape and her eyes transfixed on their backs as they sauntered away with their towels floating like capes from their broad shoulders.

But the truth doesn't. She chewed the words up as she eyed the food. Glancing over at the novel beside her bag, she thought of Josh and she felt that she was sinking further down into her past.

A woman dived into the deep end and the loud splash diverted her attention.

CHAPTER TEN

A horn beeped as Cassandra stepped out of her car onto a tree-lined street in the town of Angaston, in the heat of Thursday morning. The town was at the highest point of the valley and had a rural feel. Many of its old buildings were still intact. Cassandra placed the strap from her bucket bag over her shoulder and marvelled at the cosy town that encapsulated so much history from the Cornish first settlers, mainly miners, as well as other British settlers, that had settled in that part of the eastern side of the Barossa Valley. A German presence was also greatly felt in areas that circled the town, but this portion was largely influenced by the English pioneers compared to other parts of the valley which had a predominantly Bavarian history.

Cassandra admired one of the many grand Romanesque Lutheran churches made of soapstone. She then strolled into Murray Street and stopped to gaze at the old Flour Mill from the mid-eighteen-hundreds.

Walking along the Heritage Walk, she pondered how life would have been like back in the day. She pictured the old butcher shops, English pubs, blacksmiths, bakers, and banks, with people carrying about their day. The town provided a similar feel with shops still operating out of the old buildings. She looked at her watch, stopping in front an historic Methodist church. Cynthia was meeting her at a local cafe near the famous Barossa Brauhaus Hotel. She continued walking, excited to see the rustic Doddridge Blacksmith Shop again.

The heat was persistent as it burned the footpath under her sandals. She was wise to have chosen a white, linen shirt around her emerald green, strapless jersey dress.

Gazing at all the buildings, she couldn't help but think of how much fun she'd have with Connor when he finally joined her. She couldn't wait to give him a tour of all the lovely and nostalgic shops and businesses from long ago, and many of the charming shops still operating, such as the delightful cheese shop that was known for its artisan hand-made cheese.

For the time being, she had agreed to meet her friend for lunch in one of the many coffee shops. She'd decided to let Cynthia know that she was back at the Barossa Valley and that she'd be driving into Angaston that morning. Coincidentally, it just so happened that Cynthia happened to be running errands there. Cassandra looked forward to seeing her again. She decided she couldn't hide anymore. Afterwards, she would drive back to where she grew up. She wanted to work herself into the idea of dealing with her past on her own, as she had planned when she'd abruptly flew solo.

"Cassandra," Cynthia called out from across the street as she stepped out of one of the lovely homeware shops.

Cassandra waved and gave her an affectionate smile from across the wide street. Cynthia crossed over to her. She eagerly ran up to where Cassandra stood on the footpath, laughing whimsically from the excitement. She embraced her the moment she reached her.

"Cass … you look amazing! It's so great to see you again."

"Hi Cynthia. You look positively radiant. I think you've been in your element. You've always loved organising parties, even back in high school. What am I talking about? Even when you were a little girl. Remember that tea party you planned for us when we were five-years-old? I just thought about it the other day. You had set everything up with your little toy tea set and you even had your mother make fairy bread. And she helped you make place cards for everyone."

Cynthia cringed and then began to laugh, as though realising how cute and sweet it sounded now that she was older. "I even invited some boys to the tea party and ensured they sat in their allocated seats. Josh had spilled the orange cordial all over the table, and I became so angry with him. I told my mum. He was so sorry though."

Cassandra smiled at the image. "That's right. I can't believe we remember all that. We were only five-years-old. That Simon boy that lived near our house for a while took the colourful hundreds and thousands from the fairy bread and wiped his hand all over my hair."

"Until Josh tried to wipe it off with one of the pink, polka dot serviettes. My mum told me she had seen Josh push the small chair out from under him when Simon went to sit back down, and he'd ended up on the grass, bawling his eyes out."

Cassandra's heart felt like it was melting. He had truly always been there for her. She vaguely recalled Cynthia's mother telling them about Josh wiping her hair, but she hadn't known that Josh was the cause of Simon's tears.

"Well, I certainly knew how to throw a party," Cynthia said in between laughter.

"Yes. And no one can say that your parties were boring."

"It's so great that you're back, Cass. You've been away too long. You're back where you should be, where you belong."

Cassandra managed a half-smile. It was funny how Cynthia looked at it that way. She felt like she never belonged, but hearing all these stories awoke something inside of her. The more she thought about her life back then, the more she was beginning to realise that she couldn't hide from it. Those memories served a purpose; they were too valuable to ignore and they were part of her. The main aspect she couldn't ignore was the little boy who had tried to wipe the sprinkles and butter out of her hair. He had always been part of her and who she was; those memories could not be erased.

They sat in a cosy coffee shop that smelled like vanilla and custard. The sweet aroma enveloped the small space with a warmth that promised gracious hospitality.

"So, tell me about him … tell me about Connor. How is he doing? I only met him briefly when I was in Sydney."

Cassandra took a deep breath before answering. "He's wonderful, he's gregarious, and he's passionate about helping people. I fell in love with him the moment I laid eyes on him, and I still feel that thrill when I'm with him. I think it's important to be able to truly say what you feel with someone you love, to have no restrictions and to know they'll understand where you're coming from." Cassandra looked across the table at Cynthia's thoughtful hazel eyes. She was really paying attention to what she was saying.

Cynthia's hair was neatly swept away from her face, tucked behind one ear as though she didn't want to miss a word.

Cassandra felt guilty. Up until now, those words had rung true. Now she had uttered them without giving them much thought. Josh made her a hypocrite. She couldn't even show Connor the picture of Josh. She hadn't been able to talk about him. She didn't think she needed to for so long.

"So, how's Ryan? You two must be really excited about the wedding. I'd imagine you'd be stressed as well?"

"Yeah … it's stressful, but I love the excitement. We're having so much fun with it. We can't wait to be husband and wife. I've always been certain that Ryan and I would stay together. I had no reservations in my mind. Sure, we had our time away, but I knew deep in my heart we would, one day, reunite."

"That's great," Cassandra replied. The unease wrapped around her, strangling her.

"Anyway, it's also great that you found someone like Connor. Ryan and I are the same. I can talk to him about anything. I know he won't judge me. Not that I have anything to hide. It's not as if I have a dark secret or … thoughts of a lost love."

Cassandra looked up from her menu. Cynthia studied her then leaned forward and placed her hand on hers. Her face softened and she smiled. "I'm really happy we both met wonderful guys that we feel comfortable being honest to. It's the best way to start a life together. A marriage." She sat back in her seat. "Anyway, let's order our food. Everything is so delectable here."

A short while later, one of the waitresses brought their orders: a mixture of small quiches and small fresh pies, some sparkling water, and coffee.

"I can't believe we're both in our early thirties. Where has the time gone? Part of me thinks that Ryan and I wasted so much time being away from each other, but he came back home. Maybe if we hadn't separated for a while, we wouldn't be together now. I think the time away from each other really made us realise that we were meant to be together. Do you know what I mean? It's as though time gave us the answer. Time reinforced that it can't keep two people away from each other if they truly love each other."

Cassandra looked up from her cup of coffee. "I'm really happy for you. I knew you two were always meant to be. Um ... you were so in love ... how could you not be together?" she managed, with a nervous smile.

"You did?" Cynthia asked.

"Sure. I think we all did," she added, suddenly remembering Bella's words from the other day about her and Josh.

"It's funny. Many have told me that. I think we knew it too, but we felt that we had to pursue our dreams career-wise. Ryan had been accepted to study in New York, and I'd been accepted to work in Thailand in Tourism. We also felt that we were too young to be in a serious relationship. Ironically, we were too young to know how sacred love can be when you find it. Sure, we tried being with other people, but it was nothing compared to what Ryan and I had," she continued. He came back and realised that it was hard to find that kind of love. We're happy living here again. I always loved this place."

"I ran into Bella the other day," Cassandra said, knowing that Cynthia wasn't going to change the subject without an intervention. "She can't wait to come to your wedding."

"That's great. It'll be fun to catch up with everyone. Cass, I hope I haven't upset you or anything."

"What? No, it's just strange to be here again. I'm still getting used to it all. So many memories came back while I walked down this street and seeing the 'welcome' sign when I drove to Tanunda … all of it."

"I'm sure there are many memories for you. I'm surprised you haven't been back for so long. The last time you were here, you had worked for a few years as a teacher. Josh was also here. You two got to spend time together again. You got to hang out together, right?" she asked, lifting her eyes from the coffee cup.

Cassandra took a bite of her quiche, taking her time to answer. Cynthia seemed to be trying to prove a point. The way she said *right* so emphatically as though she knew more than she was letting on. "What made you decide to come back then?"

"I just wanted to reminisce; take stock of my life. I was thinking of changing my profession and studying counselling. I realised that counselling was more my thing. Thank God, because that's how I met Connor."

"Well, it was great seeing Josh so happy, you know? With everything that had happened with his mum. I have a confession, Cass. It wasn't a coincidence that he was back at the same time, when you came back a few years ago."

"It wasn't?"

"No … I had told him you would be visiting. He got on the next plane from where he was working in London."

"Oh, really?" Cassandra asked. Her heart raced. She'd planned to come back home hoping he'd be there, but she didn't know he knew she'd be there.

"I'm surprised he decided not to come to the wedding. Ryan and Josh were best friends."

"Like you said, it's probably out of his way. He has work commitments."

"I guess that's it then. It's out of his way. One thing that did puzzle me though was why he looked like someone had kicked the air out of him when he'd left all those years ago. It was the same look he had when his mother left; it was a weird time. It's funny how we felt so close to him, but no one could talk to him about it. I'd imagine he'd confided in you though?"

"He did to a point. It was a strange time. We all wished we could help him."

"Anyway, sorry for laying all this on you, Cass. I really hope I didn't upset you."

"No … you didn't. It's all in the past," she said with a forced smile.

"Yes, it is all in the past. Anyway, I can't wait to see Connor again. I had fun when I met all your friends in Sydney. And your sexy fiancé. He really is a wonderful guy for you. Especially since you and Josh … Sorry, Cass. It's just what everyone thought. He was always so protective of you. And you had something real."

"Don't worry about it, Cynthia. I know we were close back then."

"Anyway, I have so much planned. Wait until you see the house I hired for Ryan's birthday party. It's at Clare Valley, and we'll all be dressed up for the occasion. It is a shame that Josh won't be here though."

Cassandra looked at her friend's sincere smile and found herself agreeing. "Yes … it is a shame."

CHAPTER ELEVEN

Cassandra gripped the steering wheel later that afternoon after she drove into the driveway of her parents' double-storey, Georgian-styled house. The grand, black letter box greeted her as she drove past it. She noticed that the gardenias and camellias she and her mother had planted were thriving in the flower beds despite the intense heat. The landscaped front garden was so well-kept, and the large house which had been renovated over the years looked cheerful and inviting. Cassandra had always felt proud of their house. Even if her father frowned upon overdoing it with frivolous spending on 'useless, material things', as he called them, he and her mother prided themselves on being wonderful, house-proud residents in the area. They were always grateful to live amongst such beauty around them.

She parked her car near the garage and stepped outside. She searched for her key in her bag and looked around the property as the sun touched the ground with an intense, unforgiving heat. How much more of this relentless heat could they all endure? Surely, it had to change soon. Cynthia had said they were expecting a storm.

She unlocked the door and quickly turned the alarm off. Cassandra was pleasantly surprised. Silence engulfed the house, amplified by the ticking of one of the wall clocks. It looked so inviting. Its familiarity was actually welcoming.

She walked over the dark-stained floorboards and breathed in the atmosphere. Her mother had done a great job decorating it. She noticed a few new vases, mirrors and art prints on the walls.

Walking around the dining room, she was surprised to see photos of herself as a young girl. They weren't there the last time she'd visited. She was sure that her mother would have placed them there. She gazed over to the onyx mantelpiece and noticed another photo. It was of her and her father. Cassandra didn't know what to think of it. *Of course,* she thought, *he was always good at keeping up appearances for when guests or colleagues from the agency visited.*

The wide hallway led her to the lounge room. She walked into the spacious, grey room and ran her hand over the piano. This is where her mother had rehearsed plays, dressed up and sung, danced and played the piano. Recalling memories evoked from old photos, she wondered where the other photo albums were kept.

She climbed the stairs and walked into her bedroom. It was like nothing had changed. The desk shelf, bedecked with trophies, was still there, preserved with care. Her mother kept it clean. A tear streamed down her cheek when she noticed a photo with her and her mother. They were bowing as they stood on the stage they'd created in the garden. Why had her mother given up acting when she loved it so much? Every time she had asked her, she'd just stare out of the window and suddenly think of a chore that needed doing.

One day she'd caught her mother looking at herself in the mirror. She had placed a costume against her chest, probably imagining how she would look in it. Cassandra's heart had gone out to her. Her mother's smile had quickly faded, her jaw dropping, as soon as she'd heard the door from the study open. Her mother packed up the costume as she often did. When she heard the study door close again, Mr Jensen obviously changing his mind about something, Cassandra looked on as her mother gazed into the distance, at the mountains, just like she often did when she'd catch her cooking. It was as though the window symbolised some freedom or a yearning that gnawed at her — as if she pondered what could have been.

Mrs Jensen was made to feel that they had no time for such things since her husband started the agency.

Cassandra thought it was odd that her father had once been interested in the arts. He had become so money-driven. He made money, he helped with various charities; he was an outstanding member of the community. *Why couldn't he spread some of that generosity around this house?* she often thought, *to extend his smile to us and to be satisfied with what he had. Why do people also give up on the things they supposedly love?*

After she'd walked the grounds, Cassandra sat at the kitchen table with a glass of water and some old photo albums she had spotted on a chair in the dining room. Though that wouldn't have been their final resting place; it would be a pit stop before her parents moved them into hiding. She anxiously turned the page. It was an album she hadn't seen before. The pages were lined with photos from her parents' acting days. They had opened a theatre company in the 80s in Williamstown, a short drive from Tanunda. Her mother and father were standing outside the building with the sign on top. They had dreams, so what happened?

She inspected the photo. Her father's eyes looked more cheerful, almost dreamy-eyed. He was tall and handsome, and his blue-green eyes stood out. Her mother was wearing 80s bubble-gum jeans, a cropped, pink gingham shirt and a studded belt secured around her slim waist. Her long ash-blonde hair fell free and had a slight wave to it. Mr Jensen was holding her tight, like he was proud of her.

She gazed over another photo. Her parents stood in a crowd of other actors from the performance school. She carefully looked at each face to see if she recognised anyone. One of the men looked familiar. She had seen his kind, light blue eyes before. *Of course*, she said to herself. *It's the other actor that had performed with them in A Doll's House. I wonder, what happened to him?*

As she turned the page, her eyes fell on a photo of a beautiful, tall woman. Her mind couldn't place her.

"What?" she screamed. *It can't be. I'm sure it is! It's Josh's mum! Why would they have a photo of Mrs Sturgess? Dad never liked the Sturgess'.* It didn't make sense. Her mother never hung out with her the way she hung out with Cynthia's mum. Why was that? Nothing seemed to make sense. The more she looked at the photos, the more she realised she really knew nothing about her parents' life. They had kept her in the dark. Why did people walk around pretending? Why do they pretend to not know things when they do? Was that the truth? Was his smile and his warm eyes the truth and was he pretending the rest of the time?

She picked up an album that contained her baby photos and opened the cover. A photo of her and her father stared back at her. Her heart melted while her mind raced with questions. He was smiling at a flower and he had his arm around her waist. He looked as though he was laughing at the funny expression she was making with her mouth.

I must have been around five years of age then. But the man she remembered was always serious. He was probably caught in the moment, where he couldn't help but laugh at her expression. His guard was down.

She looked at another photo and answered her own question. Of course, he wasn't pretending most of the time. The fierce, cold look in his eyes in that particular photo revealed the truth: he refused to accept her. It was the photo that she'd taken of her parents near the lake. He didn't even want to look at her as she took the photo. He had been so angry with her the night before.

One minute the clouds were a friendly blue, and then a heavy, dark grey blanket covered the sky. She could hear the thunder, but Josh and she kept laughing. His dad had passed down his car to him since he'd bought a new one for himself, and Josh had wanted to see if it would make it up the hill. The air at the top was cold and sent shivers over her skin. She had been trembling. They were eighteen at the time and thought they were adults. He took his jacket off and wrapped it around her. He kissed her softly, and then they stared at each other for a while.

"Come on, let's go before the storm really takes hold," he had said to her, while the nearby goats bleated. The wind was fierce as it unleashed its anger. They had managed to drive down the hill but she'd insisted they go somewhere to be together.

The next day she told her parents that they were stuck in mud and had to wait for help.

"You silly girl!" he had shouted at her. "Do you ever think? You saw the signs. You knew there might be a storm, but you had to go off with that Sturgess kid, gallivanting around town, not a care in the world. You're just like … him."

"Like who?" she had finally demanded.

He had stumbled. "Like … like the Sturgess kid … Josh. Carrying that silly journal and taking photos of every little thing he sees. Of course, he knew that there'd be a storm — he knew but he chose to ignore it — he headed right to it. He wants the danger. He thrives on dreaming, doesn't he?"

"How can you talk like that about him? His mother left—"

He calmed down and headed to his room. It was as though her last comment had affected him. It was one of the only times she'd heard him scream to her. He then went back to his silent communication — showing how much he disapproved of her, stomping around the house, making even the furniture look timid and nervous, like it was shrinking into the ground.

She heard footsteps and a door open. *They're home,* she fretted. She packed up the photo albums and shoved them under a table. Her heart raced and her hands trembled as if she had been reduced to her childhood self. She heard the piano shut and the costumes being packed away in her mind before she met his eyes.

"Cassandra," her mother screamed, her long, blonde curls swayed freely as she moved towards her.

Cassandra eyed her mother, who looked quite youthful in a pair of stressed, light blue denim jeans and a leopard print, chiffon shirt … the way she used to dress. "Mum … how are you?" I was just …" she began, meeting her mother's friendly, pretty face. She glanced at the albums under the table. He noticed them. "You said you were getting back home in a few days." Cassandra adjusted her hair and straightened her dress, tidying up her white shirt, ensuring she looked neat.

"Oh … we had to cut the trip short. Your father had an urgent call from the office."

"Oh … that's a shame," she managed.

"We had so much fun though. Thanks to you, sweetie. Hearing about your trip made me want to travel. Where's Connor? Isn't he with you?"

"I decided to come here early, and he couldn't get away. I thought I'd catch up with Cynthia, and see how …"

"These dark floorboards are so hard to maintain. Look … we've left footprints on them. You can see any speck of dust," he began, as her mother examined the evidence.

"It's not so bad, Oscar. Relax. Like you were saying in Denmark, we need to relax a bit more."

Cassandra couldn't believe what she was hearing. Her father wanted to relax more? There was something different about them. She couldn't pinpoint it. They seemed closer, like the trip agreed with them. She couldn't believe they had even agreed to travel that far in the first place.

"We'd better freshen up, but first, I want to see my lovely daughter. Cass," she then looked at her with a serious look. "You need to visit more often, or I'll be heading to Sydney every few months. I always feel like I'm bothering you. I know you're busy with the practice. I'm so glad you're back," she said, giving her a big hug. She met his eyes. He instantly looked away.

"Good to see you again," he managed and gave her some type of weak handshake. "These photo albums should be taken to the storeroom downstairs," he then said. "It's not like anyone looks at them."

"Leave them now, Oscar. I look at them from time to time," Mrs Jensen pleaded. "Come and have a cup of tea, or do you prefer coffee, Cass?"

"We really should air out the house," her father said. "The windows have been closed for a month."

"It is rather hot … I'll turn on the air-conditioner first, and when Cass leaves we'll air it out," she suggested.

Cassandra took a sip of her coffee, and her father took a sip from his coffee. They both looked at each other.

"So, you're a psychologist?" he asked.

"Um … no, Dad, like I've told you, I'm a counsellor," she managed. "It's going great … the practice is going great," she offered, trying to avoid another awkward pause. Her mother had left them together after making the coffee so she could change into something more comfortable.

"I don't really believe that these things can cure anyone."

"They don't perform miracles. They just guide people to express how they feel," she found herself replying, becoming uncomfortable.

"You can do that with a cup of tea and a friend. Why people would pay all their week's wage on one session? They'll have to talk to a financial advisor soon."

"Sometimes people can't talk to close friends and family about certain things," she said, her heart rate almost plummeting. "Especially if they aren't aware of how they feel or are too scared to find out. It doesn't cost as much as that anyway."

Her mother chipped in after entering the room, overhearing the conversation. "That's wonderful, Cass. I'm so proud of you. I think there are many things people can't talk about and talking to a professional can help," she commented, before turning to her husband. "They use certain techniques that draw things out, Oscar. I think it's such a commendable profession." Once more, she turned to face Cassandra. "You've done really well for yourself, Cass. It must feel good to help people."

"It does feel good. It was only just the other day that a woman I had counselled came up to me in the street and thanked me for everything I had done for her. It felt so good to be able to help. I didn't even recognise her. She was so confident. And she told me I have a gift, that I should never stop helping people. It did something to me. Made me realise—"

"I really should call William and see how the office is faring without me. There's a new property on the market that's in great demand."

Cassandra looked at her dad with her mouth agape. Her mother fidgeted with her jewellery. She looked embarrassed. "Oscar, that can wait. Cass hasn't seen us for so long. Isn't it wonderful to have her back?"

Cassandra looked at her wedding ring, sparkling in the timid stream of sunshine peering in through the window. She wished Connor was now with her. Could she feel any smaller than she did right now? Her dad didn't want to hear about her accomplishments. She felt so foolish even attempting to try and talk to him about something he never understood. Part of her thought she might be able to talk to him, that he may have missed her while she was gone, and he did seem more talkative than usual. Obviously, she was wrong, though.

"That's okay, Mum. You just got back and you're both tired."

"No, I want to hear all about your life in Sydney. I always knew you would do something like that. I mean, you even used to set your dolls and stuffed toys in a line and try to help them. You would ask them what was wrong, and you would either make them have a nap or tell them how they could feel better."

Cassandra smiled. How different was her mother? How did she choose to marry someone so different to her? she found herself thinking. "I was just stunned that this woman went out of her way to stop me. She really wanted to tell me how much her life had improved. Apparently, I helped her follow her dreams—"

"Dreams?" Mr Jensen laughed. "Dreams … that's right, everyone has dreams. Heaven forbid if real life gets in the way of that. That's part of the problem, having counsellors telling people to follow their dreams. Okay, I've heard about enough. It just baffles me that people pay money to hear things they want to hear because the reality of life might be too much for them to handle—"

"So, what do you think they want to hear?" she demanded, her heart rate increasing. It was as if he wanted to push her to this point. Her career was not the cause of his anger.

"That they are allowed to waste everyone's time and live selfishly for themselves regardless of the consequences and the danger they may inflict on others," he raised his voice slightly.

"Oscar …"

"It's all right, Mum. I really have to go now anyway. You're both tired." She stood up before her mother could stop her.

"Cassie, please stay. We'll tell you all about our trip … we even went to one of the greatest theatrical performances. It was spectacular. It reminded me of the time when we were on stage …"

"That was a long time ago, Isabel. That part of our life has been over for a long time," he said in a voice so final.

"Yes … but it was a great time in my life … and I believe it was yours too," she said, matching his tone.

Her mother had changed. It seemed that they seemed to communicate more with each other in a healthy way, as though she wasn't scared to voice her feelings like she was back then. She guessed that there would have been more stability between them before she had made her unexpected presence.

"I really have to go," she leaned over to hug her mum.

"Cass … you just got here. We took so many photos. I can show you all the amazing sights. It was a truly special time for your dad and I."

She looked at her husband and gave him an affectionate smile mixed with a plea to be on his best behaviour, as though he couldn't help himself when their daughter was in his life. A knot appeared in her stomach.

"Stay and eat with us. I'll make us some dinner, or we can get some takeout. You're looking so thin. I hope you haven't been working too hard, and then there's the wedding — your wedding. I want to hear how it's all going," her mother continued.

"Nothing has changed since the last time you called. It's all on track. Connor's coming in a few days. He had too many clients and couldn't get away earlier. He's at a critical point with one of them … and he had a new client to see," she now found herself waffling nervously, like a shy girl who didn't know if she was allowed to smile, or be funny or be serious, or sit still or move … The way she used to feel around his scrutiny. The more she advised herself to steer the conversation away from counselling, the more she seemed to stumble back right into it.

"Critical stage? Maybe if people didn't need someone to hold their hand with every single problem, they'd toughen up like so many of us had to do," he said.

"And that works well for so many? Toughening up? Does it?" she challenged him as her voice shook. She was about to ask if it worked for him, but his face seemed to be flushing with some underlying rage.

She too began to fume, but she knew if she continued, she'd be walking into another one of his minefields.

"Another client? Do you hear that, Oscar? Many value the profession and it is a growing industry. I'm glad the practice is going well for you and Connor," she said, turning to face Cassandra.

"Mum … I'd better get back to the hotel. I'll have a look at all your photos when I visit with Connor. We can reminisce as well. Sweden and Denmark were beautiful, as was Norway. We even visited some of our relatives; your mum and dad in the city of Odense. I didn't know anything about dad's side though. Just that they live nearby … anyway," she quickly digressed. "The Hans Christian Andersen Museum is magical, and we even visited the Odense Theatre and saw … um … it was great seeing where you grew up," she stumbled as she heard her dad stirring in his seat at the mere mention of his family and the theatre. "It's a spectacular city …" She wondered if they ever had performed there and was tempted to ask, but decided against it.

"Did you say you were staying in a hotel? You can stay here, Cassie. I can't have my only daughter living in a hotel when our home … *your home* is right here," she said, a sadness welling in her eyes. Cassandra dared to glance at her dad. He was looking down at his coffee, like he too had some sadness consuming him.

After a few more pleas and hugs from her mother, she said her final goodbye, while glancing over to her father who managed a nod, and then walked to sit on the lounge to scan the messages on his mobile phone.

She walked out into the heat, which now felt comforting and liberating. Talking to him was like being in quicksand. She turned around and smiled at her mum and as she met her father's eyes, he ducked his head.

Behind the wheel, she was free to steer in any direction she chose. She pulled out of the driveway. "Oh no! I forgot my phone!" she screamed out. She'd have to turn back and get it.

She stepped out into the sun-drenched driveway and pushed the front door, which had stood ajar. She grabbed the phone and checked the messages. Connor had left a few. She was relieved to get it without being noticed, but stopped when she heard murmuring from the kitchen.

"Oscar …" her mother said. "You're tickling me. We're not on holidays anymore. It was great to see Cassandra again, wasn't it? You need to be more kind to her … she's my only child."

Cassandra couldn't hear his response. Her mother had turned the tap on.

When the tap stopped, her father suggested, "Let's have a quiet night. We can order some food from that Nordic restaurant and pretend we're still on holidays."

"That sounds great," her mother responded.

Cassandra walked towards the door, as she heard their footsteps nearing the lounge room.

Outside, she jumped in the car and drove out of the driveway, out of her family home, out of her parents' world which she was still so distant from. She didn't even hear his response. Maybe it was for the better. A heaviness in her chest made her feel like she would collapse. It had been a long day. She turned the air conditioner on full. The clouds in the distance looked ominous. Would the rain wash all the heat away? Her eyes were stinging from the tears. She had to stop crying. She wiped them away, not able to reach the tissues in the glove box. *It's okay*, she told herself. *At least mum looks happier with him.*

The highway was busy. A horn beeped at her as she swerved into the other lane. They were so happy. *Could I be the reason he was always bad-tempered? He'd been an actor, living a bohemian lifestyle from one theatre company to another, until they created their own theatre here in the Barossa Valley. He must have had the same passion as mum did at one stage.*

But now he didn't believe in dreams. Did she wipe his dreams away like heavy rain drowning wildflowers that had been thriving? Did they then try to plant more of those wildflower seeds, only for them to be blown away by a gust of wind, carrying them to another place that is dull and not so fertile, making it almost impossible for them to thrive there? Was it because of her that he was forced to move away from the theatre to a life that was far less interesting?

Was that why he resented her so much? He had been forced to become responsible and earn a proper wage as their acting dreams would mean living humbly.

If he resented her for these things, then why did he resent Josh and his family?

She concentrated on the green fields and robust vineyards around her. They lived amongst a sea of green and waves of gold as nature's slopes wrapped around them with life, vitality, hope and dreams. That was never enough though. They didn't fit in with the happy picture. The happy nuclear family; did that exist for anyone? Was it a myth, made up to keep kids aspiring to be the best in life? Did these kids wait for the promised sunshine, the promised acceptance and freedom, or did they grow up into naive adults? Were they still waiting for their turn to have the family dinners and the heartfelt laughter indented into the walls and permeating the air like fragrant room mist, in their cosy homes with manicured lawns?

Was her dad right? Is that why he resented the family life? Did he fear it? Did he have things promised to him that he never got? Had he given up on waiting? He knew something that the other poor, naive people didn't know.

No! I won't let him take away my hopes, my passions, or my dreams. They keep me alive.

She had passed her hotel and the cheerful 'welcome' sign to beautiful Tanunda. She was heading to an area that she had many fond memories of: Eden Valley. It was known for its promise of rich soil and a new beginning for the early German settlers. Her father told potential home buyers of nearby property about how it came to be called Eden Valley. Rich land had meant harvesting grapes, which created beautiful vineyards and a new beginning amongst nature. Its history was ingrained; it would always be part of the modern Barossa.

Cassandra drove up the steep hill, which seemed to ascend forever, and wondered if the car would make it. She was now committed. She had to keep travelling along the dirt road. She hadn't even stopped at a service station to refuel. It was now almost dusk, but she wanted to feel the cold, crisp air in her lungs, to be truly free from it all.

Stepping out of the car, she listened to the eerie sounds of bells as the goats stirred in the nearby hills. She buttoned the top of her shirt, protecting her chest from the crisp chill in the air as best she could. She wasn't prepared for the cold — she never was prepared for it — she thought it would be different this time.

The enormous wooden cross stood tall. She walked over to it. It was mystical, almost surreal. Its size made her feel powerful and humble at the same time, as it towered over her. What was it about this mystical place that comforted her so many times when her life seemed to reach a crisis point? Here she was at an extremely high peak, where the air was so cold, where life further down in the streets was remote. She never expected such coldness, and yet again she wasn't prepared. Her linen shirt was too thin. The high altitude was heavenly though.

Why did she expect her father to be different? She had hoped for kindness and warmth.

Thunder spoke to the valley with a loud roar. The raindrops fell heavily. The land, the valley and ranges below were hit with aggressive lightning. Cynthia had told her about the imminent storm, but she ignored the signs — the danger.

"You're just like your mother," he had told her when she had sprained her ankle. "You never estimate the danger." *What do you know that we don't, Dad? What danger are you referring to?*

The rain tore through the valley. She rushed to the car as another bolt of lightning hit the earth. She shut the door as a gust of wind threatened to take it and turned the ignition on. Nothing happened. She turned it again. Complete silence came from the car. It too was betraying her and abandoning her. Had she betrayed herself by not stopping to refuel?

Tears streamed down her face. Why did she come back? She should have waited to be with Connor. He was her rock. Why did she not confide in him? She was judging her father, yet she was pretending like her father ... like Josh.

"Josh!" she screamed, petrified. It wasn't him. Her mind was playing tricks on her. The memory was too clear. They had been together that night. They had driven to a farmhouse far from there. They had spent the night together. It was her first time with him. Of course, she had lied that their car was stuck in a muddy path due to the storm. She had to lie to everyone, even to Cynthia; too much was at risk. Her father would never let her live it down.

"Cassandra." He called her name. Josh? Her mind ran rampant.

"Josh! What are you doing here?" she screamed, shaking all over. She opened the window and as rain washed her tears away, she came face to face with him and looked deep into his shining hazel eyes.

"Josh ... it's you. You came back. You're here."

"Yes, Cass, it's me. I came back. I'm here. Don't worry! Everything will be okay!"

CHAPTER TWELVE

"It's not the fuel. I think it's the battery," he finally said as she watched him check the engine. "We're going to have to call for help."

Cassandra couldn't find her words; they seemed foreign. Why was Josh there? He said he couldn't make it. "Do you want me to call? I'll just get my phone from the car," she suggested. The rain had temporarily stopped but the wind was treacherous.   "You'd better get in as well. You'll freeze out here," she instructed.

He jumped in the car and she reached for her mobile in her bag. Her eyes caught sight of the book. It had started out as a sad story, but her heart had been full of hope that her own story would become more positive. She took her phone out and sat back in her seat. It was nice and warm, and quite cramped sitting together in the back seat.

"We'll be lucky to get anyone up here though. With the hill being so steep and the conditions remaining unchanged, it would be dangerous to get a car here. We might have to wait a few hours."

Cassandra looked at him. She self-consciously combed her damp hair back away from her forehead. She found herself wanting to look her best. He watched her as she flicked a strand away. His eyes sparkled like beacons in the dim lighting. He glanced at her ring as his jaw tightened.

He then looked her in the eyes. She saw the Josh she knew: at times vulnerable and lost, at other times focused and determined, as opposed to the care-free aloof and confident boy he used to be. "Congratulations," he finally said.

"Thanks," she said, not being able to look away from him.

"You're shivering." He took off his denim jacket and placed it around her. The musky aroma of his cologne teased her nose — her senses.

"Thanks, Josh. You must think I'm such a cliché: the damsel in distress. You saving me again. This time not with your bike but with your car." She gazed over to his car, which was parked a fair distance away from hers. "Maybe you'd rather wait in *your* car. It's more spacious."

"I'm fine here. It's pretty cosy, besides we need to ensure they notice us when help arrives. Anyway, it's not your fault. It's the battery. It could happen to anyone — although the hire company should have ensured it didn't. I ignored the warning also. I thought the storm would start much later. Besides, they didn't predict it'd be this bad. I think something was calling me up here. I just had to see the view, like we used to, and so I drove straight from the airport."

"You haven't even been home yet? You must be exhausted. I'd better make the call," she said, still looking at him.

He gave her a smile that lit up his face and seemed to illuminate the dim space even more. *How handsome is he?* she found herself thinking. He looked like he belonged in an old movie. He had that quiet, rebel look about him.

After she ended the call, he moved closer. His nearness felt right. "I hope I didn't startle you," he said.

"No … I was so relieved to see you. You came when I needed you … I mean, needed help. How silly of me to come up here knowing there'd be a storm. I haven't changed, have I? You're usually very observant, but apparently I've always been like this …"

He looked confused. "Haven't changed? What do you mean, Cass? If you're referring to your looks, no, you haven't." He touched her face. "You're the pretty, kind, and warm Cass I remember. Your cheekbones are more defined though, more womanly." He stroked her face with his long, smooth fingers. She backed away; he retreated. "You're letting someone else's words place doubt in your mind.

Don't let anyone do that to you. You were always the first person to tell us that. Compassionate Cass. Always looking out for everyone. Someone had to look out for you ..."

Cassandra felt a rush throughout her body. The smell of his cologne and his caring, concerned gaze. It was too much. She glanced at her ring, and then at him. He was looking at it as well. He looked up. "He's a lucky guy. He'd be crazy to let you go."

Cassandra froze. The stare was too strong. It held her captive for a while. She looked at her phone, finally managing to free herself from his mesmerising hold on her, but she couldn't check Connor's messages while his eyes were on her. As she placed her phone back in her bag, he raked his gaze over her.

"So, what made you come here, after all?" She decided to dig deep and become mature again. She'd have to take charge, because he seemed to be in some type of trance. She sensed a longing in him, a yearning.

"I thought it would be unfair to skip their wedding. Ryan was my best friend and Cynthia sounded so upset when I'd told her I couldn't make it. Besides, have you heard about all the parties she has lined up? How could I miss one of Cynthia's parties? I miss them ... I miss a lot of things."

Cassandra teared up. Why was she feeling like this? All sorts of feelings were coming to the surface. She examined his features. His hair was slightly shorter round the back, but he still had some loose and wavy strands falling over his forehead. He had let his stubble grow, ending neatly at the start of his neck. How many times had she wrapped her arms around that neck? His chest rose and lowered as he waited for her answer.

"What is it?" He tucked a strand of hair behind her ear and gazed into her eyes.

"I was just worried ... being stuck here."

"It's okay now. I'm here for you, as long as you need me," he said.

Feeling that it was getting too deep and intense, she decided to change the subject. "Speaking of parties, Cynthia and I were discussing the tea party she threw for all of us when we were little. I can't believe that you pushed the seat from under that boy Simon. Remember him? Right when he was about to sit down …"

Josh smiled mischievously. "That's right. Simon. I wonder how he is now. I don't regret it. He shouldn't have bothered you like that. I'll always stick up for you, especially with sticky butter in your hair." He smiled at his play on words. "You and I have always been friends."

"Yes, we had been great friends for many years. It's very rare for that to happen."

"As I recall, we became a lot more than that though," he said, searching her face for some sort of acknowledgement.

Cassandra glanced at her watch.

"I have an idea. I'll be right back," he suddenly announced. He paused before opening the door. "So, where's the lucky guy … your fiancé? I'm surprised you're here alone."

"I decided to come here earlier and spend some time … You know how it is when you're away from something so long, you want to savour it on your own."

He looked at her sceptically. "I know exactly what you mean."

Cassandra looked away, finding it hard to breathe. He seemed to be making a point. Did he mean about her? The way they left things last time? Why would he say such a thing?

He then decided to continue. "This place has so many meaningful memories for me, for us, I guess. Do you remember it? The time we spent here? Supposedly we were stuck in the mud. Well, that's what they all thought. Instead we drove far away, just the two of us. We were so young and so in love. Cass, you can't deny the past. I remember that night so well. We were consenting adults. You know … I often wondered why you felt the need to hide it from everyone … why you insisted we look like friends to the outside world. It actually said a lot to me … about us."

Cassandra was confused. What did it say about them? She hadn't told because of how her father would react. But, of course, she never told him that. She couldn't hurt him more than he already had been hurt, to make him feel more unwanted and unloved when his mother had left him. It would be too cruel.

"Tell me again, Cass. You and I? Why didn't we work out? I've been thinking a lot about that lately, especially with Ryan and Cynthia getting married."

Cassandra moved in her seat. She wasn't ready for this conversation. It felt wrong to be there discussing their relationship.

It was as though he could sense her uneasiness. "I'd better run back to my car and bring us the food. You won't believe what I've got for us. It couldn't have been a more ideal time."

Before she could answer, he opened the door and a gust of strong wind practically broke the door off from the car. He forcefully shut it before running to his car.

Cassandra watched him as he heroically sprinted. *He was always there for me … and here he is again just as I'm about to get married.* Strangely, she felt so close to him.

"Why didn't it work out between us?" he had asked her. How could he not know the answer to that? Didn't he remember what he'd told her the last time they met, a few years ago, when they had both returned! She had hoped that they might finally get their chance, but they didn't. They broke each other's heart again. It was strange. They loved each other but they couldn't be together. Did they have an answer to that question?

He's right. What is the reason? What was she thinking? It didn't matter. She'd moved on since then. She wondered if he had.

The door swung open, and the wind forced its way into the car again, chilling her face. Eden Valley Lookout was cold, but the air had become icy as it pierced her skin. Josh shivered and she placed her hand on his back to warm him up. His eyes said it all. He was touched by the gesture. He leaned in closer. As he moved to sit comfortably in his seat, his stubbled face rubbed her skin. Cassandra felt a tingle and guilt washed over her as he searched her eyes. She didn't want him to read what they said. She didn't even know what they were telling him.

She looked at the picnic hamper. It was a basket full of gourmet treats: fruit, pesto dip, bread, cheese, green olives, and salad wraps. "Wow!" she exclaimed. "You have dinner for us?"

"Yes, and I even have this. It might keep us warm," he said, revealing a bottle of red wine.

"Very impressive," she said. It was almost perfect. "How?"

"How did I have all this? It's like it magically appeared when we needed it. I don't know about you, but I'm feeling rather hungry. I actually wanted to come up here and look at the view. It was always so spectacular, so I had decided to buy a gourmet hamper from one of the local delis, and here we are …"

"Yes … here we are," she replied. He spoke to her like he used to, before the world broke his heart. Why did his mother leave him? He was so close to her. Cassandra had so many unanswered questions. Did he even know? Would they ever know?

"Cass? What's wrong? You seem a million miles away."

"I was just thinking how wonderful what you've done here is. It reminds me of all those picnics we had when we were young. Remember you, Ryan, Cynthia and I all brought something from home and we had our own picnic by the lake? I, of course, brought my mother's Viennese pastry which she was famous for and you brought … um … I think it was an apple pie type of thing …"

Josh looked down at the bottle of wine he was holding. His jaw tightened and his body tensed. The hurt was still there after all these years. He looked up and met her eyes. "You can say it, Cass. The pie my mother made. It was actually raspberry. Yes, I remember. I remember it all. I've thought about it for so many years, I could write books on it. It's okay. I've been seeing a professional to talk things through. I remember it all so well."

"That's great, Josh. I'm glad you're getting help, that you have someone to talk to," she said.

"I had to, especially when the only person I really felt comfortable with on a deep level had gone, again. But like I said back then, everyone leaves in the end. It's never enough for them."

Cassandra tried to process what he was saying. Did he mean his mother and her? Her heart shattered. He lost two women in his life that he could talk to. But he was wrong. From what she remembered, *he* left *her*. He'd decided to leave her.

His previous words spoke to her heart: "I got my answer then." He got his answer when she chose to hide their relationship from the world. But he didn't know what it was like for her at home and she really didn't know what happened in his home either. Maybe that's the answer he was talking about. Maybe they both got their answer.

"Cass … it's really okay. I've learned a lot of things lately, about myself, about what really happened. Perhaps, I'll tell you one day. Perhaps we were both guilty of not telling things, of keeping a distance between us. We were scared. Maybe that's why you were here the same time I was here. Maybe we were meant to find things out that we were never told back then."

The majestic cross appeared in her peripheral vision as she processed his words. *Maybe we will find out the truth*, she thought to herself.

***

130

Josh reclined in the front of the car. They had hopped into the front after they ate, to finish their glass of wine while gazing at the stars. They wanted to savour each sip.

"It's amazing that you're a counsellor. I always knew you had an innate ability to help people. Counselling is more valuable than people give it credit for. I think many who dispute its credibility aren't ready to face things they may not want to face. They could solve things on their own, like through art, music, or doing things that liberate them as they explore their feelings towards themselves, towards life and towards others. But I know for myself, I didn't want to acknowledge its merits for a while because I think I blamed the world for my problems. I didn't trust those who promised to take care of me. I thought it was a promise that no one could keep. Especially when the person who bore me couldn't bear living with me ... so ..." he trailed off, his eyes shining.

"Josh ..." She placed her hand on his shoulder. They could see the same thing at that moment.

He looked deep in her eyes and took her hand into his. His skin was smooth as he squeezed her hand. She felt warm, from the wine she assumed. The taste of it lingered on her tongue, on her lips. She pressed her lips together and his eyes fell to them. She had to say something.

"I'm glad you came back for the wedding, Josh. It'll be great for you to be amongst friends. And you can talk to me if you want. I'll listen."

"I know you will," he said stroking her face. He quickly took it away and continued talking. "You always did. You have a gift for that. I'm proud of you for helping others. You don't know how much it means to many people who are damaged."

Her heart felt like it was touched by an angel. He always said the right things, especially when her dad had tried to take her strength away from her.

"You're wrong though," he said, as his eyes combed her face before meeting her eyes again.

She gave him a puzzled look.

"I didn't just come for the wedding. I also came back for you, Cass. I came back for you." His hand moved over her lips and she inched away.

"I'd better stop drinking. Half a glass is enough for me if I'm going to be driving," she digressed.

Lights lit up the car and Cassandra sat up from her seat. "Looks like help is here," she said, relieved and shaken.

She turned to face him. He was still looking at her. A car door shut and footsteps drew near. She looked down at the diamond on her finger and saw Connor's smile in it. As she took Josh's denim jacket off, she noticed him looking away with a tight jaw. Cassandra opened the window. A roar of thunder reminded her that conditions were still hazardous.

"Looks like I've arrived just in time," a middle-aged man with a bright orange work hat and vest said.

Cassandra's heartbeat raced as an unknown, unexplainable lingering took over her chest. She knew the man was right. He *had* arrived just in time. With that realisation, she handed Josh his jacket.

***

Cassandra stumbled into the corridor on the 10th floor where her hotel room was situated. What an eventful day it had been! Josh had said goodbye to her amongst the commotion of having her car battery changed in the heavy rain. The time was now nearly 1 am. She looked forward to sleeping in her comfortable hotel bed. She was glad room service had come around earlier in the day; she had fresh towels and other essentials so she could really unwind.

A whiff of familiar cologne touched her nose. It was coming from her skin. She reached into her bag, nearly tripping in her sleepless state. She looked up and noticed someone at her door, sitting uncomfortably on the polished tiled floor.

"Connor?"

"Hi … I've been waiting for you. I thought you'd never get here. I left you messages. Anyway, you're here now. I couldn't get in because I'm not booked to stay here yet. I'm sure we can sort it out with the hotel. So, where were you anyway? It's pelting out there."

"I had just stepped outside and … and my car was stuck in the rain. What are the chances? The battery was flat. It wasn't even due to the storm," she waffled.

"Oh, I hope you had help." He walked towards her.

"Yes, I did," she managed. "I had lots of help"

CHAPTER THIRTEEN

He kissed her before she opened the door. The guilt made her nervous. But what was she really feeling guilty about? *It's not as though I had planned it,* she reassured herself. Connor walked behind her as they entered the suite.

"What a day!" she announced to the lounge room, avoiding looking at him.

"You certainly look like you've had quite an ordeal," he said. "I hope seeing me has brightened your mood."

"Of course, it has, Connor." *Why was he asking that? He must be teasing like he always does,* she reassured herself. Her nerves were making her paranoid.

"So, you were waiting there for a while? I mean, you must have. Why would you be out so late unless you were visiting your parents, or maybe you ran into one of your friends?"

Cassandra placed her bag on the coffee table. Yes, I actually did. Lucky, I did … they helped me so much. I thought it was my fault when the car wouldn't start."

"They?" he queried.

"What?" She turned to face him.

"You said *they* helped you. Did you run into a few of your friends?"

"Oh no, it was just one friend," she said, dismissively. "Anyway, I'll have to take you to the Eden Valley Lookout one day. It's just as spectacular as I remember it being. I think I'll have a shower before bed."

"Sure," he said, coming close to her and wrapping his arms around her. He kissed her lips, but she uneasily backed away.

"What is it?" he asked her.

"I think I'll have a shower before we do this. I can't wait to be near you," she smiled.

He kissed her further down towards her chest, before he backed away. His aqua-blue eyes peered into hers. They seemed so observant, like they were searching for something.

"What is it, Connor?"

"You just seem different, that's all."

"I feel different. I went back there today, to my parents' house. They ended up coming back early. I was hopeful this time. I don't know what it is about my dad. He just makes me feel so small. I've been avoiding him for years. I'm a grown woman now and I thought I would be able to handle him. I thought it didn't bother me. I convinced myself it didn't, but I realise I can't keep running. I can't help thinking there's something hiding behind his cold facade. With Cynthia's wedding coming up, I realised I needed to tidy up some things I've been avoiding," she finished.

His eyes softened. "I'm here now, Cass. I'll help you deal with your parents, and whatever else you feel you need to tidy up. I'm here now."

She kissed him urgently, feeling a need to show him how much she loved him, but he pulled away again. "You better have a shower. I'll call reception and sort things out with accommodation, okay?"

"Sure," she said, surprised by his response.

She walked towards the bathroom and turned around. The aroma from the cologne was still there, leaving its mark. She looked at him as he sat by the couch and as he picked up the phone. He looked up at her. His jaw was tight. His eyes exuded a vulnerability she had never seen before. She smiled at him. He reciprocated with a half-smile, slowly revealing his affection and warmth.

She remembered the man's voice as he spoke through the car window. "Looks like I've arrived just in time," he had told Josh and her. She eased, knowing that Connor was back. He always kept her grounded, like the aromatherapy oil blends and candles from Eventually You were able to do. He too had arrived just in time. With that thought, she continued to the bathroom. Everything would be okay. She would find her balance again.

A while later, as Cassandra began to doze off, her mind drifted to the time she'd returned to Barossa Valley when she was twenty-seven. She was determined to give Josh another chance. He had first noticed her at a wine party that Josh's uncle hosted to mark one of the new wines. It was a rather lavish affair as guests sipped wine and mingled, while caterers walked around with plates full of gourmet *hors d'oeuvres*.

He had noticed her from across the room and had approached her, looking dashing in a dark grey suit with a navy shirt underneath and no tie. The chemistry between them that night was so potent. His hand was smooth and he grabbed hers tightly, leading her to the downstairs cellar. They reminisced about the time they got drunk in the same cellar after leaving school. They giggled when Josh's uncle walked downstairs to where they were seated, continuing his conversation with some potential buyers. They heard a whole conversation about the fermentation process. She'd nearly burst out laughing when Josh gave her an impressed look, like he'd just learned something new, regarding how sweet wine was made.

"We stop the fermentation process at the right time … before the yeast turns the grape sugar into alcohol," his uncle had explained to the buyers.

Josh had remained thoughtful with his chin resting on his hand as though he was in a wine class, nodding emphatically. They remained hidden behind one of the storage shelves for a while, like mischievous teenagers, hidden directly behind a display barrel.

They then spent days going for walks and driving to the beach with the top down on his father's vintage Mustang. Taking things slow was difficult as she was soon to start her counselling course, so they had spent many nights in a hotel suite, spending precious moments in each other's arms.

"What is it, Cass?" he'd asked her one night in between crisp, white cotton sheets.

"I was just thinking how close I feel to you at this moment. How I don't want it to end," she'd said.

"It doesn't have to end. Not if we don't want it to. We have to want it to work though; no more holding back."

"Then, I won't. At least, I don't want us to hold back anymore. I want to be with you always, not just in this hotel room, like we're hiding from the rest of the world."

He leaned over and navigated her lips and her body expertly.

"We won't hide, Cass. We won't pretend anymore," he'd told her.

Cassandra abruptly rolled over to Connor's side. He was breathing heavily, as though his mind weighed him down. He seemed to be dreaming of something. He had pushed her back when she'd kissed him after her shower. She felt that she had to hold him and convince him. Her face warmed. Before leaving Sydney, he had asked if she was trying to convince …

But he hadn't finished his sentence. She had to show him how much she loved him. He was now the man for her. They had been so happy together in Europe, sitting by the lake, walking on cobblestone streets in Rome, and now they gelled with their practice. She kissed his forehead. She kissed him again on the chest. He opened his eyes and kissed her lightly on the forehead. He then turned away.

Cassandra felt disheartened. *He's half asleep*, she reassured herself. *He's just really tired from waiting all night. I wasn't there for him … I was with Josh instead.* With that thought she fell into an uneasy, restless sleep.

"Hey, wake up sleepy head," Cassandra heard Connor's voice and her senses were pleasantly awoken by the aroma of fresh coffee and cinnamon.

"We've got a lot to do today," he continued in the same jovial tone. "I thought a bike ride might be what we need to rejuvenate. I can visit your parents later or some other time. They don't even know I'm here yet so we can have some 'alone time'. How does that sound to you?"

Cassandra forced herself up from her sleeping position and adjusted the pillow behind her as Connor passed her a cup of coffee, and a peck on her forehead.

There was an image of the Barossa trail on the iPad he held. She could just make out the picturesque scene between her squinted, tired eyes. Cassandra had fond memories of cycling or walking with her friends along this trail, which explores the beauty of the North Para River and many of the rural settings between the Barossa Ranges and the Adelaide Plains.

"We can start our bike ride at Angaston. It then states here that it ends in Nuriootpa. Wow! Look at all the cellars on the way. It's so beautiful," he said, enthusiastically.

"You're all energy today. I'm glad," she finally spoke. "You seemed a bit glum last night?"

"Glum?" he teased. "Maybe I should use that word with my clients. I've decided to start on a positive note. I was tired from waiting so long for you last night. I was beginning to get worried. Maybe I could have checked into another room, but I so wanted to surprise you."

She took a sip of orange juice and stroked his face. "I'm glad you're here. I'm sorry I didn't look at your messages. The visit rattled me and then the storm … Anyway, this looks great. It's a great idea to go for a bike ride. It's such a scenic trail. Why don't we have our breakfast on the balcony? Have you seen the view?" she exclaimed, excitement building in her voice. *Things will be back to normal,* she told herself, *now that Connor is with me.*

She jumped out of bed and drew the curtains. "Isn't this view of the vineyards and the mountains magnificent?"

"It is magnificent," he said. "All of Rowland Flat and the areas surrounding it are so beautiful." He walked over to her and wrapped his arms around her while they both marvelled at the scene in front of them.

"Come on, Connor? You're going to fall behind," Cassandra playfully called out even he'd stopped to adjust the seat on his bike. The sun had returned, revealing a glorious day. The temperature had dropped to 29 degrees Celsius. Cassandra opted for a peasant top, a pair of shorts, and plenty of sunscreen. She loved wearing summery clothes whenever she did the scenic bike ride trail, even if they weren't the best choice for cycling. It wasn't a gruelling trail and she was used to it. Besides, she hoped to stop at some of the well-known places to rest and perhaps find some local produce to eat. She and her mother would often cycle together before her mother fell deeper into her own cautious world, and, of course, she had cycled many times with Josh and their friends. Today was different though. She was with her fiancé and they would create new travelling memories, just like they did during their other trips.

"Isn't this place breathtaking?" Cassandra exclaimed a long while later. They had reached Bethany: a beautiful village close to Tanunda. "Bethany has so much history. It was the first German settlement in the Barossa Valley," she explained. "The name itself means 'fertile place'. There's so much to see here. We should stop at each place and look around a bit."

"It's breathtaking," Connor shouted back as he caught up to her.

They rode side by side for a while. All her problems melted away in the fresh, country air amongst natural beauty. Cassandra swung her feet away from the pedals for a few seconds and screamed out loud: "Bethany, you're beautiful."

Connor laughed and she admired him as he rode past her. Fond memories of their time in Sweden came to her mind. She was experiencing the same adrenalin rush, and a familiar peaceful ambience which blended beautifully within her soul. Being there together was what they both needed.

They passed lofts, sand cottages, resplendent wineries, old trees, and Lutheran churches that marked the past for the German settlers.

"Wow … look at that grand old church," Connor shouted, slowing down. Cassandra nearly bumped into him.

"Sorry, are you okay?" he asked. "I was just mesmerised by that church. How many are there? We've seen so many churches around the Barossa."

"The first families that migrated here were Lutheran families. They came from Silesia, bringing their trades and a lot of their culinary skills with them," Cassandra explained. "That particular church dates back to the late eighteen-hundreds. The workers would return from the vineyards and fields after a day of work when the bell was rung," she said.

"Fascinating," Connor said, still gazing at the church. He then turned to look at her. "Just like you are," he said, and kissed her on the forehead. "It's great to see where you grew up, to imagine you as a young girl, or in your youth. I want to know everything about you, Cass. I love that we can share things about each other's life. Our past can't escape us. It'll always be part of us. I love that you feel that you can share it all with me," he added. "Anyway, let's continue. We can stop off and have something to eat at that nice restaurant you mentioned earlier."

"Sure," she replied. The heaviness in her heart threatened her peaceful state. She was having such a wonderful time with Connor. She did feel guilty about not telling him about Josh. Sure, she had mentioned him a few times since she and Connor had become an item, but she wasn't sure if he knew how serious they had been, if her words painted a more platonic picture of them. She planned to tell him over lunch.

"You should see how delicious the food is. A lot of the German cooking methods are still used by many. Of course, a lot of improvising is done by using fresh seasonal produce from the area."

"Sounds great," he shouted out as he rode ahead of her, taking in the glorious views of the village.

A while later, they were both seated at a cosy outdoor restaurant with a glass of local, chilled Riesling, and a spread of freshly baked bread, a selection of cheeses, a salad, and two slices of *Rote Grütze*, a red berry pudding from North Germany.

"This dessert is one of my favourites," she enthused to a content-looking Connor from across the table. "The difference with this is that the Germans use berries and this one also has grapes. My mum used to make a Danish version that her mother had passed onto her." She took a sip of her wine and sat back in her seat under the shade of a gum tree. She gazed at the view of the vineyard, feeling a stream of gentle sunlight on her hair and face. As she shewed a fly away from the food, she heard her phone beeping. It was Cynthia.

"How amazing?" she screamed.

Connor gave her a curious look. "What is?"

"I just saw where Ryan's birthday party is being held. Isn't it so grand? It's a huge house in Clare Valley. Of course, we'll be staying there for a few days. It's on next week. Everyone should be here from Sydney by then.

"In the meantime, you and I can spend many glorious days like this," he said. "This day has been surreal." He then kissed her from across the table. She felt his soft lips, and the taste of sweetness from the wine. He was right. They were having such a wonderful day. Maybe she should tell him everything now. She opened her mouth to talk but was met with another sensual kiss.

"Lucky we're at a secluded table, near the vineyard, and not further back towards the restaurant where most people are sitting," she said. It wasn't the right time to tell him. Connor looked so content as he sat in his seat with his glass of wine in his hand, admiring the view.

After they devoured the delectable food, Connor took her by the hand, and they strolled around the grounds of the restaurant.

"Just think about how much fun we'll have at the party. Oh no!" she fretted. "What will we wear? It's an early twentieth century theme, from a time when garden parties were the in-thing. Oh well, we'll have to go into town at Nuriootpa, and buy something for that, and the wedding. I was supposed to do all that in Sydney."

She looked at him with a smile as they passed a rusty, old-fashioned tap and old bench. They sat down and a butterfly created graceful motions as it fluttered around them. The mention of parties reminded her of Josh. She should tell him now, she thought. She felt bad for not even mentioning that she had seen him last night. As she was about to speak, the blue and white butterfly landed on her bare knee before it fluttered away. She could see the smile in Connor's eyes. They simultaneously burst into child-like laughter. "I know. Could this day be any more perfect?"

"I don't think it can." He moved closer to her and looked into her eyes, stroking her sunlit hair. "This is what we needed," he said.

She looked at his chiselled jaw. She stroked his face and placed a hand on the nape of his neck. He was close enough for her to feel his stubble. "You're right, Connor. It's exactly what we needed," she said, as an urgent desire took over her, to make it all okay. She couldn't tell him now. She couldn't. The moment was too precious. They didn't need a third party to ruin it. Even if that third party had been the love of her life. *Had been,* she said to herself. *What I have now is this, and I need to live in the moment and enjoy it.* With that thought she pressed her smooth, rosy lips onto his. She paused and looked at him for a while before he took over and gave her a kiss that spoke so much about who they were together, what they have together, and what they will continue to have. *I'll tell him later,* she told herself. *A few more hours won't make any difference.*

***

Connor and Cassandra giggled about the butterfly scenario as they walked away from the car parked in the guest carpark.

"You wouldn't believe it if you wrote it in a book," she laughed.

"I think that moment may be up there with our daisy moment at Lake Vänern," he said with a smile as they sauntered hand-in-hand towards the hotel foyer entrance. The pebbled pathway crunched under their shoes. Cassandra walked as though she was drunk from the pleasantness of the day.

She had to tell him everything about her past as soon as they freshened up. As she lifted her head, leaning into Connor, so she wouldn't lose her balance, she saw *him* stand from the bench. He looked at her, then at Connor who was laughing as he held her close.

Josh boldly walked towards them. "Hey, Cass," he finally said in that smooth, masculine way.

She met his intense hazel eyes, and then she looked at Connor who had stopped laughing. He searched her eyes like he had the night before.

She turned away from Connor and faced him. With a tremor in her voice and in her heart, she replied. "Hi, Josh."

CHAPTER FOURTEEN

Cassandra tried to steady her breathing as she awaited his response.

He smiled at her — at both of them. "So, this must be your fiancé … Connor?" he innocently queried.

"Yes … this is Connor." She quickly turned to Connor. "This is the friend I ran into: Josh."

"Yes, although we couldn't have met in more intense circumstances," Josh said.

Cassandra's heartbeat increased as soon as he uttered the words. Connor gave her a puzzled look.

"Yes, it was intense, the storm last night," she blurted out, placing her arm on Connor's shoulder in a reassuring way. "Luckily, I ran into Josh though. He helped me a lot."

Connor remained silent for a few seconds before speaking. "Well … I guess I should be thanking you then." He looked pointedly at Josh.

"Well, I didn't do much. I just stayed with Cass until help arrived. You know, so she didn't have to wait alone," he said, keeping his eyes on Connor. "We were also lucky that I had a whole basket of gourmet food and a bottle of wine to keep us warm. It's freezing up there."

Cassandra gave Josh a curious look. She felt uneasy at how easily he was disclosing the information.

"Have you been to the Eden Valley Lookout yet?" he asked Connor.

"No, I'm sure we'll get to visit it during our stay here," he replied, studying Josh.

"Yes, we will definitely visit the Eden Valley Lookout. We'll have to remember to get some jackets to keep warm. It's so icy up there," she waffled.

"Yes, you definitely need jackets if you go there," he said to Connor. His gaze then returned to Cassandra again. "I'm just glad I was able to offer my jacket to you. I hope it kept you warm." He stared at her. She could feel Connor's discerned look. She quickly turned to face him and gave him an affectionate smile.

"I was surprised that you weren't together when I ran into Cass," Josh said. "I heard the news about you two being engaged. Cynthia told me. We all go way back! We were all friends: Cynthia, Ryan, and, of course, our lovely Compassionate Cass, and me. She's always listened to other's problems." He turned to Cass. "I'm glad that hasn't changed. Thanks for listening last night."

"Sure …" she stammered. "Any time."

Connor's phone beeped. "I'll have to make a call. It's one of my clients," he said. He held her hand, guiding her towards the hotel foyer, just like they were before.

"Um … bye Josh," she managed.

"Yes. See you," Connor added.

Josh intercepted, stopping them in their tracks. "Um … Cass. I was hoping to talk to you. It was so easy to talk to you last night. I thought I might need some help. I know you're not working and I'm not a client, but you and I are friends. So … is it a good time for that? For you to listen?" he asked, meeting her eyes with a boyish, fragile vulnerability.

"Um …" she looked at Connor. "Josh was having some family issues …"

"Sure. You do what you need to do," Connor responded, letting go of her hand. He glanced at Josh. Then he took her hand back into his and leaned close to her. He sensuously kissed her on the lips. He caressed her hair and looked deep in her eyes. "I'll meet you back in our hotel room. I've got something special planned for us. Remember those essential oil massage blends from Maria's shop. Well … I've brought some with me," he said, while caressing her hair.

Cassandra smiled at him, but she felt awkward knowing that Josh's piercing eyes were on them. She glanced over at

Josh. His gaze was solely on her now. His jaw was tight, but he managed a smirk.

Connor broke away and smiled at Josh, shaking his hand with a confident, firm handshake. "It's great to meet you," he said, before walking quickly to the entrance of the hotel with raised shoulders.

They both watched him leave before Josh decided to speak. "I hope I didn't catch you at a bad time. You two look like you've had a fun day seeing the sights. I think it's great that you're showing him where you grew up. He never really knew that part of your life, well, not like I did, I guess. We grew up together. We've been through everything. Together."

Cassandra guided him to an outdoor table around the back. Kids playfully screamed as they splashed in the pool nearby. She wondered if Connor would be able to see Josh from their room's balcony. She wished that she had told him about Josh helping her the night before.

"So, I'm curious, why didn't you tell Connor about running into me last night?"

"Sorry?"

"Connor … he didn't know I was the one who helped you."

"I told him that I ran into a friend, but it was so late, I guess. He was waiting at my door to surprise me."

"And you didn't want to ruin his surprise … you thought it might upset him?"

"Um … I don't know if he'd be upset. He knows about you. I told him about you."

"You did? Okay, I'm surprised. He seemed to think I was just a friend. That's why I didn't say more. I didn't want to upset you or anything. I'd hate to do that. I also didn't want to come between you two," he said, looking into her eyes at the moment the words left his mouth. "I hope I haven't said anything I shouldn't have."

Cassandra didn't say anything for a while, instead opting to gaze at a family passing by carrying beach towels. She'd been surprised that he had said as much as he did. But then why wouldn't he? She hadn't told Connor that he was the friend who had helped her. How would he have known that? Still … being that he was her ex, she did find it a bit presumptuous that he didn't check with her first.

As she moved away from the sun, her bare knee touched his bare leg. Her face warmed at the touch. He smiled at her. "So, first, you look great in shorts, like you always did," he said.

Cassandra laughed. "Thanks … I guess? So do you." She smiled and scanned his outfit. He wore a smart pair of charcoal shorts and a casual, white shirt. His long arms revealed strength, and she couldn't help but gaze at the veins protruding from them. She remembered those strong arms wrapping her into him as they longingly searched each other's eyes. Cassandra looked away from him.

"Now that the formalities are out of the way, I was hoping to grab a coffee. I think I need one. How about you?"

"Um …" Cassandra looked towards their room. As she turned to decline the offer, she felt like all the emotions from long ago were welling up in his eyes, in the form of repressed tears. She felt a huge sense of compassion wash over her. She had to at least grant him a coffee and a conversation, after all that they had meant to each other. "Sure, one coffee should be fine."

They sat at one of the outdoor tables and Cassandra watched Josh order a coffee. He had such confidence and a calm, cool aloofness about him.

"The same?" he asked her, while the waitress waited patiently.

Cassandra acknowledged her with a smile, recognising that she was the same blonde waitress that had taken her order. The young man's words came to her mind, but she repressed them. Had she broken Josh's heart?

Josh had come back for her. Guilt crept up on her as she processed his words. *Why am I having coffee with him?*

"Cass, I'm so glad you mentioned the hotel you're staying in. I had a really restless night. It all came back to me, what we talked about … you know, about her … about my mother."

Cassandra looked at him at the mention of his mother. *He needs me,* she told herself. *How can I reject him? He couldn't confide in me back then. Maybe he needs to now. Maybe he feels that I'm the only one that can understand him, apart from the counsellor he's seeing.*

Her compassion pushed down any guilt about the situation. She was a mature woman. She could be friends with him without romance. Besides, he may have not meant it in a romantic way. "What is it, Josh? You can tell me anything. I'm here for you."

"I know you are, Cass. Some bonds can never be broken. They're just too strong. Anyway, when you left yesterday, I don't know what came over me. I started thinking about the day … the day she left. Perhaps seeing you brought everything back. I know I've been seeing a professional and I'm coming to terms with it all, but I feel like you know what I'm thinking before I even say it. The way you look at me makes me feel like everything will be okay."

Cassandra smiled at him. "I'm just glad you're able to talk openly about it. When we came out of our pizza hangout, I remember you telling me that … you told me that …"

"That some people aren't really pretending to be okay because they already know what the other person is thinking before they say it. I remember it well, and I also remember what happened after. I kissed you."

Cassandra looked around as she stirred awkwardly in her seat.

"He does know about our past, doesn't he? I mean the extent of it. It's okay, Cass. You don't have to worry. Connor isn't going to catch me kissing you or anything like that. I can tell that you're uneasy. That must be the third time you looked around. I'm guessing your hotel room is on that side?"

He pointed to the direction she had looked at. The room was hidden directly from view so she had chosen a great table, but she wasn't sure if Connor would come downstairs to find her. They'd had such a beautiful day and he was still probably upset about her not disclosing who she ran into last night. He knew that she and Josh had dated, but she had never gone into any intricate details about their relationship.

"He knows about us dating," she replied.

"Dating?" he queried, as though it was the most ludicrous thing ever said. "I'd say we were a lot more than that: lovers who couldn't keep their hands off of each other and felt a deep connection. Such a deep love that it sometimes hurt … I think that's how I would describe it. I'm not going to hide what we had, Cass, not for anyone. Those days meant a lot to me. I've never met anyone who I can connect with on such a deep level, and we were so young. That says a lot. You were twenty when you left for Sydney."

"Josh … you know my situation. I haven't forgotten how we were together either, but that was a long time ago. We've both moved on with our lives." She had to be firm with him, she decided, no matter how much her heart jumped at the mention of what they had together. She was a mature counsellor, and she had found that deep connection with Connor. Besides, she had tried to rekindle what they had when she'd returned a few years ago, but it didn't happen. Her heart hurt for him though; he obviously didn't have that connection with someone special anymore, like she had. He looked like he needed it.

He looked down at the table when the waitress returned with their coffee and a big smile on her youthful face. "Thanks," he said with his sexy, husky voice.

Cassandra noticed a small freckle near his jawline. It brought back her worry from that day at the school gates and her eyes welled. She sipped her coffee and grabbed her sunglasses from her bag. He placed his hand over hers.

"Cass ... do you remember that day in front of the school gates, when you had returned from holidays? God, I thought you were the most beautiful girl I had ever seen. I always thought that though, probably from when we were five."

Cassandra smiled and relaxed, moving her hand away from his, taking a quick look around as she did this, before turning to face Josh again. "I thought you were so handsome ... mischievous, though, but in a fun way."

He matched her smile. "I remember that day so well. I found out my mother had left us while I eagerly anticipated seeing you. It's as though one woman that meant so much to me left me and I fell into the arms of the girl I loved. If it wasn't for you I don't know how I would have survived it."

"Oh Josh," she managed.

"It's okay. I just want to share this with you, although I know you knew how deeply I was hurting at the time. I was devastated, Cass. My whole world as I knew it through those young, optimistic fourteen-year-old eyes, had crumbled to the ground. Without any indication. Dad told me. After seeing you, I went home and asked what we were having for dinner. My dad was outside, sitting on the concrete fence. It was odd. He hadn't done that before. He was looking at the ground. His eyes seemed transfixed on a pot plant. It was as though he couldn't look away from it, like some unknown force was holding him hostage. The pot was broken. He and my mum had argued about it the day before. Well, he didn't really care about it, opting to try to calm my mum down with, 'it's only a pot, love ... you can't be upset about that. I can make another one. There are more important things in life. We can't let houses or cars, or any object own us, even something we make ourselves. It's the art ... the freedom to express ourselves that's important. I never cared for perfection. Never!'

She had shouted back, 'You just don't get it, do you? Some things that are broken can't be fixed. Once you break them, you can't go back. You just can't. And you wish to God you did something to prevent it'. My dad had shrugged it off. Now that I think about it, we thought she was exaggerating more than usual. But that was mum. She was always fussing about things like that. I used to think, how could my parents be so different? I ran that day, after my dad told me. He told me that she wasn't returning. She'd left a note. Some reason that my dad didn't really explain: she felt like she was broken inside and had nothing left to offer. She said we were better off without her. I was so angry with him that I blamed him at first for not listening to her about the pot. She seemed to think he ignored her, that her concerns were self-imposed. Maybe she'd had enough, I thought."

Cassandra reached over to touch his face, but drew back before he took hold of her hand again. He caressed her fingers.

"I felt so lost. I ran and ran until I couldn't breathe. I then realised that that's what she'd meant. My mother couldn't breathe anymore. She felt like she was suffocating because she was broken inside. I never understood why I didn't see it coming. She was irritable that morning, but it wasn't that strange. What was it about that morning that she'd made her decision? I kept asking myself. It was that damn pot. It symbolised all that was broken inside. The roots of the plant were dying because the pot wouldn't stay together."

Tears streamed down Cassandra's cheeks. "Why didn't you tell me everything word for word like you are now? You only told me snippets of this. You had even told me that she would be returning at one stage. We all knew after the years passed that that was not happening."

"I wanted to tell you, but there you were all smiles and sunshine. I didn't want to ruin your happiness. You were my rock. Seeing you smile, letting me get closer to you as we grew older, and that night in the farmhouse … Cass, you knew my pain. I knew you could feel it by the way you looked at me. But I was too ashamed to say the words. I didn't want you to look at me with pity, like I wasn't good enough for my mum. I don't really even know why I couldn't tell you. I think I had repressed it, like some coping mechanism … like it didn't exist if I didn't acknowledge it. And what about you?"

"What about me?"

"Why couldn't you tell me why your parents wouldn't accept me? I thought, at the time … I thought that you too wouldn't accept me. Like you validated the fact that I wasn't enough for her … or any woman I cared about."

"I never thought that. Josh, I would *never* think that! You have to believe me! I can't believe I didn't confide in you …"

"About how much your dad despised me and my family? How he, too, looked down on us? Like we were not worthy of you? I know my dad was laid-back. He loved making pottery and sculptures in the shed. He really enjoyed it though. It was his dream to live like that."

Cassandra felt a pain in her stomach. She remembered what her father had said about Josh and his family, and about the dreamers of this world. Josh didn't know that she felt like she was a member of that category in her father's eyes as well.

"You understand. I don't know how, but you really feel what I've felt for so many years. You know I got in touch with her recently."

"You did?" she asked as her phone beeped. Connor had ordered dinner. She looked around: Parents, children, and other resort guests were packing up, ready to get dressed for dinner at the restaurant or on their balcony, or perhaps they were going to one of the many restaurants at the many cellar doors at the wineries. It was getting late. She met his sad eyes. How could she leave him like this? She felt so conflicted. Her concern made her heart hurt. She wanted to help him.

"Cass … I've spoken to her many times lately."

Her eyes combed the pool area. The downstairs bar was closing. The upstairs restaurants would now open for dinner. She watched as the resort staff worked quickly: clearing plates, delegating, wiping stains from tables. The clatter of cutlery and dishes being packed distracted her.

He reached over for her hand again. She had to know about his mother. Why she felt broken inside to the point that she'd abandoned a precious child — why she would leave her whole family. She looked around the premises again and then she saw him on the top balcony. Connor looked down on them. She had to leave. She released her hand from his strong grip. "Sorry, Josh. I want to hear all about it, but I have to go now. I have to go," she practically pleaded with him.

He finally released her hand and looked at her with sad eyes. "Sure. I'm sorry. You can go back — to him, Cass. You can leave me."

Cassandra froze, his words repeating in her ears. "She left us", he had just told her. "She won't be returning", his father had said to him. "Josh … I'm sorry. I'm not leaving you. I'll see you again to hear what you have to say, but another time. Not now. I'm here for you, like you were for me," she said. The wrench in her heart returned. She was abandoning him at a vulnerable moment. All she could see was the little boy who kept running. Not just for that afternoon, but all his life. And yet the last time Cassandra had returned, *he* had left *her.*

"Bye Josh," she said, her eyes now on the balcony. Connor was no longer there. She walked quickly, racing away from him, his sadness enveloping her. She ran. She had to run back to her new life. Although she felt like her heart was still with Josh and the life they once had together. She had to leave him.

How could she disconnect from him when the connection had been so strong? The man's words invaded her brain: "But the truth doesn't". She thought he was a nuisance. She was wrong. *Am I still pretending?*

***

153

"Connor, this is so beautiful. When did you get to do all this?" Cassandra's eyes combed the lounge room of their suite, which was adorned with candles, red and pink roses, and a table dressed with a white cloth and the finest crystal glasses. A bottle of champagne sat in a chilled, silver ice bucket and the plates on the table were of the finest porcelain. The air was laced with the smell of rosemary and garlic.

"I organised it with the concierge while you slept this morning."

She walked over to him. "You are the sweetest man. Connor, thank you, for all of this. It's a wonderful end to a wonderful day. Wasn't it fun today?"

"You don't have to thank me, Cass. I just want you to be content, to be close to me, close enough to tell me everything. You know me. I don't care about material things or believe that romance is just about dinners and flowers. I know it can only complement a connection that a couple already has with each other."

She paused before speaking. "You saw us talking? I could see you from where I was sitting at one of the tables by the pool. He really needed to talk. His mother left him when he was very young. He still looks lost when he talks about it ... even though he's getting help," she blurted out.

"Cass ... relax. You don't need to tell me all that. It's between you and him. Yeah, that's pretty heavy stuff. I get it, though. Sure, I was shocked to see him there, but I know you were childhood friends and dated, but who doesn't have a childhood love story? We all had our school crushes."

He moved towards her and offered her a glass of champagne. She took a sip and then gazed into his eyes. *He thinks we just dated? I'm sure I told him we were a tad more than that. I'm sure I did,* she tried to reassure herself. "Um ... we didn't just date, we were a bit more than that," she managed.

"Sure, Cass … he was your high school boyfriend. Look, I'll admit, I was jealous that he looked like he could be on the cover of a magazine, but I trust you, Cass. I know I have no reason to doubt your love for me." He looked into her eyes for a while. "You didn't just date each other. I get it."

"No … Connor. I want you to understand. He was my first …"

"Love? It's sweet … it really is," he said.

She opened her mouth to clarify, not sure if he understood, but his lips caressed her lips. He quickly placed their wine glasses down on the table and wrapped his arms around her, smothering her with kisses.

"How about we have dessert first?" he asked between heavy breaths.

"Sure," she responded, wanting desperately to rid the uneasiness she felt inside. She wanted to forget about it. It was too intense and they'd had a wonderful day. Besides, he didn't want to know what they had discussed. He was a mature counsellor who valued confidentiality and trusting that personal information wouldn't be indulged to him like frivolous gossip. She surrendered to her desire. There was no need to say anything. It's not as though she would do anything to jeopardise what they had together anyway. Connor would always be the man for her, she told herself. He was her present and her future.

CHAPTER FIFTEEN

The next few days were blissfully relaxing. Connor and Cassandra had driven around Tanunda and the neighbouring towns and spent the day shopping at Nuriootpa, the major commercial centre in the Barossa Valley. They managed to find a costume shop after meeting up with Cynthia.

Cynthia had drawn their attention to the vintage shop and hoped she wasn't putting them out by having them hire or buy costumes. They reassured her they weren't the least bit bothered by it and thanked her for letting them stay at the grand, old mansion she had hired for the party in Clare Valley, and commented on how generous her dad was to pay for all the guests while having lunch with her in the garden of her newly renovated, contemporary home which boasted views of rolling hills. Ryan had joined them later. They were taken with Connor, just like Cynthia had been when she'd visited Cassandra in Sydney a while ago. Cassandra had wondered why she cared so much about her old friends accepting her fiancé. Bella's words constantly entered her mind: "We always thought you and Josh would end up together."

Surprisingly, Ryan hadn't mentioned Josh until he received a message from him. "Well, what do you know?" Ryan said as he'd shown her around the garden while Connor and Cynthia talked about some of the historical sites they should visit. "It's Josh. Would you believe he's here, in Tanunda? He's also coming to our wedding, after all." He stopped talking and looked at her intently. "Did you know he was here?"

She gazed at the lemon tree. She was trying to calm her heart rate which had escalated at the mention of Josh.

"Cassandra?" he'd continued while she turned to glance at Connor and Cynthia. She was so relieved that Connor wasn't with them, that he was preoccupied. At that thought, she felt silly about hiding any mention of Josh. But she couldn't help how she felt, how her heart jumped at the sound of his name. Connor seemed to be okay about Josh being there, but the question he'd asked her the previous night was still torturing her with guilt and confusion.

"Cass?" Ryan had persisted.

"What? Oh … Josh? Yeah, I actually bumped into him at the Eden Valley Lookout," she'd managed.

"Oh? You did? You bumped into him … at a lookout that's quite difficult to get to … where it's usually so quiet? What are the chances?"

"I actually *did* run into him. I was there at the same time he was there. I know it seems odd, farfetched even. It's not like it's a crowded shopping centre where you'd expect to bump into anyone from your past …"

"Relax, Cass. I understand. I wasn't implying anything. I just meant it's odd," he'd said, searching her eyes.

"Oh, I agree, it is rather odd." She'd flicked her hair to one side and felt that he was still not satisfied with her response when she noticed him looking at the lemon tree with a furrowed brow. He was deep in thought. His short hair revealed a tight jaw from his side profile, and his eyebrows were raised. He and Josh had been best friends. She wondered what he was thinking.

He then looked back at her. "I'm surprised that you didn't tell us anything. He's been my best friend since we were kids. And you and he … well, you know what you were to each other," he said, as he now glanced over to Cynthia and Connor. "I was really upset that he couldn't make it, but now he's here and he went straight to you and not one word. Don't get me wrong, I completely understand it. It just puzzles me. I'm surprised that you didn't mention it."

"I didn't think it was necessary. It wasn't my place, and he didn't intentionally come to see me," she said, scratching her nose. "He ran into me during the storm at the lookout, like I just told you."

"He never got over you, you know? Josh. He never got over the relationship ending."

She'd looked up at him, her eyes meeting his eyes. "It's all in the past now, Ryan."

"Is it?" he asked, trying to coax her to look back at him with his watchful eyes.

She turned to look up at him again, after being fixated on a trail of ants marching in line on the soil between a patch of slightly dry grass. Cassandra watched as one deviated from the line, as though it was lost. She looked at Connor and Cynthia who were approaching them.

"I understand," he said, placing his hand on her shoulder reassuringly. Cassandra didn't understand what he'd meant by that. He then changed his tone the moment Connor and Cynthia reached them. "How about some coffee? We can have it on our newly renovated porch."

Cassandra watched his back as he confidently strode to the house in his cream shorts and slim-fitting grey polo top, guiding them all to follow. She laced her hand with Connor's and smiled at him. He returned the smile, but it seemed forced. Why was she even reassuring him? Is that what his smile was asking? Is that why he couldn't commit to a full smile? It had occurred to her that she was doing what Ryan had done to her. He'd reassured her, but he seemed to understand something she was unwilling to understand. She was now reassuring Connor. Perhaps he was unwilling to see what her reassurance really meant. Perhaps Connor knew what her reassurance really meant but was pretending that he didn't.

The next day Connor and Cassandra spent their time amongst the shops of Nuriootpa. Any doubt she'd felt was, once again, put to bed. After they had tried on costumes in the quaint vintage shop that Cynthia had told them about, they had lunch and then walked around to admire the historical sites of the town.

Connor was most impressed with the meaning behind the name Nuriootpa, which Cassandra had eagerly told him was an Aboriginal word for 'meeting place'. They took numerous photos of many of the Lutheran churches, and visited distilleries, and boutique shops. Luhrs Pioneer German Cottage was the perfect place to take more photos. Cassandra, acting as tour guide, told him the cottage was built by Johann Heinrich Luhrs after arriving to South Australia in 1844. He was the first German school teacher in the Barossa Valley. They ended their marvellous day at many of the cellar doors and sampled some wine before watching the sun say goodnight to the vineyards as it rested for another day.

The next day, they had spent a lazy day by the pool, sipping cocktails. They were having such a wonderful, languorous day, that Cassandra couldn't help but look over her shoulder occasionally in case she saw him … *Josh*.

A few days later, at the front doorstep of her parents' house, on that overcast but humid late afternoon, Cassandra's uneasiness returned. She was still fixated on a question Connor had asked her. She couldn't get it out of her mind despite the beautiful moments they had shared.

After she'd left Josh by the pool, the day he'd been waiting for her, she and Connor had their romantic dinner. She had sipped her Champagne before taking another bite in the candle light on the balcony.

"So, you told Josh where you were staying?" he'd asked, casually.

"Yes," she'd replied, matching his casual tone. "I told him the hotel we're staying in. He asked me while we ate in the car at the Eden Valley Lookout. He was wondering why I wasn't staying with my parents," she quickly added, becoming aware that her giving too much information may, in fact, make her look like she was hiding something, but she'd felt so uneasy about the topic and couldn't help it.

"The hotel *you* were staying in at the time. I wasn't staying there yet, remember? I surprised you. You didn't know anything about me coming over," he'd corrected her.

Cassandra had met his unflinching eyes. They stayed that way for a while. She finally broke the silence. "Yes, I know Connor. You surprised me and I'm so glad you did—"

He had interrupted her after finishing a mouthful. "So, you were saying earlier, he's your first love?"

Cassandra had begun to feel sick. He was looking straight at her now, awaiting her response, holding his fork in the air as though he wouldn't continue to eat until he knew the answer. "He was actually the first man that I was intimate with," she had blurted out, trying to remain confident. It was so long ago. It meant nothing.

He had nodded. "Oh, and here I thought you two had just gone out on a few dates."

Her confidence had failed her. "It was so long ago …"

"Cass, it's okay. I'm not thrilled about it, but I trust you. I trust what you and I have. Nothing can come between that, right?" He stroked her face from across the table.

Cassandra had felt like her heart would explode when she'd responded. "That's right," she'd agreed. But the moment she looked away, she felt his watchful eyes on her. As she turned back to face him, she saw something in them that she'd never seen before. A stream of darkness eclipsed the light.

"It'll be all right, Cass," she now heard him say. "You need to deal with all aspects of your past. Didn't you come here to fix things with … with your dad?"

Cassandra saw that same look in his eyes.

"Yes, I did," she managed. "At least Julie and Maria will be here tomorrow morning. We won't stay long. We need to pack our things and move to the shared house. At least that's something to look forward to. It'll be fun to see the sights together. I called Julie earlier and they're excited. I think she really needs this time with George. Anyway, here goes," she continued. "My mum organised dinner for us, and I'm sure she doesn't want the food to get cold. She worries about these things. I don't know why she's become so obsessive with her cooking when she only ever wanted to be on the stage."

Connor took her hand in his, in a reassuring way. "It's like what we learned: lots of people do that when they suppress their inner desires. They become fixated on something else."

Cassandra felt another pain in her heart when he said that. Even his genuine reassurance was drawing guilt out of her.

"I'm here for you," he continued, whispering. "If he says anything to undermine you or your job." Cassandra had told him everything about the counselling snipe the other day.

The door swung open.

"Hi dad," she managed.

He looked at her like she was an imposter.

"You scared the life out of me," he replied. "How long have you two been standing there?"

"We just got here, Mr Jensen," Connor said, offering his hand. He managed to quickly shake hands before he let them in.

"Well, come in, we don't want the flies entering. Your mother's gone to a lot of trouble for both of you," he said, in his usual irritable way. Whenever she spoke to him, it was always like she was bothering him, like he had somewhere to be even if he didn't. Cassandra gazed up at Connor. He gave her a knowing smile and placed his hand on her shoulder. Her dad uncomfortably noticed the gesture.

"Connor!" her mother announced his name like he was a royal prince with a glass slipper. Her mother had been ecstatic when she'd heard about their engagement. Cassandra hadn't expected her to be so enthralled especially since, at the time, they hadn't met him yet. It's strange how they never accepted Josh, but she'd accepted Connor before she even knew anything about him.

"Mrs Jensen," Connor offered his hand, but her mother leaned in for a hug. "It's great to see you again."

"Likewise, and I hope you two are hungry. I even made Cassandra's favourite dessert," she said with pride.

"You didn't have to go to too much trouble, but I'm happy to try Cass' favourite dessert. It's been lovely getting to know where Cass grew up," he said, jovially.

Cassandra caught her father suspiciously eyeing him. "Cassandra should show you the new properties in the area. We're very proud of this place. Sure, it's not as fancy as Sydney but some people are always looking for something. I don't know why they think they'll find it amongst all the noise and swarms of people buzzing by in their noisy, fancy cars, in narrow streets full of concrete monstrosities and asphyxiating pollution."

Cassandra hesitantly walked towards the lounge room. The fear that consumed her as a child came back to her. *And why did he always insist on calling me Cassandra even if everyone calls me Cass or Cassie, or any other name that conveys affection and closeness?* It was as though the way he said her name was another way to control her. The mere mention of her name when it was uttered from his mouth made her feel as though the school principal was summoning her to the office because she did something wrong. Again.

"I'm so glad she went to beautiful Sydney. She wouldn't have met Connor, otherwise," her mother chimed in, giving her husband a pleading look. It seemed to work because he sat down on the other couch, as though he would actually talk to them instead of leave and go to his office to hide behind the guise of urgent work.

"Yes, you seem like a responsible chap. Although I would have chosen an occupation that has a lot more clout," he said in a matter-of-fact way.

Cassandra's face warmed, wondering how Connor would get himself and her out of this one. She knew he wouldn't get defensive like she often did; he hadn't invested his heart and emotional security in this man since he had been born.

He wouldn't give him the power by answering such a loaded question.

"This is quite a great place you have here," Connor digressed.

Cassandra sighed inwardly, relieved that he had taken the reins away from her father.

"I was reading something the other day about this investments CEO. He started out laying bricks, but took a chance. Apparently, he always wanted to open his own business, and he did. It really took off, and now he's become a multi-millionaire, and contributes huge donations to charity."

"Sounds like this man has his feet firmly on the ground and his head where it should be. Sounds like he's getting the job done," Mr Jensen commented.

"He sure did. He had hit rock bottom and given up hope, he says in the interview. He'd given up hope to follow his dreams. Funnily enough, he thanked his therapist in the interview. He said without her guidance to gain clarity and valuable insight into what his values were, he wouldn't be where he is today."

Cassandra sat back into the couch with her mouth agape. She wondered how her father would react to Connor's comment. She was amazed at how he'd taken the power away from him in such a clever and rather sly way.

Mr Jensen cleared his throat before speaking. He began to talk but couldn't seem to find the words. He gave Connor a look that almost seemed like he had been defeated in his own game. If Cassandra wasn't mistaken, he seemed rather impressed with Connor.

"See, Oscar," her mother interjected, adding more salt to his wound. "A lot of people would not have even tried anything outside their comfort zone if it wasn't for counsellors."

Cassandra smiled at her mother's comment.

"Let's eat … we can't sit around chatting all day," Mr Jensen digressed.

Mr Jensen's skin broke out into a rash and he stirred in his chair. Traces of perspiration appeared on his forehead. Mrs Jensen's comment had also obviously stung him, making him look like someone had just fried eggs on his face and courteously asked him if he would like salt on them.

Cassandra felt like laughing. She wasn't expecting to have him outsmart her father in his own game. She was also, once again, noticing that her mother was showing signs of her young, bold self: challenging her father instead of passively accepting it all and repressing her feelings further, baking in the kitchen.

As her parents stood up to make their way to the outdoor table, Cassandra gave Connor an appreciative smile. He whispered in her ear when her parents were out of earshot. "I know it's not like me to undermine anyone, but some people refuse to see things clearly if you don't call their bluff, if you don't serve them a slice of their own game, or should I say cake?" he teased as a whiff of sweet vanilla enveloped the hallway as they passed the kitchen, making their way to the outdoor verandah. "The intention behind it was one for self-growth and clarity. Not revenge."

"Nice one," she said, giving him a quick kiss on the cheek. He kissed her on the lips. She instantly backed away. He held her hand and she was positive he could see the fear and pain in her eyes. He didn't know the expected rules that she knew so well. She then remembered her mother laughing when he hugged her a few days ago, when she'd returned to pick up her phone. He would never have done that in front of her. It was almost as though he told himself that he would never tear down the walls for her, to offer her some affection like a father would to his daughter.

"Let's go eat," Connor said, reassuringly rubbing her back.

As Cassandra stepped outside into the warm sunlight, her mother stopped sorting out cutlery and gazed at Cassandra. "You look so beautiful, Cass. White always brought out the colour in your eyes."

"Looks can only get you so far," Mr Jensen commented.

"You look beautiful," Connor whispered in her ear. "Your mum's right. White definitely suits you. I can't wait to see you walk down the aisle." He touched her hand with affection.

She met her father's eyes. He immediately looked back at his food.

Surprisingly her dad offered some wine and sipped intermittently from his own glass. Connor lightened the atmosphere as he launched into a conversation about his parents' farm in New South Wales, how well their local produce was selling: olives, cheese, strawberries and many other fruits. Her father was always impressed with stories of the land, of working hard. Of course, if it crossed the line and became something that involved any creative outlet where one could express themselves, ironically his defences came up as quickly as the curtains came down on his and her mother's acting careers.

When they'd had their coffee and Cassandra had helped her mother tidy the kitchen, Cassandra and Connor strolled the grounds. Her father had been called to help one of the new agents with a difficult client who had changed his mind on a property, so with the security that he'd be gone for at least an hour, they planted themselves on the comfortable, brown leather couch with a few of the photo albums. She wanted to show Connor how her parents used to be. Perhaps he could help her uncover why her father was bent on treating her like she was a stranger.

"That's my dad," she pointed out one of the photos.

"Wow ... your dad looks like quite the debonair actor in this photo. I really can't believe it's the same person. And who's this woman?"

"That's ... um ... that's actually Josh's mum."

"It's okay, Cass. You can say it. I can see how you all were tangled up in each other's lives."

"Is it?" she asked. "Is it really okay?"

"Of course, it is. I understand. You were close as children. I can see it by looking at some of these photos. I'm sorry if I seem like I'm questioning you lately. I know it's hard for you to reject people when they're in need."

Her shoulders lightened. Letting him into her world seemed to be helping them. He could see that Josh had played an integral part in her life.

"I'm surprised they even have a photo of his mum. My parents never socialised with her or with his father. Lana and Ben Sturgess were always treated with disrespect in my family. I don't know why. Josh could feel it every time he came over."

Connor paused for a while, fixated on a photo of her and Josh at one of the local vineyards. Cynthia and Ryan were walking in the background as she and Josh posed for the photo. Cynthia's mother had taken it. He then turned the page.

"Who's this handsome dude?" he asked.

"That's one of the other actors. I don't know his name. He's in one of the plays that my mum and dad performed back in Denmark. That's them at one of the theatres in Copenhagen. Speaking of Denmark, my mum is hoping to show us some of their holiday photos before we leave."

"It's strange, don't you think?"

"What is?"

"That they decided to come to Australia. I mean, why would they do that when everything was going so great? They were performing at some of the best theatres in Europe and then they came to the Barossa Valley and set up their own theatre? At Williamstown? Only to close it soon after."

Cassandra processed what he was saying. It was strange. "That's the theatre," she said. "Maybe we should go and have a look at it one day. I think it was difficult, financially, to keep it going."

"That's what I mean. Why would they take such a huge risk when things were going well with their acting careers?

Anyway, it's a great idea. I'd love to see the theatre," Connor said, still deep in thought. "*A Doll's House*. That's the book about a woman who is sick of the humdrum of life and then another man causes all sorts of drama for the couple. Interesting."

Cassandra heard footsteps and eyed the piano. She heard the sound of the lid shutting in her mind.

"Hey, are you okay? We're not making out or anything. We're just looking at albums."

"I know you think I'm acting weird. My mum was supposed to pack these up. The last time I was here, my dad suggested they take them to the spare room. It's as though he doesn't like to look at them."

"To be reminded of the past? That's very odd, don't you think?" he asked, gazing back at a picture of Josh's mum.

"What is it, Connor? Do you have a theory?"

"No … I just feel like this woman, Josh's mum, looks familiar. It's nothing," he dismissed the thought.

"Here you two are," her mother sprung into the lounge room with her mobile phone and her digital camera. "Maybe we should look at the holiday photos on a big screen. I think the cable is here somewhere." She searched one of the cabinets, before Cassandra's father's footsteps could be heard marching into the house.

"Oh Oscar … before you go, I forgot to tell you. Would you believe I ran into the Sturgess kid, Josh, the other day, Lana's son?" She stopped herself, a blush forming on her cheeks as she met Cassandra's eyes. Cassandra was surprised that she would even mention him.

"Did you know he was in town?" Mr Jensen irritably asked Cassandra. "I ran into him in Angaston just now. He was coming out of a coffee shop. He's some photographer or something like that. Of course, he is. We've got enough photographers with everyone taking selfies."

Connor opened the album she'd shut and looked at a photo of her father, mother and the other actor. He scanned the photo of Josh's mother again. He then looked into Cassandra's eyes.

"Isabel … I thought you'd already put those back in the storeroom. They take up too much space. There's no point being stuck in a moment. Even you two counsellors would agree on that. Life keeps going. It's pointless just looking at moments that have already passed."

"Did you talk to him? Josh?" her mother asked, obviously desperate to know, even if the topic was an uncomfortable one. Besides, her father seemed to want to pursue it, so they might as well all contribute.

"Yeah I talked to him. He's as arrogant as ever. I always thought he was trouble," he snarled. "It's great that you moved on from him."

Cassandra's heart rate increased. *Sturgess kid?* she thought dismally. He was a grown man. She was shaking all over. "Why do you hate him so much?" she blurted. "He lost his mother! She left him. Don't you feel at all … don't you feel …?" she stumbled on her words. Memories of her asking a similar question in her youth came flooding back to her. After all these years, he still rattled her.

Her father looked as though a lightning bolt had struck right through him. It was as though his face was on fire. "I have my reasons," he said in a deep voice.

He then awkwardly shook Connor's hand as Connor stood up, sensing his need for solitude. "It's been good seeing you again," he said, earnestly.

"Cassandra," he then managed in a deeper voice. She stood up feeling that it was the thing that most daughters did when saying goodbye to their dad. He, of course, just walked on as though it never occurred to him that it was what fathers did. He would rather touch burning coal than touch her hand and treat her like she mattered. Yet she had witnessed some carefree, warm moments between her and her dad in the old photos she'd looked at.

She stifled a tear, and smiled at her mother, who seemed to be blanketing her with warmth after the cold breeze that had snuck into the room. "It's all set. We can begin with Sweden since you two also had fond memories of it," she said, with a slight tremor in her voice as Mr Jensen closed the door of his study.

***

"Well, that went well," she said as Connor pulled out of the driveway an hour later.

"It did?" he asked.

"Well … it wasn't great but at least he was talking more now. He'd hardly utter a word to me back then, unless he was really angry with me."

Connor seemed confused. He made a sharp turn and turned the ignition off. He faced her and placed his hands on her shoulders. "It wasn't great at all, Cass, so stop trying to convince yourself that it was. He treated you appallingly. He's narcissistic and his behaviour is abusive."

Cassandra searched his eyes. She always suspected that of him, but she couldn't pinpoint what it was. She always felt there was something more, something directly underneath the facade that would explain why he treated her as he did.

Connor voiced her thoughts. "I think there's something more though. I think it's odd that they came here out of nowhere when their life back home in Europe was going so well. Your father looked so proud on that stage in those photos, playing the role of Nils Krogstad."

"It's a role he played in real life too, causing so much grief. At least my mum and he are acting healthier; she stands up to him, challenges him."

"Yeah," he said in an unconvincing way. "But it seems like she's also not revealing something. I don't know why I get this feeling. It's ironic that they came to this part of Australia."

"Why would you say that?"

"The history. Many Lutheran Germans had run away from religious oppression. They came here to be free."

Cassandra smiled. "That was definitely not why my parents came here."

Connor also smiled. "I know … but it's as though they were running from something and wanting to start anew, otherwise why would they come here?"

Cassandra nodded. Connor seemed to be onto something. "Thanks. For getting me through this … and for not getting upset that I stuck up for Josh."

"I understand … why you feel protective over him. He lost his mother, and you too lost someone — your dad. He was never there for you, Cass, so you felt like you, too, lost someone special in your life. The difference in your case is that you never really had him in the first place. You were, and I can see that you're still, hoping that you'll finally meet your father. That he will finally talk to you and see you as you are."

Tears streamed down her face. He understood exactly how she felt. At that moment she couldn't possibly feel closer to anyone else. She pressed her lips onto his, and he stroked her back as he kissed her with longing.

"I guess it wasn't that bad though," he said with a mischievous smile as their lips parted.

She gave him a puzzled smile. "It wasn't?"

"No. He did have some good points, especially when he said I'm a lot better for you than 'that Sturgess kid'."

Cassandra messed his hair up. "I can't remember that he used those precise words, but, yes, he is right. It's great that I'm with you." And her heart truly believed it.

CHAPTER SIXTEEN

"This place is spectacular! You did a great job, Maria," Connor enthused as he inspected the spacious, contemporary double-storey house.

Cassandra admired the views through the large white framed windows. From where she stood, she could see sweeping gold and emerald hills and a plethora of trees in the distance. "The gardens are immaculate, and I love the concrete feel of this place. I think Julie will approve. It's so minimalist, yet surprisingly cosy. Living amongst concrete and surrounded by nature really does take away the clutter from your mind."

"I agree," Connor said. "Having too many things in my living environment can, at times, narrow my mind. The right amount of clutter within a space can invite individual expression, but this type of setting really invites you to look within."

"Yeah?" Maria queried. "But I don't know if you'll get much thinking done. If you haven't noticed already, we have become a pretty noisy little family. I'm sure Thomas will love running through this room, and these wide corridors, they're perfect for him. I'm glad you approve, though. I didn't know if you'd like a contemporary house like this one, or one of the more traditional ones. I just couldn't resist the views and the pool. Not to mention the tennis court ..." she trailed off as they gazed through the large windows.

"We can burn off the calories we consume after we all cook up a feast," Cassandra offered. "Or better yet, we'll just pick up some gourmet hampers and bring them back here." She eyed the long glass table positioned near the wall where large windows faced the pool, garden and tennis court. There was also a long, grey table on the contemporary designer patio, next to an outdoor lounge and coffee table.

Cassandra noticed the *teppanyaki* grill. It looked very inviting to say the least.

"There's also a great restaurant at one of the well-known cellar doors nearby. Tanunda has many gourmet finds. I'm sure you'll love staying here," she said with pride.

"I'm sure we will. Driving up here was a wonderful experience in itself. Sorry we got here late though," Antonio chipped in. "Thomas wanted to see as many air dancers as he could while on the freeway."

"Yeah? Is that so?" Cassandra asked Thomas, who was eyeing the pool and the garden. "Did you stop to see some of the air dancers?"

Thomas laughed as she tickled him. "I did. I saw a blue one, and a red one, and a yellow one." He emulated the movements of the air dancers he was so fond of. "Look, I'm an air dancer. This is how they move," he said in a jovial voice. They laughed as Connor joined him.

"Don't get Antonio started. There's no stopping him when it comes to swaying his hips," Maria teased.

Antonio began to dance much to Thomas' delight.

"I think you're supposed to move your arms more, not your hips," Maria said in between laughter.

"What have we missed?" Julie asked while musing over her surroundings, as George and her made their way into the large open-plan lounge and kitchen area. Julie looked at them as she awaited their response, but her eyes moved to the tall ceilings as she appreciated the dramatic silver light fixtures. She then looked down and eyed the polished, concrete floor again. "This place is like a contemporary museum," she said, taking off her fedora and sunglasses.

Cassandra admired her grey and white striped, wide-leg jumpsuit and edgy Roman-styled sandals.

"I love the feel of this place … it's surrounded by nature. The juxtaposition between all the concrete, natural timber, and nature encircling the house works so well. It speaks to your mind and soul." She strolled around the room.

"And we'll also get to stay at a grand, old mansion in Clare Valley, so we'll have the best of both worlds, architecturally speaking," Cassandra interjected. "I'll show you the mansion we'll be staying in for the birthday party and the garden party the next day."

"Sounds fascinating, if I do say so, madam," George said in a tone that was even more formal than usual. "So many parties and, of course, then we have the *pièce de résistance*: the wedding ceremony and the wedding party."

Cassandra smiled at him. He was obviously trying to be in character for the grand *soirée* they would be attending in a week.

"Wow! I didn't know there was a tennis court!" he suddenly exclaimed, snapping out of the role. He hugged Julie as he guided her to the window. He affectionately stroked her arm. They'd just started their holiday, and it already seemed to bring them closer. Julie had been so concerned that day they' played tennis. She had nothing to worry about, Cassandra thought as she eyed George pulling her into him, sneaking a kiss on her forehead as they gazed at the court, manicured lawns and garden. She also remembered how anxious she had been that Sunday.

Connor's arm brushed hers and she knew that everything would be okay. She was facing her concerns, and Connor would help her deal with her issues with her dad. The image of Josh tightly holding her hand by the pool flashed in her mind. His grasp had been desperate, as though he was scared she would leave him. She had left him. She had left him when his eyes revealed the fear of a little, lost boy. She had told him that she wasn't leaving, that now wasn't the right time. But when would the right time be? A sadness washed over her. *How is he? Is he okay?* she thought to herself. She felt like she was abandoning him. *But he left you when you returned a few years ago,* she told herself. He abandoned you …

"Hey, are you okay?" She felt Connor's warm breath as he whispered in her ear. He smelled of bitter citrus. "Why don't you try one of the mocktails Antonio made earlier?"

"Sure," she said, following him to the onyx kitchen bench, pressing the guilt and fear down again. As much as she tried to laugh and enjoy herself with her friends, she couldn't help feeling like she had ignored the man she had at one stage in her life considered to be her best friend. Her boyfriend. Someone she loved so much.

Everyone gathered outside with some light snacks and refreshments.

"So, what do you think of this house?" Cassandra asked Julie, showing the image on her mobile screen.

"Wow! It's so grand! How exciting! The party is in a week, right?"

"That's right. On Saturday. I called Cynthia earlier to let her know where we're currently staying. They might pop over later. She hopes it wasn't too much trouble to get outfits."

"No way! No bother at all. I love getting dressed up," Julie reassured her.

Maria then approached the table and grabbed a few grapes for Thomas who was riding his scooter.

"Who's ready for a game?" George called out from the far end of the court.

Cassandra and Julie stood up at the same time, already having changed into their sneakers.

"Sure. Why not?" Julie called out.

"Come on, Connor! Maria and Antonio can have their turn after," Cassandra suggested, noticing they were both busy with Thomas. "I'll be happy to look after Thomas."

"That's okay," Antonio called back. "Thomas wants me to watch him perform some stunts."

Cassandra smiled as she watched her long, slim shadow forming on the concrete as she walked onto the court, the sun casting a beam of light in her path. She straightened her cap as she marvelled at the emerald slopes in the distance.

Connor took his spot as the server. Cassandra eyed Julie intensely on the other side of the net. Julie laughed while trying to match her intense expression. The ball tore through the air like a whip, and Cassandra's heart rate increased with excitement as she watched Connor slice it towards the corner of the court, managing to get it right on the line.

"Nice one!" George screamed.

Connor served again and Cassandra ran after the ball when Julie returned it with skill and finesse. Cassandra then managed to manipulate the ball, making it land in the opposite direction from where George and Julie were heading.

"Very clever," Julie said, as she caught her breath from trying to outsmart her play.

"Yes, but don't get too used to it," George said with a warm smile.

She then heard some clapping from behind her. Maria and Antonio had stepped into the kitchen, so it couldn't be them, she thought.

She turned to see Cynthia and Ryan. They stopped clapping when she came face to face with them, but she could still hear slow applause from the person standing behind them. Her jaw dropped and her heart rate escalated to the point that she thought she would collapse. He finally stopped clapping.

An awkward pause followed. It seemed like an eternity before anyone said anything. Connor's stare combed the side of her perspiring face. He then looked at Josh, who beamed with pride and confidence. The tension in the air was palpable. Even George's powerful serve wouldn't be able to tear through it, to decimate the delicate undercurrent that threatened to reveal itself and come to the surface. She could taste its bitterness in the suddenly thorny air.

"He's right. It was very clever play," Josh finally said, looking at her eagerly.

"Hey everyone," she finally managed, with a dry mouth that felt like sandpaper. "This is my friend, Josh." The inelegant, rattled manner with which she spoke contrasted

Connor's steady gaze: his tight jaw, his dubious, unwavering eyes which managed to remain still and focused, while she quivered and fidgeted nervously with her racket.

Josh sauntered towards her and somewhat unceremoniously placed his hand on her shoulder, as though sensing her agony. Connor's unflinching gaze seemed to encourage his confidence; it seemed to tell him it was okay to approach her, as opposed to the opposite. Cassandra was, once again, taken aback by his candour.

"It's great to see you again, Cass. I just went over to visit Ryan and Cynthia, and they were on the way to see you, so here I am again. I have the privilege to see your beautiful face again. I guess some things never change."

"Oh? How so?" Connor quipped, his unfaltering gaze still on him as he too walked closer to where she stood. Connor's tone unnerved her even more. He'd seemed to be okay with Josh being back in her life when they'd visited her parents the other day. Was Josh now becoming overbearing? It was the second time that he knew where she was. *That's it!* she thought. *He probably thinks I told him where I'm staying again. Or Josh appears too comfortable, almost as though Connor isn't even a threat.*

She now caught a glimpse of Julie's perplexed face. Her eyes were also fixated on Josh. Cassandra could feel George stirring on the other side of the court. He was hitting the under-soles of his shoes with his racket, obviously itching to continue the game. Julie turned around to meet George's eyes. Both of them gave each other a seemingly knowing look.

Josh turned his head to look at Connor in a way that surprised Cassandra. His shoulders tensed and his jaw tightened as though he had been strung like the racket she was latching onto. Why did he have such an effect on her? He had a presence about him. Even the slight breeze that she felt on her warm face seemed to have become timid and stifled. However, despite this, its gentleness felt like thorns pricking her skin.

It was all too much for her. The outside world became small and stuffy. She saw blurred images and everything appeared green, then grey, and soon enough she saw darkness. Even the friendly shrubs and vibrant flowers became black in appearance, more like sinister shadows. Her eyes felt heavy and her head ached. She was shivering, yet hot. Her knees buckled.

"Cassandra," Connor screamed, his voice louder as he caught her. She fell into his arms, leaning all her weight onto him.

"I just need some water," she managed. "It's the sun. It's intense."

"Slow down … just take deep breaths," she heard another soothing male voice. His strong hand touched her other shoulder. They were both helping her to the outdoor table. Her legs were so heavy. The patio had blurred. A hammer pounded inside her skull. Thoughts ran rampant inside her mind. *I nearly fainted,* she told herself. *I'm a counsellor and I'm acting like some weak, love-sick adolescent.* Embarrassment took over as her body began to respond to the ice pack that Maria had placed on her forehead.

"I hope she's okay." She was sure it was Cynthia's voice.

"Have a drink," she heard Josh's deep, husky voice. Her vision was still failing her. Things around her now looked green. Perhaps she was coming around again.

"I'll take you to the sun lounge," Josh said.

"I'll do it. It's okay, we're fine," Connor responded.

"Mummy … Mummy, is Cassie sick? I've got Mr Potato Head … he'll help her," she heard Thomas' voice. It was all it took to will her way back to consciousness. The last thing she wanted to do is worry a little boy.

Moments later, resting her head on the sun lounge under the comforting shade, she sipped the cool water from the glass Josh held. "Thanks," she said, his features clearing.

"I'll take it from here," she heard Connor saying.

"Sure, man, I didn't mean to overstep. We're cool, right? I mean, we've got the same goal here. To take care of someone that means a lot to us," he said, emphatically.

Josh's eyes appeared in front of her. She could see the hazel in them. They matched the hills in the distance. His stubble brushed the skin of her warm face as he leaned close to adjust the backrest and the pillow from the back of her head. She flicked her hair away from her face with trembling hands. Josh assisted, moving another ash-blonde strand away. His eyes looked at her with intent. "Cass, I've been so worried about you," he said. "You're in safe hands though. You always were, and you still are now."

Connor held her hand firmly. Her vision had returned.

Josh smiled. "Hey, sleeping beauty. I know you found me irresistible in the past, but to faint … I mean, that's a first," he managed with a sexy, dimpled smile. A look of genuine concern washed over his face.

On other occasions she would have laughed at his playful comment, but Connor was now sitting right next to her. She snapped out of her trance-like state and she turned to Connor. "I'm fine now. I'm just so embarrassed. I can't believe I ruined everyone's fun. You can all continue; I'll just rest here for a while. Some fruit juice should help."

Josh stroked her shoulder. "I'm so glad. Seriously Cass, I hope you're okay. I'd hate if anything happened to you. I couldn't bear it …"

"It's okay, I've got it from here," Connor repeated in a louder voice.

"Sure man. She's … she's yours," he said and moved away. Cassandra's heart and head throbbed, but she was glad her vision had returned. She had to get it together.

"I'm fine now, Connor." She stroked his hair and leaned into his chest.

Connor kissed her on the lips tenderly. "You need to take it easy. Just rest for a while."

"Sure. I can watch the game from here. Please don't stop on my account. I'm feeling so much better already," she said with a forced smile. She dared to look in Josh's direction.

He was still looking at her. He looked vulnerable; the confidence had abandoned him. He looked like he did that day by the pool, when he'd told her about his mother.

"Don't worry about the game," George offered as he neared them.

"Yes. Just rest. Maybe you should go inside," Ryan suggested.

"No, please! Thomas was having so much fun, and maybe the food will help. I'll just eat something. I already feel so silly. I'd hate to think I ended all the fun."

Josh's eyes beamed with confidence. "Well, you heard the lady. How about a game? I'm in. How about you, Connor?"

Connor sat up and glanced at Cassandra. She nodded.

"Sure. Here, you can borrow one of the rackets," he said, practically throwing it at him.

Maria eyed Cassandra as Cynthia sat next to her, handing her a glass of orange juice. "Cass, I'm sorry. I hope I didn't cause any trouble," Cynthia said in a low voice meant only for Cassandra's ears. "He just turned up when we were leaving … and I thought, since we were all friends … Now that I think about it, it was insensitive of me. He seemed a bit terse with Josh. I thought everything was okay between them."

"They are, I mean, it may have not looked like it now, but Connor and I had a big talk the other day and he's fine with it all. He actually felt sorry that his mother left. Connor is mature when it comes to these things. We'll just have another talk about it, to clarify things. We'll be fine." She scratched her nose.

"Phew … I was worried for a while. So was Ryan. He's the one who had asked him to come along."

"It's all good, Cynthia. Everyone is excited about your wedding and the party in Clare Valley. Why don't you tell them all about it?"

"Sure. You know, I'm also excited about your wedding too," she said, slowly, her eyes studying her carefully.

"Me too. I mean, we are as well … Connor and me," she said looking towards the court at the two men.

Cynthia also looked at them, rather sceptically. She held the stare for a while, and then glanced at Cassandra again, who looked on as Josh tied his shoelace. He gave her a quick smile as their eyes met. She smiled back, only to meet Cynthia's eyes before taking refuge with a sip of her drink. Cynthia cautiously smiled at her before she stood up and walked back to Ryan.

Cassandra noticed her whisper something in his ear before looking at her and smiling. Their eyes went back to the court, glued liked everyone else's.

Julie sat next to her on the other lounge chair. "You okay?"

"I'm more embarrassed than anything," she reassured her before her eyes, too, became fixated on the court.

"Looks like we're in for an intense game," Julie said.

Cassandra faced Julie. "You and George seem to be at a good place right now. Is everything okay with the new coach he hired? What was her name?"

"Samantha … he calls her Sam," she trailed off. "Anyway, George and I have always been good together. George has just made her the head coach. She's that good. He often tells me about her athleticism … her prowess. He keeps saying how great she is at the game. That is … at tennis, Cass."

"Oh?" Cass asked, trying to stifle the innuendo that her uttering the word "Oh" may have implied. Julie seemed to be confident with George going on about Samantha's athleticism. She was obviously right. They were in a good place. The last thing Julie needed was for her friends to cast doubt and fear on a healthy relationship. Cassandra was glad for her and anything disparaging may be damaging to their stability.

"That was just Maria trying to warn me to have my eyes wide open," she continued from her previous comment. "Just because I've been working with some renowned designers who may be okay in the looks department, as if

George would hire a fit and attractive coach just to get to me!" she laughed. "George is a fair guy; the only games he plays are on the court."

Cassandra gave her a smile that communicated that she agreed with her. Connor was also mature in that respect, she reassured herself. He didn't harbour any resentment towards Josh. If he did, he would have told her.

A loud bang on the court got their attention and they gazed towards the tennis court. Connor had hit the tennis ball with such power, it flew past Josh's head and landed on the fence with great force.

Josh wasted no time. He bounced the ball before serving. It landed straight at Connor's sneakers. Connor dominated it, responding with a powerful aggressive backhand. Josh ran as fast as a fox chasing a rabbit and managed to return the ball with just as much gusto. They were both perspiring in the intense sun.

Cynthia turned to Ryan. "This is turning out to be quite the match. We might have to intervene before someone gets hurt."

Cassandra caught her gaze as Cynthia looked in her direction. It was as though Cynthia was wondering if she was thinking the same thing. Behind each joke lays an element of truth.

"Speaking of relationships," Julie said. "I think this game is fast becoming a rally for your attention or perhaps to prove a point ... to perhaps back off? I've never seen Connor hit the ball so vigorously."

"Wow ... what's going on out here?" Maria asked as she stepped out onto the patio. Antonio followed her with Thomas close behind. "We might need to keep Thomas out of the way in case he gets hurt. It's intense out here."

They continued to watch, everyone's eyes moving from side to side as the ball flew from corner to corner in a steady, yet vigorous rhythm, steered by a contemptuous force and male bravado.

Cassandra nursed her glass of orange juice. She could feel Maria's watchful eyes on her now. It felt like she was responsible for what was happening on the court. She hated the way it made her feel guilty. As a counsellor she knew how debilitating such emotions could be. Surely, Connor wasn't doing it intentionally, he was not the passive-aggressive type. He was good-natured and confident, always ready to talk about his feelings.

The ball flew across the court sounding like a gust of bellowing wind tearing through the air. Connor hit the ball so hard, and it made it straight down the line.

Josh gave him a sage smile. He knew it was a near-perfect return.

Julie glanced over to George with an expression that said, *Do something.*

"Looks like you guys have worked out quite a sweat," George managed.

Connor did not want to stop. He was waiting on the other side of the court, racket firmly in hand awaiting an impending shot; an alpha male awaiting its prey.

"It's just a friendly game," Connor shouted out. "Right, Josh?"

Josh didn't take the bait. His smug smile spoke volumes. It revealed that he had unveiled Connor's pretences, like he knew what game he was really playing.

Cassandra felt sheepish. She would put an end to these childish antics.

"Why don't you have something to eat?" she suggested.

Josh looked at her and replied with an affectionate, warm smile.

"Sounds good to me," Connor replied, after smashing the ball one final time across the court to a stunned Josh, who'd just turned to find it at his feet.

***

Two hours later Connor and Cassandra were seated in their hire car. "Connor, we're fine aren't we? You and I?"

He leaned in and kissed her forehead.

"Sure, Cass. Why do you ask?"

"The game. You weren't using that as a way to show that he'd better back off, were you?"

"It was that obvious?" he asked, taking her completely by surprise.

"Yes … it was that obvious. To everyone. I felt so silly. First, I faint and then I have my ex-boyfriend and my fiancé nearly destroying the net with their *friendly* tennis game. It was like a war zone," she exclaimed.

"Well, since my friendly fiancée is too polite to be firm with him, I thought I'd clarify some things myself, in case there's any ambiguity."

Cassandra's stomach turned as he said this. *He thinks I'm not giving him a clear message, that I'm not setting boundaries. Is that what he's saying?* Her mind speculated.

"I'm just glad you're feeling better now. What made you faint anyway?"

"I don't know what came over me."

"The moment you saw Josh … that's when it happened. Is it because of me? Were you worried about how I'd react?"

"Maybe, but you're fine, right? You understand that we have a lot of history, that I can't just ignore him? And then there's the issue of his mother …"

Connor clutched the steering wheel. "Yes."

Cassandra noticed that his eyes weren't blinking as he stared in the distance; they were unflinching as he uttered the next words. "Of course, there's that issue. We can't ignore his feelings. Even though he's seeing a professional and it happened so long ago. But you're right, he needs his ex-girlfriend to talk to as well."

"Connor? Do I detect a bit of passive-aggressiveness?"

"Perhaps, just a little," he said, a smile forming. "I think under the circumstances that's to be expected, don't you?"

She looked out onto the road as his hand rested on hers. "I trust you, and that's all that matters. As for him … that's another story." He pressed the accelerator and merged with the other cars on the way to one of the local wine cellars.

Before Josh had left with Cynthia and Ryan, Josh had grasped her hands in front of everyone and said, "When do I see you again?"

Cynthia had instantaneously guided Connor and the others approaching them out to the front of the house. Julie seemed to follow her cue without much persuasion, guiding everyone away from the scene.

"I don't know, Josh. It's a bit difficult now."

"I need to talk to you about her … about my mother. Cass, you're the only one I have ever felt that I could trust with my feelings …"

She questioned him with her eyes. Josh and she knew all too well that he hadn't completely confided in her over the years. What she knew had come from his touch, not audible words. But the chemistry could not have been stronger. She knew what he meant.

He'd read her thoughts. "Remember what I told you. Sometimes people refrain from saying what they already feel; what they already know about the other person is more intense and real than words could ever reveal."

She'd heard a rustling of leaves as Thomas sped through the path on his scooter. She could hear Maria running after him as Thomas neared the pebbled path at the side of a landscaped water feature. The path led to the garage where the others were heading.

Josh's skin and strong hold he had on her hand revealed his desperation. "When?" he'd asked again. When she didn't respond, he held her hand tighter and moved her closer. He kissed her lightly on the forehead, but quickly backed down as if it was nothing, as if it was just a friendly kiss between friends. "At Ryan's birthday party … at Clare Valley. I'll see you then," he said before disappearing and blending with the others as they headed towards their car.

Cassandra had been in shock. It had just occurred to her that he'd also be staying at the old mansion at Clare Valley. They'd all be staying at the house. The peck on her forehead told her he could behave himself.

Connor's hand was now on hers. He looked at her before placing it back on the steering wheel.

"Cheer up, Cass. I trust you with all my heart. You have nothing to worry about." He searched her eyes.

CHAPTER SEVENTEEN

Over the next few days Cassandra showed her friends the sights, taking the reins. They visited the historic town of Kapunda, where they took photos with the famous statue, Map the Miner, also known as Map Kernow, or the Son of Cornwall. The statue was erected to commemorate the Cornish mining history of the town and they all marvelled at its gigantic size. Cassandra explained that the Kapunda copper mine of 1844-1878 was the first successful metal mine in Australia. It had relied heavily on Cornish immigrants.

They strolled around the vicinity for a while, learning about the historical significance of the town. Focusing all of her attention on acting as a tour guide liberated Cassandra. While they explored, memories of Cynthia, Ryan, and Josh flooded back.

The next day they drove to the picturesque town of Gawler, the oldest country town in the mainland of South Australia, where they had lunch at one of the outdoor restaurants. They explored old mansions and sandstone cottages. Wide, open spaces with nostalgic remnants spoke to them about the town's history.

The next day, they decided to unwind by the pool, and then they drove to some of the famous cellar doors to taste some wine. This was followed by tasting some of the local, artisan cheese, and other local produce in Tanunda's boutique shops.

Surprisingly, when Cassandra took her friends to her family home, her dad seemed to be taken by them. He had even enthusiastically talked with Maria and Antonio about their trip to Greece, especially the ancient sites. His amazement increased when Maria told him about how great Eventually You was doing. He was even impressed with some of the hotel projects Julie had worked on overseas and in Australia. George challenged him to a game of tennis, and Cassandra was sure that her dad stifled a laugh. He seemed to acknowledge that she had done well for herself. Having such wonderful friends that often spoke highly of her and how she'd helped them with their problems seemed to convince him further. It would have to do, she'd thought, since she wasn't able to gain any such approval on her own.

"I have to see it," Maria had shrieked, when Mrs Jensen had told them about their performance of *A Doll's House*. It had been one of their most celebrated performances back in Copenhagen and Vienna, she'd told them all. Mr Jensen remained silent but did not oppose the suggestion.

He'd nodded to his wife when Maria wouldn't take no for an answer, but when they had gathered around the lounge with trays of coffee and her mother's acclaimed Viennese pastries, Mr Jensen kept himself busy in his study. It was almost too much for him to be included to such an extent. The fact that he'd agreed was more than enough to endure.

"It's so strange that your parents settled here just when they were becoming successful in Europe. Why would they settle here? Why would they open an acting school here? Mmm ..." George had pondered, his blue eyes deep in thought. "Was it a known place for acting or was there an abundance of theatre goers here?"

Her father entered the hallway from his study. He had caught the tail-end of the conversation and looked as though he was frozen. His eyes were glued to the television, where he was playing the character of Krogstad.

Her mother walked in with glasses of water when Antonio said, "I remember reading the play ... it's from that Norwegian writer, who was it? Ibsen. It's such a tragic and sad story. Why a mother would go to such drastic measures," he'd added, as Mrs Jensen looked at her husband, who now stared at a scene where the other actor who played Nora's husband Torvald, threatened her. On the screen, the actor told her that the children and he had suffered enough.

Mr Jensen had gone back towards his study, looking sullenly at the floor. The comment that Antonio had made hit her hard. It had just occurred to her how ironic it was, how the performance had transcended somehow to their real life. And it, to some extent, mirrored the plight Josh was experiencing with his mother.

When they were leaving the property, Cassandra watched her father take off in his car as though he was on a mission. She got the feeling that he was about to do something he'd been planning to do for a while.

They headed north to Clare Valley. The beauty of the horizon invited her back from her reverie. It wouldn't be long before they were there. Lovely, yellow daffodils coated the large, open fields shared by sheep and cattle, and water glistened from the streams. Cassandra looked on in quiet admiration at the scenes that unfolded as they drove. It was just as she remembered it: authentic, charming, rustic, and real.

"We definitely have to go to Sevenhill Cellars to see the old vineyard I was telling you about. The Jesuit monks used to make sacramental wine there. We can see the wine making cellar. We might as well regroup today and take it easy before we dress for the evening's festivities," she said in an old-fashioned lady-like way. "I might even get to read some of my novel."

"I must say, I'm looking forward to wearing a vest and the suave, beige suit," Connor admitted.

"It will look so elegant with the white, vintage shirt. You looked just like George Emerson in *A Room with a View*."

"And you look like Lucy Honeychurch from the same novel. That governess-inspired dress with the shirt and tie also looked sexy on you though."

"Oh, I loved that one too, but I couldn't resist the one I chose. Besides, it'd be more fitting for the uptight character in that novel, Charlotte Bartlett. I've always wanted to wear an embroidered, cream dress with puffy sleeves and that broad-brimmed hat goes with the outfit. I think the pearls and short, lace gloves will look so lovely and they're all so fitting for the era. Perhaps I'll wear the hat to the brunch garden party. By jove, won't we look grand? First rate, as they used to say," she joked, slightly uneasily when she remembered Josh asking her when she'd see him again.

She decided to be mature about it. She would have the much-needed talk and not make an issue of it. Connor already knew how much she cared about her friends. Besides, she was certain that he'd be preoccupied with catching up with old school friends. Even Bella would be there. She could even guide him with her counselling knowledge and the many skills she had learned.

Mrs Sturgess … what had become of her? She would find out about her, his brother, and his father.

And why did her dad react so suspiciously when Antonio commented on how tragic it would be for a mother to act the way the mother in the play acted?

She caught Connor glancing at her, before looking back at the road. "You're really getting into this, aren't you? It's great to see you like this, Cass. I know things have been tense, but I shouldn't let anything destroy the time we have together. We always have fun on these trips. You look out for people, even Josh Sturgess," he said in a formal way.

"We don't have to worry about him this weekend," she said, succeeding in sounding flippant. "Have you seen the size of the house? He'll probably be eyeing all the lovely ladies, and I'll be admiring you while we're dancing, when I'm in your strong arms," she said in a distinguished way. "I also can't wait to show you all the beautiful, rustic vineyards. There's around fifty of them if I recall correctly. It's so exciting, Jo—"

A loud horn cut her off as a truck cut someone off. The guy in front of them tooted hysterically. Her face warmed. Connor hadn't heard her. She looked at him and smiled.

"Looks like the guy in front of us needs to meet someone like you. He wouldn't let trivial matters get to him then. So, you got cut off," he said to the guy in front of him who obviously couldn't hear him, and muttered, "There are worst things in life."

"Yes, there are," Cassandra agreed, relieved that he hadn't heard the name she almost called him.

Soon they were standing at the front lawn of the grand, heritage mansion.

"Wow! This place is immaculate. I wonder when the others will get here," Cassandra enthused. Maria and Antonio had decided to take their own hire car to see the sights in case their plans — or Thomas' needs — impeded with anyone else's plans.

Julie and George had hired a four-wheel drive intending to take everyone, but with Maria and Antonio pleasing a toddler and Cassandra and Connor deciding to leave early, they would have the car to themselves.

The lawn was manicured and damp to the touch. The smell of freshly cut grass hung around them. The sprinklers made a sound like a rattlesnake as they jetted out water intermittently, reminding her of lazy summers from her youth. As they walked across the lawn, passing rustic outdoor tables and benches, the wide, black and white tiled balcony welcomed them with grace. The house carried a nostalgic, romantic vibe reminiscent of the regency era it belonged to. Black, old-fashioned wicker armchairs and small, round wicker tables were strategically placed amongst the long, cream stone wall. The detailed, wrought iron rails complemented the walls around it. Enormous cream columns on a smaller Juliet balcony reflected both Georgian and Victorian architecture. Cynthia had told her that the mansion was built by a wealthy English man back in the day.

"After you, madam," Connor said as he wrapped his arm around hers, while the porter placed their luggage on a brass trolley.

Candles and infusers perfumed the air with the scent of rose adding to the vibe, as they stepped inside the grand entrance. Cassandra marvelled at the parquetry as she wandered around the foyer, admiring the huge, antique chandeliers on the tall, ornate ceilings. The mahogany front desk was bedecked with porcelain vases of flowers, and a brass bell. A yellow candle illuminated the desk, its delicate flame swaying soothingly. Plants, ranging from ferns to palms, in huge, black and gold planters were scattered throughout the foyer which led to an open plan lounge area. It all looked so decadent and exotic.

A huge, red Persian rug blanketed the centre of the lounge room, and a velvet, cream and pastel pink velvet lounger with gold legs faced an onyx fireplace. The tearoom could be seen from the black French doors where two planters with indoor ferns stood tall as though they were obediently waiting to open the doors for the guests.

Cassandra could see the charming tearoom from where she stood: little square tables were covered with crisp white tablecloths and the French windows shared views of the grand balcony and the manicured lawns. Outside, nature circled the house and a water fountain invited attention to the centre of the garden. Cassandra's heart raced with excitement. She felt as though she was in a chateau in the south of France or in Florence. Memories of Europe comforted her and eased any turmoil that threatened to unhinge her. This would be another great memory for both of them. She couldn't wait for the party in the ballroom that night.

Cassandra admired the view from their bedroom. "Wow! You can see Sevenhill from here. I recognise the church. How beautiful is this, Connor?"

"It's all wonderful, Cass, especially being here with you," he said, wrapping his arms around her waist as she gazed outside. "And tonight will also be another wonderful experience for us."

She watched more guests arriving in taxis and cars. A smartly dressed couple stepped out of one of the cars. Connor encircled her waist and turned her to face him. He pressed his lips to hers and stroked her back. She couldn't help but strain her neck to glance at the lawn. A woman admired the flowers near a neat, maze-like hedge that led to a meandering path where a rustic tap and a statue sat. *It's not him,* she thought as she saw a tall, older man and woman step out of the other car. She wondered when he'd get here. Connor held her tighter and kissed her neck.

"When do I see you again?" he'd asked her. *Enough!* she scolded herself. It wasn't her concern. With a bout of confidence, she stroked the loose, light brown curl that fell onto Connor's forehead. She leaned in and let him take her on a journey, one that was only for the two of them.

CHAPTER EIGHTEEN

"I wonder when they'll get here," Connor whispered loudly, trying to talk over the jazz band. "I hope they make it."

"I know. I'm surprised they didn't get back earlier. Surely, they didn't get lost. I'll try calling them again," Cassandra offered. "Maria needed to get some of Thomas' favourite snacks. He won't settle without them."

"I just called Maria and she's not answering," Julie said from across the long table.

Cassandra noticed the place card next to her. It was for Maria. The table was elaborately dressed with porcelain black and gold plates, crystal glasses, tall and thin candles in silver candle holders, and small crystal vases housing red and pink roses.

"Well, at least they were already dressed," George said, pouring a glass of wine for Julie and then refilling Cassandra's and Connor's.

"Can you pass me the bottle of Merlot?" a smartly dressed young man asked her from the far end of the table.

"Certainly," she said and stifled a smile when she realised how in character it sounded.

The tables were filling. The dance floor was brimming with people, who talked with glasses of wine in their hands.

Cassandra straightened her hat. "Isn't it rude to wear hats indoors? Or was it okay in this particular era?"

"I think it was okay for women but not for men. And maybe women didn't wear them to a ball," Julie said with a smile. "Don't quote me on that though. I'm more versed in matters involving the decor and furniture of that era. Anyway, it's just a dress-up … it's not as if we're really in the era."

"I should have worn a ribbon through my hair instead. I don't think my hair will stay in place for much longer with this huge hat on it."

"You look gorgeous. We all do, it's safe to say," said George proudly. "Now if only the others will get here so we can really let our hair down, and that means your hats too, ladies."

Julie gave him an affectionate kiss on the cheek. "You beautiful man," she said with joy in her voice. "How romantic is this night? And I can't help talking so formally dressed in this outfit. We're all beginning to sound like you, George. You've always sounded like you just stepped out of the pages of a classic novel."

George affectionately smiled. "And you love that about me, right? You thought, and still think, it's sexy."

"Well, I thought it was obnoxious actually and that you were smug, but of course, that's all in the past. It is rather sexy," she said, leaning on his chest.

Cassandra admired their love for each other. "I know. This place is magical." She scanned the large ballroom. Cynthia sat at the far end of the table with Ryan and waved to them with her laced, champagne-coloured silk glove. "You all look so elegant," Cynthia said as she approached them. "Thanks for coming, you guys."

They stood up to greet them both. "Happy Birthday, Ryan," Cassandra said, giving him a hug. She didn't realise that they would be sitting at their table. After all the formalities were done, Cynthia and Ryan headed back to their seats.

Cassandra caught her looking at the place card next to her with dismay. She quickly swapped the place card from the table behind her with the one next to her. "I can't believe I mixed up the place cards. I've been so busy planning all these parties, and of course, this particular guest had told me that he wouldn't be coming," she told one of the male guests across from her.

"I got Maria on the line," Julie shrilled. "They've got a flat tyre. Would you believe it?"

"Oh no!" Cassandra replied. "Have they got a spare?"

But she didn't hear Julie's reply as a tall, handsome man dressed in an elegant, charcoal, tailored coat, a white shirt with a tall collar, and smart grey pants, with a black top hat on his head walked in. His chiselled jaw was accentuated further by the tall hat, so much so that he looked like he'd been carved out by Phidias, the ancient Greek sculptor.

"They're having problems with the spare tyre. This is awful. When will they make it now?" Julie cried. "It's such a great party. I mean, look at all the trouble they went to. I just can't wait to take a tour of the whole house. Even the balcony has been decorated with such care. Tea lights are everywhere."

George laughed and pulled her onto his chest. "I love it when you talk design, you get this hungry passion in your eyes."

"Sorry, I can't help it, but you all have to admit … is this place incredible, or what? I just don't want them to miss out on anything."

"Don't worry. We'll keep in contact and see if they need help," George reassured her. "It's not like the car has broken down."

Cassandra managed a nod, but even though her mind was with the conversation, her heart was with the man striding towards his table. He came to a smooth halt at the table where Bella and her husband were seated. She sighed in relief. To her dismay, however, he proceeded towards another table, where he would, no doubt, be sitting.

Oh no! she panicked. *It must be near our table or on our table!* she thought as he kept walking toward them. *He's probably just going to greet Cynthia and Ryan,* she reassured herself. But then she thought about how Cynthia had made a mistake with the place cards. She said someone had changed their mind …

Oh no! Of course, they were referring to him; he was Ryan's best friend, after all. Her thoughts were hysterical.

"Josh, Ryan and I are so glad you could make it," Cynthia exalted. "Of course, our closest friend is sitting right here."

Cassandra had forgotten how to breathe. She glanced over to Connor. He gave her a reassuring look. She wondered if he was as confident as he appeared.

"Nice to see you again, Cass." Josh said as he kissed her hand. "That's what they did back in the day, isn't it?"

"Hi Josh," Cassandra said, much too quickly.

"Yes, they did," Connor replied. "You've obviously arrived in character. So generous of you."

Josh smiled a broad, dimpled smile, his eyes revealing the depth of his soul. He took his place by Cynthia and gazed over to Cassandra from across the table. "You look so beautiful by the way, as do you, Julie."

"Thanks," Julie replied. "You look quite dashing yourself."

Connor finally looked down at his phone as a beep alerted him to a message.

"It's so good to have all the gang back again and to have your new friends join us as well," Cynthia shouted from across the table.

"Yes, last time you came back here, you hadn't met Connor. I remember you confided to me about your counselling aspirations," Josh said, intently. He then turned to Connor. "She was at a crossroads career-wise. I was glad to lend an ear," he said before turning back to Cassandra. "I mean, how could I not, when you were always there to listen to me as you still are now."

Connor's jaw dropped. He looked like he was eager to hide the confusion that was shining through his eyes.

She urged him to snap out of it. She had vaguely told him about the trip home, but had omitted the 'spending the magical days and nights with Josh' part. She took Connor's hand into hers.

Julie decided to chime in. "That's our Cass. She's always offering an ear to all of us. Maria and I have had our share of issues, and she's always ready to help. Connor and Cass make such a great couple, the way they're both passionate about helping people." Julie finished her sentence practically in the same breath. She gave Cassandra a satisfied look and glanced at Connor as though checking if her words had the desired effect.

Ryan looked concerned from across the table as he gazed at his friend. Josh hunched his shoulders.

"Hey, Josh Sturgess? Is it really you? Wait! I knew it! You and Cass—"

"Hi, Brandon," Cassandra interposed, standing up from her seat to greet the former football star of their school. "Meet Connor, my fiancé."

"Oh … fiancé? So, you're not … I mean, nice to meet you, mate," Brandon stumbled and played with the buttons on his silk vest.

Connor's phone beeped again. "It's Maria and Antonio. They really need some help. I'd better go since George has already had a few drinks." He moved closer, whispering, "I understand … it's okay," before continuing in a louder voice, eyeing Josh. "I won't be long." He kissed her, careful not to ruin her carefully applied lipstick, before playfully straightening her hat. "Madam," he said with a nod before walking away.

Cassandra smiled at his attempt. She met Josh's eyes. "He was just acting …" Josh did not share her adoration for the attempt.

"Yes, he certainly was," he said, emphatically.

Cassandra stirred and played with her long, pearl necklace. The band lifted their music, switching to a contemporary tune and Josh poured more wine into her glass as he moved to Connor's seat. She thanked him, as Julie and George stood up and headed towards the dance floor. Julie looked back over her shoulder, frowning.

"You really do look beautiful. So, who are you? Which character?"

"Perhaps Lucy from E. M. Forster's *A Room with a View*? My mum was in a production of it back in Europe. He was such a great writer."

"That's quite fitting. You're trying to be polite under such intense circumstances, trying desperately to hide your desire for the rebellious, lyrical photographer. Like it's so improper to voice your feelings or to show how you truly feel about me. Not too dissimilar to how Lucy felt about George Emerson."

Cassandra was stunned by his directness. She went along with his humorous tone, even if it carried a lot of weight. "Josh, you were always funny. And yes, you were always the lyricist. I was surprised when you didn't become a writer. But I can also see you as a photographer. You carried your camera everywhere and had quite a portfolio."

He processed her words. "I remember you and your mum acting out scenes from many of the greats of our time. I valued that about her. I hear that your dad used to be like that. Not that I saw many of the performances. Your parents resented the sight of me. You practically snuck me into your back garden. It's so strange that the people we thought we knew turned out to be completely different. Even your parents changed. They went from artists to keeping up with the Joneses." He looked at his glass. "I was also thinking that it's funny how the most observant people see things on a microscopic level, like they have a third eye, and how the other half have their heads in the clouds and routinely carry on with their day as though they're doing the most important thing they could for the whole of humankind. They're more in the clouds than the dreamers. From where I'm standing anyway."

"Oh, Josh," she managed.

"Please, don't look at me like that. I've never wanted your pity. I got that from everyone else, but I couldn't bear it from you, Cass."

"I've never pitied you, Josh. I truly felt for what you were going through. I also relate to what you just said more than you know."

"So then, do you think it would be inappropriate to have a dance? Especially since you are a lady and I am a gentleman and we are in 1908, or something like that?" his tone lightened.

Cynthia and Ryan blended with the crowd on the dance floor. No eyes were analysing their every move. "Sure, why not?"

He took her hand and guided her to the dance floor where a modern waltz was playing. His fingers intertwined with hers, making her uneasy. If felt too familiar.

She kept her distance as they danced, even when his eyes invited her in on a deeper level. They shone with feeling. She knew he hated being there without the freedom they once had.

"Let's go to the balcony," he suggested, already guiding her. "It's a beautiful night."

They brushed shoulders with women in lace and silk frocks and men with smart pastel and dark suits. A sea of feathers and colourful hats blended with the huge paintings on the panelled walls. They walked out of an arched door draped with gold curtains, onto the balcony. The black and white tiles reflected those in the ballroom and lower level. Green hedges twisted into a maze-like structure, and the nearby vineyard added a charming touch to the grandiosity of the mansion.

They sat at the outdoor armchairs, a coffee table separating them, and contently breathed in their surroundings.

"Cass, tell me, how did we get here? Why are we here, dressed like this in such a romantic setting, and we're apart? Why are we not together? I saw my mum yesterday

… she was at my dad's. It's been so hard for him. I couldn't bear to see him so lost, but his passions have kept him busy. She's a mess. I can tell the guilt is consuming her. When I saw you, I thought about her choices, how she's now living a life with regret. I thought about my own life. About how different it could have been had I chosen a life with you." He leaned close to her, meeting her eyes, and placing a hand on her silken knee. "I love you, Cass. I'll never stop loving you." He refused to look away from her as he searched for an answer.

She froze at his words, taken aback by his directness. Her heart rate increased but she had to ask, "Then why did you leave me that day? I told you I loved you, and that …"

He eyed her. "It's funny how we get used to things. Even the beauty around us. Then we feel like it's never enough." He leaned back in his chair when one of their old classmates peered over at them.

Cassandra frowned. How did that comment answer her question? He seemed to think that it had.

He continued. "That's what you said to me before you said you loved me. I wasn't enough for you. You'd made it clear that we shouldn't continue as a couple. Why we wouldn't work. Your leaving me to go to Sydney cemented this. Hiding me from them —your parents — cemented this. This place would never be enough for you. I would never be enough for you. You were broken inside, just like the planter my dad had made; it couldn't be fixed. It hadn't been made with love, but with fear of following one's dreams. It lacked resilience. My dad had made it when he could sense that she would leave him. He wasn't enough. And then it broke …"

The wind cooled the wetness of her cheeks. "You don't know me, Josh, not like you think you do. I'm not her. I'm not your mother! It's not my fault that she walked out on you. You know nothing about me. You say you do, but you don't."

His jaw tightened. He wouldn't meet her eyes. "Well, show me then, Cass. Show me who you really are. Maybe then I could have also shown you who I really was, and we'd stop pretending, as you'd say. You are more like her than you think. You're running … You ran away." He paused, studying her. "It's strange, sometimes we run far away from what we really want. We explore new lands, new cities, taste them, breathe them, until we realise they too can suffocate us if we let them. Sometimes what we leave behind is what we always wanted. But we're scared of it; we're scared that it may not give us the stars. We're scared it may be just what we crave but that's all — nothing more. Isn't it better to have a life that gives you joy most of the time than to keep looking for something you're unsure that exists? Maybe then you'll realise you could have enjoyed what was always there?"

Cassandra couldn't find the words. She tried to process the message beneath his words.

"Anyway, I don't know what's worse; who's braver. Some people stay but they're not really there, while others leave but they're still held back like a magnet; it's as though they haven't really left even though their passport tells a different story."

"*You* left *me* … You left me when I returned, Josh," she said, her hands trembling. She looked around the faces of the few people who looked at them. She had to get away from him … from them. It was too tense between them. Standing up, she headed down the wide, concrete steps towards the garden.

The loud music buzzed in her ears, embellishing the sound of a familiar birdcall. It was the bird she'd heard in Sydney. Her heart sank further. It then dawned upon her. Was she still running from Connor as well? Was she scared to settle into the dullness; is that why she detested the bird's monotonous sound? She had so feared the silence, the hidden expectations, day in day out. Part of her knew he was right; she had left him even if he was the one who had uttered the words.

Coldplay's "Viva La Vida" played over the speakers as the band took a break. The dramatic violin strings picked at her heart. The rhythm tuned her heart; it was necessary to feel what she was supposed to feel. *Supposed to? Just what am I supposed to feel? Since when do I listen to what I'm supposed to do? I'm a counsellor. I follow my instincts, my dreams, and my values, the things my father mocked.* But she didn't know what her heart was telling her. She was scared to listen to it.

Josh didn't know her. Even if he sensed it, he hadn't lived it. He never really saw how her dad had treated her. She needed to go it alone and see who she really was away from his scrutiny. Josh had been her sacrifice because she wasn't ready to give her heart to him. She was afraid he would treat it the same way her dad did, that he would close the shutters in his eyes and only invite the darkness.

The violin's lamentable crying continued, tugging at her heart. Her heels pressed into the dirt. She held her long, silk and lace dress in her hands as she ran. Some of it draped like curtains over the dirt path. Memories flooded back; the yellow and white petals. It was there, outside the school gates, under the frangipani tree, where she lost him, her heart … where they lost each other.

Josh followed her and turned her around, the moonlight shining in his deep eyes.

"Why did you stop looking at me like that? They lost their light, Josh. Perhaps that's why I gave you mixed signals. Perhaps I was afraid that you'd become like him, like my father. He lost hope just like your mum did," she said, trying to catch her breath.

He stroked her hair. "I know, Cass, I know. I lost both of you under that same beautiful tree! Cass, it was that day at the school gates that I said my final goodbye to her! I loved the smell of its flowers … they're sweet and enticing, but the scent left a bad taste in my heart. It was a curse and a blessing. In a strange way it always made me feel safe. It will always remind me of what I had. I know it seems weird, but its sweet familiarity is comforting."

Without thinking, she stroked his hair, feeling his heartache. He moved closer and teased her lips with his.

"Don't let it end like this. I love you. I have nothing to hide. I told you I came back for you. He doesn't know you like I know you. He never will. I want you so much. I haven't forgotten breathing you in. What we had was real, and pure, and bold. You're right. I've been unfair to you. You're not her and I'm not him, Cass. I'm not your father. I know a lot about all of us, more than you think I know."

Cassandra gave him a puzzled look. What did he mean by that? "I can't do this now, Josh."

"Then when, Cass? When you're walking down the aisle; when you wake up to a man you love but you realise that you've lost that deeper connection? That love so intense it scared you. Yes, you love him. Your heart has a lot of room for love, but you can't deny this unbearably intoxicating connection we have." He brushed his lips over hers and she moved away. Her breathing had become heavy. He stroked her hair and rested his forehead on hers. "I need you, Cass. Please, let this be our final chance to make it right. You know if you listen to your own heart, that it may give you the answer you fear, that you still love me."

"Josh, I do love you. I can't hide that from you or from myself, but I found the person that I can spend the rest of my life with—"

"The safe option. You found the safe option. Someone less complicated with less baggage, right? Perhaps, I was, in fact, wrong about you. You are running away just like she did, because you're scared to face the truth: you love another man. What makes you different, then? Prove that you're not. You have a chance to be brave and not pretend like most of your clients do. Be the role model, Cass, or you'll leave him too. Eventually. When you get bored; when you're reminded of the love you had. Your cheeks blush at the intensity of it. I can see it. You'll never have this with him. He's acting like he's fine with it, but he's threatened by me because he sees it in your eyes, what you feel for me. I know you in a way he never will, and that frightens you to the core." It was as though his eyes were coaxing her to feel what he was feeling.

"Cass, where are you? They're already cutting the cake. Cass!" Connor called out.

She walked away from Josh.

"Don't go to him, Cass. Don't leave me. It's not too late for us. You need me as much as I need you." He took her by her hand and turned her around. Leaning close, he snuck a kiss.

Memories of a time long past came to her: His lips pressed urgently against hers and her legs buckling under the pressure, the sweet smell of milky flowers, the shade blending with the sunlight in her hair, the strawberry-sweetness on his breath. She had savoured his kisses and caresses, but he had told her the words that broke her heart: "I love you, Cass. So much that it hurts, but sometimes that's not enough. I can't be the man you want me to be. I will never be enough for you. Like I said, they all leave in the end. Everyone does, even the ones that remain. You know that better than anyone. I've never pretended. Like I said, your eyes have told me your stories, your fears, and your braveness. I could write them down. They would make the most beautiful literature."

"Cass!" Connor's voice grew louder.

"Stay," she had told him. "Please, Josh. I love you. Don't leave me. We can go anywhere together and start anew as ourselves, without any scars from our parents. We can leave their fears and shattered dreams. We're ourselves and we don't owe anything to anyone."

"You say it, Cass, but your actions show that you don't truly mean that. If you did you would have told them about me! You wouldn't have kept me in the dark. Your eyes revealed the truth. The way you looked away when you told me to hide what we have from the world showed me everything," he'd said to her.

"Cass?" Connor's voice drew closer before the sound of Happy Birthday filled the air.

She remembered the way Connor had communicated only with his eyes by the lake in Sweden. She couldn't lose what they had for something she doubted would ever be attainable. She didn't need to search; she had already found the stars and he was wrong about their relationship. They were intense, and bold, and Connor loved her. Connor brought out her desire in another way. He invited hope and sunshine into their lives and made their troubles seem like something they could work on together.

"You're doing the same with him …" Josh pleaded. "You're lying to yourself. You haven't found the real thing. You're building walls with your loaded smile. If you really want him to stay in your life, you'd also show him your fears. Don't you see, Cass? You're just like a frangipani tree. You're sweet and caring and offer solace to everyone around you. But you know, even such a smile which offers hope continues to smile even if something threatens it. Even when dreams are shattered, the smile continues to pretend."

"I'm not doing that." His words twisted her heart. The wrench came back. Maria's words echoed his: *You're a frangipani tree, Cass.*"

He wiped a tear from her cheek. "Cass … you didn't even tell him about what we shared. The poor guy is acting just like you are. I see through his fear; you kept it from him. Why? Why do you keep the truth from him? You didn't even tell him about running into me that night at Eden Valley. You're scared to show him the happy and sad stories from your past. Your darkness. Because it might turn out to be the light that will guide you to where you should be … with me."

She had to be firm. Things had gotten too intense. She felt a slight chill in the air. "I'm not your responsibility, Josh, and you're not mine. We've had our turn and now it's gone forever. I've found my light and although I see glimmers of it in your eyes and in your words, I was right. It's what we *could* have had. Josh, we've missed that chance. It wasn't our time. Your light is fickle. It's scared to shine on us. You need to heal before you can see clearly. You need to stop seeing her in me."

His grip weakened and she freed herself, running towards Connor. His voice guided her out of the dirt. The rows of vines were lit up by the moonlight. His voice guided her towards the hedged maze. She ran but the confusion and the light now failed her.

I do love you though, Josh. I feel for you … for your plight.

The birthday song rang in her ears and she followed it. Her heels dug into the manicured lawn as the band played louder. The hedges were tall, dark, and imposing as she tried to find her way around them. She leaned onto the damp leaves and held on when she nearly lost her balance.

Mosquitoes flew around in the floodlights. She was close to the start of the maze and could hear the trickling water from the fountain. She couldn't miss the cutting of the cake. The band added a jazzy spin to the song. Cynthia had gone to so much trouble. Shame washed over her. She hoped Josh hadn't decided to follow her. She picked up her pace. He'd probably feel guilty about missing Ryan's birthday speech. Although the light in Connor's voice guided her to him, her feet moved forward, but her heels dug stubbornly into the soil, like they were holding her back.

"There you are," Connor said. 'What were you doing back there? You didn't get lost in the maze? Cass, you're shaking. One of your ex-classmates had seen you here. I was looking for you."

"Oh, I was just running so I wouldn't miss the speech. I had gone for a walk, and yes, I did actually lose my way. But only for a moment. I'm not lost anymore. I finally found my way back." She sucked in a few breaths. "I'm where I belong."

CHAPTER NINETEEN

Cassandra fidgeted with her dress as they stood around the table and clapped. The tall, colourful cake sat proudly in the middle. Candle smoke lingered in the air as she, once again, looked at the traces of dirt on the hem of her dress and heels of her shoes. Thankfully, no one seemed to notice in their jovially tipsy state.

Ryan began his speech as Josh walked in. The air quietened, feeling his presence as he approached the table. He caught her eyes before he met Ryan's. Ryan gave him a knowing and concerned look. Bella stood near Ryan appearing like his loyal servant, rather than her friend and partner-in-crime from French class. Bella glanced over to Cassandra. *She must have told Connor where she saw me,* she speculated. She steadied her breathing as she thought of Bella's remark about their kiss on the school oval. *Were her actions innocent?*

Soon after the speech, they were seated and the mains arrived. Maria and Antonio launched into an explanation of the tyre ordeal and how thankful they had been for Connor appearing when he did with a new tyre since their spare was also in need of repair. Thomas jumped next to his chair, dressed in a cute, old-fashioned suit of his own, eyeing the cake as one of the waiters wheeled it to the kitchen.

"Your dress!" Maria shrilled. "Why on earth would you go anywhere near dirt in a cream dress?"

Connor also looked at the hem of her dress. "I thought you just took a stroll through the maze."

"I did, but I couldn't help myself. I had to walk towards the vineyard. I was feeling adventurous. This dress makes me feel like roaming amongst the vines," she said with an awkward laugh. "Of course, we're not allowed to touch the vines." The last fact stunned her as much as seeing the dirt on Josh's shoes did.

"You look like you've been in a football field, mate," Brandon laughed.

This got Connor's attention. Ryan, Cynthia and Bella looked at Josh. Ryan seemed concerned as he gazed at him.

"It's a nice walk along the vineyard. Looks like we all had the same idea," came the voice of one of the guests who had been introduced to them as a long lost, yet recently found, distant cousin of Ryan's.

The night carried on with the same chatter and some curious glances. The guilt made her uncomfortable. Connor suggested to go to the balcony to have tea and coffee after they devoured their mains.

"You know how to throw a party," Bella shouted to Cynthia.

"She always did," Josh said.

He was getting chummy with Antonio, talking about graphic design and photography, moving on to Julie, and even entertaining Thomas with a magic trick using one of the serviettes, a five-dollar note, and Thomas' old-fashioned cap.

Cassandra wondered about the game he was playing. Was he trying to score points?

Bella decided to share how Josh saved Cass from remaining behind on a school excursion after acquiring a fear of heights due to a bad dream.

"I just knew which buttons to press with Cass," he said, instantly meeting Connor's eyes. "I knew what made her tick, what upset her, and how to bring her out of her shell. I think it came down to trust."

Cassandra's face warmed. She hated being discussed as if she weren't there. What would her clients think of her actions?

For some reason, Josh's remark caused Connor to look at Josh's dirty shoes which he had partly wiped with a napkin. His jaw tightened.

"I also knew what made her smile and what brought her joy," Josh continued, meeting her eyes, and then looking away innocently, smiling at Thomas as he tried to perform the magic trick he'd shown him. He shared the smile with the rest of them, bathing them with its warmth. An outside observer would think they were ready to hold hands and burst into a rendition of *Kumbaya*.

"We knew each other's quirks and idiosyncrasies. And how to have a good time," she tried to clarify, attempting to break the awkwardness.

"Yes, we especially knew how to have a good time, as you put it," he agreed, a dimpled smile returned to his handsome face.

Julie cleared her throat rather nervously before speaking. "Remember the time in Sydney when Connor ran to the field to save Cass from falling after trying to show off her football skills? She slipped!" Julie launched into one of their own stories. She then ended her reminiscing by saying, "You two have so much in common. It won't be long now until you walk down the aisle. Did I show you where the reception for Cassandra and Connor's wedding will be? At Sydney Harbour!"

Connor gave Julie an appreciative, knowing smile. It had worked. It had been the last strike and Connor didn't look that smug when he watched a tense, defeated Josh head back inside.

"What a night!" she said as they stepped into their room a few hours later.

"Yes, it was," Connor replied as they threw themselves onto the opulent bed, after taking their shoes and hats off. They looked at each other for a while.

Cassandra spoke first. "I hope he didn't get to you. I just went for a walk and he happened to also pass ..." she began but refrained when she remembered Josh's words: *Why do you keep things from him?*

He kissed her forehead like he understood something she was struggling to understand herself. "I get it. Don't worry, Cass. I have you here, with me now, and that's all that matters." They struggled to keep their eyes open.

Cassandra soon woke up to the sound of footsteps outside the door. She couldn't sleep without taking her makeup off, so she got up from the bed where they had fallen into a deep sleep with their clothes on. She decided to put the "Do Not Disturb" sign on the door in case room service came by early.

She quietly opened the door and placed the sign on the brass doorknob before she noticed Josh pacing, his shoulders hunched and hands in his pockets. The suit really did flatter him, she found herself thinking. He looked noble and distinguished yet rebellious, walking his own path. She wanted to reach out to him, instead he stepped inside his room — alone.

A few hours later, the sunshine woke them and they stumbled out of bed, drawing the curtains and revealing the large, French doors to the balcony. Waiters and caterers were preparing a lavish outdoor brunch for the tea party. Cassandra laughed as she saw some of the staff preparing equipment on the croquet lawn.

"Croquet? Wow, Cynthia hasn't lost her touch. Her parties were always so carefully planned," she commented.

Connor and Cassandra strolled arm in arm into the huge reception on the first floor balcony where many had already gathered. Some sat on the black wicker chairs, while others sat on picnic mats or fold-up chairs on the freshly mowed lawn. The sun wasn't too harsh. It was ideal weather for such an event.

Cassandra and Connor noticed Maria, Antonio and Thomas having a game of croquet, or rather attempting to as Thomas had just moved the hoops and balls around and ran around each piece of equipment.

Cassandra held her hat in position as a breeze threatened its place. She caught Connor giving her a look of admiration.

"You're looking splendid in that hat, madam," he said.

"Why, thank you. The suspenders you wore last night looked so fine on you. Especially with your shirt off," she replied, before bursting into heartfelt laughter.

She had decided to wear the fancy hat with her summer dress that morning, feeling like she still wanted to be in character. As she combed the garden, she realised that many had done the same. Some female guests still had their pearls around their necks, ribbons and feathers in their hair, and the men still looked suave with chino pants or shorts and linen shirts, some even sported caps that many would wear for leisure activities back in the day.

Cassandra and Connor reached Thomas. "Can I have a turn?" Cassandra asked him after wrapping her arms around him.

"Yes. Maybe Cassandra and Connor can show us how to play. Mummy and Daddy don't seem to know how to play so maybe your lovely godmother here might have some idea?" she queried.

"Hardly. Let's just pretend we know what we're doing. Just look confident and everyone will think we know," she suggested with a smile, as she eyed the wooden mallets on the ground. "Should the posts be there?"

"Is that what a counsellor advises her clients?" Antonio teased, matching her smile.

"Yes, just bluff your way through life. No one really knows what they're doing anyway," Connor added, light-heartedly.

As she lifted Thomas into the air, she caught sight of Josh — standing near the hedged maze, admiring the view of the vineyard. Thoughts of the lone kookaburra warning predators invaded her mind. He seemed a million miles away, until he turned around and met her eyes. She was still laughing while Thomas giggled as she spun him around. She paused, feeling the warm, approving smile radiating from his face. He then looked away and stared at the view again.

She wondered where his mind was at. Was he still thinking about what they'd said to each other?

"Hey, Josh!" Ryan called out to him.

Cassandra knew that he knew something had happened between her and Josh the moment Josh had entered the building the night before.

She turned to look at them both. Ryan ran over to him and placed his hand on his shoulder. Connor also noticed the scene.

She gave Ryan a half-smile, not sure what she should feel, or how she should act when she felt responsible for the desolation that had befallen Josh.

Cassandra couldn't help the sudden bout of guilt that washed over her. It was amplified when Ryan gave her a rather non-committal smile.

A bell rang with a chirpy jingle. It sounded like a school bell of long ago, and it invited everyone to look at the head caterer: a short and eccentric middle-aged man dressed in a pink bow tie. "The kitchen is now open for omelette requests. The buffet consists of sandwiches and other gourmet treats made from fresh, local produce. High tea stands with sweet offerings will be brought out soon, and I urge you not to miss our friendly caterers serving tea and coffee. The bar will be open until the afternoon," he shouted out much too enthusiastically as though he too approved of the last statement.

The last announcement got many cheers and whistles from most of the guests, including Julie and George who approached.

Cassandra laughed. Julie and George seemed to be having such a great time.

"This is so surreal, you guys. I feel like I'm in a film or some novel. I'm so grateful that we were also invited. I can't believe Cynthia's parents paid for all this."

"It's part of their wedding gift," Cassandra said. "Her dad admired her passion for party planning. She was so excited to host them." Cassandra stifled a tear. She had talked to Cynthia's parents the previous day while running into them at the foyer lounge, and her father's face was beaming with pride when he spoke about his daughter. Connor had squeezed her hand.

After they ate, they headed out to sit on the picnic mats. Cassandra sat down, grateful for the rest. She had seen Josh intermittently as they ate on the many small, round tables, and she had even accidentally brushed his elbow while trying to reach a biscuit for Thomas. Her face warmed from the mixed emotions. Cautious of the stares around her, she'd quickly looked away, noticing Ryan had glanced over.

"How about a game of darts? There's a child-safe dart game set up," George suggested.

"Why not?" Antonio replied.

Connor kissed Cassandra as he sped off to join them after she reassured him that she'd be okay on her own. She had been looking for an excuse to read her book.

"I'm just going to take Thomas to the miniature golf section first," Maria announced.

"I'll join you," Julie decided.

Cassandra stifled a yawn. "I feel a bit tired. I might just grab another cup of coffee and read my book. I was hoping to get some time to read and relax before we head to Sevenhill Cellars and to the winery later to show you the old vineyard I was telling you all about."

"I know what you mean. It was such a great night. I haven't felt this exhausted for a while. The wedding will be so much fun," Maria enthused as Thomas dragged her away to where his dad was heading with George and Connor.

She smiled as Julie floated behind them in her beautiful summer dress.

Cassandra sat comfortably on one of the fold-up pool chairs with her book and a cup of warm coffee. She stared at the cover of the novel for a while. How strange was that afternoon when she'd seen it out the front of their practice? She'd been anxious until Kelly had told her how much she'd helped her. It had rekindled her hope. She wondered who the book belonged to. It didn't even occur to her to tell Connor about it. Perhaps he knew who had lost it. Or Ava might have known. She'd enquire later.

She opened the book. The story had touched her the moment she'd read the first page. It had struck a chord inside of her. Someone had left the little boy. She thought of Josh, just like she had a few days ago while watching her mother and dad acting out scenes to *A Doll's House*. Why was everything diverting her attention towards him lately? It made her feel even more guilty that she was abandoning him. She read the next scene:

"Peter, pick up your bag. We're going to be late for school," Peter's mother screamed, her anxiety obvious as she frantically looked for her car keys.

"Okay, okay, Mum. I don't care if we're late today. The teachers have a staff meeting in the morning," Peter screamed out from his bedroom, whilst ploughing through the mess to find his soccer boots.

For some reason, he felt elated. He would be meeting Sandy before their late morning class started. He wanted to see her. He missed his best friend. It had been two weeks since he had last hung out at the local hangout. Not being with her felt strange, like things weren't like they were supposed to be. His male friends always teased their relationship. They asked when he would kiss her. The usual teen stuff. He didn't care. Sandy had always been part of his life. She was his neighbour and they were only one year apart. The fact that she was one of the prettiest girls he had ever seen was a small part of why he loved spending time with her. Her genuine warmth and concern for the world around her floored him at times. He could say anything to Sandy. His feelings were safe with her. She never ridiculed him. She treated his feelings with the utmost care, the way she treated everything around her.

"Peter, hurry up. I have an appointment. I need to see someone about something ..." his mother's words trailed off.

Peter simply ignored her. He did a lot of that lately. She was trying to get back into the workforce.

"Found them," he muttered as he grabbed his soccer boots from under a pile of washing that he should have placed in the laundry basket but, of course, didn't. His mother would definitely let him know how disappointed she was in him if she saw the state of his room. If he didn't start cleaning up the empty soft drink cans and packets of Doritos on his desk, ants would not only build colonies, they would build a whole universe.

"Peter, please ... you know I have an appoin ..." She stared at his room. "Let's just go," she finally said.

"I'll clean my room later ..." he began.

"That's okay. That's not important now," she reassured him by patting his hair.

It was as though her dismay had turned to affection in the space of a few seconds. He wasn't used to the affection. Maybe she was beginning to see things from his point of view and realised mess and cleanliness were trivial matters. Life was meant to be about having fun, not house chores.

His dad and he were on the same team when it came to housework.

"You can't win the battle against dust," he would always tell her. She, of course, would ignore him and continue cleaning around him as he stared at his laptop, shrugging to himself.

Guilt would get him though. So much so that he would pretend he was helping by moving things. It was difficult to clean something that was already tidy.

Peter had learned the word 'neurotic' from these experiences, as his dad would utter it under his breath when his mother was out of sight. Peter knew his dad loved her though. Peter would catch him sneaking a kiss while she cleaned. His dad thought her fussing was sweet. He loved seeing his parents interact when they were affectionate towards each other. It made him feel safe.

"Told you that I'll be ready soon," Peter said, smiling. His mother would not ruin his mood. He couldn't wait to see Sandy before class. They passed the kitchen and Peter was surprised to see that the dishes were still on the table. Cereal bowls still half-filled with milk and glasses of orange juice were illuminated by the morning sunlight. His mother was letting her standards slip a bit, he thought to himself, his stomach turning slightly.

"I shouldn't have had jam on my toast," he blurted out as they walked out of the front door and onto the timber porch. "Sweet things always burn my stomach in the morning."

They walked to the four-wheel-drive which was still packed with his boogie board and his older brother's surfboard from their Sunday afternoon at the beach. It had been such a fun day. The ocean made him feel as though he could do anything, like he could fly. His mother laughed when he courageously attempted to ride a boogie board in a ferocious surf beach when he was a three-year-old.

"This one was born to swim," she had said proudly, holding him firmly, as she guided him back to the sand, telling him he was too young to swim in a surf beach. Peter had a determination to succeed, and to be just like his older brother, Dean.

"What time did Dean leave for camp?" he asked, as he dragged his sports bag to the car while trying to carry his ever-so-heavy school bag. He couldn't believe how many books he had to carry ever since he started high school. What would happen when he was in his senior year? Would they need a trolley to carry them? He laughed when he visualised all the students pushing trolleys throughout the corridors of his school.

"Peter, stop dragging your bag. I can't buy you another one. It'll tear. You know that we also have to pay for your soccer camp ..." She had a blank look on her face.

"Mum ... Mum? You're daydreaming again. You've been daydreaming a lot lately."

"Oh, sorry. I guess I have been," she stared, unblinking at him.

"Mum ... you're doing it again."

"Oh, I'm sorry, darling. I was just admiring how big you've become. It was only yesterday that you were this high," she said, as she placed her hand next to his stomach. "Anyway, what are you laughing at?" She flicked a soft, dark brown strand of hair away from her face. Her blue eyes looked teary as she gazed at him.

Peter looked at his mother with admiration. She was by far one of the most good-looking mothers at his school and that morning she looked fresh and young in her long summer dress. She was forty-three-years-old but she looked like she could pass for thirty-years-old. Her height made her stand out.

"She could have been a model," most of his female friends often told him.

"I was just thinking of something funny about school," Peter shrugged it off.

"Anyway, we'd better get going," she said, panic-stricken once more as she glanced at her watch.

Peter loaded his bags into the boot of the four-wheel-drive and gazed over at Sandy's house. Her father was pulling out of the driveway on his way to work. Peter hid behind the car as he drove passed them before entering it. He didn't want to see him. He was intimidating.

The February summer sun caressed Peter's back as he leaned up from his crouched position. He loved summer. He loved everything about it. Even if the Christmas holidays were over, and autumn would be upon them before too long, it wouldn't get cold for another two or so months.

"Where are my sunglasses?" he heard his mother talking aloud, desperately looking in all the compartments of the car. She owned so many pairs, and yet, could never find them. "Here they are," she said, as she grabbed a pair from the glove compartment.

Peter struggled to put his seat belt on around the school books. Having had no time to pack them into his bag earlier, he had carried them under his arm. He was lucky he had found them at all in the 'No Man's Land' that his room had become.

"You need to be more responsible." His mother's voice had an authoritarian tone.

"Mum ... not another lecture. I know, I'm in high school now so I need to be more self-sufficient."

"You say it, but you don't do it though. How many times did I tell you to clean your room? I mean, I can't keep doing everything. I have to plan my career now. I'm not always …"

"I wonder what Sandy bought for me. She said she has something special to give me. I wonder what it is. She's so cool. She's always thinking …" Peter's face warmed. He didn't feel comfortable discussing how he felt about Sandy with his mother. He knew it was healthy, and he shouldn't keep things bottled up. His Physical Education lessons covered topics like feelings and relationships. Lately, he felt that he couldn't recognise his feelings though. He was beginning to feel differently around Sandy, and girls in general.

"Peter, have you heard anything I said!"

"What?" Peter looked at his mum, with defensive guilt. He was thinking about how nice and tanned Sandy would look. His mother's eyes were upon him again as she stopped at the lights. Gulls scavenged as chips and empty cardboard boxes were tossed out of bins onto the footpath by the deviant creatures.

His mother turned and looked as she heard their screeching squeals; fixated at them fighting for an ice cream cone. She then looked at the mountains in the distance. "It's beautiful, isn't it? Living here. It's so beautiful …"

"Mum, the lights are green. Mum …"

"Oh, yes. We'd better hurry. I have a lot to do after I drop you off."

"I can't wait to get to school. It's going to be a fun day today. I can feel it."

A soft hand touched his skin. Feeling the affection instantly, he gazed into his mother's kind, blue eyes as she brought the car to a halt outside his school. She looked at him with pride and love.

Peter looked away, feeling awkward. It had been a while since his mother looked at him like that. He felt loved and accepted when she looked at him like that. It reminded him of the days when his mother was less stressed and more attentive. Of course, he too had pushed her away. He had his friends now. He was a teenager and a mother's love wasn't cool. He also had Sandy. She listened to him. He could say anything to her.

"I love you so much, Peter. I hope you know that. I know I don't often tell you anymore, but you need to know that. Always remember that!"

"Mum ... someone from school will see you." He pushed himself away from his mother's perfumed embrace. He then sneezed from the floral scent. She always wore the same one. It was really expensive. He knew it cost more than the new pc game he wanted. Why did they frown at the cost of his games when scented liquid cost more?

Cassandra read the last few words, her heart racing. She had forgotten where she was, too engrossed in what she was reading.

"Hey, what are you reading?" Cynthia asked.

Cassandra looked up at her in a daze. Brandon was with her with some other people she didn't recognise.

Then he appeared like an imposing beautiful statue demanding attention. His chiselled and somewhat serious features softened the moment he saw her. Her tears blurred her vision. "It must be a really good book," he said.

"What?" she asked, realising that they were all looking at her. She quickly closed the book and placed it back in her bag.

Josh tried to catch a glimpse of the cover. She felt that he was part of it; the little boy she used to know. Surprisingly, she felt as connected to him as she had when they were bright-eyed, fourteen-year-old students.

"So, are you enjoying the garden party?" Cynthia asked as Brandon headed to the croquet game, the others in tow, including Bella's children.

"It's great. Julie and George are enjoying it and are grateful for the invitation," she said, feeling Josh's watchful eyes on her.

Ryan passed with another group of family and friends and grabbed Cynthia by the hand as they giggled their way to a table under a tree with a few bottles of chilled sparkling wine.

"Looks like the party hasn't ended. Cynthia sure outdid herself this time," Josh said as he sat next to her. "I hope I can still talk to you. That's allowed, right? After how I carried on last night? I've had a good look at myself this morning and I feel so embarrassed. I hope I didn't cause trouble between the two of you."

She looked at the vulnerability in his eyes. "Of course, you can talk to me. We'll always be friends but ..."

"But you're taken, and I need to respect that," he said in a voice that had started out strong but wavered at the end. "Your father visited."

Her heart practically stopped. "What? When? I mean why would he visit you?"

"Well, he actually visited my dad, but he was glad I was there. He asked about how my brother is going in Queensland. He's a diving instructor now. You remember how he was into water sports and things like that," he drifted slightly. "He also asked how my dad was doing. It was the strangest thing, Cass. He actually seemed regretful. He even looked at some of my dad's sculptures, his poetry. He knows my mum came back and that my dad and she are actually on speaking terms for now ..."

"What? You never told me—"

"I've wanted to, but I can't help feeling a connection with you when I talk about these things. I know I'll probably overstep again. I can't help how connected I feel to you when we touch on our past. When we touch ... You were the only one who was there, and I see the young Cass I fell in love with when I talk to you about this stuff. I can't help how I feel, Cass. You can't punish me for loving you."

She looked over the nearby hill where the golf and dart games were set up.

Josh noticed her looking in that direction. "You don't have to worry. I'm not going to cause a scene. Anyway, they seem to be on good terms ... our parents. Your mother even called my mum the other day."

"Why?"

"They haven't told you yet? Obviously not. It's a delicate situation, Cass. You'll find out a lot of things soon. I just want you to know that I'll be there for you when you do. I'll always be here for you. You can count on that."

Her brows furrowed. She had to find out what he meant. It wasn't the right time or place though. Connor would be back soon. She had told him she wanted to read her book. How would it look to find them together again? Just as she contemplated this, she caught Ryan glancing over at them.

"Don't worry about him. He's just worried about me. He knows how much I still love you." This time he refused to look away. Their eyes were locked for a few seconds. She felt the wrench twisting in her heart again. She couldn't let him get under her skin again. She would always love him, but Connor was who she wanted to marry and spend the rest of her life with.

"Josh, please understand that you're placing me in a difficult situation."

"Doesn't that say a lot to you? That you still care for me and you're torn between two men?"

"No, it says that I still care for you as a close friend and that I don't want Connor to think there's more."

He wasn't buying it. "Sure, Cass. If that's what you need to tell yourself to get through the days … and nights."

"I have to get going. I promised them we'd visit Sevenhill." Her nerves had taken hold of her mind.

This got his attention. He looked thoughtful as she stood up. He also stood up and looked down into her face, almost studying her every move. "Relax, you're a free woman. Does he have a tight hold on you? You need to be free and live life to the fullest. I'm not sure he's right for you if he thinks he can keep you in a cage and only let you fly when he allows it. I know what makes you free, what makes you feel. I'm worried that you're making a big mistake with him. It's not too late, Cass. You're not married yet. Our parents have deep regrets. My mother certainly does. She always liked you. She even regrets that we're not together. She's felt responsible for me not being able to commit to any woman. But I've told you that I'm working through all that. Please, don't make me beg."

"I thought you'd seen the light this morning … that you regret what you told me last night. I can't keep doing this to Connor. I have to go," she cried, trembling.

She knew she was being brutal, and she knew she was breaking his heart, but she couldn't upset Connor anymore, especially in front of all their friends. She already felt like everyone was sussing them out when they were together. "I'd love to find out more. I'm really confused about my dad and the visit and what you mean by finding things out. I need to know why so many things were what they were, but not now. Josh, please respect my wishes. I have to go."

She grabbed her bag and sped off to the others without looking back. Too much was at stake. She had to be strong even if that nagging feeling that she had abandoned him killed her. She couldn't help but think he was feeling what the boy in the book was feeling.

CHAPTER TWENTY

Cassandra and Connor crossed the grounds of Sevenhill Cellars later that afternoon.

"The town of Sevenhill was founded in 1851 by Austrian Jesuit Fathers and Brothers," she told Connor as they gazed up at St Aloysius Church. The church was made with local stone exemplifying the architecture with intricate, stained-glass windows. It stood tall amongst the vines in the gardens. "I remember learning that it was homage to Seven Hills in Rome. You know, how Rome was built on seven hills?"

"Fascinating," Connor replied softly, respecting the sacred place.

They continued walking around the paved grounds which circled the enormous church and peered over to the old vineyard.

"Sevenhill Cellars was established by the Jesuit brothers to make sacramental wine," she continued as they gazed at a shrine amongst the vineyard. "It's the oldest winery in the Clare Valley."

Julie, Maria, Antonio and George walked slowly behind her, while Thomas tried to match the adults' sombre mood. They stepped out of the old church and Thomas ran to the park where tables and chairs were positioned. They followed him and talked.

When they walked through the cellar doors, they admired the historical space and then they climbed down the stairs to where the sacramental wine was first made. The barrels and equipment were there for tourists to see. Old bottles of wine were displayed amongst photos of the Jesuit brothers.

"This is so surreal," Julie whispered as though she was still in the church.

"I know, you can only imagine what it would have been like," Maria replied.

Soon they were seated at one of the outdoor tables and Cassandra walked with Maria and Thomas around the outside of the church, which was surrounded by lovely landscaped gardens. They sat on an old, stone bench and took a few photos with Thomas.

"So, you've been seeing Josh a lot lately," Maria mentioned.

Cassandra sighed heavily at the mention of his name.

"Is everything all right between you two? I don't want to point out the obvious, but he is rather handsome … in a rebellious, movie star way, you know, because of the way he carries himself. All eyes are instantly on him. He's almost got a James Dean walk," Maria said, stifling a laugh.

Cassandra was relieved that she'd lightened the mood. "I'll admit to that," she retorted.

"Anyway, since he's all that and he is your ex-boyfriend, do you think it's getting to Connor?"

"It's complicated, Maria. I can't just abandon him. I actually care for him. He's had a hard life," she managed. She wanted to confide in her friend the way they had confided in her on many occasions. That anxiety seemed to be coming back. Why had her father visited them?

"Cassandra, I need to be frank with you. Connor seemed really upset when we were at the outdoor games area. He saw you talking to Josh. He seemed really tense but he pretended that he was okay with it all. I don't think he is."

"He saw us? Oh my God! Why didn't he say anything? I can't believe it! I told him I wanted to read a book. *Maria*, it's not what you think. Josh was about to reveal something about my parents. Connor knows how much I need to work things out with my dad. I'll have a word with him. I'll explain everything." She meant it. She had to confide in him about how Josh kissed her, how he wanted her back. She hadn't forgotten Josh's question regarding why she constantly keeps things from Connor. She didn't want to be like her parents. He was right; she had to be honest with Connor if they were to have a solid marriage. Cassandra looked at Maria's concerned, focused face. Behind her she noticed Thomas reaching over to something under a massive tree.

"Anyway, I just thought I'd bring it up since I saw how worried you were when that photo of him fell out of your bag back in Sydney. I know you two used to be really close."

"No, don't touch those, Thomas! You can't touch those mushrooms," Cassandra screamed when she saw that Thomas' hands were nearing some mushrooms that had grown near the bench where they had been sitting.

Thomas cried, thinking Cassandra had scolded him. Maria took him in her arms and tried to explain that his godmother was just looking out for him, that he can't touch certain things from nature.

Some people turned to look as Thomas' cry got louder. Cassandra stroked his back as Maria carried him.

"Let's get some food then," Cassandra suggested.

Maria took Thomas by the hand and guided him through the landscaped path. She walked quickly, nearly tripping on a long stick.

"Sorry," Cassandra said as she bumped into a tall man. *It can't be*, she thought. "Josh?"

Connor's shoulders were tense as he noticed the exchange. Thomas was still crying.

"*Josh*, what are you doing here?" Cassandra practically shouted.

Maria looked just as shocked as she did; her eyebrows were raised and her mouth was agape as she gave her a questioning glance.

Cassandra glanced to where the others were seated, and she was thankful that Maria was with her. It was becoming quite difficult to dig herself out of these impromptu encounters with her ex-boyfriend, especially after what Maria had told her about Connor.

Maria guided them towards the others, obviously finding it odd that he appeared out of nowhere, trying to play down the incident.

"Are you okay, Thomas?" Josh asked him with a smile.

Thomas seemed to be mesmerised by Josh. He looked at him with eyes wide open. Still uncertain if he could trust him, the tears began again.

They reached the table where everyone was sitting.

"What's the matter, Thomas? Would you like to see another magic trick?" Josh asked him.

"Yes, you're the magician. Mummy, it's the man with the magic tricks," he screamed, remembering the night before.

Miraculously, Josh's magic worked on Thomas, a grin settling over his face.

"Thanks, Josh," Maria said, looking relieved.

Cassandra was impressed with Josh's ability to soothe Thomas. It reminded her of Connor. She met Connor's eyes as she thought of this.

"You were great with him," Antonio acknowledged.

Julie decided to intervene, sensing the tension. "Connor is also great with kids, isn't he, Cass?" she asked, flicking her light-brown hair away from her face.

Connor seemed appreciative of Julie's attempt but also irritated by it, especially when Cassandra added her own comment. "Connor always manages to bring children out of tantrums. He has a knack for it," she added. When she'd finished her sentence, she realised how lame and childish it sounded, but for some reason, she felt guilty again, even if she hadn't planned for Josh to be there.

"So, Josh, what a coincidence that you're here. Again. Did you just decide to come here out of nowhere?" Connor asked.

Cassandra thought of Josh's words: "Why do you always keep things from him?" She had to say the truth. She didn't want to give Josh the wrong impression. "Um … I actually told Josh we'd be here."

Josh was surprised by her revelation. He gazed over to her, studying her next move.

She then met Connor's eyes. They seemed distant.

"You did?" Connor asked her with a tight jaw. He then looked at Josh. "And you couldn't wait to come here …"

"Yes, it's wonderful here. We used to visit this place frequently. The Riesling bike trail is so beautiful," he replied with surprising confidence.

"That's where we're going now," George said innocently, before meeting Julie's scolding eyes.

"Yeah? I'd love a ride before heading back to Tanunda. I miss this place. I might just join you. If that's all right with all of you?" he queried, looking at Connor.

Connor didn't answer.

"That's fine," Cassandra found herself saying, feeling that she had to protect Josh for some reason. She couldn't believe that she'd said the words. It may have been better if one of the others answered instead. She was being silly, she told herself. Connor would understand everything when she'd explain.

Josh gave her an appreciative smile. Cassandra looked away, feeling that she couldn't reciprocate under the intense circumstances.

A half hour later, they were riding past the charming views of the vineyards they passed: the colourful gardens, lovely meadows, rustic houses, and the many historic churches. Cassandra's thoughts were tangled, however, and she couldn't enjoy the scenery around her. The sun was thankfully not as intense. It made her feel safe as it covered her with its gentle warmth. Connor was further ahead as George and Antonio challenged him to pick up speed. He had, at first, waited for her but her daydreaming kept her behind and she still felt lethargic from the party from the previous night.

As Josh appeared beside her, she tried to catch up. He did look so sexy in his grey shorts which revealed toned, muscular legs. His crisp, light-blue, linen shirt also revealed toned, tanned arms. She then wondered what he wanted to tell her about his mother and her dad. She had so many unanswered questions that plagued her mind.

Cassandra's mind went back to what she'd read earlier that day, and the look in Josh's eyes the night before. He had kissed her and pleaded with her to stay with him instead of Connor, and here they were again. Together. She had to put a stop to it, to tell Connor everything sooner or later before he found out from someone else.

He kissed you and you're now riding a bike with him like you're both on a romantic date, she told herself. She had to catch up with the others. Her mind was in turmoil.

"*Cass!*" Josh screamed as she bumped into his bike. He veered off the path and headed for a sharp piece of rock on the side of the trail. Cassandra managed to stop herself from falling and quickly placed her foot on the brake, stopping just before the fence.

"It's gone. The air's completely gone out of the tyre," he said.

Cassandra couldn't believe it was happening again. What were the chances? She looked up at the trail. The others were so far ahead, out of sight.

"Wow! Remember that?" he said, peering over at a beautiful cottage surrounded by trees. He took his camera out of his bag. "I just love how the sun teases everything it touches, creating patches everywhere."

Some things never changed, she thought. "You still bring an actual camera along wherever you go? You never told me. What made you become a photographer? Why do you love taking photos? I felt like you were always looking for something you couldn't find."

That got his attention. "And you keep telling me we didn't really know each other. I told you we know more than we think. I was right, just like you're right now. I started taking photos to see the truth, not the lie in everyday life. A good photographer can capture the stillness within when all the trivial white noise is gone. An experienced photographer can capture what they're looking for. If it's beauty, they'll find it. If it's ugliness and pain, he or she will find that too. Even a good writer can do that ..." He looked down at the ground, his words fading. He then looked at her again.

They had faded to the background somehow, she thought. Her mother did when she stopped talking, when she stopped sharing her dreams. She spoke to her as her mother, but not as Isabel.

Even though there was beauty around her, her mother didn't see it. She only saw the imperfections and what she didn't have. Cassandra had caught her off guard when she thought no one was looking, staring far into the distance, but not seeing anything around her. Perhaps that's what her father and Josh's mum did.

"Cass, I thought I wasn't enough and that you would feel that I wasn't enough for you."

"You ran away too," she challenged.

"Yes, I wanted to taste it all, to see if I could fill any empty void. I agree I wasn't brave enough to stay with you either. I thought I would find it in New York, in London, anywhere but here. We all have our own stories to tell, and they're always different even if the same experiences touched the same people. We're affected by the same stimuli but it affects everyone in a different way. Each of us saw what we were searching for. That's why I was steered to art, to photography. Behind a lens, every subject might be in the same environment, but their mood is different in the photos. We might have been tied together at one stage, Cass, but our circumstances forced us to see life differently. Like at this moment, your eyes reveal so much. You're still hiding. I'm ready to see it all. I want to capture it all." She heard the camera go off. "I wanna capture this beautiful moment to keep it forever. I'm choosing to see the beauty."

It was getting too intense again. Why was it always so intense with them? Did she need her life to be so painfully intense? Maybe they were both too much for each other. Maybe that's why it didn't work between them.

She quickly looked at her watch and slid her mobile out. "I'd better tell the others where we are."

"Looks like I'll have to walk it. You can go. I'll be fine," he said.

"No, I feel bad. I can't just leave you! I'll just let the others know we've fallen behind." The minute she said the words, she wondered why she always attached herself to him. It was as though she couldn't let go.

"Cass, I've travelled this trail often. We both have. It's not exactly a gruelling trail."

"I know … but …" she looked into his hazel eyes.

"What is it, Cass? You'd rather be here with me. Tell me. Is that it?"

"I just can't leave you like this, especially since you've always been there … especially when you helped me after I sprained my ankle. You came to me with your bike. My dad was furious that day," she said. She felt overwhelmed by the memory and drained by the thought of her father's disappointment. "What do you know that I don't?"

"You'll find out soon, Cass, I promise you. It's not my place to tell you."

"Why? They won't tell me. My father treats me like I don't exist, like I don't matter."

"He does? You never told me that. Not even when we were together. Like I said though, whether I knew it already is a different story. I could tell by the way you often changed the subject when I mentioned him."

"You placed me in this 'happy' role. Everyone did, when I started listening to everyone's problems … when I smiled and laughed at everyone's jokes. I was always on someone's pedestal and I felt that had I shared who I really was I wouldn't be worthy of their attention …" Her voice quivered.

"Cass, I'm sorry you felt like that. You always seemed so hopeful, joyful and compassionate, but you had other sides that you were scared to show the world. I would have loved to hear about them. It would only make my adoration for you stronger."

"Even now, I hate being placed on a pedestal where no one can reach me. But for him, I was never good enough. He only saw my trophies, not me. I wanted to succeed on my own, away from his expectations. You can never please a person who only offers conditional love. Nothing will ever be enough. I need answers, Josh. I've been anxious about coming back. Nothing has changed between us …"

He gazed up. "I know it hasn't changed between us."

"That's not what I meant, I mean, sure I still care about you, a lot. My dad, he's still the same, at least towards me he is."

He pondered this. "Why him? Why Connor? Why do you think he'll give you more than I can?"

"Josh, I've already explained. You left me the last time I came back."

"You know, this is unfair. The timing of it all. Now you're ready to confide in me, and I to you. As a counsellor, doesn't that mean to you that we're finally ready to commit to each other? Don't answer that yet. You might see things differently in a few days. Just remember, I'll be waiting for you. Too many people settle and throw true love and passion away because it may be too complicated. I believe things that come out of adversity turn out to be strong at the end … like the diamond on your finger."

"Josh …"

He walked over to her and placed his finger on her lip. "Shh. Don't say it. I don't wanna hear your voice uttering words that push me away. Is it okay if I wrap you in my arms right now and tell you it'll be okay? I know you can look after yourself and you'll be able to use the skills you've learned. I hope you can heal and use those skills to finally help yourself instead of just the people around you."

Cassandra gave him a puzzled look. "I don't understand, Josh. You're scaring me."

"That's the last thing I want. I admire how you've grown, but it's okay to feel that you may need help. I just feel like taking you in my arms and hugging you right now. Can I do that, Cass? Can you, at least, give me that? I've always been there for you and you've been there for me. It's hard to let go of that role and I feel that you need to be protected right now. I figure you're going to need it soon. You might be losing a piece of you, or you might be finding a missing piece. Like I said, it depends how you look at it."

He put his strong arms around her and stroked her hair gently, breathing as though he was breathing in a flower. He lifted his head and she too lifted her head from his safe, warm embrace to turn around. It was Connor. He had come back for her. They locked eyes with each other. He broke the stare.

"Are you coming with me? Are you going to move forward with me? Or are you staying back here with *him*? What's it going to be?" He gave her a look that she had never seen before. Her heart was torn into two. But it couldn't be torn anymore. It was too much to bear. She came back home to make things right. She wanted her heart to beat with ease again. She wanted to give it wholeheartedly to the man standing in front of her who now, too, looked like the young boy she read about: scared and confused.

CHAPTER TWENTY-ONE

They rode quietly with Josh walking on his own behind them. When they reached the others, Maria and Julie guided her to a quiet spot under a tree as the men sorted the bikes.

"He was so upset, Cass. He couldn't believe you had fallen behind with him again," Julie said.

"I had collided into him while daydreaming."

"You collided into him? Don't you see how that sounds? You've always told me there are no accidents."

"I would never do that ..." she began. "I even nearly collided into Connor on our bike ride the other day."

"Not consciously. I know you wouldn't but it's almost like you're holding onto him. Be careful. Connor can only be so patient. Can't you see he's the man for you? He's always been the man for you. You were beaming when you told us you were an item a couple of years ago. You said you couldn't imagine being so true with another man, remember?" Julie pleaded with her. "I was so envious that you were so sure about him. I was in a confused place, being steered towards my ex and my past. Trust me ... it's a terrible place to be in. The anxiety can hide what's in front of you."

"Are we all ready?" George called out.

"Yes. We're ready," Cassandra replied, her future becoming clearer. Julie's words filled her heart with hope. She had been positive about Connor; he was the man she wanted to spend her life with. She would face the music. She was ready to tidy the mess and be true with the man that gave her so much joy. She had her answer. She had been scared to commit to Josh. It was clear who she had chosen.

As Connor and Cassandra made their way to the historic house, passing the maze and the massive water fountain, they remained silent. He turned so suddenly that she reeled back. His eyes looked fierce, like he desperately wanted her to understand.

"Don't you see what he's doing? He knows that you feel obligated to be there for him. I don't think he's a manipulator by design though. I'm not unfeeling. I get that he's been through a lot, but he's … he's so desperate to cling onto the past; he's probably so desperate to have you back that he's willing to try things that go against his values. That's what desperate people do. Unless they're given a reason to hold on … Unless he isn't just appealing to your decency, to your caring side. Unless he's appealing to your heart for other reasons!"

"Connor, please, everyone will hear us. Let's just go back to our room. I'll tell you everything."

"I already know everything. I know how much he wants you back. I'm really not sure where you stand though. I know why you came here. I saw the message."

Cassandra felt like someone had slapped her.

"What message?"

"The one that you sent Cynthia, when you agreed to finally go to their wedding. You were in the shower and you told me to send a message back to Julie? I inadvertently saw Cynthia's message. She had just informed you that Josh would also be coming, after all. You weren't certain until then."

"No, Connor, that's not why I came back. Remember, I was a mess? I felt like something was missing. I had looked at the photos because Cynthia and Ryan's wedding made me realise that I couldn't move forward until I sorted my past … to find out why my dad treated me like he did. I felt guilty all the time, like I wasn't living up to some standard. That's how I still feel around him. It led me to believe that I may have been insecure at the thought of being in a relationship because I felt that something more of me was expected. I was always searching for something. I wanted to fix things with my dad …"

"And with him … especially with him. That's why you couldn't wait to leave. I mean, Cass, you left a few days earlier than planned. You couldn't even wait a few more days for us to leave together? How would you read that if the tables were reversed? There are too many of these re-occurring incidents: running into him at Eden Valley Lookout? I saw how remote it looks up there. What are the chances? Even if that truly happened, you didn't even tell me that he was the friend that helped you. The love of your life, not just your high school crush as you made it sound. How many things have you kept from me? I'm not stupid, Cass, so please stop treating me like I am. For God's sake, we're both counsellors; we should know better."

"I didn't plan on running into him at the bike trail today; that was another thing that just *happened*. All those incidents were accidental, Connor. I know it seems suss. When we realised that his bike had a flat tyre, he told me something about my parents that he hadn't completed yesterday. It's something big, Connor. It might explain everything."

"You mean the conversation you had earlier today when you were supposed to read your book? Let's not forget that you did tell him we were going to Sevenhill today, and also where your hotel was that first night, and he appeared at the tennis court, and you conveniently fell behind today …"

"I didn't tell him about the house we're all staying in at Tanunda. Cynthia and Ryan did," she stumbled on her words, knowing how incriminating it all sounded, almost like he had been right about the rest of the accusations.

"Well, gee, one of the incidents weren't due to you!" he said in a sarcastic way. "Here's another one then to replace that one: you both coincidentally had dirt on your shoes last night? Why would you run in the vineyard with a cream dress that you loved so much? I think most of your ex-classmates knew that you'd been with him. I think they weren't even surprised. They did know what a passionate love affair you had together. It seems to still exist …"

"No, that's not true, Connor. Please, let me explain!"

"Please do. Maybe you'll clarify why you also carried a photo of him in your bag?"

Cassandra froze. "You know? When did you see that? It's not what it seems … I know it looks bad, please, I can explain … everything."

"By the way, did he tell you this big secret he apparently knows about your parents?"

"No …" she began.

"Of course, he didn't, Cass. He wants you to beg it out of him. It's another hold he has on you; another chance to play on your emotions, to talk privately with you. I'll bet you still don't know the full story about his mother. He's keeping you close to his heart until you give your heart to him, until he has you where he wants you. Until he breaks us up!"

Cassandra was trembling.

"Be brave. It's quite simple, really. Do what you set out to do with your parents. Find the answers. Take charge. Don't give him that power over you. It's not healthy for him, for you, or for us …"

"You're right. He wants me back," she finally confessed.

He looked stunned but relieved that she was honest with him. She could see the hurt and fear in his eyes. She did that to him, ironically when she was trying to rid the fear and confusion inside of herself.

"Why did we waste our time pretending we weren't hurt? That's why I became a counsellor. I wanted to stop pretending, to bring out emotions, beautiful or ugly. I just want to tear down the walls and see things as they are from now on, Connor. Can we start doing that now? Both of us? There's no time like the present. I want you to know how much I have always loved you!"

"Cass, you didn't even tell me you had seen him when you came back a few years ago. You met me around a year later. Was he still in your heart? Did you convince yourself to love me? To settle because it didn't work out with you and him? I don't even know if he broke it off with you. He does look like a man with regrets."

"No, we broke up with each other. He found the answer in my words. He knew it wouldn't work. Love wasn't enough for the two of us and I think it might have been an unhealthy, desperate love — one where we were both broken inside. We need two solid halves to make a whole, Connor. I'm so close to being that complete half for you. I'm working on it. It's always a work in progress, just like we tell our clients. I never had reservations about you, not like I had with Josh. I see it clearly now. You came into my life for a reason. So I could taste a healthy love, not a desperate one that promises so much but keeps falling short."

He pressed his lips to hers, scratching her cheek with his stubble. He smelled like roses, like the foyer in the magnificent mansion. The water trickled in the fountain as they kissed softly, respecting the moment. She felt that she could tell him everything and she would, especially about Josh trying to kiss her. It would be okay.

They parted their lips and he stroked her tear-stained hair from her face and kissed it. "You don't need him to solve your problems with your parents. Just go talk to your dad. I'll be there right by your side. I think if you do that, it may solve a lot of issues that have been plaguing you with Josh, as well. I do get it, Cass. Throughout your whole childhood and teenage years, even in your early adulthood, Josh was the only man that stood by your side. Your father never did, but is that all you want? Someone in the sidelines? Where was he all these years before he found out about us getting married? I think he needs to heal so he can finally move on. I'm here now. I've got you."

"How lucky am I? If I hadn't changed my mind about becoming a counsellor, I never would have met you, Connor."

"Let's go inside. We'll need to relax before dinner, and then we need to pack so we can head back to the Barossa Valley in the morning. It's been an interesting weekend, madam," he said, slowly coming out of his sombre mood.

"It sure has," she agreed, a smile now forming on her face. They would be okay, she told herself as they made their way to the house. Walking hand in hand, leaning on Connor's shoulder, she caught sight of Ryan looking at them from the second floor balcony. He acknowledged her with a nod before walking away from the balcony's stone rails. Cassandra then thought of Josh's words: "I think you'll need a hug. You might need it when you hear the news. It all depends how you look at it", he'd told her. "I'll be here for you. You might think differently about us after you find out". He had said those words with such confidence.

Did he still think there was a chance after she talked to her dad? Her head spun. "Many people throw away love and just settle", he'd said. *No*, she told herself. Maybe Connor was right. He was unintentionally, and against his better judgment, desperately clinging onto her, feeling that he was lost without having her on the sidelines. The fact that Cynthia and Ryan were also taking the plunge might hurt him. It would be a reminder of what Josh and Cassandra could have had. Unless Cassandra gave him that one last chance. His words were supposed to rattle her and lure her in.

***

Later that evening, Cassandra sipped a cup of tea in the lounge area after they had dined in the dining room. Connor had gone to get them some martinis to celebrate their last night at the historic mansion. She peered outside the large, French windows and noticed a figure walking despondently towards the house. *He's just arriving … he mustn't have come back after the bike ride.* She wondered where he'd gone. Her heart went out to him. He looked so lost, even when he appeared strong.

"You have to let him go, Cass," she heard a familiar male voice.

Panic-stricken, she turned to meet Ryan's brown eyes.

"You don't need to keep worrying about him … unless you want to go back to him? Is that a possibility? If the answer is no, as much as you care for him, you have to let him find his own way, Cass. You have to do it for both of you … and for you and Connor. No good will come out of it."

"There's no chance, Ryan, but I can't help it. He looks lost, the way—"

"He'll be okay. He's stronger than he has been in a long time. Of course, we'll always be there for him, for each other, but not in the way you used to be. He has had a few offers back in New York … a chance at committing to a serious relationship. I think he came back to see if he should move on or if you and he would become an item again. That's why you have to let him go. If you truly love him, you'll let him go."

"Sure. I mean, yes, I do love him," she said and watched him walk back to Cynthia who gave her a warm smile as Connor came back to her, to take his place by her side.

CHAPTER TWENTY-TWO

Back in Tanunda on Monday morning, they all relaxed by the pool of the rented contemporary house after unpacking their overnight bags from their weekend getaway. Cassandra had promised to show Connor the acting school her parents had started back when they were in their early twenties. The building was still there but now operated as a cinema. The town had a lot of history and was another great tourist attraction.

Connor and Cassandra were, once again, on good terms. In fact, she felt that they were in a better place than they were a day ago. Connor even understood that she had put a stop to the kiss as soon as it started. Everything was out in the open. There were no more secrets between them. Despite that, she wondered what Josh had meant about her parents, and why he still had hopes for them.

Later that afternoon, they were in the car approaching Williamstown. They decided to stop so Cassandra could get them both a cold drink. She stepped out of the small shop and was startled to hear her name being called.

"Cassandra, I can't believe it's you!" she heard the male voice.

She instantly turned to see who the familiar voice belonged to.

"Mr Dennison," she exclaimed. It was her father's friend and colleague from the real estate agency.

"How are you? It's been so long since I saw you in these neck of the woods. How's Sydney life treating you?"

Before she could answer, a woman came out of the shop.

"Lynette, come and meet a friend of mine. This young woman is Oscar's daughter Cassandra. I haven't seen her for a while. This is my cousin Lynette. She's in town for a while."

"Oscar's daughter? You're his daughter?" she queried.

Cassandra felt like an object on a display shelf. "Yes … I'm his daughter," she said, feeling foolish being inspected in such an unceremonious way.

"I don't see the resemblance. I think she takes after her mother, probably … although, I don't see that either. Most people take after one or the other," she insisted.

"She takes after both," Mr Dennison interjected, rather adamantly.

"Nice to meet you. I have to go. My fiancé is waiting in the car."

"Yes, you go," Mr Dennison said in the same way, if a little flustered. "Let's not keep her away from her fiancé. They're on holidays. Young people are always doing so many things all at once these days."

Lynette was still not satisfied and looked at Cassandra like she was studying a foreign specimen in a lab. She could feel their eyes on her as she walked back to the car with the chilled drinks cooling her hands.

"I have to say, it's great coming back home, running into some people, but God, some people can make you feel like you're five again with the way they analyse you."

Connor laughed and they continued on their merry way.

"I still can't believe your parents had established an acting theatre and an acting school. It's such a bold and innovative idea, even risky. How could your dad have been so different back then? Do you think something happened to make him question their venture?"

"I wouldn't have a clue. I do know that something happened when I was around thirteen or fourteen. Things were tense at times, but then it was like the darkness stayed for good. They drifted apart and my mum created her own world in the kitchen, while he went to work and then craved solitude in his study. He never liked talking about the past.

It had suddenly become even more taboo than before. My mum would get the photos and videos out but only when he wasn't around. It was coincidentally around the same time Josh's mum left. Things really became weird then. Maybe they felt bad for treating her as though she didn't exist."

"Coincidentally?"

"Yeah, you don't think it's a coincidence?"

"Maybe, but why was there a photo of Mrs Sturgess in the photo album? They obviously spent time with her. I remember I even thought I knew her. I've been racking my brain since I saw it."

"That's weird. I wonder why you would think you know her. Anyway, my feet are killing me. I was thinking we can go back home and take it easy. It'll give us a chance to relax. I can also read my book while you go over the brochures we collected. It was such an exhausting weekend," she said, looking at him cautiously.

"We're good now, you and me?"

"Better than good, Connor."

He kissed her forehead. "Your idea sounds good to me. What book are you reading, anyway?"

"Trying to read. I haven't had much of a chance. It was getting interesting. I felt like I could somehow relate to the story. It moved me in some way. I can't explain it."

"I can. It's who you are. My Compassionate Cass? They were definitely right to name you that. You feel things on a deep level."

She leaned closer and hugged him.

"Speaking of books, Ava called and the client that I had just started seeing … I'm actually not sure if she's coming back … she was really upset that she lost some novel. She's been looking everywhere for it, and it just occurred to her that she may have left it in the practice."

"What? What's it called? I should have checked when I found it, but everything happened so fast, so I just threw it in my bag. I feel awful for keeping it. I've been meaning to check with you or Ava."

"Don't worry. At least it's in safe hands. I'll let her know. You love literature and feeling each word in a story. Well, feeling in general, evolving though the arts. I've always loved that about you. Maybe you're more similar to your parents than you think. Even your dad?"

Cassandra pondered what Connor had said. Pride, surprisingly, took over her at the thought. She had something in common with her parents. Maybe she could reach him on that level? Even if he had closed the doors to that life.

"Anyway, show me the rest of the building," Connor said. "Look, there are some photos from the past. They show what it's been used for over the years."

"I can't believe they put these photos of my parents and the other actors up. They weren't here the last time I came around," Cassandra said. Her chest inflated as she looked over her parents' photos. "Look, that's my mum. Is there a photo of my dad?" she queried aloud, scanning the photo with all the actors in it. After a while, she finally saw him and he looked much different. "That's why I didn't recognise him. He looks different in this photo. It must have been taken when they just arrived, when he was young. It's strange."

"What is?" Connor asked the question as though he already knew the answer. "That they don't talk about him … the other actor. Yet he's in a lot of photos."

"Yes. I wish they were clearer. They seem to have faded. Maybe there's too much sunlight here," she waffled, uneasily. Glancing up to the small, arched window, the intense stream of light blurred her vision.

She looked away and came face to face with Connor. They locked eyes. "I'm so glad," he began. "I'm so glad that I have you back, Cass. I thought I was losing you for a while. I'm here for you, if you need a shoulder to lean on. I'm here to wrap you in my arms and help you get through it."

Cassandra smiled appreciatively. "You never lost me, Connor. You're the only man for me. Like you told me in Sweden … by the lake."

They walked hand in hand around the room as Cassandra's uneasiness returned. Connor's words reminded her of what Josh had said, that he'd be there for her, that she'd need someone to lean on.

An hour later, they were heading back to Tanunda.

"Connor!" she called out to him. "Can you stop the car for a second? This place … it looks familiar."

Cassandra jumped out of the car, feeling Connor's curious glance on her back.

"What is it, Cass?"

"This place … I've been here before. It looks familiar. She kept walking towards it. She could practically hear the chatter and laughter from long ago.

"Do you want some of this Viennese pastry?" she'd asked Josh.

"Sure, what about some of this pie? My mum made it. She used the freshest ingredients and told me to tell you all that. My mum's always fussing about these things."

"Tell me about it. I don't know why they care so much about the most trivial things," she'd said.

"Maybe we should have a cricket game after?" Ryan had suggested.

"After we have all this food?" Cynthia had exclaimed.

"Has anyone had that new French teacher yet? She thinks we're all going to major in French and live in France. I don't know why she cares if we pronounce everything with an accent," she'd said. "I'm actually scared to go to her class tomorrow. Bella and I got in trouble last week. We had to stay back until we read a page from our textbook with the correct pronunciation and accent."

Josh stroked her back. "At least she gave you sweets after. Let's go sit on that log by the lake," Josh had suggested, taking his camera out. Looking defensively at them, he'd said, "What? I like taking photos."

"Take it easy. We've all noticed your new hobby. First, you start writing things in a journal, and now you take photos. I think it's cool. You're like some rebellious artist," Ryan had said.

Cassandra's breathing reached a detrimental level.

"What's wrong, Cass?" Connor shouted from the car.

"Nothing. I mean, I just need to take a look at something."

She kept walking. In her mind, Josh wore his summer board shorts, revealing tanned legs. She saw his messy hair, his smile guiding her to the lake. Cynthia was laughing, her long brunette hair covering her sun-kissed shoulders, her youthful smile revealing perfect white teeth. Ryan lifted her, pretending he'd throw her in the lake until they rolled on the grass giggling like small children. She followed Josh's footsteps in her mind. She stopped where he stopped. She was now looking at the stone bench and the log near the lake where he'd taken photos of nature and of her.

"It can't be!" she cried to the trees around her. "It can't be."

He had run to the grass and knelt down by the log adjacent to the old, stone bench near the lake, *the lake where he'd had many picnics with friends and fam ... he couldn't breathe anymore ...* They were the words she had read in the novel, or something to that effect.

"Cass, we'd better get back. Antonio needs help with something," Connor called out again.

"Sure," she said, trying to gather her thoughts. It was the scene described in the book. The log next to the stone bench near the lake. "I'm coming, Connor," she called out as she turned away, seeing Josh's friendly eyes and hearing Cynthia and Ryan's laughter. Leaving them behind, she walked to the car.

***

They had finally arrived at the house, but Cassandra couldn't remember how they got there.

"Are you sure you're okay?" she heard Connor asking her. "You were silent in the car."

"I was just thinking of something," she said.

"Do you mind, Cass? I'll talk to you later. You seem a thousand miles away. Antonio's waiting. I'll see you, okay? Go in and relax. He thinks it might take a while. I might be gone a few hours. I don't even know what it's for, but he said it's important." He kissed her as he headed to the garden. He then stopped in his tracks and turned around to meet her eyes.

"Now I remember who Josh's mum reminds me of. You know, when I saw her in the old photo album? She reminds me of my new client … the one I was telling you about … the one I had an appointment with that day when you left. How weird! She looks just like her. It's an old photo, anyway. Just forget I said anything," he said, and kept walking towards the garden.

Cassandra stood still, looking on with her mouth agape; an overwhelming uneasiness taking over her heart.

CHAPTER TWENTY-THREE

Thomas' cheerful laughter could be heard from the lounge where she closed the large, glass sliding door. They had gone shopping and Maria was preparing a snack for Thomas in the kitchen. She snuck past them as Maria looked in the fridge and Thomas was preoccupied with a new toy he'd hastily opened from the cardboard box, which sat in tatters on the coffee table. She had to be alone. She needed solitude.

Comfortably seated on a contemporary lounge in the bedroom, she scoured the book. Any clue, any new piece of information would suffice. She scanned the words with trepidation.

"I'd better go, Mum," he said, as he noticed Kevin, one of his friends, in front of the school gate. He was talking to her. He was talking to Sandy. Her hair glistened in the hot sun, its light illuminated each strand on one side of her head while the shade from the tree stroked the other side, making it look a darker shade of blonde. She was one of the prettiest girls in school. Peter didn't care about that though. He connected with her. More than anyone he knew.

Cassandra's heart throbbed violently. She caressed the page protectively with her quivering hand before continuing to read.

"Okay, Mum ... I'm going, or I'll be late. Didn't you have some appointment?" He grabbed his bag with one hand and his sports bag with the other, then looked into his mother's eyes. They looked paler, as though they were hazy. Her caramel hair almost covered her whole face as she leaned over and kissed him on his forehead.

"Have a good day. I'll miss you," she said, and stroked his hair away from his face, combing it with her long, slim fingers. "You need

a haircut. Make sure you get one this week," she added, softly. She then looked to the steering wheel. "Go, or we'll both be late."

"Okay, Mum, sure. I'll get a haircut. I've gotta go, bye." His focus was now on Kevin and Sandy who were still under the frangipani tree. He opened the door, and immediately felt the sun on his head. The air looked hazy from the intense heat. The scent of flowers, freshly mowed grass, and the humidity in the air, made him feel free, even if he was obligated to go to school. There was something magical about summer. Living amongst nature, he always felt like it was holidays.

"Peter ... Peter ... wait!" he heard his mother's voice. He turned and peered in. She looked different, almost vulnerable.

She must be worried about entering the workforce again, he speculated. "What is it, Mum? Sandy is—"

"Just that ... I love you. I love you and your brother. Go now. Go and see your friends and fix your tie."

She then turned on the ignition and covered her eyes with her sunglasses.

"Okay? Bye, Mum," he replied, turning his back on her and straightening his tie as he took in the strong, sweet fragrance from the white frangipani tree. As he walked towards the school gate, he heard the car drive off. He turned to wave to his mum once more, but the back of the four-wheel-drive was already turning at the end of the street. She was gone. "Bye, Mum," he said to himself. He then turned to his friends and felt a sense of comfort when he looked into her eyes — his best friend's eyes. He couldn't wait to hang out with her again. He had so much to tell her — things he could only tell her. Today would be a great day. He could feel it!

The tears cascaded down Cassandra's face. The words shook her to the core. It was the last time he'd seen her.

"Please, don't look at me like that. I never wanted your pity, Cass", he'd told her at Ryan's birthday party. But how was this possible? Were these words on the pages his words? She could think of no other explanation. He had changed the names. Was this how he felt? What he saw as reality through his fourteen-year-old eyes? Her heart raced. She turned the pages and searched for the author's name. There was no photo. It was a proof copy. *But why?* Guilt washed over her. Should she be reading this?

She recalled thinking that the woman looked familiar. It wasn't supposed to fall into her hands, but it had to be fate that made it possible. Fate was against what she'd learned.

Mrs Sturgess … Why would she be at their practice … with Connor? An awful feeling consumed her. Why would she pretend she was a client? Was she really a client, or was she working with Josh? He, too, had said his mother regret that she and Josh weren't together. And why would her father despise them all? Josh had told her they were talking now. She needed answers. She had to read the rest of the book. Even if the name on the front page wasn't his, she knew that there was no other writer that would know how significant that day was.

Sandy … Her mind went into overdrive. One day at the beach he'd told her that her hair resembled the colour of the sand. He'd laughed affectionately when he'd called her Sandy. Cassandra; it was close to her own name.

She continued to read. She had to find out more. Maybe then it would all make sense. There were no accidents. Perhaps Mrs Sturgess, on a subconscious level, wanted her to find it. Why would she not be more careful about something that meant so much to her?

Cassandra turned the last page and closed the book with trembling hands. Her face felt warm but the rest of her was shivering. She had skipped through the book, reading parts of it that stood out. A strange numbness took over. She always thought it was ironic that people would appear as though they were unaffected when they'd been hit with the most catastrophic event. An event that would change their life. But when the most trivial things would happen to them, their eyes revealed passion and fire.

Everything seemed blurry, yet crystal clear. The book explained a lot; what she'd read in a book that carried the words that had changed her life as she knew it. Was she supposed to have seen it? Josh warned her that she'd need him … that she'd need someone to lean on. She now knew what he'd meant.

Where would she go from here? Who would she talk to? They all owed her an explanation, one that they should have given her a long time ago. She had felt like it was her responsibility to make everything seem normal. As a child she wasn't sure what normal was, except what she'd seen on television programs catered to families just like hers. The movies were pretentious, assuming they knew what the ideal family should look like. It was meant to torment those that didn't resemble the families they portrayed. To tease them. To emphasise the fact that they didn't resemble perfection.

She needed to see him. What would he tell her? She combed her hair and applied some lip gloss. She ran a brush through her hair, a habit that was difficult to break. It had started, of course, when she was young, when she thought little girls must always look their best: they must look their best while studying, while playing a game of soccer or softball on the field, even when they were eating their dinner. She had hoped it would distract her father from when she wasn't bathing in her post-match victory glow, or when she was holding a report card with a lesser grade. Would he have noticed if she'd sat there as she was? Foolishly, she assumed that the awards would be enough, but they were never enough, and she realised, with this new information, that they probably didn't provide him with even a moment's ounce of joy and pride either.

Glancing out of the large window with a heavy heart, she watched as everyone prepared for the outdoor dinner they had planned. It promised to be a gloriously fun evening. Connor and Antonio were still not back and George was near the outdoor grill talking with Julie. Maria was still inside with Thomas. Perhaps Thomas was taking a nap, she thought. Her eyes remained unflinching. A few hours earlier, it would have been a fun idea. There was nothing she enjoyed more than letting her hair down with her friends and Connor. It all seemed so different now.

Her mind went to Josh. Josh was excited to see her at the school gates that day. "He had a good feeling", the page had read. He had a good feeling about that particular day. It was right after the summer holidays, when he had routinely said goodbye to his mother; he thought he would see her later that afternoon.

Her tears became uncontrollable and she quivered. "Why do they always leave?" he kept asking her. Now she had the same question. Why do they all leave in the end? *Why did you leave me, Dad?*

CHAPTER TWENTY-FOUR

Parked outside, she admired the friendly camellias and gardenias. The curtains were drawn over the kitchen window. No doubt, her mother was cooking a wonderful dinner for the two of them. She hoped they weren't planning on having guests. She couldn't bear the thought of running into some family friend from her past. They would analyse how she'd grown, if she'd changed her hair colour, whilst gifting them with a smile that would make her mouth ache, but hide her pain. She despised the pretending, yet she continued to pretend. Not anymore! She would put a stop to it once and for all. She had become her own woman, and she had faltered lately, but she would face it all now so she could continue striving.

"Cass!" Her mother seemed surprised as she let her in a few moments later. "You didn't tell me or your father that you'd be coming over. I'm surprised to see you."

"My father?" she queried. "I'm sure he won't care. Or maybe he'll care too much. Not about me, of course, more about me bothering his peace and quiet."

"Cass, are you feeling all right? You don't seem like yourself."

Yourself, she thought. What self was that? She was made from lies and pieces of memories and notions that she'd made up. She had wondered why the pieces wouldn't fit. She'd forced them to fit, but it was obvious they didn't belong, because it was the wrong puzzle.

"So, where is he?"

"Who, dear? You're scaring me, honey. You're shivering. Did something happen to you? To Connor? Please tell me that's not the case."

Cassandra's heart went out to her. Her mother always went along with it. Why? Why didn't she make it messy, loud, like she did on stage? Why didn't she invite her to feel, to accept, to heal? Was she made to feel ashamed of the choices she had made?

Was her mother even glad to see her? Or did she cause problems for them? They seemed so happy now … now that it was just the two of them. Was she only able to exist as part of him? Part of Oscar, the actor she'd fallen in love with? The one she had followed to South Australia? Connor was right. It was strange to be so successful and happy and then just move to foreign shores. It was all an act though. They were extremely good actors. She could see why they had succeeded in their chosen field.

She opened the door to his study without knocking and he looked up from his desk. She could feel her mother's worried expression behind her as she stood in the hallway.

"I know everything," she said.

He took his reading glasses off and paused for a while before he spoke. "You know nothing."

Cassandra was caught off guard. She was used to his tone but was taken aback at that moment. She stifled her tears. She wouldn't give him the satisfaction.

He stood up from his chair. "She came around to see me. You just missed her."

She gave him a perplexed look.

"Josh's mother, Lana. I know … about the book. She's worried about whose hands it's in. Now we know," he said. "She did lose it in your practice, after all, after she saw Connor."

Her mother stirred behind her. "Oscar, perhaps we should sit down." Her voice broke.

"It's okay, Isabel. It's time … it's time to let her in to the room. It's time for Cass to see it."

Cassandra's heart felt like it would break. He called her Cass. Was he trying to get to her? To make her think he was accepting her because she now knew the truth? When she didn't give a damn what he thought of her anymore?

"Cass, dear … your father can explain …"

She turned around, trembling all over. "My father?" she managed. "My *father*?" Her knees weakened. "My father can't explain anything, Mum! He can't explain anything at this very moment because he isn't even in this room," she screamed at the top of her lungs. Her voice shattered the residue of silence that had quietly and steadily built. It had become thick, resembling foam-like scum on a shower screen that had never been cleaned. Layers of secrets, of silence, of fear, of hidden expectations, of what she should say or do, or shouldn't do or say to appease him, all scurried away fearfully at the sound of her screeching, commanding voice.

Her mother looked at her in that numb way. Strangely, it was as though her mother was relieved. Maybe they all felt that it was that time to be free of the lies. Maybe Josh's mum felt that it was the right time as well; that's why she had been so careless.

"So, you read it all? The book?"

"Most of it. I may have missed some sections but I think I got the gist of it. The 'you're not my father' part was clear, even if it wasn't exactly spelled out."

"Josh, as you probably know, had gone to therapy to deal with his mother leaving …" her mother began to explain. "He wrote the book as some sort of therapy. He also wrote a poetry book, since he loved writing; he obviously took after his dad. His therapist thought it'd be a cathartic task for him … like art therapy. He avoided mentioning too much about those around him in the book. He included more about his own family situation instead. He never intended to publish it. He knew too many people's lives might be exposed if they looked into it. Lana explained it all. She was really distressed with the idea of it landing in your hands, but we all agreed it might be the time to tell you. He gave it to his mother to show her how he saw things. She's been living in Sydney for some time now. He told her he needed to disengage in order to reveal how he really felt through the characters …" she waffled as Cassandra looked at her in disbelief and shock. Her mother had completely ignored the most important part: The man she was married to was not Cassandra's father!

Her mother seemed to read her mind. She moved closer to her. "I'm surprised you worked it out. Lana said it didn't explicitly give out the information."

"I worked it out. The references about the colour of his eyes sort of gave it away. It was one of the hints. I ran into Mr Dennison. Even his cousin picked up that I don't really resemble you or him. Now I know it's because I took after him in the looks department. I felt it when I'd see him in that Ibsen play you were in. All it took is some mild hints to work it out."

"Cass, I'm so sorry about what you found out. We never felt the need to tell you. Oscar had agreed to raise you as his own and we wanted to protect you …"

"You never felt the need to tell me? Oscar agreed to raise me as his own? He could barely stand to look at me," she blurted out, shaking. "Had you told me, maybe I would have understood."

She turned to face him as she heard him stir.

He finally spoke. "Your so-called father wanted nothing to do with you …"

"Oscar!" Her mother pleaded. "You don't have to knock her while she's down."

"It's the truth, since everything is out in the open, she may as well know the whole truth. The parts that aren't in the book. He chose to leave you. He knew about you. The only man who stayed is the man standing in front of you. I decided to take you in. I loved your mother and I wanted to spend my life with her, even if she made that lapse in judgement. That's all it took to change our lives as we knew it. Of course, he'd made sure she was intoxicated with alcohol and he had her believe that I was planning to leave her. He even made it look like I was seeing someone else, going to the trouble of taking photos that insinuated that was the case, but that wasn't true. He made up wild, ugly stories about me. He said that I had become too good for everyone and was seeing some of the other actresses behind Isabel's back. It was all very well-orchestrated, almost like he directed a play."

Cassandra didn't know if she could feel any smaller. He excelled himself this time. It was as though she'd done him a favour, given him a reason for his resentment towards her.

Her mother's regret and protection could be felt behind her, standing like a fragile flower in a strong breeze.

"Well, you can say it. Shout it out from the rooftop. You've practically said it already. He's the reason I was born. So, where does that leave me? Am I part of the mess? Is that why when I left everything seemed so much neater for both of you? The constant reminder of him was no longer here. After all, I do have his eyes. Now I see it: the kind blue eyes that looked at me from the screen. I was always drawn to those eyes. I felt comforted by them, like they knew me, and I knew them. It was fitting that you played the character that caused so much grief to others. You could relate to the character. Although, it wasn't much of an acting challenge, was it?"

She saw that her words stung. He looked into her eyes. It was strange that after all these years that he finally looked into them. Was he hurt? Did he have feelings? Had her words mattered to him? How could they matter if she was invisible to him? Finally, he noticed her. It took lowering herself to his cruel standards to get noticed.

"Have I caught you off guard? You didn't think I had it in me, did you? This minuscule, nuisance who walked around with her head in the clouds. A dreamer. Say something. You owe me that. Just don't pretend I'm not here, like I don't matter because the way my heart is beating now, I know I exist, and I matter to someone out there. I matter to *him*. I won't let you tarnish his name. I can't believe anything that comes out of your mouth anyway ..."

"Cass, honey, please ... don't do this ..."

"Don't do this, Mum? Don't talk? Don't bother him? He needs his space away from the burden that's standing before him, lest the dust is disturbed by some noise. I've suffered all my life because of your choices. You could have told me why he resented me! I thought something was wrong with me. I thought I was unlovable. I couldn't even commit to any man."

"You've found a sweet, caring man now. You found Connor," she said, sheepishly.

"Don't talk to your mother like that! She's suffered enough over the years," he dared to instruct her.

"My mother … that's right … you always referred to me as her daughter when you talked to my mother."

"Enough! I can't hear anymore," he said.

"Oscar," her mother said in a blunt voice. "We don't get to call the shots anymore. We gave up those privileges a long time ago. She suffered because we weren't brave enough to face our own damn feelings. You will talk. It's time to stop hiding. You will talk to our daughter. Remember what you'd told me when I gave birth to her?" She turned to face Cassandra. "You need to hear this, whether you want to or not. He told me that it wasn't your fault that he'd left you … that he would love you as his own … unconditionally. He would find it in his heart to treat you with the utmost respect and to give you every opportunity you deserved."

"Then what happened?" she asked, turning to face him again. "What happened? Why couldn't you do what you said?"

"He caused so much grief for us, sweetie. He didn't want a family. He wanted to act and tour the world and never settle. He fooled us all. He somehow had a way of manipulating everyone. It started in Denmark when he met Lana."

"Lana?"

"Yes, Josh's mum."

"I never knew Lana spent time in Europe."

"She kept that part a secret. It was too painful for her. She was in the audience. She would watch us perform every night. Her parents were very influential in the theatre world. He, your biological father, had promised her the world. She had to get back home; her parents were setting up acting schools all over the country. They were very philanthropic, believing that the theatre should be for everyone, as should the arts, not just for the elite. All children should be introduced to the arts, to see how liberating they can be. He applauded their generosity; he made their daughter so happy. They valued him and could see him as a future son-in-law. Everyone thought they were the most romantic couple."

Cassandra nervously sat on the chair, unsure what she'd hear her mother say next. "Josh is not related …"

"No, God no! It's nothing like that, honey. We would have warned you otherwise. We'd never allow you two … anyway, a healthy relationship, of course, can't exist or last with a person who doesn't even know what love is. He replaced the void in his heart with superficial things instead of spiritual needs. He craved material things: eating out at the most lavish restaurants, country club membership, the best car, clothes.

Lana was in love with him, but he seemed to truly reciprocate that love. He pretended to in the beginning, until he had lured her in, and then he broke her spirit. She was never good enough for him. Other women wore better clothes than her, he'd tell her. They were prettier, more well-spoken. At one point, she had become like him: spoilt, selfish.

"For years we thought she was like that: selfish. We know now that she was made to feel that she was nothing without the material life around her. I think he made her doubt herself. He had a way of doing that to people. Her parents had invested so much of their time and money on him. He'd convinced her to ask for copious amounts of money; she would demand it of them because of the pressure he put on her. He made them think that they could believe in him. They, however, didn't fall for his lies for long. They despised what they saw and Oscar became the star in their eyes.

"He went away for a while, unable to face the facts that his star was not shining as brightly anymore. When he returned almost a year later, his hatred had reached a detrimental level. By then, we were the star couple. Our acting was thriving. Droves of people came to see us. He couldn't handle it. He wanted the adoration, the applause, to fill the void. When he didn't get that, he tried to fill it with material things. He couldn't see that they wouldn't fill the void. It was as though he was determined to prove a point, that he was the best actor, so he set out to destroy Oscar and me and he nearly succeeded, but we realised we couldn't do without each other."

"What do you mean? How did he succeed?" Her heart raced. If she heard any more, she would be sick. She'd only seen him on the screen as a young girl and had wished someone like him would be her father instead of the man who raised her. Now they were telling her that he was no good to her either. Her small glimmer of hope had been taken away just when she thought she had found it.

Mr Jensen turned around from his stagnant state and took his hands off from his face. "He set his eyes on your mother. Lana had been tossed aside by that time. He had left Australia and headed back to Europe, to make it on his own. To show us how it's done. To prove that he could make it without us. She had met Ben, Josh's father, and she was with him for a year before he'd returned. By then, Ben and she had their first child Drew, Josh's brother. Of course, this also threw him into one of his jealous tirades. He hated that Lana wasn't doting over him and had moved on with her life. Ben seemed to be what she'd needed at the time. He was down to earth, real, and the opposite of him. And he truly loved her. She seemed to reciprocate, but she couldn't keep it up. She had much baggage. He had made her doubt every decision. She became a perfectionist in an attempt to succeed, but I think she convinced herself they'd be better off without her. That's what she told us."

"But what makes you so different? You've destroyed every ounce of confidence I had whenever you had the opportunity. I was only worthy if I was the best at everything, and even that wasn't enough. You're not different than him. You have no right to judge him."

"I stayed for you …"

"You were never there, except when I left. Then you finally got to be the couple you always wanted to be, without the constant, ugly reminder."

He froze as though her words kept him hostage.

"You're right …" he finally said.

"What?"

"You're right. I'm no better than him. I failed you too. I thought I could love you as a father without being reminded of him. He'd taken everything from us, including our dreams. He took all the profits from the business and gambled them because he chased that one allusive dream that he could never attain because it was unattainable. He always wanted more than he already had. He was his worst enemy and ended up destroying himself in his aim of destroying those around him."

Cassandra had forgotten to breathe. "I can't listen to any more of this. I have to see him, talk to him, hear his side. To find out why he chose to leave me." She headed for the door with trembling hands.

Her mother's hand touched her shoulder. She stroked her hair. "Cass, you can't talk to him. He's no longer with us. He's gone."

"What do you mean no longer with us?"

"He lost everything one night … his house, his car, he had become the person he feared and he didn't know who he was without the adoration, without the material possessions. How he loved that car … treated it like a status symbol, like it represented his self-worth."

"How?"

"He refused to hand his car over. So, in an alcohol-induced state, he drove it into the river."

"No, you're lying. You've always been great actors; it can't be." Her heart felt that it would break. How much more heartache could she endure?

She ran out of the house and tried to remember how to breathe. Her head spun. "Why did you leave me? Why, Dad?" she asked the sky where she saw his pale blue eyes, where she saw her pale blue eyes, only the sky now appeared dark and she thought of Josh running up the hill, crying on the grass near the lake, asking the same question. But, unlike him, she hadn't met her real father. He had been acting as a kind, caring character. He, too, was obviously a great actor.

She heard footsteps behind her. Of course, it was her mother, trying to explain, always trying to explain — to maintain the peace that said so much about how things were. Only it wasn't her. She turned and saw him approaching through her tears.

"I never wanted to make you feel like you didn't belong. I felt like I lost myself, like I was a weak man letting him destroy us all like that. I projected it onto you. But I didn't want to abandon you as well. You were the daughter of the woman I loved. You are part of her. But I shut it all out. I shut the world out: my hopes, dreams. I told myself that they didn't matter; that I didn't matter, but I realise now that you can't love those around you when you forget to love yourself."

She remained silent, trying to steady her breathing.

"Cass, you're right. I'm no better than him. I did the same to you and your mother for so many wasted years. Please, don't hate me. I wouldn't blame you if you did, but I couldn't even give your mother a child. When you were in your mid-teens, we were hopeful because your mother was pregnant with my child. But your birth wasn't without complications and those complications made pregnancy hard for your mother. I tried not to blame myself for not keeping him away. I even blamed Lana; it wasn't just you. I felt that if it wasn't for her convincing us all to come here to work with him, we wouldn't have allowed him into our lives. He had resented her and her parents for wanting us to become part of the promising venture. She brought him into our lives. We hardly knew him back in Denmark. We were in one successful production together. By the end, Lana wasn't even talking to her family because he made them lose so much money, and turned their only daughter against them."

"*I* made it difficult for you to forget him! You tried to accept me, but it was too hard because my being on this earth was the reason you had lost all your hopes and dreams … all the light in your eyes."

"You don't know how much he manipulated us. On the surface, he was so kind, charming, handsome. When Lana left, she opened up old wounds and I didn't want you making the same mistakes. Her son seemed rebellious and he reminded me of your father's carefree attitude. We now know why she left. We judged her and her son unfairly. We thought her life with her family wasn't enough for her, that she wanted more of the glamorous life, and her husband couldn't give it to her. Why else would she have been madly in love with someone like Carl?"

"Carl? That was his name?" His name made it real.

"Yes … Carl Lassen," he replied before continuing. "She blamed herself for everything. She never forgave herself. She had lost her self-worth and had deep anxiety. I thought you were a bit like him too, not the bad parts, but the reckless, rebellious parts of him and I was scared you'd destroy your opportunities. You were too young to be so passionate and in love with that … with Lana's boy. He had gotten under your skin. You were both too dependent on each other. You were so talented in many things. I felt like I had to stop you. Like you were my responsibility."

"You mean I was your obligation. Do you see how all this seems to me? It reveals that had I not been born you and mum would have lived the life you wanted. I took away your dreams just like he had."

Cassandra ran away from him, away from it all. She had to see Connor. To talk to him, to have him wrap her in his arms. She drove away from the house, watching her father … the man she thought was her father … who had never really been her father in any way. His head was in his hands as he sat on the front steps.

She braked, her heart aching at the sight of him. He looked lost and weak. She was used to seeing him in his smart suits, dressed in an air of confidence, his shoulders always lifted and straight, his eyes focused. It was too much to see him fallen and broken. An image of Josh's father sitting on the front steps with the broken pot next to him entered her mind. It was the night that they'd realised she'd left them for good.

She pulled into the driveway of the shared house. She'd left the book in her room. Her life had been so different before reading it! Desperate to find Connor, she ran through the open back door. Someone was talking in the garden. It was George on his mobile. She could hear his suave voice, focused on what he was saying to someone on the other side of the line.

"I don't think I can go on like this, going behind her back. It's torture. I need to talk to you again … to go over our plan," she heard him say.

She froze in her tracks. Her tears had stained parts of her hair, and she flicked it away from her eyes with a nervous tremor. *Who is George talking to?*

"Sam, just cancel the dinner. I've changed our plans. It's too risky to discuss it now, but I'll call you soon. I can't wait to talk to you and explain." He hung up as Julie stepped onto the patio. As she got to him, he embraced her. Cassandra saw the expression on his face. His mind was still on the call with Sam.

Casandra's heart accelerated. George was seeing the new tennis coach.

She snuck back out of the house. It was too much to process. She had to get out of there, fast. She was in no mood to deal with it. Too many thoughts clouded her thinking. Where could she go that was safe?

She jumped into her car and took out her phone. She called Connor, but he didn't answer. Without thinking clearly, she reversed out of the driveway and headed to nowhere in particular. How liberating had it been on that first day to be on the open road! She was apprehensive about seeing her family, but now that she had answers, she didn't know what to do with them.

He's not my father. But my real father caused grief to everyone around him. Josh's mum had suffered greatly. The scars of his emotional abuse caused her to doubt herself and led to anxiety. She left not because of her family, but because of Carl Lassen.

Because Lana hadn't healed the scars, Josh had suffered. Drew had been away at an elite school for sports and athletics and was therefore able to deal with it. Their father had been a mess all because of Carl.

Josh ... oh, Josh, we've both suffered because of him. My mum probably blamed herself. She would have been grateful that her husband stayed with her, but also indebted. That's why she always seemed to be apologising.

The thought of him crying on the front porch, looking defeated, seemed as though he too had suffered. Surprisingly, her heart ached at the image. It felt like the wrench had tightened. *I never really knew you, Dad.* As she uttered the words in her mind, she saw the father she had known all these years, the one that decided to stay.

CHAPTER TWENTY-FIVE

Turning into a familiar street, she wiped another tear from her eye. Her throat was sore from all the information she'd been fed.

She parked the car outside the school gates without thinking. There it was, standing as robust and lively as she remembered it. How many precious moments had they shared under that sweet, nurturing tree? In her numb state, she shut the door and crossed the street. She ached for a taste of those sweet moments, to savour them again without the bitterness, not knowing at the time why she was made to feel shame for seeking them, for thriving in their fruitful aura.

She meandered under its blissful beauty. 'You're a frangipani tree", he'd said to her. *What did he mean by it?* She knew Maria thought she was as kind and sweet, generous and warm as the tree was. Did he really think she was like the tree in a less positive way? That she was pretending, always looking lovely and happy even if her world was crumbling?

"I understand what you're going through," a male voice beside her proclaimed.

Shocked, she turned and watched him as he walked over to where she stood by the gates.

He stopped in front of her, eyeing her carefully. "That's why we might need each other. We don't want to live like them. We don't want to have regrets. If anyone can understand that, it's me. We can help each other. We can talk to each other without restrictions. It's all out in the open now."

"Josh … the book …"

"Yes, Cass, you were reading a book I wrote. I didn't even know. I was as shocked as you were when my mum told me it may have landed in your hands. She confirmed her suspicions today. I never wanted you to find out something so sensitive in such a way. Yet, I don't know when you would have found out if you didn't read it. My mum even told your parents about her suspicions. They almost seemed relieved, like it was bound to happen one day. We all deserve the truth. After all, doesn't it set us free?"

She looked at him through blurry, tear-stained and tired eyes. She paused for a moment to gather her thoughts before she spoke. "One man affected us, Josh. You knew it and I didn't. Which is worse?" she asked him, her voice breaking.

"Hey, you're shivering. The shock's obviously still fresh. It breaks my heart to see you like this, Cass. I know it's too soon to see it now, but maybe in a few days, when the shock wears off, you might think it's better you finally know everything. We were the victims of one man's manipulative ways. I found out many things over the last few months. My mother and I have had many long talks. She regrets so many things. One of her many regrets was that I had lost the love of my life. You."

"How did your mum even end up at our practice?"

"It wasn't planned or anything. She lives part-time in an apartment in Sydney and travels to New South Wales to her parents' house. They've been helping her; they're, once again, on good terms. She decided to see a counsellor and your name popped up. I guess she felt that things were coming full circle, that it was meant to be.

"Her hope was shattered when she heard you were engaged. She went to see you … to talk to you and gage where you stood, but you weren't there. And then Connor greeted her, thinking she was ready for a counselling session. He'd organised the appointment and told her he would take care of the administration later. She was stunned and then she felt that she could really talk to him. She wanted to show the book, to explain her situation, but she hadn't mentioned that you were a part of her story. She didn't know how to tell him without him being suspicious of her. I mean, he would think she was stalking you or something. The mother of your ex-boyfriend, regretting the fact that her son lost the love of his life?" He paused before continuing.

"It all happened so fast, Cass. She never meant for you to see it, but then some things, I believe, do happen for a reason. She doesn't want me to suffer anymore. I was deeply affected by her abandoning me. We were so close. One minute things were great and the next ... she was gone ... out of my life. I was scared you would do the same, Cass. So, I left you before you left me. I choked."

She attentively listened.

"Anyway, she feels responsible and she realised it was too awkward, so she ended her sessions. But she did want to know if there was a chance for us before I moved on ..."

"With this other girl in New York?"

He looked at her, perplexed. "How did you know? Oh, wait, Ryan? He's been worried about me. He told me that you and Connor were really tight, unbreakable, that I should move on. But Cass, do you want to live with regrets like our parents did? Now we know everything, we're ready to give each other another chance ..."

"It might also be a chance to start something new, now that the unfinished business from our past has come out into awareness. We can think clearly now without carrying the baggage; ours and our parents' baggage, without letting it hover in the background. You need to let go and move on, Josh. With that special girl in your life."

He looked at the tree the moment she said the words, breathing its sweet scent as he sighed heavily.

"I still can't believe the man I thought was my father ..." she trailed off. "He made me think I had to meet his criteria to be loved, to be accepted. All I wanted was for you to love me like I loved you. I was scared, Josh, of the silence. It was in your tight jaw. And you never let me in. It's time to move on. We've been drifting back and forth for a while. Now we know the truth and maybe when I too come to terms with it, it may set us free. Finally."

"Cass, I loved you … I still love you. I can't bear to think it's the end of us. I thought you'd see that you're someone that deserves a chance at true love. You misunderstood what I meant that night at the party in Clare Valley."

Cassandra's eyes searched his.

He looked away from her to the tree before he continued to talk. "I said it all wrong. This tree … it reminds me of you. I'm the man I am today because you were in my life. I would never have survived it if it weren't for you. Even if I didn't tell you, the fact that you were there ready to listen meant the world to me. You were there for a reason. Like the frangipani is always there to create beauty, to bring a smile to one's face, to spread warmth and kindness and to provide safety. When I look at it, I see you. That's who you are and what makes you *you*. You're one of those people who has that gift to make anyone in their presence feel like they're worth it, like it'll be okay. Seeing you always brought back the sun, the summer. No matter who the person is that stands under this tree, they can't help but feel its beauty, its friendliness. It brings back hope."

She smiled at him. "I'm glad you see me in such a positive light, Josh. I couldn't bear it if you looked at me and thought negative things. You were, and still are, a great part of the woman I am today. You helped me to become that woman. I want to learn and keep growing and see life through the lens, to find the beauty if I want to find it because of you. But I realise it's also okay to find the things that aren't as beautiful, because once I finally deal with them, it won't be that hard to find the beauty again. I will always think positively of you, Josh. You helped me. For a long time, you were the only man that helped me. You washed away the shame and guilt I felt about being who I am. I loved you … so much, but …"

He wiped her tear away and pressed his lips onto hers, kissing her gently. He embraced her as though the action gave him strength. As he pulled away, his eyes focused on something behind her. Before she could turn around, he held her by the arms, and looked her straight in the eyes. "But you've found someone else that you love now. Someone that can give you what I failed to give you: stability and security. I gave you strength, but I also made you uncertain. We weren't strong enough for ourselves. The timing was wrong, but now the timing is right for us to start anew with someone else. I know we're both ready. Go be with him. He's the man for you, Cass. You're right, I may have also found someone I can give my heart to."

Cassandra watched him as he reached up and grabbed a flower from the tree.

He smelled its sweet scent then placed it behind her ear. "I hope the beauty you seek is always with you, in your mind and in your heart. You don't need to tell me anything. Your eyes reveal that you've already found what you've been searching for: a place to belong where you're accepted for the beautiful, amazing, giving woman you are. I couldn't be happier for you. I can't deny you that happiness."

"Josh, I do love Connor ... so much. You can see it too ..."

"I won't be the man that ruins your life, like the man that manipulated everyone's lives, pretending to care, only to make them feel scared to love the person they already had in front of them. I won't make you run."

Her skin warmed at the mention of her biological father.

"Hey, his actions are not your fault. You're your own person," he said with a soothing voice.

"For years, I was scared to love someone because I felt that I wasn't worthy of love. I couldn't accept myself, so how could I accept someone else?"

"Cass ... you can only become who you are when you accept who you are," he said, a hesitant smile forming.

She smiled at his words. "Or when you accept who you are, you can become who you are?" she said with a faint laugh. "I have. I hope you have too, and I hope we keep evolving and do great things in our lives."

"He's right, you know." A familiar voice startled her. "He's right. You are an amazing, intelligent, caring and beautiful woman."

She turned. "Connor? How long have you been here?"

"Long enough to hear what I needed to hear. I saw you leave the house and then Josh left. So, I followed. I saw the book and I knew it broke you. Josh's mother had called me and told me everything. I was worried about you, so when you called, instead of answering, I raced out to talk to you. I knew you would need me. I wanted to be there for you. You had already driven out of the driveway, and I saw Josh right behind you. I had to see if you were all right, so I borrowed George's hire car."

"Oh …" Cassandra's heart ached at the thought of George.

"There's another thing that you're right about though," he said.

"Oh? What's that?" Cassandra managed.

"That he really cares about you. Josh really cares about you. I can see it now, and I can't take that away from him. It was really clear to me when I saw how eager he was to reach you."

"Connor, I ran to see you, but something happened. I heard something else. Anyway, you were the first person I thought of. I needed to talk to you," she said, looking sympathetically at Josh. Josh gave her a knowing half-smile before looking down at his feet.

"It's okay, Cass. I know you did. I noticed that you had called me. I don't blame him for caring about you. I'm here now, so we can talk, and find some solution to moving forward."

She heard Josh stirring as her eyes were still searching Connor's face. She could hear the pebbles crunching underfoot. He turned her around and gently kissed her on the forehead. "I'll give you two space to talk. Stay strong, Cass. You deserve the best in life. I'll see you both at the wedding, right?"

"Sure, Josh."

"It's okay, Cass. You can let go. I'll be okay." Josh stroked her hair one more time. He turned away sooner than he used to, as if that would be the normal now. "I'm okay with it. I have no regrets. Like I said, I may have not survived it without you." He looked at Connor, lest he become too sentimental and risk losing his momentum and courage.

"Connor …" Josh then said in a formal way, reaching out for his hand. He gave him a firm handshake.

"Thanks," Connor replied.

"For what?" Josh asked.

"For being there when I couldn't be. I think it'd be fair to say you both helped each other when you really needed it."

"I think it's more than fair to say that. Look after her. Congratulations on your engagement. I hope you're there for each other for a long time to come. But you can't blame me for trying, man. I missed her."

"No, I guess I can't," Connor said before Josh hunched his shoulders and walked to the car.

Josh straightened and walked with more confidence, as though acknowledging that their time together was officially over.

"You knew … about my father. That's why you also said I might need you. You knew from his eyes, like I always suspected but never dared to contemplate."

He hugged her. "I'm here now, and that's all that matters."

They looked at each other for a while. Connor's eyes revealed genuine concern and reassurance. He would be there for her and they would make things right, together.

***

They pulled the cars into the driveway and Cassandra recalled George's phone call. Her nose was greeted with the smell of grilled prawns the moment she stepped out of the car.

"Connor," she rushed over to him as he locked the car. She whispered, "I heard something."

She heard the piano and moved closer to Connor when a man with a big, white box, wearing a smart-looking white shirt and black pants passed her.

"Who's he?" she asked.

"One of the caterers. I helped Antonio organise them. That's where I was."

"What are you talking about? What caterers? Anyway, I have something more important to tell you. It's about George. I heard him talking to that new tennis coach. You won't believe it, but I think they're having an affair. I left the house because I couldn't handle it."

Cassandra couldn't believe that her comment got a smile from Connor. "Connor? How can you smile about it? Did you hear what I said?"

"Cass, I'm smiling because I can't believe how incredible you are. You just found out the most devastating news and you're concerned about Julie and George. It reminds me of why I fell in love with you. Come here. I have a surprise for you," he said, taking her hand into his. Cassandra's heart beat rapidly in anticipation.

"Aren't you worried about what I told you?" she asked as she walked beside him, trying to keep up with his long strides. She began to talk, before she bumped into another woman dressed in black and white. "Another caterer? Like the man at the driveway? Why are there caterers here? What's going on? Connor, I'm so confused. Is this what you helped Antonio organise? Is that what you meant? You organised some type of grand party for all of us?"

"Not necessarily. Don't worry. You'll be okay once I show you," he said as he led her to the tennis court, where she noticed dim lights flickering ahead.

The violin joined the piano, their sounds melding together. She stopped in her tracks, mouth agape and her puffy eyes wide. "Wow! This is so beautiful! But … why is the tennis court decorated like this?" she asked as she stared in amazement at the rose-covered fence around the court.

"We helped George set this up. Of course, Julie couldn't find out. It would ruin the surprise. We, of course, made sure they were out of the house when the caterers and the florist set it all up."

He held her hand tighter and leaned over, planting an affectionate kiss on her lips. The door to the tennis court was ajar, just enough for them to peek through.

"Sorry," she said when she was in the path of one of the caterers, stepping back to allow the young woman out of the tennis court. Gazing at the court, Cassandra felt like she was in a different world. Candles housed in white lanterns were everywhere. She could see the view of the distant vineyard from where she stood, and the mountains shared the majestic beauty of the scene. Julie and George sat in the centre at a small round table with an ice bucket full of champagne. The candlelit table was adorned with wine glasses and plates filled with food. Julie beamed as George raised his glass. Cassandra looked on as Julie reciprocated the gesture. They leaned in and passionately kissed each other.

"I don't understand," Cassandra said, softly.

"We all helped," Connor continued. "Even the new tennis coach. What was her name … Samantha? Sam? You know the one that George was talking to earlier? He told her to cancel the similar plans they had at one of the tennis courts in Sydney. You know, at the tennis school? He decided this would be a perfect setting to propose to Julie instead."

"Oh my God!" she screamed. The violin reached a peak, the pace vigorous. Cassandra leaned over to Connor. She had screamed much too loud. "Thank God the violin masked my voice," she said. "I don't want to get in the way of this beautiful moment."

Hope suddenly filled her heart as she looked at the couple who beamed as brightly as the stars in that balmy summer's night in the Barossa Valley. They beamed as much as her diamond ring beamed. She waited for the anxiety, but all she felt was pure joy.

CHAPTER TWENTY-SIX

The sun rose with the same intense vibrancy as it had done the days before, but Cassandra had lost her own vibrancy as the glow from Julie and George's announcement slowly became part of their everyday life. The adaptation to the news, however, highlighted the woes that continued to torment her with relentless uncertainty. Connor managed to bring a smile to her face every so often, as did Julie and George who seemed to be walking around with permanent smiles plastered on their faces.

Cassandra pondered the events of the last few days while holding the book. Josh had told her to keep it. He had sent her a text message informing her that it couldn't be in safer hands. She felt that Josh was still struggling with the fact that they would no longer be a couple, and this, perhaps, was his way of giving her part of his soul. Cassandra accepted it, deciding that it was part of her and that she would accept every disowned aspect of who she was, even the lies and betrayal that had constituted her childhood.

Josh would slowly come to terms with it. It was different this time. He had accepted how strong Connor and her were. He would not jeopardise her happiness. He cared about her too much. He always had, she told herself, so he would always have a special place in her heart. She especially knew this from the words he had written in the book. The pages spoke of how sacred their love was and how they had each other's back.

She had to plan her next move regarding her parents. She couldn't go on with the uneasiness consuming her. She had lost her appetite, and she couldn't socialise, even if she was ecstatic about George and Julie's announcement.

"You've hugged that book all morning," Connor said.

Cassandra didn't respond, instead opting to peer out at the garden.

"Cass, we're only here for a few more days, so we could join the others and go to explore Kangaroo Island or we can face your parents and see if we can find a way to move past this."

Cassandra turned to look at him. "I don't think I can do anything. I still don't know what to feel. The wedding is this weekend, and there will be a bachelorette party, and a pre-wedding breakfast, and how am I supposed to deal with seeing them again on Cynthia and Ryan's wedding day? It'll be so uncomfortable. The last thing I want is to ruin their special day!"

"Your mum's been calling though. She desperately wants to talk to you. She's lost. I'm sure you can find it in that generous heart to …"

Cassandra gave him an accusing glare. "What? Connor, do you know how lost I feel? How lost I've always felt? Do you really think I can just forget about this? My father isn't my father … and my biological father was a complete jerk. I can't even seek closure because he's dead. I have to deal with my denial and come to terms with it …"

"Yes, only then can you move on from this. At least he stayed, Cass. He wasn't perfect but he stayed by your mother's side, and by your side. He raised you with fear and regret, loathing and self-blame. He's willing to accept responsibility for his mistakes and that counts for something, in a world where the notion of the perfect family is just that, a notion. Don't you think?"

Cassandra looked up from the book stupefied, and locked eyes with Connor while her stomach turned at the thought of her weak and defeated father. She had to protect him. *Why would I want to protect this cruel, lying man?* she thought.

She contemplated Connor's words. Yes, he had stayed, but he had damaged her self-worth. Her counsellor side saw the logic: he had loathed himself for allowing Carl to betray them. He couldn't have his own child, but was she so unlovable?

Her mother had hidden her guilt in the flour, and sugar, and milk; she had sugar-coated her feelings, instead spending countless hours in the kitchen, baking sweet pastries, in an attempt to be forgiven. It seemed that he had forgiven her, but Isabel hadn't forgiven herself.

But her mother did love her. Surely, she didn't regret having her. Connor sat next to her on the couch, facing the garden and tennis court. They heard laughter from the pool.

Cassandra and Connor looked on as Maria, Antonio and Thomas splashed around in the water, resembling the allusive notion of the perfect family. Cassandra had to remind herself that there was no such thing. Maria's struggles and conflict with her mother over the years was a perfect example of how dysfunction could lead to healing. It was never too late. Cassandra had a strong memory of laughing with her father as a little girl.

Connor continued his previous thought, "Even now, he's not giving up on you. He could have but he hasn't. He wants to make it right. In my eyes, he's your father, Cass. He wasn't perfect by a long shot, but he'll always be your father."

Cassandra's heart warmed and lightened. He was her father.

A timid knock caused them to look towards the hallway. Connor's walk became decisive and bold as he approached the door. Cassandra remained still, her legs refusing to continue. The door opened, revealing her father. As he stepped inside the wide hallway, his shoulders shrunk and his walk was rigid, as though *he* was now the deviant student called to the principal's office. Usually it was she who took quivering steps to his study, staring at the door as though it would help her to make him less severe, and allow him to acknowledge her with kindness, instead of a judgmental sneer.

A nervous cough heralded that he was ready to say what he feared to say and had seemingly rehearsed. Cassandra shifted from foot to foot, instructing her limbs to do what they were supposed to do.

Her legs were weak as she walked towards the lounge and guided him to sit, even though that would mean she would be plastered to the lounge if the situation became awkward. She turned and his shoulders relaxed as he combed the large space with curious eyes.

He walked over to one of the white walls and tapped it with his knuckles, testing if the house was brick veneer or double brick. He seemed impressed. "I know the architect that designed this house. It's a modern gem. This would sell quicker than a glutton accepting an invitation to a medieval feast." He cautiously chuckled.

Cassandra awkwardly looked around the room, her shoulders tense, knowing that they'd have to move on from the comforting wall that the topic of architecture and real estate had constructed for the two of them to hide behind.

Surprisingly, he planted himself on the armchair adorned with the grey, throw-away, faux fur rug that looked like it belonged on the aristocratic shoulders of a European Countess boarding the RMS Titanic. Her heart sank at the realisation that there was really nowhere to go but down from here. What could he possibly say to her that would eradicate all the years of lies and heartache? Surely not this faux reconciliatory visit that her newly bold and fierce mother had obviously enforced on him.

"Your mother doesn't know I'm here," he began as though reading her thoughts.

Connor retreated from the encounter as he excused himself with the altruistic diplomacy of a selfless missionary. "I'd better leave you two to talk."

Cassandra glared at him. How could he abandon her so easily while she was on a sinking ship? He gave her a reassuring smile, which promised she would survive this. She was quite capable of saving herself, especially since the threatening and obstructive iciness in the air was melting away.

"Yes, we're okay. You can go, Connor," Mr Jensen now said, resuming his usual confident, authoritarian stance. Although it was now more like a friendly schoolteacher than a megalomaniac dictator.

Connor's footsteps withdrew as her thoughts became louder. Thomas' whimsical laughter from outside lightened the heavy silence, its warmth generously gifting her with an ounce of strength.

"Do you want something to drink?" she offered, not knowing what she should be feeling. She was angry with him, but Connor's words appealed to the purity of her heart.

"No thanks," his voice broke, unveiling his vulnerability.

Sitting down for a conversation that wouldn't end in a tumultuous argument was new to both of them.

"Despite what you think, we had some good times ... you and I," he managed in between an awkward cough.

He tidied a strand of pepper-coloured hair from his slightly wrinkled forehead. She remained silent, eager to hear his next sentence, as she pondered the fact that he was still rather handsome in a serious way. Perhaps if he smiled, a warm glow may iron out the creases in his forehead. He did look tired though, his eyes puffier than usual. The relaxed, checked blue shirt looked rather cheerful as it fell casually over his beige pants. It seemed to reflect his humanity; his vulnerability was real, which made him approachable.

"The photo ... on the mantelpiece. Did you see it?"

Cassandra moved at the question. She recalled the photo he was referring to in her mind. "The one that mum placed there? Yes ... I did. I haven't seen it before ..."

"I put it there. I thought it could be seen better from all angles of the room."

"Oh ... you did?" she managed, trying with great difficulty to envision him performing the act, trying to imagine how he would have examined the photo as he placed it on the mantelpiece. She couldn't picture it.

"I love that photo. It always makes me smile. The day it was taken was beautiful."

Words failed her, so she continued to listen with uneasy wonderment.

"It was taken when we were about to go to one of the animal farms. You were so excited. I told you that you could pat them, and even feed them. We were all happy." He stopped talking and looked at the faux fur throw-away. He patted it without thinking, as though he was retrieving the memory more clearly from the annex of his mind. "We were happy that day … and many other days. I remember the good times. There were plenty. I choose to remember them when I feel I've failed in life. That couldn't be more true now than any other time."

Cassandra looked on in disbelief. He looked away, clearing his throat. "I wanted to protect you from it all. I tried, but I couldn't even save myself. I blamed myself for not preventing things, but I've just realised something. You clarified it the other day. I … I wouldn't have those precious memories if I had prevented him. My only regret now is that we didn't create more of them … as a family," he said, lifting his head and meeting her eyes.

Cassandra's heart rate escalated. It throbbed violently. Unshed tears stung her eyes. She wanted to look away. It hurt too much to look at him and hear the words she had longed to hear.

"It shocks you. I can see it," he finally said. The intensity of his stare decreased. "That's what pains me. Those words are so foreign to you; they make you uncomfortable … as though they're hostile. Your comfort has been a familiar silence. It built safe, but hostile walls between us. I can see it clearly now. That photo is the image I want to remember. Its gentleness can melt away the coldness I chose to live in. Why on earth would I choose to live in the cold, when I had a little girl that invited the sun to shine on us every single day? Just like your mother always did! You take after her so much. I hurt you both deeply. That wasn't my intention. How can I make it up to you? Tell me what I can do to make things right between us."

She wiped her tears away with a quivering hand, taking deep breaths to steady herself. They were quiet for a while. She could feel his nervous gaze on her, but she couldn't find any words.

"He made my life miserable," he digressed, filling the silence. Cassandra instantly looked up. "It's not your fault though. You were an innocent victim in all of this and you're nothing like him. He wasn't all bad though; he had many endearing qualities. As do you. If you do take after him in any aspect, it would be that. I think he was emotionally crippled. I think he was stuck in the past. Maybe when he was wronged. There were stories … there were always stories in those days. People speculated. I heard one of the actresses say that his father was brutal, so I guess he decided to be the aggressor rather than the victim. But, then again, who am I to talk?" he drifted as though he was floating in his own thoughts.

Cassandra didn't know why she couldn't find the words. Lament leaked from her heart, but she couldn't seem to construct a sentence which would express what she was truly feeling. She had never seen him so animated.

He, once again, cleared his throat. "I'm so proud of you. Of the woman you've become and of the girl you used to be. What a fool I've been … hiding behind my pride. You have to understand, he had made me look like a con artist, like I was the one stealing funds from the acting school. It took years to gain the community's trust. I lost myself in the process, feeling like I had something to prove. I had to ensure that I raised you right. Please … talk to me. Is it too late? Can I make amends? Show me how to be a good father. I owe you that. Your mother is so worried. She's starting to look weak. I don't want her to hurt like this …"

Cassandra met his eyes as a burning feeling tugged at her heart. She felt for her mother, but was that the only reason he was there?

He gave her an awkward smile that seemed to belong to some other man's face. "I also don't want to hurt. I've made a huge mistake. I … I don't want you to hurt anymore either. I'll do anything you ask. You don't know me the way I wanted you to know me, the way you saw me when you were a little girl. Like in that photo … the way I was when I was on stage. I can see you don't remember the good memories, only the bad …"

Cassandra couldn't swallow. Her eyes welled with tears at the words that were ready to enter her mouth. She combed away a strand of hair from her face. Her lips trembled under the pressure. She dug deep and looked up into his eyes. Josh told her a photographer saw what they wanted to behind the lens; that they saw what they were looking for. Gaining courage and noticing Connor's smile from the garden, she dared to look straight into her father's eyes. "Are you serious? About making amends?"

His gaze moved from his feet to her and shot her a shocked look. He narrowed his eyes. "Of course, I am. I've never been more serious in my life."

Cassandra saw the man behind the hopeful look. She could see Oscar, the passionate young actor who had so many dreams for himself and for her mother. Years of failed attempts at fulfilling his dreams had cast a shadow in his eyes. For years, his eyes were dark; now they glistened. Taking a deep breath to steady her heart, she said, "If you really want to be a good father, there is something you could do for me. I'd be more than honoured …" she faltered.

"What is it?" he asked, his eyes now vulnerable and apprehensive.

She cleared her throat. "I'd be honoured if you could walk me down the aisle on my wedding day. Can you do that? Can you find it in your heart to do that for me … Dad?" she asked him as tears welled in her eyes and her mouth trembled. Her heart raced.

She waited for a few seconds, feeling fragile and exposed.

He was stupefied. A shy smile formed, alighting his face as it grew, taking over his tired but hopeful face. His eyes shone. "Yes ... of course, I can. I'd be more than honoured, Cass. Nothing would make me happier than to walk with you down the aisle, to stand by your side. After all, you are my one and only daughter."

CHAPTER TWENTY-SEVEN

A fountain in the centre of the tranquil garden wept tears of joy as it sprinkled water playfully. A crowd had filled the open space with merriment. The sun created streams of warmth and light on all the graceful, peach and white roses adorning each cream silk covered seat. Cassandra breathed contently as she held Connor's arm.

"Wow, okay, this will definitely be another one of Cynthia and Ryan's great parties," Cassandra said as she looked at the spectacle around her.

"It'll be your turn soon," Julie said as she walked by her side, glancing over at George.

"And then it'll be your turn," Cassandra replied, looking at Julie and catching the quick kiss George planted on his fiancée's forehead.

"I wonder where my parents are," Cassandra said, peering around. Familiar faces caught her eyes, yet her parents were not to be found.

"So, you're okay with it all?" Maria asked from where she stood behind her, fussing with Thomas' shirt.

Cassandra turned and smiled at Thomas who looked adorable in his formal wear. Antonio stood beside him looking just as dashing in his slim-fitting suit.

"I'm okay. I think I'm slowly coming to terms with it. It explains a lot," she said as they made their way to the available seats, the sound of a trumpet ushering calm and order. "I think we're at a good place, right now," she whispered in Maria's ear.

Connor took her hand and whispered, "I'm so proud of you."

"Thanks. I wonder where they are though. I can't find them anywhere."

Connor looked around at the other row of seats. "There they are. They're sitting next to Josh and his mother. That's her, or should I say my ex-client?"

"What?" Cassandra raised to look. She noticed her father, who seemed to be straining his neck to see her. Her mother quickly waved to her. She smiled back, adjusting the strap of her dress self-consciously like she had as a young girl who fussed over her appearance. She stopped when she caught the awkward warm smile her father shot her.

"I can't believe they're sitting together," she said, catching Josh glancing over in their direction. Connor waved to him, as he always would with a friend. Josh seemed to be taken aback, but then reciprocated with a smile. Cassandra waved to him and when Josh turned back to speak to his mother, she whispered. "I'm so proud of you."

The wedding march began and Cassandra smiled at Lana: the woman who had left their lives all those years ago, the woman who had shattered their lives as they knew it in an instant. But also the woman who came back and repaired it all.

A few hours later, "What Is Love?" by Haddaway blasted from the speakers. The DJ had shifted to play some retro dance songs. Maria and Cassandra couldn't stop laughing as Antonio and Mrs Jensen performed a few tangos together, and now matched their tempo to the dance music.

"Wow! Your mum's pretty good," Maria enthused.

"I guess. She is a performer," Cassandra said with pride.

Her father glanced with knitted brows, but a smile smoothed his features. The sorrow, regret and tears would be in the past.

Her mother had profusely apologised for shutting her out and keeping the truth from her. She had included her in her past though, showing her the plays and the photos when her husband wasn't looking. Maybe, on some level, she had wanted her to know her biological father. An overwhelming guilt had consumed her over the years, not too dissimilar to Josh's mum.

"Cass … are you sure you're okay with everything? It was shocking news. It would be understandable if you were still troubled by it. I must say though, the way your dad is admiring your mum right now is so sweet," Maria said.

"You think that too? He is admiring her, isn't he? That's what I thought. Anyway, yes, I'm still trying to get my head around it all, but I'm really okay. Seeing my dad looking at my mum with pride for who she really is: a person who lives life to the fullest, a performer, a woman with dreams and desires … I'm at a good place right now; better than I have been in a long time."

"I'm glad to hear that," said a female voice beside her.

"Oh," she said, her mouth agape. "Mrs Sturgess … how are you?" Seeing her standing there was still so surreal. She was, after all, the woman they talked about without ever mentioning her name.

"I know … many have given me the same reaction. I know it's awkward, shocking even, but it was time for me … it was time for all of us. Dear Cass, I'm so sorry for what I put you and Josh through. He was fond of you, so fond of you, but now you're engaged to a man I have been fortunate enough to have met … in rather strange circumstances. I hope I didn't cause any more problems for you. You see, I blamed myself for many things."

"It wasn't just your fault … it was …"

"It's okay, dear. You don't have to say it. He's gone now and I know a part of you will miss him even if you didn't get to know him. I've learned not to blame anymore, to reclaim my power, like you teach your clients … like Connor does. Yes, things could have been very different, but you're not to blame for any of it. And I realise, as I hope you and your parents have, that they aren't to blame either. I mean, look at your mother … she's glowing. It's good to see her like that again. And your dad … I'm glad I came back in time to …"

"To fix things … That's what you did, Mrs Sturgess. It might have taken us a while, but things are as they should be now."

"My daughter is a smart woman," her father said from behind her. "If you hadn't come back, we wouldn't have our family. Thank you, Lana. You've done a great thing. For all of us."

"Oh Oscar," she said, clasping her hands.

"I'm glad Ben and you are together again. The sod has been miserable without you."

"Hey Cass … Come on. You loved this song back in school," Cynthia called out and grabbed her hand and then Mr Sturgess' as well. She gestured for Connor, who had just joined the conversation, to follow. "Come on … on the dance floor."

"Of course, I'll have a dance with the beautiful bride," Cassandra shouted over the music as she stepped onto the dance floor. "Groovejet" by Spiller blasted from the speakers.

When the dance was over, Cassandra walked outside with a glass of Champagne. She moved over to the pebbled path between the huge, black planters housing blushing peach and pink flowers. This was where Cynthia had stood, where she had shown Cassandra where the wedding reception would be held. It was dusk now, as the sun set with majestic grace over the mountains. And she saw him, sitting with a beer in his hands, gazing at the mountains, the lake, and the nearby vineyard.

She approached him. His raised shoulders under his slim-fitted suit jacket, and his pondering gaze brought back memories of them together. She savoured those memories although her future was now very clear.

"I always thought the slopes in the distance looked like arms ready to embrace anyone in their path," she said.

He turned as a kookaburra roused attention. They smiled at the sudden intrusion.

"Should I stay away?" she found herself asking, playfully.

Josh gave her a knowing smile. "It is dusk after all. A time when the stillness of the night invites everyone to feel, to take stock of what life is really about. It's also a time when loved ones come together."

"So, speaking of loved ones … your mum was really sweet to me. I'm so glad she's back in your life, and I'm glad you have someone waiting for you back in New York," she cautiously said, nearing him with the crystal flute of bubbly.

His eyes became serious, still like the night. The guests tried to match Agnetha and Frida's strong vocal cords as they sang to "Dancing Queen". Where they were positioned, the inside festivities contrasted with the still night. A blend of sounds from the evening's crickets, cicadas and birdlife brought with it its own mirth: sleepy, mesmerising, and natural sounds. The croaks from the frogs near the tranquil lake sounded rehearsed; their synchronisation was almost perfect and could give the singing guests a run for their money.

Josh finally spoke. "Yes, I do. At least I hope I do. I had to try once more, Cass. You understand that, don't you? I had to make sure before I get involved with someone else. I've been working with Chloe for a while. I get the impression that she likes me. I think she's sweet, but we'll see how it all goes. After searching for a while, you get tired of looking for something you might not find and you realise what you have in front of you may be what you've really been looking for but didn't know it. We had our chance for that and, although we missed it, we'll always be connected, you and I. I had decided to go wherever the road took me, only to realise that I want the stable life I never had."

"Josh …"

"You don't have to say anything. I just want to look at you, to remember you like this. It gives me peace." He looked into the distance for a while. "You know, Cass, Kookaburras don't just call because they're warning those that wish harm to stay away. Sometimes, at odd times of the day, their call is like a chuckle which usually implies that they might be lonely or looking for lost loved ones.”

Cassandra looked up in wonderment. “And when they call out loud enough, those who love them find them?” she added. “Josh, I’m so glad you found your loved ones …”

He stood and pulled her into his arms. “I’m glad you did too, Cass. You discovered your dad, the one that raised you, but you never had the opportunity to truly meet.”

“Hey, you two. Just like old times, hey?”

They moved away from each other, and caught Ryan’s speculative, tipsy gaze, as he and Cynthia approached them with their own glasses of Champagne.

“It’s all good,” Josh managed.

Ryan and Cynthia wrapped their arms around them as soon as they reached them.   “Can we join you as well?” Cynthia asked, emotional, festive laughter ringing through the night air.

“Yes. Is there room for us?” Ryan matched her tone.

“Of course, you can,” Josh replied with a laugh, the walls slipping down. “We’re friends and that will never change.”

They raised their drinks and as the night sky of Tanunda blanketed them, they shouted in unison, “Friends for life.”

EPILOGUE

Three months later, Cassandra fiddled with her hair in front of the antique mirror in the North Sydney terrace house. The soft, white silk fabric of her wedding dress brushed her skin and fell freely around her ankles. Her French manicured nails shimmered alongside the diamond ring on her long, slim finger.

The make-up artist and the hairstylist had finished, leaving her with Maria and Julie. They were there to help her with last-minute preparations. They thought it would be fitting to get dressed and ready in the terrace house, with all its sweet memories. The church being nearby was just another bonus. And, after many photos with Sydney Harbour in the background, they would go to the reception venue they'd hired at Circular Quay. The white, 1950s Bentley would arrive soon to pick them all up for the long, exciting day ahead.

"We'll need to take a few more shots," a young man with well-gelled hair that shimmered in a shiny, slim-fitting shirt, tight, black pants, and pointy shoes, announced from the garden. "This garden is a great setting for some shots of the bride with the bridesmaids."

Julie stifled a tear. "I can't believe we're in this house together after all these years. And you're getting married to Connor. I was an emotional mess during Maria's wedding, and now your wedding … I mean, Cass, you were just sitting on that dining room chair when I saw you with him. I knew you two were more than study partners. Isn't it wonderful that you're finally getting married?"

Cassandra tried to stifle her own tears so as not to bleed her mascara. Peace had come over her, despite the stress of the day. She leaned over and hugged her friends. "I'm so happy you're all in the bridal party. You look adorable in yellow dresses. I thought they'd look summery, kind of like how the sunshine warms the place up."

"I actually love the colour. I didn't think it would be me, but it is! It even has a bit of a bohemian feel to it, which you know I love."

"I knew you would, Maria. I also told the seamstress to add a unique touch to the collar by adding these unique pearl buttons just for you, Julie. The bracelet you got from Amsterdam adds an elegant and edgy feel too." She scanned the dresses with approval. "I hope Cynthia's dress fit her. She should be here any minute. They flew over to Sydney yesterday."

"Oh my God, Cass. It's your wedding day and you're more worried about how we look. Enough caring for others today … Well, maybe you can care about Connor."

"I think what Maria is trying to say is to try to take care of yourself on your wedding day. It's okay to be selfish sometimes, and it's our turn to tell you how gorgeous you look. I love the design of your dress. It fits like a glove and you're glowing."

"I think you two have used the word *gorgeous* to describe my appearance a hundred times today."

"And we'll tell you a hundred more times. I just hope Thomas is okay with his page boy duties. He's so excited to wear the same suit as his dad. It's great that we're all in the bridal party."

"He'll be great. He's too adorable. No one will even notice if he stuffs up …" Cassandra began until she heard an impatient cough from the French doors leading to the garden.

A knock at the door startled them.

"Great, it's Cynthia!" Cassandra enthused.

"Ladies … I'll need you all to step out into the garden," the young photographer said.

An hour later, Cassandra breathed deeply as she waited at the church, which throbbed with chatter from the guests who had arrived early. While she pondered if Connor and the groomsmen were okay with preparations, she heard her mobile beep. She halted; her little, velvet bag hung suspended between her and her mother. She pulled her phone out and skimmed the message:

Cass,

I wish you all the best in your new life. I can almost imagine how radiant you look right now. It hurts not to be part of it, but things are going great with Chloe, and it is difficult for me to get away. Just know that you'll always have a special place in my heart. That is a given because you gave me so much of your love, and I intend to keep it in my heart so I can keep evolving and giving love to others.

My best wishes to you and Connor. I wish only the best for both of you!

Your friend … always,

Josh. xxx

Cassandra smiled at the message.
"Cass, dear, you'd better give me your bag now. The priest is ready. You look so beautiful, honey."
"Yes, she does," her father chimed in.
She turned to him.
"Your mother's right, you look beautiful. White has always suited you. Are you ready?" he asked with a warm smile, offering his arm.
She looked between his eyes and linked arms. "Yes. I'm ready … Dad."

"Have a great honeymoon, you two." Mrs Olsen wrapped her arms around her daughter-in-law as they stood outside the reception venue, the lights of Sydney Harbour sprinkling their magic around them.

"You both look dashing," Mrs Jensen said, hugging Connor and then her daughter. "What a venue! I'm coming to Sydney more often."

"Oh, you both should. They have some of the best theatrical performances here as well," Mr Olsen suggested.

This got her father's attention. "Maybe we should go to see the production of *A Midsummer Night's Dream*. You know, we always wanted to act in a Shakespeare play."

"Cassandra and Connor actually visited Verona and saw the Juliet Balcony when they went to Italy. Did they tell you?" enquired Mrs Olsen. "It's also amazing that they're going to Denmark for their honeymoon."

"They say the Danes are the happiest people," Mr Olsen remarked, still obviously intrigued by the topic since the last time they spoke.

"Yes …" Mr Jensen agreed. "We better not ruin their reputation then," her father said with a laugh. "Let's go see that play," he said to his wife. "We'll all go together. We'll organise a time while we're in Sydney. So, who's the Danish one in your family? Or is it Norwegian?"

"It's actually from my …"

Mrs Olsen intervened. Mr and Mrs Jensen stood back as they debated for a while.

The photographer called out for Connor. Their driver would take them to the hotel soon and he wanted to take some more photos of the bride and groom by the Harbour.

Cassandra leaned over to her dad and gave him a hug. "Bye, Dad," she said and confidently planted a big kiss on his cheek.

For a while, he looked like a fish out of water. To her surprise, a tear streamed down his face. He swiped it away. He was still learning. It was fairly new to both of them.

He took her hand. "Bye Cass. You make a wonderful bride and daughter. I'm so proud …"

"Mr and Mrs Olsen ..." The photographer was becoming impatient, as he stood with a hand on his hip.

"I think they mean Cass and Connor," suggested Connor's mum.

"Yes ... that's us now," said Cassandra, taken aback. "Thank you so much, Dad, for everything."

He smiled, content.

"You better go," Maria shouted so that the photographer could hear. "Your photographer is summoning you. Make haste!"

The others followed as Cassandra and Connor walked hand in hand to stand in front of Sydney's Harbour Bridge. The Opera House stood tall in the distance.

"Happy Honeymoon, you guys," shouted Cynthia as Ryan's whistling rang out through the Harbour.

"What a night? Sydney Harbour looked breathtaking. It was such a great venue. I wish everyone could be as content as I feel right now," Cassandra said to Connor as they sat inside the stylish Bentley, heading to the hotel.

"We'll try our best to ensure that happens to our clients. After all, we're not miracle workers, and we can't neglect ourselves," he added. He was then deep in thought. "The cake with the daisies looked great. Maybe we'll call our first daughter Daisy," he smiled.

"Okay, if your parents heard you, they'd tell you not to scare the girl. We haven't even started our honeymoon ..."

"It's such a kind gesture that you would want to honeymoon where your biological dad grew up. You have such a forgiving heart."

"I want to visit the town he grew up in. What was it called? Indre Byen? I want to feel that he was part of my wedding somehow. I'm sure we'll love it. It has many historic buildings and historic universities. I've learned that we sometimes have to see beyond what we see blindly. We see what we want to see; we just have to adjust our focus. I choose to see that he was a man that made wrong choices because, perhaps, he wasn't taught how to make the right ones."

"I think that if he'd survived, he would find a way to be a part of your life. He'd see what an amazing daughter he had," Connor said as he leaned over and kissed her on the lips. "You don't need any sunny, pretty, and nurturing flowers when you already are one."

"Aww," she replied and giggled. She kissed him again. "I can't believe we're now officially married. Maria, Antonio, and Thomas are a wonderful little family; Julie is about to get married to the love of her life." Sentimental tears welled as she glanced at the North Sydney terrace ahead. It would lead them to their hotel. "We all go through trials and tribulations, and heartache and uncertainty, but with love and hope and navigating the path for ourselves, it all works out — eventually."

The driver stopped the car, announcing that he needed to make a quick call. While they waited, Cassandra glanced out of the window and was astonished to see that they had stopped right next to the white frangipani tree across the street from Maria's house. She inspected the tree. Its friendly, white and yellow petals were illuminated by the street lights, and she was left wide-eyed with shock to see that someone had carved something on the trunk of it. She leaned closer to the window. It was a heart. Her chest warmed like she had just taken a sip of soothing, herbal tea from Eventually You.

Smiling to herself, she thought of one of the many wedding gifts Maria and Antonio had given them. Connor had told her how much they enjoyed the massage oils and diffusers, so she had gifted them many boxes of many different oil blends, each with unique healing properties and a diverse array of exotic scents. Maria had hinted that their gift might be fun to have on their honeymoon.

Cassandra then took out the small photo of the actor she used to see on the video that her parents kept. The photo of the troubled but charismatic man known as Carl. She had carried it in her bag to ensure he didn't miss any of it. There was room for everyone on their special day. His deep, kind-looking eyes hid so much envy and malice, and from where Cassandra sat, she could also see a lot of pain. She placed it back in her bag for safekeeping.

The Bentley moved past the house and continued its journey. She was finally steering her life in the right direction.

Connor took her hand and affectionately kissed it. He looked at her and smiled, his eyes full of love and warmth. "You're right, Cass, there will always be uncertainties and challenges, but for now I feel that I can confidently agree with you. It will work out for all of us … *eventually*."

ACKNOWLEDGEMENTS

Writing *Under the Frangipani Tree* was such a beautiful experience as I was transported back to my holiday in the Barossa Valley and Clare Valley in South Australia. It was very enlightening being there and learning about the history of the land: how the early pioneers established the vineyards and imprinted their history in the soil of many towns and villages. I was also so fascinated with the modern towns, how they incorporated the old with the new.

I thought it would be so wonderful to base the story amongst such gloriously beautiful and natural settings. Mother Nature symbolises growth and evolving; the characters in the Julie & Friends series each embarked on their own journey of self-growth and being true to themselves, just like the land and nature are true — authentic. Similarly, the organic shop Eventually You, which features throughout the series, symbolises authenticity and healing.

I was so sad to say goodbye to the characters of this series. I am also proud of the series: all the hard work, drafts, rewriting, and the vigorous editing that I ensured took place so that I can offer a series that was as refined as possible, without losing its authentic voice. The wonderful characters have been with me for many years and I've grown to love them. I think they may represent various aspects of myself and the individual I aim to evolve into; one that accepts all aspects of herself and keeps learning. I had thought of incorporating some of what I'd learned during my counselling studies in the first book, Eventually Julie, and like a plant thriving, all three friends, and new friends that were introduced along the way, right into *The*

Greek Tapestry and now with this novel, have thrived within a nurturing environment. It was a fun series to write, and although it does deal with some serious, universal themes, it was also written in a light-hearted way, as I believe that in real life many of us use humour in times of insecurity: when facing adversity. I hope the reader has taken something positive from this book, and from the whole series if you have read all three books.

I would like to thank my husband, once again, for his continuous support, motivation, and his boundless help with all things technical. I'm extremely grateful for him encouraging me to follow my dream of becoming a writer. His support has meant so much. Writing can be a lonely, yet rewarding life which enriches the soul and the mind and it can also gift the writer with a sense of accomplishment and self-awareness. It is easy to feel defeated at times while writing, and even if tears are shed and uncertainty may loom in the air, there are times of pure elation and joy, as writing, just like reading, can be so liberating and cathartic.

I'd like to thank my children for being part of this journey and allowing me to talk to them about the stories and characters, book cover designs, and anything relating to the writing process while writing this series. I've talked about the characters to the point that I feel that they are real. I hope that my children, like the characters, will learn to persevere with their dreams, and face obstacles as they arise.

I would sincerely like to thank Peter and Caroline at Bespoke Book Covers for all three beautiful book covers. Their continuous assistance and professionalism are to be highly commended. Thanks, also, to my editor at The Expert Editor for her professional proofreading, and for all her honest, positive and encouraging feedback.

I would also like to thank my family, my friends, and extended family, for all their support.

Thank you to the readers who have taken a chance on a new author and have made my dream of having my work read come true. There is nothing more rewarding for me than to have you read my books, and to enjoy them and be affected by them in a positive way. I thank you from the bottom of my heart for being part of this world I created.

If you enjoyed reading this book or my other books, I hope that you can leave a review with your thoughts, even if it is a few lines. Other readers may, too, enjoy it/them as much as you did, and it's the only way to spread the word. As reading can be subjective, a review may highlight things in a book that other readers may also look for in a story. It means the world for new writers to have their work acknowledged and discussed by readers, and reviews are essential for this to occur.

Thanks, once again, for reading this book. You can find out more about me and my writing on my website: **antheasyrokou.com** where you can follow me on social media and also subscribe to my newsletter.

You can also have a read of the blurb for my book *True Colours* on the next page.

My warmest wishes, Anthea.

Also by

ANTHEA SYROKOU

True Colours

Twenty-six-year-old Tess Harrington is comfortably content with her life in the city. Originally from a small country town, Tess now works in a hair salon she part-owns with her friend Pamela, located in a quirky street full of culture, art, and plenty of tea and coffee. She couldn't be happier spending her days interacting with the locals who work in the wonderful shops that line the street, and indulging in quiet nights in her nearby apartment, where she reads her many books, sips tea she makes with her prized teapot, and eats delightful gourmet sandwiches from the local deli.

She treasures the antique finds which adorn her apartment, attends her monthly "shop girls" soiree at a swanky club called Vinnie's, and is never lonely, for she has her books, which introduce her to the romance and adventure she quietly longs for, and which satisfy her hidden desire to run free amongst storms, and to swim in surging seas.

Life couldn't be going more smoothly for Tess, and she intends to keep it that way. With one failed marriage already under her belt, Tess decides to forgo relationships altogether, as does her friend Pamela, who finds herself in a similar predicament. They tell themselves they don't need men in their lives — not even the handsome restaurateur Silvio, who swoons over Tess and calls her his muse.

But when someone threatens this almost too tranquil world she has built for herself, will she be strong enough to resist the outside elements of the "real world"? Will an unexpected surprise on her doorstep cause Tess' cosy world to change irrevocably? Or is it the change Tess needs, to finally live a colourful life, and not just read about it?

Join Tess in this endearing and uplifting story of love, friendship, and passion!

"What a great read. Anthea is a clever, witty author. I love the words she chooses, the smooth plot, and the "real" characters she creates."

R. Tramp (Amazon review)

"Readers who are fans of Author Anthea Syrokou will once again appreciate her ability to explore the psychological realms."

Jena Books

"Anthea did it again; She kept me up all night with her story-telling."

The Rambling Boho

"Anthea Syrokou's books are a delight to read, and her wisdom in life and relationships can be seen in her story."

A. Miller (Amazon review)

ANTHEA SYROKOU is an author who grew up and resides in Sydney, Australia.

Anthea's love for writing was planted at a young age when she studied Greek mythology. Her love for literature continued well into her teenage years when she enjoyed reading novels by many of the great English writers.

As a young adult, she immersed herself in reading women's contemporary fiction and writing about topics, that many could relate to, in a witty, light-hearted way, which became a passion — one that she takes very seriously.

Anthea has a BA degree, majoring in psychology and industrial relations, and a diploma in counselling. She also studied Greek literature at university and has worked in direct marketing, and insurance and investments.

As well as writing fiction, Anthea also writes articles and posts on everyday issues; often adding her dash of humour.

When she isn't writing or reading, Anthea enjoys spending time with her family, travelling, yoga, and escaping to the vineyards. A quiet house with some jazz playing in the background, surrounded by a few lit scented candles is her idea of relaxation. Anthea lives with her husband and their two sons.

For more information, please visit **antheasyrokou.com**